...and Never Coming Back

Also by Robert Evans Wilson, Jr.

Children's Fiction:

The Annoying Ghost Kid

Non-Fiction:

Wisdom in the Weirdest Places

Humor:

OFF THE WALL! The Best Graffiti Off the Walls of America

Editor:

Awaken the Christ Consciousness Within You by Barbara Wilson

... and Never Coming Back

by Robert Evans Wilson, Jr.

cover design by Kevin Tester

This is a work of fiction. All of the characters, organizations, and events portrayed in this novel are either products of the author's imagination or are used fictitiously.

...and Never Coming Back

ISBN-10: 0692389431
ISBN-13: 978-0-692-38943-0

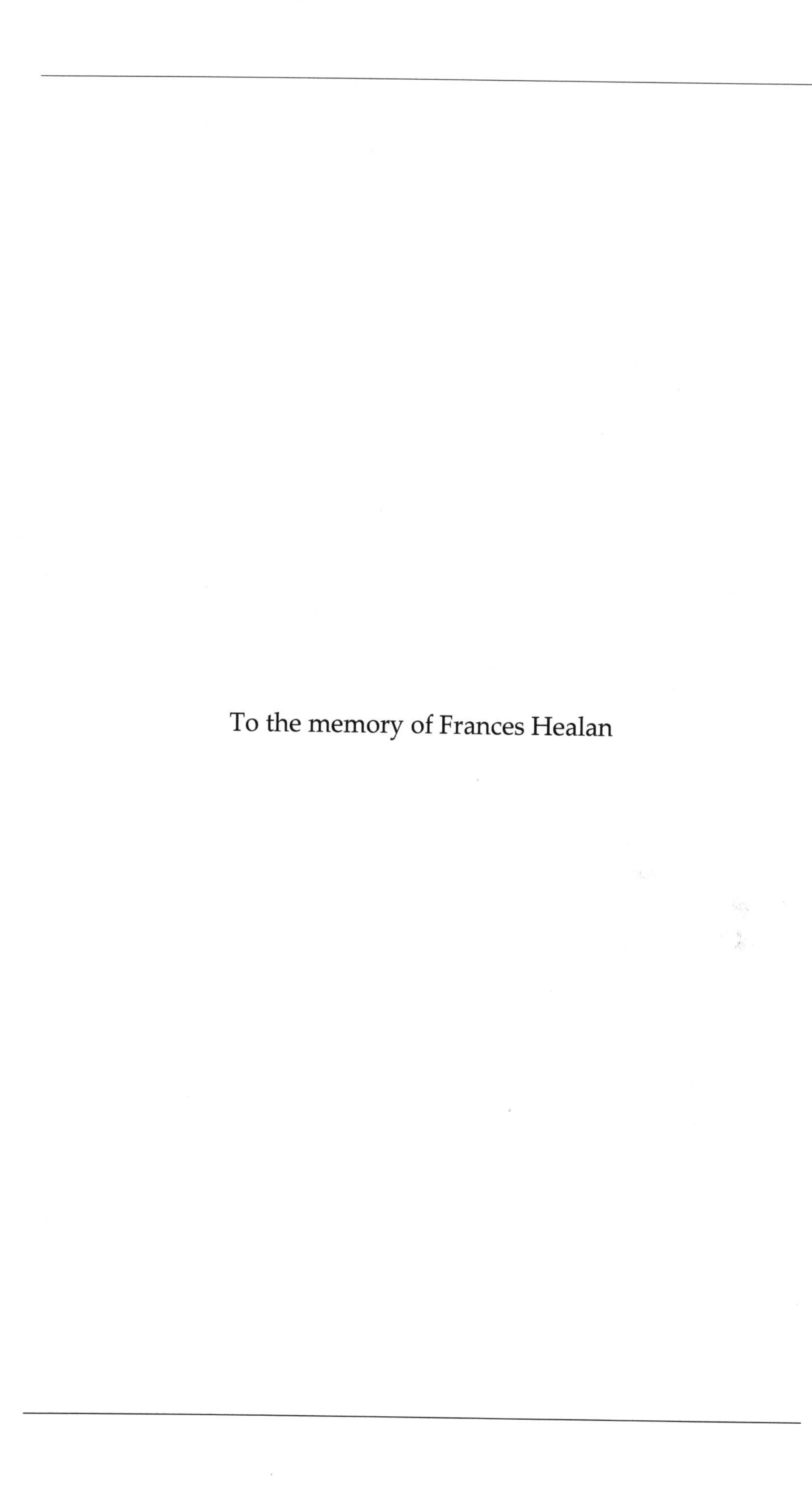

To the memory of Frances Healan

Acknowledgements

Thank you to Randy Sekeres for proofreading and helping me eliminate a host of grammatical errors. Thank you to Kevin Tester for creating the beautiful and intriguing cover art. And, a special thanks to Kent Boxberger for encouraging me to follow my highest excitement.

PROLOGUE

"... and never coming back," cried the seventeen year old boy. He ran down the front steps of the old farmhouse into the rain. His left foot slid across the algae coated bottom step. He kept his balance and did not fall, but his right foot landed in a deep puddle. The cold water rushed into his sneaker and soaked his sock. Then, as if orchestrated by his dark mood, the rain started coming down harder.

He slogged on to his car, grabbed the door handle of the late model Ford. The rusting hinges in the heavy door resisted. He put his soggy foot against the side, and yanked the door open.

A woman following him, stopped at the top of the stairs, under the protective roof of the porch. She called out over the sound of the storm, "Wait."

He turned and looked at her through the curtain of water.

"Don't do anything foolish!" she said.

"Like what?"

"You know, like hurt yourself."

"How could I possibly hurt anymore than I already feel."

"You'll feel better in time. Time heals all wounds."

"Don't patronize me," he screamed, and then turned toward the driver's seat.

"Wait!" she cried again as he climbed behind the wheel. The car engine roared. She started down the stairs, but he sped off down the gravel driveway and onto the muddy road.

#

It was May 18,1967; less than a week since the killing. The teenager sped along the dark and empty road. He slowed down as he entered the town square. The clock on top of the county courthouse read 9:07. The stores were all closed; the park abandoned, only the blinking lights around the movie house marquee showed any sign of life; it read *Casino Royale* - David Niven. At the intersection he stopped and contemplated his choice of directions.

He stared at the blurred highway signs through tears and rain, and wondered which way to go, but the painful thoughts that would not leave his head made any decision difficult.

"If I go north on 19, I'll end up in Atlanta," he thought, "No. No, too big and too scary... south will take me to the Gulf of Mexico. I could just live on the beach... west on Highway 26 goes nowhere; but east will take me to Savannah. No," he decided, "Savannah isn't nearly far enough away."

The heavy feeling in his chest made him want to curl up in a ball and do nothing, but an even stronger sense of fear and anger pressed him to keep moving. He recalled a laughing voice saying, "When the shit gets too deep, you can always go west."

"West to Alabama and nowhere," he said aloud.

The falling rain and the lonely road intensified his pain, and once again he sobbed uncontrollably. Turning on the radio for distraction, he heard Roger Williams playing, *Born Free;* unconsciously he sang along.

The farther west he drove, the harder the rain fell. Lightning flashed in front of him causing the radio to crackle. He continued on.

He drove directly toward Alabama's *Tornado Alley*. Seasoned drivers were pulling off the road, but the grieving boy kept his foot pressed to the gas pedal. The pounding rain defeated the beating strokes of his windshield wipers, but it did so needlessly for he could barely see through his tears. Visibility had ceased to hold any meaning to him; for he had ceased to exist. The static ridden tornado warnings rising from the radio went unheard and unheeded.

"Jack is dead." he sobbed. "Jack you were so free and playful. You were my best friend. Why did you die? Why? Why?"

Another part of his mind reminded him that Jack hit an unforeseen barrier head on. He never really understood what Jack did, or why, but he had watched Jack die and he only knew that Jack was good and that Jack was the only good thing in his life.

"Oh Jack, how could this have happened? How can you be dead?"

Unbearable pain penetrated his heart. The young man couldn't live in such a world -- wouldn't -- so he too, must be dead. Numbness smothered his conscious mind, while his subconscious propelled the car. A somnambulist, fueled by the laughing voice deep in his memory: Jack's voice. "In the old days when the shit got too deep, you could go west and be your own man. You could go west, and master your own dominion."

That voice, ringing in the hollows of his brain like a metronome, set his break-neck pace. "Go west... master your own dominion... go west... master your own dominion... go west... "

His car careened eighty miles an hour down the lonely highway. Hydroplaning half an inch above the pavement, his balding tires found friction only against the surface tension of the pooling rain water. Fifty miles ahead the tornado raged. Although he was not in immediate danger of the hundred-sixty mile an hour wind, its gale strength residue was visible around him in the trees that lined the highway. Branches that normally spread a peaceful umbrella of shade over the pavement snapped like angry whips. It was through this wet and windy gauntlet he traveled.

Up ahead, the powerful winds ripped through the forest taking down tree after tree. A massive hickory fell across the lonely highway, twenty-seven tons of wood did not even make a sound; the roar of the tornado, like the crashing of Niagara, drowned out all other sound.

The young man sped on heedless of safety. Suddenly a wall of bark soared in front of his preoccupied eyes. An automatic response deep in his brain slammed his foot against the brake pedal, but the tires meager tread could not dig deep enough into the water to catch the road's surface. The car's bumper ground into the tree, the young man's head into the windshield.

An hour later he returned to consciousness. Putting his finger to his forehead, he felt sticky congealed blood, but only a little pain as he poked it. Overall, his body seemed unhurt. He giggled as a silly thought popped into his head: on TV a bump on the head always causes amnesia.

Looking down, he saw glass from the windshield all over his lap. Glancing back up, his breath was cut short. A sturdy branch speared through the windshield and into the passenger seat. Wincing with visions of human shish-ka-bob, he imagined the branch a foot more to the left, and praised a god he no longer trusted. He took a deep breath and knocked the door open with his shoulder. As he climbed out, a sharp pain shot through his head. He staggered a few steps and passed out against the tree.

#

Rain spattering his face woke him only minutes later. He rose and looked around him. He saw a mangled car and wondered if anyone could live through such a crash. He looked around to see if there was anyone who needed help, but he found no one. Never questioning how he came to be there, he shrugged and assumed an ambulance must have already taken the body away. Then he thought, "It's too bad that people have to die, but the important thing is I'm alive and I've got to get going."

He felt fine. Better than that, actually, his soul was free, and his chest felt light enough that he could practically float over the tree trunk in front of him. If he'd seen himself in a mirror, he would have been confused by the rain-streaked red slash along his hairline. He would have wondered where he got it, because there was no pain in his head, only a throbbing mantra, a remnant from a lost past, beating deep inside his skull: "go - west...go - west...go - west...go - west...go - west..."

CHAPTER ONE

Middle California was hot and dry in July of 1987, hot enough and dry enough to ignite, but Frank Stacy hadn't really noticed until his wife, in collusion with his secretary, tricked him into taking a day off. To refer to Frank as a workaholic would be inaccurate. The true workaholic is a lazy man who knows that if he ever lets up, he may never get started again. The compulsion driving Frank to the office before sun up, and keeping him going until after sun down, day after day, was more intense than that.

Frank Stacy, at age 37, had achieved the admirable success of being the most anticipated movie maker of all time. The movie-going-public could not be satiated by his continuing stream of films. The typical comment, whenever a long line wrapped around theater, was, "Must be a new Stacy flick." A reviewer once said, "Frank Stacy could make a movie about toilets in Afghanistan and it would be a smash!" He apparently forgot the one movie that flopped. Forgetting, however, was easy to do, for Frank filmed constantly. It was easier to catch him on a set than off. Outsiders wondered where he found his energy, not to mention his preparation time. Envious competitors simply referred to his cameras as meat grinders.

Discovering the identity of the actors in a new Stacy movie became part of the thrill of attending one. It was the only gimmick Frank ever used. Withholding the names of the actors until the closing credits of his films became legendary. He went so far as to forbid the use of star's names in the advertising for his upcoming movies. At first his producers fought him on this. They said it was the stars who fed the box office, but Frank remained firm and his hunch paid off; for it was the excitement in seeing if they could recognize the stars before the closing credits that created the demand among the movie-going-public. One would think that would be as easy as looking at the actor's face, especially since Frank worked over and over again from his own stable of personally trained actors, but it wasn't; and after they had seen the movie, most people were good sports and wouldn't even tell their friends. The fun was in the anticipation; and Frank kept them coming back for more as fast as he could crank them out.

It was from this never-ending world of work that Myra conspired to give him a break, and to hopefully gain some new insight into her husband's essential self.

"Myra, how did you get him to stay home? Frank's appointment calendar is renowned from here to New York for being the strictest in the industry," whispered June as Frank got up from his lounge chair and headed for the pool.

"I called Connie several weeks ago, and asked her not to schedule any appointments for him today." Myra then lowered her voice slightly as it took on a vindictive tone, "She was a little too enthusiastic about it; I never thought Frank's great defender would agree that he needed a day off."

"Or maybe she needed a day off," June quipped lightly in Connie's defense.

Myra ignored the comment, "Then, last night, I turned his alarm clock off when he went to sleep."

"Wasn't he mad as hell, when he finally woke up?"

"No, but..." Myra's eyes seemed to become vacant in thought for a moment, then she said, "he did seem a little jittery until I told him that you and Zack were coming over. Then he calmed right down and seemed to accept it."

"Myra, I'll never understand what he sees in Zack; they're total opposites. Zack's parents should have named him Sack, as in sack-time, because I swear I've never met a less industrious man."

"I don't understand either, but look at them; they're playing like a couple of boys."

"Well, Zack's always been a boy; I dread to think of what would have become of him if his parent's hadn't left him so much money."

"As long as he has this effect on Frank, I'm glad they're friends."

"You must have that effect on him too, or how do you explain catching the most eligible bachelor east of the Pacific?"

"I was just lucky."

"Aw c'mon, give me the truth now," June cajoled. "I've been curious for years."

"We had mutual business that kept us together for long periods of time, that's all."

"Oh, who are you fooling? Must I quote the press, 'Frank Stacy discovered the acting parvenu Myra Mason in a prep school production and proceeded to mold raw talent into the finest acting ability ever known'."

"Okay June, I guess I'll have to tell you the truth, because if you quote another tabloid, I'll puke." She paused as if to catch her breath and then confided, "He didn't discover me; that was a ruse for the press. You know how tough it is to get into Frank's acting classes, right? Well, I wasn't good enough to get past his preliminary auditions. So, I bought my way into his office."

"You what!"

"It was when Frank needed a stake for that philosophical piece he did a few years ago."

"You mean *Resurgent Man*?"

"Yes, none of his regular producers would put up any dough. They made it crystal clear that their dollars were only available for his suspense-adventure films. Like most investors, they'd only back a sure thing."

"And they were right; it flopped."

"Only at the box office."

"Well, I wouldn't know about that."

"It actually started paying us back once it hit the video stores."

"Did you say, us? Don't tell me you backed it."

"Yes, I talked Daddy into giving me the money. When I went to Frank, I only put one condition on it: acting lessons."

"And he then let you in his class?"

"Not exactly; he told me I had to earn my way into those classes, that to allow me to buy a place would be a slap in the face to his other students, and that he had no intention of denigrating the integrity of his method in that way."

"So, there must have been a compromise; what was it?"

"He gave me private lessons until I earned my way in. The rest is history."

"You mean he made you a star because you lost your investment."

"Give me a break, June. You know better than that. I would never have demanded a condition such as that, nor would he have accepted it. He genuinely helped me find my talent. I knew it was there, and I knew he was the one to bring it out."

"He really admires you; I can see it in his eyes."

"I'm afraid - there's a kind of distance in that admiration, like a sculptor stepping back to review his work."

"Huh?"

A look of helplessness came over Myra's face as she said, "I can't really say how I know this, but sometimes I feel like I've never even met him. I know this sounds crazy, but sometimes I feel as if he's acting out some kind of role with me. First it was teacher, then it was director, finally it became lover, but now that it's husband, it's like we're stuck in a bad script. Do you want to hear a real secret, June? I swear this is true, ever since we got married he's been plagiarizing the husband from TV shows like *Father Knows Best* or *Leave It To Beaver*."

"Oh, come on Myra, now you're the one who sounds like a tabloid! Don't start getting caught up in Hollywood hype." She laughed and added, "Otherwise, we'll make you leave the peace and quiet of Fresno and move back to LA."

"But I'm not; and it's getting worse, or so it seems since we bought the house. We don't even work together anymore. It's a little embarrassing - the whole world knows he hasn't cast me in years."

"That's because you've become too famous for his pictures."

"June, now you're the one who's getting caught up in Hollywood hype. Too famous means too type-cast. Can anyone honestly say that about my work?"

"No; no one can. In fact, now that I think about it; it took me ten minutes to recognize you in your last film - and I'm your best friend!"

"But, June, when I ask him why; he tells me he's saving me for a great part commensurate with my talent, then in the same breath, he'll encourage me to accept offers from other studios. It's like a blow to the stomach. I want to cry every time I audition for another director. I do it, but only to keep working."

"What are you saying?"

"I'm saying that when we're together, I feel that his behavior is almost mechanized. I don't mean like a robot, but like a school boy reciting by rote."

"Myra, you're just suffering from normal marital blahs. It's a normal phase every couple goes through. Sometimes you just get tired of looking at each other."

"No, that I can understand, believe me, it's different from that. That's why I arranged for him to take the day off. I figured if he played with Zack all day, tonight he would be more receptive to me."

"Are you trying to tell me Frank is gay and he gets aroused by Zack?"

"No. I know I'm not making any sense to you. It's weirder than anything I've ever encountered, but somehow when Frank is with Zack he changes; he transforms... like... into another person."

"You're beginning to sound like the *Twilight Zone.*" June giggled and started humming the TV show theme song.

"I know; and it's scary, June. It's almost as if... I know this is really going to sound like Hollywood hype, but it's as if he has a tragic flaw. Except he doesn't have it when he's with Zack. With Zack he doesn't seem to be anyone else, but himself. I know that sounds strange, but what I mean is, that when he's with Zack, he isn't Frank the director, or Frank the producer, or any of the rigid roles he takes on in his business life. He's relaxed in a way I've never seen. There's not a single facial muscle held in tension; and Frank's control over his facial expression is legendary. What I'm hoping is that he'll stay in that mood after you two leave; and I can get to know my husband a little better."

"I don't really see what you're talking about," June consoled, "but that doesn't mean anything because the only time I see Frank is when he's with Zack."

Myra gave up and shifted the conversation to subjects that were less personal and frustrating. Behind them they heard the wop-wop sound of the diving board following by a splash. The two men began a diving contest in the pool.

Then Myra heard Frank yelling to Zack, "That was pretty good, Buddy, but I'm gonna show you a feat I haven't performed since I was a boy..."

She audibly sucked in her breath, and snapped her head toward the direction of the diving board. It was a reaction that caused June to say, "What is it?"

"He never mentions his childhood, in fact, it's almost as if he avoids it." Myra replied.

"...let's have a drum roll for the full gainer." Frank finished.

Zack began to slap the edge of the pool, a wet smacking sound that didn't resemble even a soggy drum. "Up, up, uuuuup!" He cried as Frank's feet left the board.

Immediately, all three saw that his take-off was wrong. Like the freeze-frame technique from one of Frank's motion pictures, their minds froze the scene into slow motion flashes. He went up, his feet floating up above his head, then completing the full circle back toward the water. But the angle was too sharp - as if his body wanted to make a second sweep - and his head fell back against the end of the diving board with a sickening thud.

Myra and June screamed, and Zack dove into the water. He swam to the bottom, following the billowing blood rising from Frank's head like puffy red smoke. He scooped the inert body into his arms, and pushed off the pool floor. As he splashed to the surface, Myra and June sobbed by the edge of the pool. Both reached out to pull Frank's lifeless mass out of the water.

Zack pushed as the girls dragged Frank out. He then pulled himself out, and quickly rolled Frank over onto his back, while Myra pushed her fingers into his neck to check for a pulse.

"His heart's still beating, but he's not breathing." She turned to the still sobbing June and ordered, "June, go call an ambulance."

Choking back her own sobs, she pinched his nostrils shut. Frank's mouth was much bigger than hers so she pressed her mouth inside of his to create a seal.

"I'm breathing for him now," she told herself as she forced her breath deep inside his lungs. His cold wet lips were pressed against each side of her cheeks; and she could feel his flaccid tongue against her own lips each time she blew to inflate his lungs. Once, as she exhaled into him, she thought of *Sleeping Beauty* and let her own tongue slide out and touch his, as if maybe she could kiss him back to life.

June returned, still crying, and sat by Zack who was keeping Frank's bleeding skull cushioned in a folded towel. Myra continued her litany of resuscitation: her head bobbing frantically. Up to suck in air - down to blow it back out. Up for herself - down for her husband. Up to sustain life - down to give it. Up to look for the ambulance - down to pray. She had to keep Frank going ... going ... going ... just a little bit longer.

Twenty minutes passed, and Myra's steady persistence was making her red faced and dizzy. Her tears were beginning to interfere with her own breathing; and Zack offered to take over. She shook her head, it was more than air she was giving Frank: it was love; possibly the last love she would ever be able to give him.

She could feel her diaphragm cramping, as she exhausted her body. "Don't die!" she screamed in her mind. "Not after you mentioned your childhood; not when you've just broken the silence that may give me the key to your love. I love you Frank, and I desperately want your love."

Then, as her anxiety was reaching its peak, she felt the resistance of life as it forced back the breath she was trying to give. Frank was coughing; his body was gasping and heaving as his autonomic system pulled in a lung-full of air. Myra leaned back in relief, and her tears broke loose and flooded her face. She sobbed freely; and loudly blubbered, "He made it. He made it. He's breathing."

Zack cheered, "All right, Myra!" Then he put his arm around her to steady her quaking shoulder.

Five tense minutes passed while the three watched the movement of Frank's chest, until finally his eyes opened. His eyes focused first on the satisfied smile on Myra's wet face then, his sight roving, he took in the faces of June and Zack.

Pushing up onto one elbow he faced the pool and woozily started to fall right back in. Zack grabbed his shoulder and said, "Easy boy."

Frank's glance moved slowly around the perimeter of the mosaic pool. He looked at the oasis-like landscaping blending palm trees and cacti, and then he looked across the length of the yard to the house. Rising at the top of a small hill was a three story pink stucco Spanish villa with a roof of red, yellow, and orange tiles sparkling in the noonday sun. He looked back to the three faces and exclaimed, "Where the hell am I?"

Zack snickered, and June gave him a dirty look.

Myra took his shoulders and gently guided his head back down to the towel. "Lie still, honey. You've had a bad accident."

"No kiddin'!" he replied. "I must've totaled my car."

"Car?" June gasped.

"Yeah, I smacked my head into the windshield. Wasn't it cracked?"

Zack laughed, "Your head or the windshield? It must have been that thick skull of yours that was whacked cause you're drawling just like a Georgia cracker. Where the *hail* am I." Zack mocked Frank's accent then slapped his belly and laughed again, "Oh, you are just too much -- making jokes when we were all worried you were dead."

"Well, I don't reckon I can help where I come from." Frank responded indignantly while pushing his way back up against Myra's prodding hands.

Zack's laughing stopped short.

"Now, I appreciate y'all helpin' me out, but I've got to be gettin' on." Frank said as he stood up. Then as he looked down, he saw he was clad solely in a dripping wet bathing suit. He cried, "Hey, where're my clothes?"

Myra reached for him, "Honey you need to sit back down."

Frank backed out of her reach while looking around him on the ground as if he'd find his clothes lying there. Suddenly noticing the bright California sun shining, he demanded, "When did it quit rainin'?"

Pausing briefly, to take in more of the daylight or perhaps the surrounding topography, he looked carefully around, then asked, "Say, how long have I been out anyway?"

There was no reply only three silent faces staring at him.

#

"Hold it." Hooper Johnson said as he leaned back into the sofa. He stretched his long legs out on the living room floor, then gesturing with the script he held in his hand, continued, "Sally, I'm not hearing any meaning, any soul in your voice when you say, 'I love you' to Markus. You've got to feel the emotion or it sounds awkward and unbelievable. Now don't give me that look; I'm not trying to make you feel bad. I'm trying to teach you. Saying, 'I love you' is the most difficult line any actor will ever have."

"How about I try it again by substituting the word *rhubarb* for 'I love you?' That's what my last acting teacher told me to do. He said it neutralizes preconceived attitudes my brain associates with certain words. By using *rhubarb* instead, I free up my natural emotion, so that it may enter my speech. Then once I'm feeling the correct emotion, I replace the correct words."

"Yeah, like surf's up, dude," Hooper said in Valley Speak, "and I suppose next you'll tell me that the best warm-up exercise is barking like a dog and crawling around the room on all fours."

Resuming his normal accent, Hooper continued, "Sally, that's absurd, if you need an exercise try saying, 'I love you' as if you mean, 'I hate you' then reverse it, and say, 'I hate you' as if you mean, 'I love you.' Always use the opposite to get the proper perspective on elusive emotions. Besides, it makes more sense than articulating with weird vegetables."

Sally dropped to one knee, and ran her hand along the inside of Hooper's outstretched thigh, and said tenderly, "I hate you, Hooper." Then in the same voice, said, "I love you, Hooper."

"Great!" Hooper answered, pulling his legs out of her reach. "Now tell it to Markus."

"I love you, Markus. I worship you. That's why I take private acting lessons from you."

"Stick to the script," Hooper ordered, "or I'll charge you double."

"Charge me triple, only let me stay and cook your dinner."

"Come on Sally, get serious."

"I am serious, because I love you - I can love Markus; thinking of you puts me in the right frame of mind."

"Good, whatever works for you. Now let's get on with the lesson."

"Not until you promise me I can stay for dinner."

"Okay, dinner; but no promises beyond that."

CHAPTER TWO

Myra was first to react. She grabbed Frank's shoulders and gently forced him to sit back down. He did not resist this time. The disorientation seemed to momentarily upset him. Myra took the opportunity to guide his head back on the towel to rest.

"Frank, just lie still; the ambulance will be here in a minute."

Frank pushed right back up on his elbows and said, "Look ma'am, I don't mean to be rude, especially since y'all stopped to help me, but I don't have time to be going to no hospital."

"Frank," she cried, "you've got to have your skull x-rayed."

"Ma'am, why do you keep callin' me Frank? My name is Eugene Eastly and my father is Jim Eastly, the plumber. You might've heard of him before; he's done work as far as Opelika. If you have, you know he's a real son of a bitch, but that don't matter anymore cause me and my best friend Jack are on our way to California to make movies. Say, where is Jack? Wasn't he in the car with me?"

June gasped again, and Zack whispered to Myra, "It's like when he's acting. Do you think that whack on the skull has thrown him into a role from one of the scripts he's reviewing?"

"I was thinking the same thing." Myra whispered back. Then to Frank she said, "Snap out of it, Frank, this isn't a script. You've hurt yourself, and you're going to the hospital."

"Look, ma'am. Just don't call my old man, cause I'm not going back."

"Oh, God. Oh, God." Myra started crying again. "Oh, I wish that ambulance would hurr-- Oh, there it is; thank God."

The paparazzi were already laying-in-wait, when the ambulance arrived at the hospital. Like predators, they pounced at the first sight of their prey. Someone listening to a police scanner recognized the address when the dispatcher called it out, and tipped off the press.

Zack reacted violently to the camera flash greeting, but Myra grabbed his arm before he could hit the nearest nuisance.

"You'll just make it worse," she whispered to him. "We've got to appease them, or they'll never leave us alone. I also don't want them to hear Frank talking until his head clears. Why don't you take him in, and I'll stay here." Then removing her scarf and sunglasses she added, "I'm a veteran at handling these guys."

Myra turned to the crowd, parted her silk swimsuit cover-up, and flashed the photographers with a classic Betty Grable leg-shot.

It worked, someone cried, "It's Myra Mason!" The statement caused the photographers to wheel away from Frank's stretcher and stumble over each other in the attempt to capture her pose.

"Miss Mason!" ... "Over here, Miss Mason!" ... "Miss Mason!" they cried.

"Gentlemen, today I'm simply Mrs. Frank Stacy, middle-age housewife. Frank had a little accident while swimming today. He bumped his head on the diving board. He's conscious, but I'm afraid he'll have to have some stitches. Let this be a lesson to all you forty-year old boys who think you can still show off."

The crowd laughed, and Myra offered one more poster-girl shot before saying, "Fella's, if you'll excuse me, I'm going inside to be with my husband. If anyone's interested, I'll notify Frank's office, and you can call in for the number of stitches he had to get. And guys, try not to embarrass him too much."

The crowd laughed again, and she disappeared into the emergency room replacing her scarf and sunglasses.

Two hours later, the doctor came into the waiting room.

"Mrs. Eastly, your husband seems to be suffering only a minor concussion. I've run a complete set of skull x-rays and a brain scan, and neither show any damage. I have advised him to take it easy for the next couple of days. He had to have eight stitches and with the lump he's got on the back of his head he won't be sleeping on his back for a while."

"But, doctor, what about his confusion?"

"I haven't noted any confusion."

"Dr. Thomas, my husband's name is not Eugene Eastly, it's Frank Stacy."

"Frank Stacy! I heard he'd been admitted, but when I didn't see his name on our roster, I assumed he must have been a direct admission to one of the surgical floors."

"Doctor, when he regained consciousness after the accident, he didn't know who I was. He didn't know he is in California. And, he didn't know his name is Frank Stacy."

"Come on, let's go back and take another look at him."

In the examination room, the doctor asked his patient, "What is your name?"

Frank answered, "It's Eugene, sir."

"Eugene what?"

"Eugene Eastly."

"Eugene, do you ever go by any other names?"

"No, sir."

The doctor turned back to Myra, and said, "People who are confused seldom show this much confidence when answering." Pausing he looked at Myra for a moment then said, "Is this some kind of hoax, because if it is, I won't stand for it another minute. This is a busy emergency room; and this hospital has a reputation to uphold."

Myra reached into her purse. Then handed him her driver's license, Frank's license, her S.A.G. card and Frank's Director's Guild of America card. Then, once again removing her scarf and sunglasses, she said, "Dr. Thomas, my name is Myra Mason, I'm also known as Mrs. Frank Stacy. Why don't you just ask him where he is?"

He stepped back into the hallway, then after examining the documents, said, "Pardon me Miss Mason; I'm sorry I didn't recognize you, but it isn't like L.A. up here. We don't see many stars, and you must admit you look different in every movie."

"It's okay, but will you please go in there and ask him where he is?"

"Yes," he answered. Then pushed open the door.

Inside the room he asked Frank, "Mr. Eastly, can you tell me where you are?"

"Yes, sir. I'm in the hospital."

"In what city?"

"I don't know."

"Do you know what state?"

"Alabama, I reckon."

"Alabama? Mr. Eastly, can you tell me what day it is?"

"No sir, not exactly, because I don't know how long I've been out."

"Then just give me the last day you remember."

"Sure, it was May 18th."

"Mr. Eastly, you are in California not Alabama. And, it's July 14th."

"Holy Cow! I've been out for two whole months? ... Say, how did I get to California if I was unconscious?"

"Dr. Thomas," Myra whispered, "if we could step back outside, I may have an explanation."

Dr. Thomas followed her out, and she said, "Doctor are you familiar with Frank Stacy's work?"

"Well, I've seen some of the movies he's directed."

"I'm talking about his approach to method acting?"

"No, I can't say that I am."

"He's the best teacher of method acting since Stanislovsky. When he studies a role, he meditates on the character's psyche and inner motivation until he practically becomes that person. Without changing his clothes or even applying make-up he can become another person so convincingly that people who have known him for years won't even recognize him."

"So you're saying--"

"That somehow this accident has kicked him into some role he has recently studied."

"Well, I'm neither a neurologist nor a psychiatrist. Your explanation is as good as any for now. As long as he is suffering from any type of amnesia, I believe we should admit him for observation. Hopefully, a few days rest will bring him back around."

"That's what I was hoping you'd suggest."

"In the meantime, I'll arrange for a neuro and psych consult. For now, I'm going to give him a sedative and a bed. Sometimes it only takes a good night's rest to abate simple traumatic disorientation."

#

Sally poured more wine into Hooper's glass.

"Are you trying to get me drunk?" he taunted.

"Yes, it's the only way I know to take advantage of you."

"Your acting has improved quite a bit," he said; changing the subject.

"I attribute it all to you. I'll never forget my very first lesson with you. You were so serious, and even a little intimidating. I mean, you've got a really good reputation; and I know you don't take that many students."

"You mean, I can't get that many students." he laughed.

"Don't try to deprecate your ability with me. I can still remember how you sat me down, and tried to act so stern. You were just like that professor in *The Paper Chase*, when you said, 'Lesson number one: acting is a moving force, and good acting follows a path of motivation. If a role requires you to touch a hot stove: you do not play getting burned. You play to escape the pain of getting burned.' I'll never forget that Hooper. I apply that theory to everything I do; including playing up to you."

"Enough with the flattery, I want to hear whether or not you've heard back from Warner's yet. After all, they were the ones asking you to make the screen-test."

Sally hesitated, and sipped her wine before answering, "Yes, I got a call back, and it looks like I'm going to get the part."

Hooper's face broke into a grin, "That's wonderful, but why haven't you mentioned it? You should have told me right away. I'm so proud of you; this is easily your most important accomplishment."

"Oh, Hooper," she started to cry. "I didn't want to say anything because you haven't worked in a while."

"Don't worry about me, in fact, my agent is sending me to audition for a supernumerary role this week in a picture called *Runaway Grandparents*."

"Hooper, you can't fool me." she put her hand on his and continued, "I know a supernumerary is the same thing as an extra. That's chicken feed, and you deserve better. Why won't you audition for Frank Stacy? At least he'll appreciate your ability."

Hooper shook his head.

"Look," Sally insisted. "I know you're good enough. I auditioned for him once, but I didn't stand a chance. I saw the people he picked. And, Hooper, you're as good if not better."

"You're flattering me again." He squeezed her hand gently; but then pulled his hand away from hers.

"No, not now. I'm serious. Why won't you at least give it a chance?"

"I guess it's a matter of pride, a sort of standard or goal I set for myself. I want to make it in such a way that people will ask me if I was ever a student of Frank Stacy. I want them to ask it, just so I can say I'm not."

Sally nodded toward a poster tacked to the dining room wall. It was a still of Myra Mason from a scene in *The Tangled Web*. It was the sole adornment to his walls. She asked, "Does it have something to do with her?"

"Yes, she's the talent I intend to surpass."

Sally folded her napkin, dropped it onto her plate, then stood up.

"You're not leaving?" Hooper asked with surprise.

"Yes I am; I know when I'm out of my league."

Hooper stood up, and said, "Sally don't be ridiculous."

"Sorry teacher, but you don't sound sincere. Try it again by saying 'Myra don't be ridiculous.' Then maybe, it will sound like you mean it."

Hooper stood silently as she walked out the door.

#

The morning sun on her eyelids gently awakened Myra from an uneasy slumber. She rolled over to put her arm around Frank, but her hand fell on an empty sheet, and she recalled the reason for her nightmare-ridden sleep.

Frank had not wanted to stay at the hospital; he argued vehemently until the sedative began taking effect. Myra wanted to be beside him when he woke up. She hurried out of bed to get dressed. The phone rang as she was walking out the door. It was bad news. She grabbed the edge of the credenza for support as Dr. Thomas said, "We have a problem, Frank disappeared from the hospital sometime during the night."

CHAPTER THREE

"Cars sure look different out here in California," Eugene said to the man driving the truck.

"Whadda ya mean?" asked the driver.

"Well, they're a lot smaller; and I don't recognize most of the makes."

"I thought you said you were from Georgia?"

"I am."

"I been through Georgia plenty of times; and I never noticed any difference."

Eugene pointed to a *Volkswagen Jetta,* and said, "Look at that car; that's about the strangest car I've ever seen."

"What are you crazy? That's a VW."

"A VW? Well, the only VW's we got are the regular ones. Like that one," he said, pointing to an old beetle.

"Buddy, you're mighty strange, but I suppose if you're going to live in Hollywood and make movies you gotta be strange."

"Have you been to Hollywood much?"

"Nope, mostly just pass through. So, what kinda movies you wanna make? Something like *Rambo* maybe?"

"No, I don't want to work for Disney. I'm going to be an independent."

"I said *Rambo* not *Bambi*."

"I'm not familiar with that movie; it just sounded like a Disney title to me."

"Not familiar with it! What are you kiddin' me?"

"My home town is pretty small; we don't get all the movies."

"Maybe, but it don't seem likely. So, what kinda movies does an independent make?"

"Oh, I could make movies about anything. For example I've been watching you use that radio to talk to the other truckers, so you'll know where Smokey is. It's like you're talkin' in code, and I'll bet

Smokey means the cops. It's like a cat-and-mouse game! I could make a movie about--"

"It's been done."

"You're kidding?"

"No, but I think you are. Look if you don't want to tell me; you ain't gotta. I was just trying to make conversation."

The truck passed a sign reading: Los Angeles 90 miles. Eugene was too excited by the thought that he could be in Hollywood in less than two hours to worry about making conversation with the trucker.

Several hours earlier, around 2 A.M., he woke up in his hospital bed. The only clothing he had was the half gown the nurses put on him. He poked his head out the door until he could see the nurse's station at one end of the dimly lit corridor. At the other end he saw the fire exit. Seeing no one in sight, he started down the hall toward the fire exit stairwell. As he was about to open the door, he heard steps. Quickly, he backed into the shadow formed by the shallow alcove framing the door. As he listened to the sound of steps grow distant, he felt the cold metal door against his bare buttocks. It was a rude reminder that he would have to procure better clothing, or he would not be traveling far.

Peeking out of the alcove, he saw it was safe to make his exit. Then as he descended the stairs, he stopped at each landing to look out onto the floors. On the second floor down, he saw a sign reading: *Doctor's Lounge*. He reconnoitered the hallway, and then ducked inside the lounge. It was empty; along the wall was a row of lockers. One was unlocked. Hanging inside was a baby blue sweat suit with dark blue stripes on the sleeves and legs. He thought the outfit looked like, what his father would call, 'sissy clothes,' but it beat being naked. In the bottom of the locker was a pair of sneakers with thick wedged shaped soles with the word *Nike* embroidered on the back. He felt a little guilty about stealing the clothes, but taking a cripple's orthopedic tennis shoes was really low. When he tried them on they fit; so he talked himself into it, and tied them on.

The hallway was still clear, and the door at the bottom of the stairs led out of the building. Outside, he started running to put some distance between him and the hospital. As he ran, he found the odd looking shoes he'd stolen actually helped him run faster; it was as if he were bouncing with each step. By 6 A.M. he found himself at a truck stop at an intersection of Interstate 99.

His stomach began to rumble. He dug his hands down into his pockets. He felt a few coins, and they counted out to ninety-four cents.

"Well," he thought to himself, "at least I'll be eating for a couple of days." He pushed through the door, sat at the counter and ordered coffee. When the waitress set the cup down, he slid a dime across the counter to her. She looked down at it, and said, "What's that?"

"For the coffee." he replied.

"Coffee's a dollar."

"A dollar!" he cried.

"Look at the sign." she said, jerking her thumb over her shoulder to point at the menu plaque on the wall behind her head.

"Good golly, California sure is expensive," he said as he pulled out the rest of the change and put on the counter in front of her. "I'm sorry, it's only ninety-four cents" he said, and then pushed the cup back to her. "I should have looked at the menu first. I didn't realize it could cost so much."

She started to scowl as she would at any normal dead-beat, but paused when she noticed the look of sincerity in his face. She chuckled, shoved the coffee back to him, and gently mocking him, she asked, "Good Golly? Where're you from kid?"

"Georgia."

"Okay, the difference is on me this time. You can make it up to me next time."

"Gee, thanks." he replied; and she scooped up the ninety-four cents and dropped them into her tip pocket.

A few minutes later a trucker came and sat down beside him, and then ordered coffee and a hot apple Danish. Eugene watched as the waitress removed the pastry from a glass and stainless steel refrigerator. She then put it into what looked like a chrome plated bread box. Seconds later a bell rang and she removed it steaming with heat.

"Holy cow!" he cried out. "How'd you do that?"

"Do what?" she asked.

"Heat that turnover up so fast?"

"Kid, you're weird." she said, and turned to another customer.

Still curious, he asked the trucker, "I've never seen anything like that before. Can you tell me what she did?"

"Sure, she nuked it."

"Wow! You mean that box has a miniature nuclear reactor in it?"

"Say Pal, are you on drugs or what?"

He didn't say anything; he didn't know what to say. Between the doctors and nurses at that hospital, and the people here, it seemed that every time he opened his mouth he was speaking a different language. He turned back to his coffee, and contemplated how he would make movies. Moving pictures that would depict exciting stories of action and romance, but more than that. He wanted to tell complex stories of individual men and women who stood apart and caused the rest of mankind to either crave their death or create gods in their image. He would pry the spirit from deep inside such characters, then expose it, in all its glory, on the silver screen. That type of person did not seem to exist anymore, but Jack could speak of them, and Eugene could picture them in his mind. They would capture it. They would create the role models for a whole generation; but first, he paused and reflected, he would have to find Jack.

He wondered if Jack had gone on to Hollywood. They must have gotten separated after the accident. Was Jack injured too? He only remembered himself getting hurt. Jack must have gone on ahead. He learned from the waitress that he was somewhere just south of Fresno. She pointed it out on a map taped to the window. He studied the map for several minutes, and then concluded that he needed to continue south. So, he returned to his seat, and asked the trucker sitting next to him. "Pardon me, sir. Could you tell me how I might find a driver on his way to Los Angeles? I'd like to see if I could hitch a ride."

"You're not supposed to be doing that around here." the trucker began gruffly, but again like the waitress, he saw something in Eugene's face that make him soften. "But, I'll tell you what. I know of a fellow going your way; and if he hasn't left yet, I'll ask him for ya. But, you better not let anyone know about this, you hear?"

"Yes, sir."

"Then, come on." He rose, and Eugene followed.

It was several hours before the driver was ready. While he waited, Eugene caught up on his sleep. Once they were under way, he found that making conversation with this latest benefactor was just as difficult as it had been everywhere else. Eugene contented himself to ride in quiet and watch the road.

About dusk the truck pulled off the Golden State Freeway near Griffith Park.

"End of the line, Kid." The driver wondered why he called him, Kid. He seemed like a kid, but somehow looked a little older. He pointed west and said, "Hollywood's that-a-way, just on the other side of this mountain." He pointed to a dusty scrub covered hill. "That big cement ditch we just crossed is the Los Angeles River, if you want you can follow it all the way to Universal Studios."

"Isn't the Hollywood sign on the other side of this mountain?"

"Yes, I believe so."

"Then that's the way I want to go. Thanks mister, you really helped me out a lot." Eugene shook the driver's hand, then turned to climb down.

He was not quite sure why, but the trucker found himself pulling his wallet out, and saying, "Hey, kid. Wait a minute. Let me give you a few bucks. No town seems too friendly to a guy who's pockets and stomach are empty at the same time."

Eugene accepted the forty dollars and insisted on getting the man's address, so he could return the favor.

It was too late to start canvassing the studios; he still had several miles to go, and the sun was well hidden behind Mt. Hollywood. His destination was on the other side of Griffith Park; he set off on a beeline to get there. Eugene bought the last hot dog from a push cart vendor wheeling out of the zoo; and as darkness fell on the winding road before him, he heard the plaintive roar of a lion rising within the zoo walls. He walked up for hours then down for hours; he learned that distances on maps are deceiving and memories of maps even more so. He had reached a golf course, when he heard the twelve bongs of midnight on a distant clock. His weary legs led him at last to a cozy clump of bushes to sleep under.

At 11:25 P.M. the trucker had finished his run, and was drinking a beer in a bar outside San Diego. He was chatting with the bartender while a television on the wall played the evening news. The bartender was telling him how he moved to California to become an actor, but gave it up because the competition was too tough. A familiar face on the TV screen caught his attention, and he interrupted the bartender, "Quick, turn up the sound on that thing!"

He heard:

"Recapping our top story this evening: film director Frank Stacy, who was injured in a swimming pool accident yesterday, disappeared from Fresno General Hospital this morning and is possibly suffering from amnesia. If anyone is aware of his whereabouts, please contact the California Highway Patrol."

"What! Do you know something about that guy?" the bartender asked him.

"Yeah, I dropped him off in L.A. about four hours ago."

"You sure it's him?"

"Pretty sure; it looks like him. He had a bandage on his head."

"Do you believe he's got amnesia?"

"Well, he better, cause I gave him forty bucks."

"Forty bucks! That guy must make a hundred times what you do."

"That's what I mean. He gave me some different name: Gene or Eugene. He said he was from Georgia and that he was going to Hollywood to make movies."

"Georgia! He must of been acting?"

"No, he sounded just like he was from Georgia, and I've been around the country enough to know the difference. Hell, I even thought he was a kid."

"But Stacy must be in his forties."

"Well, he did look a little old, but he thought he was a kid, so I thought he was a kid."

"Then it was definitely Stacy."

"How do you know?"

"Because that's Stacy's acting method: to completely become the character you're playing. He's famous for it. Hell, if I could've gotten in his classes, I wouldn't be standing here behind this stupid bar. I'd be a star."

"Maybe I should call the Highway Patrol?"

"Hell if I would. Stacy hasn't got any amnesia; he's just acting. It's probably some publicity stunt for some new movie he's putting out. Why should you help him get free advertising; he just skinned you for forty bucks so he could stay in character?"

"I guess you got a point. How 'bout another beer?"

CHAPTER FOUR

Eugene woke with the first light of dawn. He was a little stiff from sleeping on the ground, but his excitement of actually being in Hollywood caused his muscles to loosen quickly. He pulled the dirty bandage off his head, and then jogged out of the park down Vermont Avenue. His eyes took in the sights he'd only dreamed of seeing. Exhilaration ran in chills up his spine, and goose bumps rose on his arms. He was going to make movies - great movies.

The mountains rose behind him against the dawn and into his view came the nine huge white letters that did more than spell out the name of this place; they shone like a beacon pouring out the message: HERE DREAMS COME TRUE. His legs began to pump faster in anticipation of reaching first Hollywood Boulevard and then the Sunset strip itself. Suddenly another sign caught his eye, and caused a rumble in his stomach. It was a big yellow "M" against a red background. He stopped and stared at the name: *McDonald's*.

Could it be the same company, he wondered, as that little McDonald's hamburger stand he once ate at in Atlanta. This restaurant didn't have the huge yellow arches, but it had a dining room so you didn't have to stand outside to eat. And, it was open and actually serving breakfast. "Wow," he thought, "even McDonald's is wonderful in Hollywood."

Having sated his hunger, he continued his trek into Tinseltown; hiking west on Sunset Boulevard to the address of Nordwick Studios. Nordwick was a private studio built on the ruins of what had been the backlot of the once famous *Laskey Studios*. It was the last studio still operating within the boundaries of Hollywood proper; and it was available to anyone willing and able to pay their fees. It was the perfect place for independents because it offered a full range of state-of-the-art equipment for lease.

It was at Nordwick that Eugene hoped to catch up with Jack. He and Jack had planned their trip so they would arrive at the same time Smurling would begin filming his newest picture. They would take any job, scrubbing toilets if necessary, to be on the set with Smurling. Smurling was the director they emulated. The man who's confidence they had to win; he was the mentor they wanted. Unfortunately, Eugene was two months late; he hoped they were still shooting.

The guard at the gate shook his head at the dirty, disheveled, unshaven man standing before him.

"Nope, ain't nobody here by that name."

"Are you sure? Could you look again? Please. It's spelled S-M-U-R-L-I-N-G."

"I don't need to look. I know the names of all the directors that come through here, and I've never heard of this Smurling."

"Never heard of him? He was scheduled to begin shooting *Baker's Dozen* on July first, and he shot *The Raven And The Nomad* here last fall."

"You must have the wrong studio, because no one has filmed a re-make of *The Raven And The Nomad* here."

"Re-make? I didn't know it had been done before."

"Say, haven't I seen you somewhere before?"

"Not unless you've been to Ellaville, Georgia. I've only been in California a few days, but maybe you've seen a friend of mine. He would've arrived here about six or seven weeks ago. You might remember him because he would have asked for Smurling too. His name's Jack Franklin."

"Don't remember anyone else asking for Smurling, of course I'm not the only guy working the gate."

"Is there anyone I can ask inside? He would've also been looking for work."

"Well, you can go ask in the office, but you stay off the sets."

"Thanks."

He walked into the office, and the receptionist took one look at him and said, "Wow, you look great, but you're a little late; casting for *Runaway Grandparents* started at six. They're casting a lot of street people though, maybe if you hurry you can still get a part. You really do look like you slept in the park last night."

"I did."

"Really! Do you study under Frank Stacy?"

There was that name again, and hearing it bothered him. "Uh, no."

"That's too bad. Well, you better hurry, you need to report to stage number four."

He paused in thought. He hadn't planned on acting, but here was an opportunity for work, and he would need money while he searched for Smurling. He'd do it, but first he had to find out if Jack had been here.

"What are you waiting for?"

"I wanted to ask you if a friend of mine was here looking for work about six or seven weeks ago? His name is Jack Franklin."

"I wouldn't have any idea. Thousands of people have been through here in that time. All we do is screen them and make sure the right ones go to the right set. What you need to do is check with the union."

"Oh, may I use your phone?"

"Sorry, company use only."

"Well, thanks anyway. What set did you say that was?"

"That's Sound Stage Number Four."

That was the second blow in less than half an hour. His elation over being in Hollywood was turning into despondency. With his shoulders bent, and his head down, he shuffled between the rows of huge, round-roof, Quonset hut-like structures that were as big as warehouses. By the time he saw a line of people waiting outside a door, he was completely depressed. Above the door he saw the numeral 4, so he took his place at the end of the line. Leaning against the wall, he slumped to the ground.

An hour passed and the last group was called to walk across the set. Still depressed, Eugene dragged along following the group.

The director stood up, "You there, Blue Sweats, excellent characterization! Now why can't I find more extras like you. Who are you; one of Frank Stacy's students?"

There was that name again. He was beginning to hate it. He kicked the floor. "No, suh." he mumbled; drawled. "I'm jus' Eugene Eastly an' Ah needed a job."

"Too much!" the director cried in laughter. "He can even speak in character. What is this, a last minute audition for a supporting role?"

It looked to Eugene like he was going to get a part, and the corners of his mouth began to rise. This was good news, and his mood from the morning was returning. His shoulders followed the smile as if they were attached by invisible strings. Hollywood was benevolent and the grin forming on his face was drawing the rest of his body out of its slump, and out of character.

"Okay, Eugene and the tall guy with the felt hat stay, everybody else, thank you." He then turned to his assistant and continued. "Michael take these two, put them with the rest of the street people, and give them their instructions."

"Mr. Zienkiewicz," Michael lisped, "it's absolutely imperative that we resolve that matter with the costumes before we can give any instructions."

"Whatever."

The assistant made a snap military parade turn with his feet, but his hands floated out from his sides causing the gesture to look more like a pirouette. He then marched away with quick short steps causing his rump to twitch in a way that Eugene thought would probably get him tarred and feathered back in Ellaville. As they followed, Eugene asked the fellow with the felt hat, "What's the big deal about this Frank Stacy? Everybody keeps talking about him like he's a god."

"Where've you been, on the moon? Stacy is a god. There's not a director on earth that compares to him."

"Not even Smurling?"

"Who?"

"You know *The Unyielding, Gods Of Autumn, The Boise Affair*."

"Ancient history! Stacy is light years ahead of any of the old greats."

"I'm embarrassed to admit it, but I don't know a single movie this Stacy has made."

The man stared at him suspiciously as if he'd said, he'd never tasted *Coca-Cola*. However, after a moment, just like the waitress and the trucker, something about Eugene's face made him soften, and he said, "Then you're just not reading the credits because I know you've at least seen *American Epitaph, Furnace Of Hephaestus,* and *The Tangled Web.*"

"No, I've never even heard of them."

"But those were major box office hits; everybody has at least heard of them!"

Eugene shrugged, "What can I say, I grew up in a one theater town in southwest Georgia. The fact is, I only just arrived here in Hollywood."

"Then you really ought to see Stacy's flicks. You can probably rent most of them. Do you have a VCR?"

"Vee-cee-yar. What's that, a French movie projector?"

"Come on Eugene, now I know you're yanking my chain, even small towns in Georgia have VCR's."

Eugene shook his head.

"Man, you ought to be trying out for a re-make of the *Beverly Hillbillies*. What are you going to tell me next, that Mary Pickford is your favorite modern actress and Jeff Davis is president of the United States?"

"Why don't you just call me a dumb redneck? I know it's true, but I'm going to learn how to direct films; and I'm going to be better than this guy Stacy. You just watch!"

"Take it easy, I'm just playing with your head. I'm sorry. Okay?"

"Okay"

Michael led them to a room where all the *Runaway Grandparents* extras were waiting. He told them to make themselves comfortable until he returned with their instructions. The room had more than forty people in it. The few available chairs were already taken, so they sat on the floor against the wall.

"What's your name?" Eugene asked his new friend.

"Hooper Johnson, used to be John Hooper, but I changed it."

"Pleased to meet you Hooper. Maybe I should change my name."

"Don't bother, I don't think it matters much what a director's name is."

"I guess you're right."

"You know, it's too bad about Stacy getting amnesia and getting lost. I'd bet, just from watching you during the audition, that you're good enough to get into his classes. Then once you got in, you could have learned a lot about directing."

Eugene's hand involuntarily moved to the back of his head. "My God," he thought, "that explains it. I must have had amnesia too, from when I hit that tree; and from the way those people were acting, I must look like Stacy. Whoever found me wandering around Alabama must have thought I was him; and they sent me to his family."

When Eugene did not answer, Hooper said, "Hey man, I didn't mean to depress you."

"That's okay, it doesn't bother me because I've really got my heart set on learning from Smurling." Eugene answered.

"Forget Smurling, he's probably dead anyway."

"He's not dead; he is supposed to be filming at this studio right now, but there must have been a cancellation because the guy at the gate said he wasn't here."

"He must have retired then. You should at least consider Stacy as an alternative."

"If this Stacy is so great, why aren't you one of his students?"

Hooper paused, as his eyes lost focus for a moment, then he said, "If you're a Stacy student - you're an actor; period. I haven't decided if I wouldn't rather be a movie star instead." As he finished, he chuckled at his own answer.

Eugene studied Hooper's face for several seconds, then responded with what was more of a statement than a question, "There's another reason isn't there?"

"Jesus, Eugene. You don't even know me and you're already cutting through my bullshit, and reading my mind."

Eugene maintained eye contact with Hooper, who finally admitted, "It's because of a girl I want to prove something to. Now let's drop it."

"Sure, Hooper."

"Look, I've got an idea. Why don't you quit worrying about Smurling, and come over to my place tonight. I've got a VCR and we can rent *The Tangled Web*."

"Well, I don't know."

"Look, I'm not gay, if that's what you're worried about."

"Then why invite me over if you don't want to?"

"But I do."

"Then why did you say you weren't happy about it?"

"I never said that."

"Sure you did. You said, you weren't gay about it."

Hooper burst into laughter, "Eugene, you're a riot! I don't know how you can do that and keep a straight face. Why the hell do you want to direct? You ought to be an actor. Better yet a comedian."

Hooper reached over and grabbed a discarded newspaper, and tore off a corner. "Here, I'll give you my address and phone number. Tell me where you live; I'll give you directions from there."

"I haven't got a place yet. I just got in town last night."

"Then you can follow me home in your car." He handed over the scrap of paper with his address and phone number. "Keep this in case we get separated on the way over."

"I'm afraid, I don't have a car either. I totaled it in Alabama on my way out here."

"Must of been drinking some of that Georgia moonshine, huh?" Hooper laughed at his own joke. "I'll tell you what. You can move in with me for the run of this picture, and we can ride in together."

"Gee thanks, Hooper."

"You better wait until you see the slum I live in before you thank me."

Eugene thought about sleeping in the park and said, "I'm sure it beats my latest accommodations."

Their conversation waned as their wait continued. Hooper stretched out on the floor and closed his eyes. Eugene picked up the discarded newspaper to pass the time and saw the headline:

RONALD REAGAN PUSHES TAX REFORM BILL

He read the first line and started laughing. He punched Hooper in the shoulder and said, "Hey, look at this. The paper made a mistake. They wrote President instead of Governor in front of Ronald Reagan's name."

"Not funny, Eugene. Forget I complimented you before. Playing like you're in the *Twilight Zone* only works once. Here, give me that." Hooper snatched the paper out of Eugene's hand, rolled it up, and stuck it under his head like a pillow. "Now don't wake me up until the queen bee gets back."

Another hour passed before Michael returned. He called them up to his table in the same order they were chosen earlier. When Eugene's turn arrived Michael handed him a manila envelope, and spoke in the bored staccato of a bureaucrat, "This contains all your instructions: where to pick up your costume, where to report, etc. You'll also find your set passes; do not lose these or you will not be able to get past the police blocks when we shoot the street scenes. It also contains your basic contract. I need you to sign it now and show me your guild card. By the way, we have assigned you a speaking part. Two lines. Congratulations."

"Thank you. Is it okay if I show you a guild card later? I haven't had a chance to join, yet."

"Goddamn it!" Michael exploded in petulant exasperation. "I just knew I wasn't going to get through this day without a hitch."

"I'm sorry. If it's a problem I'll go down and join up right now."

Hooper stepped over, and said, "Michael, Eugene just got into town last night, from Ellaville, Georgia."

"Elavil? You sure that's not the name of the medication his psychiatrist prescribed him?"

"Look, I'm trying to tell you he's a bit of a neophyte, so why don't you cut him some slack."

"And, who are you, the star?" Michael snipped.

"Hey, don't get huffy. I came over here to help you out. Just tell me if Zienkiewicz will sign the form, and I'll drive Eugene over to union hall and get him on the roster."

"He gave him lines, didn't he? He'll sign."

"So there's no problem?"

"Mr. Zienkiewicz is a busy man, he doesn't like to take time to go down and sign anything, which means I'll have to go down, pick it up, have him sign, then take it back down. That's a problem."

"It's not a problem, because you can pick up the phone and tell them to give Eugene the form and he can do the legwork. Okay?"

Michael hesitated only a moment before answering, "Okay."

As they walked to the car Eugene asked, "Hooper, I don't understand. What's the big deal?"

"Oh, it's union politics; a director isn't supposed to hire a non-union actor unless he's willing to stipulate on paper that there are no union actors that are right for the part."

When they arrived at the offices of the *Screen Actors Guild*, the hall was packed with people waiting. Eugene was given a number, and by the size of it, he knew he was in for a long wait. Hooper left to go grocery shopping and rent the movie. He instructed Eugene to call him when he was done and he'd come pick him up, but Eugene insisted he could take a cab.

An hour passed before Eugene got a chair in the lobby. As he sat down, a well dressed woman walked in. A murmur of voices rose with her entrance, and a young girl jumped up and asked for an autograph.

The woman stated to the receptionist that she had an appointment, and then looking about the lobby, she added, that she had no intentions of waiting long. The receptionist assured her that her wait would be short. A man sitting across from Eugene offered his seat to her, and she took it graciously. Upon getting settled, she took a cigarette from her purse, and as she was lighting it, she looked at Eugene. She stood immediately, dropping everything.

"Frank!" she cried, running over to him. She grabbed his hands. "Frank, what are you doing here? The whole universe is searching for you."

The faces of people waiting turned to watch. Someone else recognized him, "It's Frank Stacy. Look!"

Several people gasped, and Eugene jumped up pulling his hands out of the woman's grasp. "Leave me alone, I'm not Frank Stacy!"

Another person yelled, "He's still got amnesia."

The woman tried taking his hands again, and said, "You are Frank Stacy, you just don't remember. I'm Jennifer Talbot, Frank, I was one of your students. I've starred in your films. My whole career exists as a testament to your handicraft. Look at me Frank, please, you'll remember."

"No, you're wrong. I just look like Frank Stacy. I'm not him!" he cried, and moved away toward the door.

"Somebody call the cops, before he gets away!" called a voice from the crowd.

"He's insane and needs help. Somebody stop him - grab him!"

They began to crowd around him. He jerked his hands free of Jennifer's grip, and pushed through the crowd. A man grabbed him. Eugene swung his fist hitting the man's face. He let go. Eugene ran outside, hit the sidewalk of Sunset Boulevard, and ran, and ran, and ran.

Tears burned his eyes, smearing his vision. He didn't know how to tell these people they were wrong. They wouldn't listen. He'd have to hide until the real Frank Stacy was found. He ran until he reached a gas station where he ducked into the men's restroom and locked the door. As he stood panting, inhaling the urine stench of the grimy unventilated room, he looked into the cracked mirror, and was shocked. It was not his face. It was, but it was older. There were crow's feet wrinkles around his eyes. Worry lines cut deep arcs around his mouth. His white blonde hair was longer and darker, and receded above his temples. He saw the white pucker of a scar along his hair line. He rubbed his finger across the alien scar which he could not recall getting. When he looked closer, he found several silver hairs. His insides began to shake, and cold sweat ran down his sides. He pushed the door open and ran out. He ran until he reached a busy intersection where he couldn't cross. While he waited for the light to change, he noticed a newspaper box. He leaned over, read the date, and screamed, "Jesus Christ, Oh, Jesus Christ!"

His whole body was shaking, and tears streamed down his face. He leaned against a lamp post; his legs were feeling weak. He saw a cop looking at him. So he hailed a cab. The driver asked him where, and Eugene pulled the scrap of paper with Hooper's address from his pocket and read it off.

Twenty minutes later, Hooper was opening his door, and said to him, "Well, Buddy, how'd it go?"

Then he noticed that Eugene was shivering despite the hot Santa Ana winds that kept L.A. sweltering well after sunset. When he leaned closer he saw Eugene's face was swollen, and that the look in his eyes was utter terror. "Good God, man. What happened?"

Eugene walked in and said, "Hooper, I've got a problem. A big problem and I need help, but I don't know what kind of help I need."

"What is it?"

"Will you promise not to call the cops or anyone else?"

"You didn't kill anyone, did you?"

"No."

"Then your secret is safe with me."

Eugene dropped onto an easy chair and sat pensively on the edge of the seat. "Hooper," he said, nervously twisting his hands together, "I'm Frank Stacy."

CHAPTER FIVE

Myra hadn't received any news of Frank's whereabouts. She finally sent Zack and June home, as well as her parents, who had come over to keep her company while she waited for the state patrol to phone.

Her agitation grew, and she could not sit still. She needed something to occupy her mind or she was going to drive herself crazy. She was blaming herself for Frank's disappearance; and her feelings of guilt increased by the hour.

"I should have stayed at the hospital," she told herself. "I should have slept on a cot in his room."

In the back of her mind there was something familiar about this situation. It was just a feeling, but when she tried to identify the source, she could turn up nothing. She began drifting through the house aimlessly, until she ended up in the projection room. She wandered in, and then back out; through the house, and back again. On the third time she found herself impulsively putting *Resurgent Man* on the projector. There was something about this film that seemed to match the mood of this situation, but it was nothing she could place her finger on.

Her maid, Sara, noticed that she had finally settled down, and brought her a cup of tea, and a blanket. Myra asked for the cordless phone, and Sara put it on the seat beside her. After thanking her, Myra looked at it wistfully and thought that if the rest of the day was any indication, it would remain quite silent. In the meantime, the movie began to absorb her attention, and it also stimulated her memory. She found herself returning to an odd moment in hers and Frank's lives ten years earlier.

RESURGENT MAN

ACT ONE

SCENE ONE: MASTER SHOT: EXTERIOR. DAY. Gurgling stream running through the middle of a lush forest heavy with green foliage and undergrowth. Two barefoot boys are walking along the stream (TOWARD CAMERA).

Both boys, about twelve years old, are dressed in the familiar summer uniform of cut-off jeans and T-shirts. Both have crew-cut hair. One is tall and skinny with blonde hair, the other is short and chubby with red hair and freckles. Each is carrying a bamboo fishing pole, and a stringer of fish.

As the boys reach the camera, CUT TO:

Behind the boys as they enter an abrupt opening in the forest.

MASTER SHOT: In front of the boys is a dry desolate valley extending upward several acres on either side of the stream. Tiers of rock outcropping rise out of the dryness like a cemetery of a thousand broken headstones. Nothing is growing, and if appearance is any indication, nothing is interested in trying.

CUT TO: The boys entering the wasteland, the thinner boy stops and drops his fish into the stream.

BILLY:

"Hey Jimmy, look. My fish are still alive."

JIMMY:

(looks impatiently over his shoulder) "So what. Aren't ya coming?"

Billy: "No, it's too soon to go home. My parents were drinkin' when I left; and that means they're probably screamin' by now. I'm gonna stay out here where it's quiet until they fall asleep."

Jimmy: "Well, I gotta get going. I'm hungry. See ya later."

CUT TO: Jimmy leaving. He pulls up the back of his pants with the hand holding the stringer causing his fish to slap against his bare freckled calves.

CUT TO: OVER-THE-SHOULDER of Billy squatting alone on the bank. The tails of the fish are flipping back and forth.

Billy: "Boy, you guys sure like this water; it's bringing you back to life."

CUT TO: MASTER SHOT: Billy picks up a large stone and places it just downstream of the fish. He stands and observes for ONE BEAT. Then proceeds to pile more rocks causing the water to back up.

CUT TO: a miniature bridge of rock traversing the width of the stream, with a small pond behind it. Billy is releasing the fish from the stringer.

Billy: "Okay you're free! Well, not quite as much water as you're used to, but I can do something about that."

Billy fills the cracks in his dam with mud.

CUT TO: Two girls in lightly colored summer dresses walking up. Both are roughly the same age as Billy, and nearly his height. One has long white hair, a flat chest, and pink knobby knees protruding below the hem line of her dress. The other has dark curly hair, olive complexion and budding young breasts.

CUT TO: CLOSE-UP of the blonde girl.

CASSANDRA:
"What 'cha doin'?"

CUT TO: Billy continuing his task.

Billy: "Making a pond for my fish."

CUT TO: MASTER SHOT: The girls watch for ONE BEAT as if to determine that is indeed what he is doing, then the girl with the dark hair kicks off her sandals and starts to help. The blonde hesitates ONE ADDITIONAL BEAT then joins in as well.

CUT TO: a higher, wider dam with the girls passing Billy rocks.

CUT TO: an even higher dam as all three carry one huge rock.

CUT TO: Billy standing waist deep in water with the two girls opposite him on the dry side of the dam. All three are struggling to stabilize a long flat stone.

CUT TO: Billy pointing toward the setting sun.

Billy: "Wow, look how late it's gotten."

CUT TO: the dark haired girl.

JEANNINE:
"Oh, no! I'm going to be in trouble."

CUT TO: Cassandra pointing toward the woods.

Cassandra: "Look how dark the woods have gotten. I don't remember which way to get home."

CUT TO: Billy.

Billy: "I do. Follow me."

CUT TO: three wet and muddy children running toward the woods.

FADE.

SCENE TWO: MASTER SHOT: INTERIOR. NIGHT. Living room Billy's house. Billy is sitting on a window seat looking out at a thunderstorm. Flashes of lightning reveal despair on his face. In the background can be heard an adult male and female yelling drunken obscenities at each other.

FADE.

SCENE THREE: MASTER SHOT. EXTERIOR. DAY. Craggy creek bed. Billy is standing beside the creek. The dam is no longer there. Walking up behind him are Cassandra and Jeannine.

Jeannine: "What happened to our pond?"

Billy (despondent): "Rain washed it away."

Jeannine: "Then let's build another one."

Billy: "The fish are all gone, too."

Jeannine: "Well, you can catch more fish can't you?"

Billy: "Yeah, but the same thing will happen again, next time it rains."

Cassandra (authoritative): "It doesn't have to."

CUT TO: Billy sweeping out his arm to gesture toward the rough lifeless valley.

Billy: "I don't think anything is supposed to survive here."

CUT TO: MASTER SHOT

Cassandra (protests): "We can learn how to build a stronger dam."

Billy: "How are we going to do that?"

Cassandra: "At the library."

Billy: "At the library?"

Jeannine (defensive): "Yeah, Cassy knows. She's a bookworm, she knows everything in the library."

Billy (laughing): "Cassy? What kind of name is that?"

Jeannine: "It's short for Cassandra! What's your name, smarty?"

Billy: "Billy."
Cassandra: "Like Billy-goat?"
Jeannine: "Or Hill-Billy?"
Billy (defensive): "No, it's short for William."
Cassandra: "Why not Willy, then?"
Billy: "I don't know," Billy turns and faces Jeannine. "but what about you? What's yours?"

CUT TO: Jeannine squaring her shoulders while sliding a foot backward into a fighting stance.

Jeannine: "Jeannine, and if you say anything funny, I'll make you eat mud."

CUT TO: Billy stepping closer to Jeannine.

Billy: "I'd like to see you try."

CUT TO: MASTER SHOT

Cassandra (yells): "Hey! Are we going to the library or not?"

Billy shrugs, Jeannine drops her fist, then all three turn and walk.

FADE.

SCENE FOUR. MASTER SHOT: INTERIOR. Day. Library. Billy, Cassandra, and Jeannine are sitting around a table each with several books open in front of them. Librarian sits in the background.

CUT TO: Cassandra holding up book pointing to a picture of a beaver dam.

Cassandra: "Look! Here's what we need to build." (She turns book around and reads.) "It says here that the beaver's dam can only be broken by a severe flood. Its design works to catch debris as it's washed downstream which makes it stronger."

Jeannine: "That's great, but where the hell are we going to get a beaver?"

Billy looks at Jeannine and laughs.

Jeannine: "Hey, what are you laughing at?"
Billy: "You stupid."

Jeannine starts to smack Billy with a book when the Librarian clears her throat.

Cassandra: "Hey, let's get out of here."

FADE.

SCENE FIVE: MONTAGE. EXTERIOR. DAY. Craggy creek bed. Rapid Succession of short shots intercut as Billy, Cassy, and Jeannine build dam.
BACKGROUND MUSIC: The Andrews Sisters singing *Three Little Fishes*: '... boop boop ditum datum watum choo and they swam and they swam all over the dam ...'

Billy, Cassy, and Jeannine walk through the woods carrying hatchets, shovels, and hammers.

CUT TO: Billy cutting saplings, Jeannine and Cassy fashioning stakes.

CUT. All three drive stakes into the creek bed.

CUT. All three weave saplings in between stakes.

CUT. All three covered with mud stand and admire finished dam as the sun sets behind them.

FADE.

SCENE SIX. MASTER SHOT: EXTERIOR. DAY. The bank of a river, the sun is shining bright. Billy, Cassy, and Jeannine are fishing.

CUT TO: Cassy, whose pole is bent.
Cassandra (squeals): "I've got one!"

CUT TO: Jeannine jumping up and down.
Jeannine (yells): "Reel it in! Reel it in!"

CUT TO: Billy dropping his pole.
Billy: "Easy. Not too fast."

CUT TO: Cassy landing the fish, and Billy lowering it into a bucket.
Cassy: "How many now?"
Billy: "Sixteen."
Jeannine: "Let's take 'em back now."
Cassandra: "Oh, no not yet!"
Jeannine (extends a large wiggly worm): "We'll stay if you bait your own hook."
Cassy (draws back): "Never mind; let's take 'em back."

CUT TO: Billy and Jeannine laughing.

FADE.

SCENE SEVEN: MASTER SHOT: EXTERIOR. Back at the beaver-style dam where Billy, Cassy and Jeannine are sitting beside the pond watching the fish.
Jeannine: "What do we do now?"
Cassandra: "We could raise fish, and sell them."
Billy (complains): "But that would take years."
Cassandra: "Don't you like it down here?"
Billy: "Yes, I love it. It's the only place I know where I can get completely away from my parents."
Cassandra: "What's wrong with your parents?"
Billy: "They're always drinking, and then fighting."
Cassy (pauses ONE BEAT as she looks at Billy, then answers):
"I always go the library to get away, but I like this place better, I'm glad Jeannine brought me here."
Billy: "So what do you need to get away from?"
Cassandra: "Six maniacs, my perpetually screaming and non-stop running younger brothers."
Jeannine: "At least you guys don't have to deal with the Commandant."
Billy: "The what?"
Cassandra: "Oh, that's what she calls her father."
Jeannine: "He makes me so mad sometimes, that I just want to scream. So I run outside where no one will hear me, but this is where I always end up. The woods are so peaceful I don't care anymore.
Billy: "I don't get it?"
Jeannine: "You see, it's like this, the Commandant was in the Marines, and he thinks he still is. He runs the house like it's a boot camp. He makes me and both my sisters get up every morning at five. We have family calisthenics until oh five:twenty, then it's run to the showers, make the beds, and get dressed in time for inspection at oh five:fifty, and if you haven't noticed, I'm only allowed to wear dresses."
Cassy (interrupts): "What's wrong with dresses? I like wearing dresses."

Jeannine (wrinkles her nose in displeasure): "If I pass inspection I get free-time until oh six hundred when Mom has to have breakfast ready. Breakfast is over at oh six:fifteen. Chores are done until oh six:thirty. Then we rotate in thirty minute periods for piano practice, study time, and Mom teaching us Spanish. Get the picture?"
Billy: "Yeah, then what do you do?"
Jeannine: "Why then it's time to catch the bus to school."
Billy: "Where do you go to school?"
Jeannine: "Meyer's Elementary, Cassy too, but we start at Central High next year."
Billy: "Hey, me too."
Cassandra: "Really! We should get our classes together."
Jeannine (groans): "Oh, God Cassy, how can you even think about school when it's the summer?"
Cassandra: "But high school should be fun."
Billy: "Say, Jeannine, what does your father make you do now that it is summer?"
Jeannine: "We used to have to have what he called a regimented activity every afternoon, but Mom made him stop. She said we had to have some free time of our own or we'd never learn how to make decisions. He gave in so now we're free until he gets home at six o'clock, and it starts all over again."
Billy: "But, do you still have to get up so early?"
Jeannine: "Yes, but it isn't so bad when I know the rest of the day is mine." (She flops on her back, raises her arms to the sky, and sighs.) "Oh, I wish it would stay summer forever."
Cassandra: "Gee, what happened the other night, when you got home so late?"
Jeannine: "He made me stand at attention while he yelled at me. His favorite word is 'insubordinate.' If he tells me I'm insubordinate one more time, I swear I really am going to scream."
Billy: "I thought I had it bad. My Mom and Dad fight all the time, but at least they leave me alone."
Cassandra: "We should come here all the time. It's the perfect place for all of us. Why don't we make this our secret place?"

Jeannine (excited): "I like that. Let's take an oath that we'll never tell anyone about it."
Cassandra (exclaims): "Ooh, let's make it a blood oath!"
Billy (bright and interested): "Are you serious?"
Cassandra (in a low conspiratorial voice): "Oh, yes. A blood oath is romantic and mysterious, and the pain makes it binding."
Jeannine: "I can't believe you would cut yourself when you won't even put a worm on a hook."
Cassandra: "But oaths are different, they're sacred, and worms are... just gross."
Billy (pulls a pocket knife from his pants): "Are you ready? Do you know a good oath?"
Cassandra: "I've read plenty of them so I can probably make one up, but first we've got to heat the knife until it's white hot. Do you have any matches?"
Jeannine (pulls a crumpled pack of cigarettes from her dress pocket and points to a match book inside the cellophane): "I do."
Billy (Startled): "You smoke?"

Jeannine nods.

Billy: "My father would kill me."
Jeannine: "I do what I want."
Cassandra: "You mean as long as the Commandant doesn't find out about it."

CUT TO: a small camp fire. Billy is heating the knife blade over the flames. The girls are sitting on either side of him.

Cassandra (solemnly): "Repeat after me: I swear by the gods of the pond..."
Billy and Jeannine: "I swear by the gods of the pond..."
Cassandra: "to keep the pond secret, and protect it forever."
Billy and Jeannine: "to keep the pond secret, and protect it forever."

BEAT.

Cassandra: "Does anyone want to add anything?"
Billy: "I do. May we, the protectors of the pond, remain friends for life."
Cassandra and Jeannine: "May we, the protectors of the pond, remain friends for life."

Cassandra (takes the knife from Billy): "Let us seal the oath."

CUT TO: CLOSE-UP of Cassy cutting her wrist. She grunts softly and bites her lip then passes the knife to Jeannine.

CUT TO: CLOSE-UP of Jeannine wincing silently as she draws the blade across her wrist.

CUT TO: Billy sucking air through his teeth as he takes his turn with the knife.

CUT TO: MASTER SHOT

Cassandra: "Now we pass the blood bond in a circle. The circle represents infinity. When we seal the circle the sacred oath will survive forever."

Cassy presses her wrist against Jeannine's. Jeannine turns to Billy and presses her wrist to his. Completing the circle Billy presses his wrist to Cassy's.

Billy and Cassy release each other's wrist. The three sit silently and with moist eyes look from each other to their wounds and back again to each other.

CUT TO: Jeannine lighting a cigarette.

CUT TO: MASTER SHOT

Billy: "May I try that?"

Jeannine (passes the cigarette): "Sure."

Cassandra: "Me too."

Jeannine (protests): "But you told me you didn't like smoking."

Cassandra: "I don't, but sharing smoke is like part of the bond."

Billy: "Kind of like an Indian peace pipe?"

Cassandra: "Sort of, but more because we're not supposed to smoke, and this place is where we are free to do what we want,... but mostly I just want to be a part of what you guys want to do."

Billy (passes Cassy the cigarette): "I know this sounds kind of weird, but I feel like we're a family, that is, what I always supposed a family should feel like."

Cassandra: "I think we make a good family."

Jeannine: "Cool, me too."

CUT TO: Jeannine putting out the cigarette, then passing around sticks of chewing gum.

Jeannine (standing up): "I'm afraid I have to go."

Billy: "Wait, a minute. I've discovered a new way out. It's an old abandoned logging road.
(Stands and points) You can't see it, but it's right up there."

CUT TO: Billy, Jeannine and Cassandra walking down an overgrown dirt road in the middle of a dense wood.

CUT TO: The three exiting the woods onto a two lane highway. Across the highway an old black man rides a tractor in a furrowed field.

Billy (waves): "Hi, Mr. Dillon."

CUT TO: Mr. Dillon pulling up to the fence as the children run across the pavement to meet him.

Billy: "Mr. Dillon, these are my friends, Cassy and Jeannine."

MR. DILLON:
(Using Southern Black Vernacular English/Negro Dialect)
"Pleased to meet you. I see y'all been playin' in the woods."

All three children in unison: "Yes."

Mr. Dillon: "I used to play there when I was your age too, but it was a tree farm back then."

Cassandra: "What happened?"

Mr. Dillon: "That was part of my family's farm until about thirty years ago, then the gub'ment come along and says I have to sell it to them. I didn't want to, but they said, it had to be preserved."

Jeannine: "Preserved? What for?"

Mr. Dillon (drawling): "Somethin' 'bout future gen'rations."

Jeannine (looking perplexed): "Oh."

CUT TO: Mr. Dillon cranking the tractor back up as the children wave good-bye, then start off in their separate directions.

CUT TO: The logging road.

ZOOM: To a nearly hidden sign in the brush which reads: National Forest. Emerging from behind the sign is a forest ranger in a rumpled uniform with a huge beer belly. He is pulling up his zipper.

FADE.

SCENE EIGHT: MASTER SHOT: INTERIOR. NIGHT. Dining room of Jeannine's house as she rushes to stand in line with her sisters, who are already undergoing their father's inspection in front of a table laden with food. She puts out her hands as her father steps in front of her.
Jeannine: "Sorry I'm late, sir."

THE COMMANDANT (MR. WARNER):
(angry) "You're not only late, you're filthy! This type of thing is happening all too often. Your grades this past school year were miserable, and I received far too many notes regarding your behavior. I knew I shouldn't have allowed your mother to talk me out of sending you to summer school. Now get upstairs and get cleaned up. For being tardy you have forfeited your television privileges for the evening."

CUT TO: CLOSE UP of cut on Jeannine's wrist as she leaves the room.

CUT TO: Jeannine's mother's face staring at the cut in horror.

As Jeannine exits the room her mother crosses to her husband and grabs his arm.

MRS. WARNER:
(whispering harshly) "She's slashed her wrist. Now will you finally believe that you're being too hard on the children?"

CUT TO: CLOSE-UP of the Commandant's pained face.

FADE.

SCENE NINE. MASTER SHOT: INTERIOR. NIGHT. Living room of Billy's house as he enters to find his parents asleep in front of the television with a half empty liquor bottle in front of them.

CUT TO: Kitchen as Billy removes a frozen dinner from the freezer.

FADE.

SCENE TEN. MASTER SHOT: INTERIOR. NIGHT. Kitchen of Cassy's house. She enters doorway, skipping, with a bright smile on her face as two little boys, obviously twins, push past her, running, to get outside.

CUT TO: Her mother holding a baby while a toddler was clinging to her apron.

Cassandra: "Oh, Mother, I'm so happy! I've got the two best friends in the whole world."

MRS. SIBLEY:

(smiles warmly) "You see dear, I've always told you being smart didn't matter to other children."

Cassandra: "I can't wait until you meet them!"

Mrs. Sibley: "I can't either, dear."

BEAT.

Cassandra: "I wish Daddy could have met them."

FADE.

SCENE ELEVEN: MONTAGE. EXTERIOR. DAY. Rapid sequence of short shots intercut depicting Billy, Cassandra, and Jeannine: Bicycling, Kite flying, Entering a movie theater, and Walking down city sidewalks.

CUT TO: SCENE TWELVE. MASTER SHOT: EXTERIOR. DAY. POND

Jeannine: "This is our last day of freedom. School starts tomorrow."

Cassandra: "It won't be so bad, you'll see."

Billy: "Maybe the Commandant will let Jeannine out, if he thinks we're studying together."

Jeannine: "I think he will. It's funny, but ever since I started hanging out with y'all, he's been acting different... nice even... I only hope it lasts."

Cassandra: "Billy, do you ever think about what you want to do when we're grown up?"

Billy: "Sometimes I think I want to be an explorer, and go out and find places nobody has ever seen, ... places where there aren't any drunks like my father. I think I'd like to go to Alaska."

Jeannine: "Alaska sounds great; I'll go with you. I'd like to get as far away as I can from my father too."

Billy: "The Commandant's just strict that's all. At least he's sober."
Jeannine: "But, it's more than that, Billy. It's as if he's not real, as if he's a robot. The Marine's robot, or the Union's robot."
Billy: "Union?"
Jeannine: "He's shop steward at the mobile home factory."
Billy: "That's better than my Dad, he used to be the night janitor over there until he got fired for being drunk."
Jeannine: "Yeah, but I'll bet your Dad doesn't talk like he's quoting the Official Rule Book. The Commandant doesn't even belong to himself. Everything he says, everything he does could come right out of the Marine's Handbook or the Union By-laws. I once asked my mother why, and she said order gives him a sense of security. To me it's not worth it if you have to give up your identity."
Cassandra (softly): "At least both of you have your fathers."
Jeannine: "I'm sorry, Cassy, I didn't mean to make you feel--"
Cassandra (interrupts): "It's okay."
Billy: "What happened to your father?" BEAT. "You don't have to tell, if you don't like to talk about it."
Cassandra: "It's all right. He died unexpectedly last year, at least to us it was unexpected. He must have known because he left my mother enough insurance for all of us to live on."

BEAT.

Cassandra (points to the water): "Oh, look! Babies. Thousands and thousands of baby fish."

Billy and Jeannine jump up to look where Cassy was looking.

Jeannine (squeals): "We're going to be rich!"
Billy: "Think they'll be big enough by next summer?"
Cassandra: "There's one way to find out."
Billy: "How's that?"
Cassandra: "Look it up in the library."

CUT TO: Billy and Jeannine groaning in unison.

DISSOLVE TO: SCENE THIRTEEN. MASTER SHOT: INTERIOR. DAY. A dimly lit bedroom. Roy, the fat ranger, is pulling up his pants while walking toward a door. Behind him sitting of the edge of the bed is a woman with platinum blonde hair, heavy facial make-up and wearing a satin camisole.

Roy puts his hand on the door knob.

PROSTITUTE:
(good natured) "Honey, aren't you forgetting something?"

Roy turns to face her.

CUT TO: CLOSE-UP of Prostitute smiling while rubbing her thumb against her fingers in the sign for money.

CUT TO: MASTER SHOT

ROY:
(hostile) "Look whore, you can just consider that one on-the-house, unless you want to have a visit from my friends down at police headquarters."

Prostitute (cries): "I don't understand, didn't I do what you want? Didn't you enjoy yourself?"

Roy: "Course I did."

Prostitute rises and walks over to him and puts her hand on his arm.

Prostitute (smiles): "Sweetie, isn't it worth paying for? After all, it's only twenty dollars."

Roy (slaps her hand away): "I told you this one's for free!"

Prostitute: "But... but, I've got bills to pay."

Roy (shoves her to the floor): "Shut up, slut!"

Roy exits leaving the door open. Glaring sunlight pours onto prostitute's tear-stained face revealing wrinkles, sagging flesh, and her true age of fifty-plus years.

FADE.

SCENE FOURTEEN. MASTER SHOT: INTERIOR. DAY. High school hallway. Billy is standing in front of an open locker. The girls are walking away.

Cassandra: "Bye-bye, we'll see you at lunch."

Jimmy enters from the direction the girls are exiting. With him are three other boys.

Jimmy: "Hi, Billy."

Billy: "Hi, Jimmy."
Jimmy: "Haven't seen ya all summer. Where've ya been?"
Billy: "Oh, I've been around."
Jimmy (snide, nods toward receding figures of the girls): "You been hanging around those girls."
Billy: "What about it?"
Jimmy: "Only homos hang out with girls."
Billy (nods toward Jimmy's companions): "Yeah, well I've always heard that homos hang out with boys."
Jimmy (raises his fists): "You callin' me a homo?"
Billy (grabs Jimmy's collar): "Weren't you just calling me one?"

Jimmy looks over his shoulder.

CUT TO: His three friends, all of whom are smaller than Billy, are backing up.

CUT TO: CLOSE-UP of Jimmy.

Jimmy: "No, I was just kidding. I only wanted to know who the girls were."

CUT TO: CLOSE-UP of Billy as he turns Jimmy loose.

Billy: "They're friends of mine."

CUT TO: MASTER SHOT

Jimmy (straightens his shirt): "So, who'd you get for math?"
Billy: "Mr. Jenkins."
Jimmy: "I hear he's a real jerk."
Billy: "I guess I'll find out."
Jimmy: "Well, I'll see ya around."

As they walk away Billy smiles while rubbing the scar on his wrist.

FADE.

SCENE FIFTEEN. MONTAGE (The passing of seasons).
MASTER SHOT: EXTERIOR. DAY. POND.

BACKGROUND MUSIC: *Turn, Turn, Turn* by The Byrds.
CUT TO: FALL. Billy, Cassandra, and Jeannine all wearing sweaters doing their homework by the pond. The trees at the top of the hill are bright autumn colors. CUT TO: WINTER. The pond is frozen and the three children ice skate. CUT TO: SPRING. The children throw bread to the fish. CUT TO: SUMMER. They are knee deep in

the water, pulling a net full of flip-flopping fish toward a large white pickle bucket on the shore.

SOUND TRACK: Song runs once completely then begins again, but stops abruptly on the word "die" at the end of the verse: "a time to be born ... a time to die". Replace music with Location Sound: Happy voices and water splashing.

Billy (points toward the edge of the net): "Hey Cassy, don't let that one get away."

Cassandra: "But it's slimy, can't I just hold the net?"

Billy: "Slime doesn't hurt; just think of the money."

Cassandra wrinkles her face then picks up the fish and tosses it to the center of the net.

Jeannine (cheers): "Atta-girl, Cassy! We're gonna be rich."

CUT TO: SCENE SIXTEEN. MASTER SHOT: EXTERIOR. DAY.

Alley-way behind a brick building. Three bicycles are parked in front of an open door above which a sign reads:

Simpson's Fresh Seafood Market
Deliveries 8 A.M. to 10 A.M. only.

One bike has a basket holding the white pickle bucket. The children stand around a man wearing a dirty apron who looks down into the bucket.

MR. SIMPSON:
"Yep, these are mighty fine lookin' fish you got here, and I'm sorry to have to tell you, but I can't use 'em. They got no commercial value."

Cassandra: "What's no commercial value mean?"

Billy: "It means he can't sell them."

Mr. Simpson: "That's right kid. What you all ought to be raisin' are trout, or bass, or even catfish."

Jeannine: "Which will you pay the most for?"

Mr. Simpson: "Trout."

Billy: "Where can we catch trout?"

Mr. Simpson (studies the children's faces for ONE BEAT): "Well, trout can be real tricky, but your best bet would be the State Fish and Game Commission."
Billy: "They'll tell us the best place to catch them?"
Mr. Simpson: "No, son, they'll sell you fingerlings if you've got an approved pond."
Jeannine: "Fingerlings?"
Cassandra: "He means babies."
Jeannine: "How'd you know that?"
Cassandra with Billy joining in: "I read it at the library."
Jeannine: "Well, guys let's go put these fish back, so we can call the Fish Commission."

FADE.

SCENE SEVENTEEN. MASTER SHOT. INTERIOR. DAY. Living room at Billy's house.

Billy hangs up the phone and turns to the girls.
Billy: "It looks like we're out of business."
Cassandra and Jeannine (alarmed): "Why?"
Billy: "The commissioner asked me where I lived so he could send a man out to inspect the pond. I told him I wasn't going to raise fish where I lived but in the woods off Highway 41, near the turn off for Hartsville. Then he said I must be mistaken because that area is all National Forest, and no one is allowed to use government land for a fish farm. When I asked him why; he just said, it's against the law, and that if I wanted to put in a fish pond on my family's land to have my father call him."
Jeannine: "You didn't tell him we already put in a pond?"
Billy: "No, I never got the chance."
Jeannine (emphatic): "Then let's find another place to get fish."

FADE.

SCENE EIGHTEEN. MASTER SHOT: INTERIOR. DAY. Office with green walls adorned with several wildlife posters. A man wearing coveralls with insignia on the shoulders is sitting behind a metal desk. He is talking on the phone. To his right is an open door on which a sign reads: Fish and Game Commission.

CHARLEY:
"...there's probably nothing to it ... the caller was only a boy ... I just thought you might want to have the man who works that area keep his eyes open, you know flood control and all ... yes, yes I realize that territory covers thousands of acres ... anytime, Sam ... you too, Bye."

CUT TO: SCENE NINETEEN. MASTER SHOT: INTERIOR. DAY. Wood paneled office as a man in a green Forest Ranger uniform sitting at a desk hangs up phone.

SAM:
"Roy!"

Roy enters the office; his belly preceding him.
Roy: "What's up Sam?"
Sam: "Charley, down at Fish and Game, just called; he said, a kid called wanting to put a trout farm over in your section - somewhere around U.S. 41 and Hartsville. It's probably nothing, but it could be someone trying to homestead Federal land."
Roy: "Did you say a kid?"
Sam: "Yes."
Roy: "I think I know what it's about. There's a beaver pond down off the old Dillon logging road. I've seen some kids playing down there several times. You want me to run 'em off next time I see 'em?'
Sam: "No, I don't think that's necessary, just keep me posted if you should see any adults down there."
Roy: "Will do, chief."
DISSOLVE TO: SCENE TWENTY. MASTER SHOT: EXTERIOR. DAY. Mr. Dillon's farm.
Large pond behind which can be seen a red barn. The three bicycles are parked and the children are talking with Mr. Dillon who is wearing blue overalls, a straw hat, and a grisly day's growth of beard.
Billy: "Thanks for swapping some of your catfish for our fish."

Mr. Dillon: "Any time, kids. These little pan fish have the best flavor and Lawd knows I don't have time for fishin'."
Cassandra: "We wanted to raise trout, but we found out we have the wrong kind of pond."
Jeannine: "But just as soon as we make enough money, we're going to build a real trout farm."
Mr. Dillon (drawls): "My - my, I just cain't get over it. Where did town kids like y'all learn about raisin' fish?"
Cassandra: "From books."
Mr. Dillon: "Now, how 'bout that. If'n y'all ever need any help, feel free to come ax me, but I don't think y'all need it. Catfish pretty much take care of themselves, but I'll tell you a secret. You feed 'em some grain or some bread, an' they'll grow faster."
Billy, Cassandra, and Jeannine (in unison): "Thanks, Mr. Dillon."
Mr. Dillon: "Y'all come 'round anytime, 'cause y'all is jus' about the nicest chilren' I ever know'd."

FADE.

SCENE TWENTY-ONE. MASTER SHOT: EXTERIOR. DAY. POND. Billy, Cassy, and Jeannine stand at the edge of the pond.
Billy: "There's nothing left to do now, but wait."
Cassandra: "Mr. Dillon said, he thought a few of them looked pregnant to him; I hope he was right. If we're lucky, we'll have a lot of fish next year."
Jeannine: "I know where we can get some bread to feed them."
Billy and Cassandra: "Where?"
Jeannine: "It's bread the bakery throws out when it's too old to sell."
Cassandra: "I don't think the fish will complain. Let's go get some."

The three mount their bicycles. The camera pans toward the woods; then ZOOMS on Ranger Roy, who is standing partially hidden behind a clump of scrub pine with a pair of binoculars pressed to his fat sweaty face.

CUT TO: Roy as he lowers binoculars.
Roy (to himself): "No sir, Chief, I don't mind keeping my eyes on pretty little girls like these. No sir, I don't mind at all."

FADE TO BLACK.

#

Sara turned off the projector; Myra had finally fallen asleep.

CHAPTER SIX

The words hit Hooper like a blow. A blow of instant recognition as the features of Eugene's face meshed with his memory of Frank Stacy's, but just as instantly cynicism kicked in, and he immediately doubted Eugene's claim. He had learned to be suspicious; in the movie industry, it was a survival mechanism. Hollywood was full of emotional basket cases who were devoid of self-worth, and who needed daily validation from others to feel that they had personal value. As a city, it seemed to attract more than its fair share of insecurity cases and garden variety weirdos. It was the nature of this land of dreams, and finding someone who was well grounded was rare. Hooper had become accustomed to always being on guard for nut-jobs or worse the occasional sicko. He was disappointed to observe Eugene slipping into this delusion. There had been something refreshing about his personality that afternoon. Something genuine and pure, it pissed him off to find out he had been duped by a clever psychotic.

"Hey man this isn't funny." he declared to Eugene. "I know you said you wanted to be a director, but this is crazy. And, I mean like completely over the deep end. Do you think you can just take over and become somebody else just because he's missing?"

"No. It's not like that." Eugene began.

"Maybe, but I'm sure beginning to wish I'd never spoken to you this morning."

"Please listen; I just found out," Eugene pleaded. "For the last three days I thought it was 1967. Remember I told you I crashed my car in Alabama on my way out here?"

"Yes."

"That was in May, 1967, I was seventeen years old. I was knocked out, and I didn't wake up until three days ago. When I woke up I was beside this swimming pool, Frank Stacy's swimming pool, and his wife and some other people were there. I thought they were crazy, because they kept calling me Frank. When they told me it was July, I thought I had been unconscious for two months, not twenty years."

Tears were streaming down his face again. He dropped his head into his hands; and his body shook in silent sobs.

Hooper walked over to the coffee table and picked up the newspaper. He was sorry he'd promised not to call the cops; this kid was really losing it. He'd been a little weird that afternoon, but Hooper thought he was only trying to be funny. Now he actually seemed to believe he was Frank Stacy. The kid must have learned more about Stacy since he'd dropped him off at S.A.G.. Hooper flipped through several pages of the paper before he found the story about the famous movie director's accident. He skimmed through the article and glanced at Frank Stacy's picture then looked back at Eugene and shook his head.

"No way," he said to himself, but then he felt a twinge. It was that same feeling that made him like Eugene earlier in the afternoon. He thought, "There is just something about him that makes me want to take him under my wing." The feeling continued to nag him in the back of his head. It kept saying to him, "Don't be hasty."

"Dammit," he said, and Eugene looked up from his hands.

Something about that face made him want to give Eugene the benefit of the doubt. He looked back at Stacy's picture and after a few minutes thought to himself, "Well, there's a resemblance, albeit vague, if only there was a little less dirt and razor stubble."

"Hey Eugene," Hooper said aloud, "why don't you take a shower and shave - it'll make you feel better. When you get out of the bathroom, I'll fix us a drink and we'll talk.

While Eugene was in the shower, Hooper pulled out his copy of *THE HISTORY OF THE MOTION PICTURE,* and found a few more shots of Frank Stacy. He looked closely this time at the shape of the eyes and ears, the profile of the nose, the arch of the eyebrow. Stacy was famous for his ability to transform himself, so Hooper had to take note of details most people would overlook.

When Eugene stepped out of the bathroom, Hooper was pissed to see that he hadn't shaved, but he didn't say anything - at least he was cleaner. Hooper really didn't want the boy to know he didn't believe him. So he scrutinized the face. It was close, but it was still different. Different enough that any similarity was simply coincidence. This kid, Eugene, knew he looked like Frank Stacy all along; and was going to play Stacy's disappearance to the hilt. Then Eugene turned around and through the thin clumps of wet hair Hooper saw the stitches in the back of his head, and he remembered.

"Hold it, Eugene. Don't move!" he cried, and picked up the newspaper and walked over to him.

Quickly reading through the article he found the number he was looking for: eight. He then counted the stitches. "One, two, three, four, five, six, seven, eight." It was a convincing number, and Hooper suddenly found he was shaking. He found he was both excited and nervous at all that was implied in the situation before him.

"Okay Eugene," he said quietly. "I believe you're Frank Stacy."

Hooper stared at the man before him, as he tried to consider everything he knew, and everything Eugene said. Then as realization dawned on him, he burst out loudly, "Jesus man, you've lost twenty years!"

Eugene just nodded.

Hooper recalled their conversation back at Nordwick that morning, and said, "Then you weren't kidding when you said the paper made a mistake about Reagan being President. You really didn't know."

Eugene shook his head. "It's like I'm *Rip Van Winkle*."

"You really don't remember anything about being Frank Stacy?"

He shook his head again.

"Let me see if I've got this straight. Twenty years ago you left home to come out here and make pictures. If I recall correctly, you said this morning that they would be great pictures. You were knocked out in a car crash, and somehow you got up, perhaps semiconscious, became Frank Stacy, then came out here and made great movies anyway. Then three days ago, according to the paper, you had a diving accident which knocked you out again; and when you woke up from that you became fully conscious. Actually, you don't have amnesia now. You had amnesia before."

Eugene nodded.

The poster of Myra Mason on the wall drifted into Hooper's peripheral vision, catching his attention causing him to become fully cognizant of the situation before him. "Myra," the name just slipped out of his mouth.

When the focus returned to his eyes, Eugene was staring at him. Trying to cover quickly, he said, "Well, don't you think you should at least call your wife?"

"She's not my wife."

Eugene's statement caused a tingle in Hooper's stomach, but this time he ignored it, and said, "Well, yes and no, but still she must be terribly worried. Let me call her anonymously. I'll simply let her know you're okay."

"Okay, but let's wait 'til morning. I need some time to think; to try to sort this out."

"Sure, I'll get us some whiskey, and if you like, I'll tell you what you've missed out on for the past twenty years."

Hooper came back from the kitchen with a bottle of *Jack Daniel's* and two jelly jar glasses. He sat on the sofa across from Eugene. As he set the jars on the coffee table between them he said, "I guess these glasses aren't quite what you're used to, but I'm afraid I can't afford crystal."

Eugene looked up with his tear-stained eyes and blubbered, "I ain't never drank out of anything better."

"Just testing, Frank."

"And don't call me Frank! Even if I am; I don't remember it."

"Okay, Eugene, so tell me what you do remember."

"Well, like I said before, it was in May that I left to come out here. May in 1967. I must have decided to drop out of school, because I wasn't supposed to graduate until 1968, but I can't seem to remember. Anyway me and Jack--"

"Who is Jack?"

"Oh, Jack is my best friend; he's wonderful; he's like knowing Socrates or somebody like that. He had a farm near my house, and I used to go and sit out in the field with him under this neat old oak tree. I'd listen for hours to the things he could say."

"What's so neat about an oak tree?"

"Nothing really, although Jack used to call it the Intellectual's tree. I guess it's just that growing up in South Georgia I didn't ever see many other kinds of trees than the three P's until I was fourteen years old."

"Three P's, what's that?"

"Oh, sorry," Eugene laughed. "Peach, pine, and pecan, everything else was cleared off so long ago for cotton that when the slaves were freed, the farmers couldn't afford to plant as much cotton. The only trees left to drop seed were pines which grow like weeds. Only one thing grows faster than pine and that's kudzu, but kudzu ain't good for nothing. At least you can get turpentine and paper from pine trees, which is why everyone grows them. I don't remember when peaches and pecans became popular."

"You mean poplar." Hooper laughed at his own pun.

Eugene didn't get it and said, "Poplar's a weed too. Everybody cuts it down before it can take over."

Hooper rolled his eyes, and said, "So tell me more about this young Socrates, like how old is he?"

"He's... uh." Eugene paused tried to figure the math, then giving up, said, "Oh, he's two years older than me. Anyway, he was going to help me get started in the movies before he moved to Alaska. Anyway, me and him left together on a really stormy night, but I smashed the car into a tree, and that's the last I remember."

"So, what happened to Jack?"

"I guess he's out here somewhere, still waiting for me to show up."

"All these years?"

"Oh, I keep forgetting; I guess he might have already gone to Alaska, but I'll bet he's probably still waiting for me out here somewhere."

"What's in Alaska?"

"It's like living in a colony of the United States."

"But it's a state now."

"I know, but you'd have to understand Jack. Jack was a descendant of Thomas Paine, and real proud of it. He even wished he could have lived in the American colonies at the same time."

"And since he couldn't; he decided on Alaska?"

"Yes, but it's more than that. He wanted to be a part of the new American Revolution."

"I don't see how Alaska figures in."

"Well, he always said Alaska was a frontier where people are too busy fighting nature to get involved in other people's business. He said, it's the same as it was in the early American colonies. People back then were masters of their own domain, and they got real used to it. So when the British started imposing a lot of new laws and taxes, they got pissed off, but they weren't strong enough to do anything about it. That is, until the British got into a war with France. Then because Britain was preoccupied, they were able to make the break."

"So again, what does Alaska have to do with all that?"

"Jack figures the people in Alaska are like the early colonists, and don't like being pushed around. His plan is to start an independence movement up there, and when the Viet Nam War escalates into World War Three, Alaska can announce its independence. And, the United States will be too busy to do anything about it."

"Eugene, the Viet Nam War is over."

"It is? Has anything happened in Alaska? Is it a country?"

Hooper shook his head.

"Then I guess that definitely means Jack is still out here in L.A.."

"I wouldn't count on it, Eugene. With plans that big why would he wait out here?"

"Because I'm going to make movies expressing his ideas, and he wants to help. After I'm established, he'll move on up there, and I'll take my vacations with him."

"You know Eugene, Jack might have been drafted."

"No! Jack's too smart for that," Eugene insisted a little too loudly.

Hooper raised an eyebrow, "Whatever."

"So what else has happened in the last twenty years?"

Hooper began with who had been President, "You ever heard of a Georgia politician by the name of Jimmy Carter?"

"Sure he's from a rich family in Plains which is only about ten or twelve miles south of Ellaville. His daddy's got one of those peanut permits they gave out during the Depression. If you don't have one, the government won't let you sell peanuts. They'll actually make you plow your crop under if you plant them; but if you do have one, you don't even have to grow peanuts to get rich. You can just rent your permit to somebody else."

"You're kidding."

"No, in fact the Carters make so much money, that ol' Jimmy wasted some of it running for governor in 1960."

"What do you mean by wasted?"

"He lost."

"He did? Why was that?"

"I guess because he ran on the good ol' boy, white-is-right ticket, but it was too late. Everybody was gettin' bored with it."

"Bored?"

"Well, yeah, that and his timing was off. If he had run four years earlier, it might have worked because the state legislature had just voted to make the old Confederate Battle Flag the new state flag in retaliation to the federal government passing the Civil Rights Act. By 1960, the people had over half a decade to get used to Civil Rights, but more importantly the economy was stronger. Say, Hooper, do you know anything about political economy?"

Hooper was staring at Eugene, who, undaunted by his ignorant sounding cracker accent, was beginning to orate like a college professor. He shrugged and answered, "Not really."

"Then let me make it real simple: when the economy is strong and people are making money, they don't have any reason or need to hate."

"Oh," Hooper said, awed by Eugene's insight, then added, "I guess Carter must have finally figured that out, because he changed his strategy a hundred and eighty degrees later on and won.

"So, Jimmy Carter is now the governor of Georgia?"

"Well, no; he was governor a while ago, and after that he became President."

"President of the whole country?"

"Uh huh."

"Nah!"

"Seriously."

"Well how 'bout that."

Hooper went on to tell him more; but Eugene was drinking the whiskey like it was water, and soon fell asleep on the sofa. The video cassettes he'd rented caught his eye as he rose to go to bed. He mused that he never got around to telling Eugene about what he'd become.

CHAPTER SEVEN

On Monday morning, September 15, 1975, promptly at 9:00 A.M., Constance Barnes, Frank Stacy's personal secretary, called into her desktop intercom, "Miss Myra Mason is here."

"Send her in." the box crackled back.

Myra Mason, in the fall of 1975, was as beautiful as her father was rich. She stood above average height, and walked on long slender legs. Dark honey colored hair, thick as a horse tail, careened in gentle waves away from her face then cascaded over her shoulders. Crisp lines and soft angles fashioned her face; a look that in ancient times would have driven sculptors to stalk her, and poets to sing beneath her window. Her skin was clear and smooth; silken to those allowed to touch. Her almond-shaped green eyes were warm and empathetic, yet she could look directly into the eyes of anyone including a rival without fear or hesitation. She found a great deal of pleasure in living; and when she smiled, her full lips parted to expose hard, straight, brilliantly white teeth. She was so comfortable and confident, in her person, that she was able to casually display her perfect beauty without a thought. Admirers often wondered if she had been carefully bred, and not merely the accidental result of genetic dice.

On the Wednesday before, Myra turned twenty-one. When her father asked what she wanted for her birthday, she answered: "Acting lessons from the best - the very best in the world."

He replied, "Acting lessons you may always have. I want you to ask for something special."

"This is special, Daddy. I haven't yet told you the price."

He listened as she surmised what it would take. When she finished he was stunned.

He hesitated. "Yes, that does fall into the category of special." Then with joking lilt added, "Could I talk you into settling for a house on the beach in Malibu, with a new Lamborghini in the garage?"

He stared back into her "Please, Daddy" gaze for a long moment. It was the method he'd established for gauging her determination when she was a teenager. The intensity with which she returned the gaze was one he recognized. He gave in. "What the hell. I don't mind if you spend your inheritance now."

She walked into Stacy's office wearing a crisp navy blue suit with a straight narrow skirt. Her posture was not affected, although it was borrowed; it belonged to an astute business woman she admired, and she learned to imitate it. The graceful steps, however, were her own, passed down by generations; refined in marble drawing rooms. Savoir-faire was the attitude she sought; yet her heart shivered with derring-do. Butterflies in her stomach threatened to betray her as a fraud, expose her as a nothing more than a side-show charlatan.

So, as she stood before his desk, Myra made a last minute appraisal of the man who knew how to produce actors. She looked directly into his cold blue eyes, and with her peripheral vision, took inventory of his tailored Italian suit and neatly combed dark blonde hair. For a moment her eyes were drawn away from his as she noticed a puckered scar along his hairline.

Hidden between two fingers, as a sole prop, she held a small folded piece of paper. She was playing a role for the greatest role player in history, and it had to be good. All her training, breeding, and intelligence were required for this performance. She would be, for as long as it was necessary, a cunning business person. A horse trader from a long line of horse traders. Her father, had she allowed him to attend, would have watched with pride.

"Mr. Stacy, I understand you are in need of a major investor for your current movie project."

"This is true Miss Mason, however, in all honesty, I must advise you to read *BARRON'S*, or better yet *VARIETY*'s business opinions, on my current venture. They are correct; this project is highly risky. This picture will not be one of my action thrillers, but an attempt to experiment deeper with my artistic credo. The projected returns are slim, if any. I'm content to make this picture primarily with my own funds, along with a few small investors."

"Mr. Stacy, I would like to be your sole investor."

"Have you read the reports I spoke of?"

"No."

"Then I can't advise it."

"I'm not interested in your advice on this matter Mr. Stacy."

"Then you have read the script?"

"No."

"Then I don't understand."

"I have investigated your finances Mr. Stacy; even if you use your entire net worth, it will barely cover fifty percent of your costs. You will unlikely be able to acquire the additional fifty percent you need from smaller investors. I will provide the entire amount: one hundred percent. I do not expect to get a financial return, but will gladly accept one if it is forthcoming."

Stacy scrutinized her face, while on his own face, lines deepened about his mouth, parenthetical lines enclosing his lips like a secret quote. He studied her posture, and he noted briefly that she was holding something in one of her hands. Returning his eyes to hers he said, "From what you just said, there is only one important remark: that you do not expect to get a financial return. Such a statement belies that you do, however, expect to get a return of some sort."

"You're very perceptive, Mr. Stacy. In return you will accept me as one of your acting students."

"Out of the question, Miss Mason," he said, his voice brusque. "I accept students solely on the basis of merit."

Raising her arm, she extended her hand out over his desk. Twisting her fingers, she unfolded the slip of paper she'd held between them. Dropping it on his desk, she said, "Mr. Stacy, that is a signed blank check; it will be honored by any bank in the country. All you have to do is fill in the amount, and begin production of your artistic credo. You will not have to postpone it another day."

He glanced at the check then looked into her pond-green eyes, and found his vision held in check. They held still for several seconds, shrouded in the silence of the office.

As Myra held his stare, she recalled the words of her father, who had made his fortune closing sales, "After the final offer is made, the first who speaks loses." She clamped the inside of her lip between her teeth.

Finally Frank Stacy leaned back and smiled. The lines around his mouth disappeared as he said, "You're auditioning for me right now!"

She nodded cautiously.

He wove the fingers of his hands together, and then stretched his arms outward to cause his knuckles to pop. "All right, Miss Mason, I'll teach you. My current class is full; however, I will make arrangements to train you privately. Under the circumstances, that would be best. Further, you do not have to invest in my production. If you had shown this much talent when you auditioned for me before - yes, I remember you now - you would not have had to go to these lengths."

"Mr. Stacy, a deal is a deal. I was not good enough before; and the cost of a second audition is sitting on your desk. Please pick it up."

"Do I detect by the inflection of your voice Miss Mason that I have broached a matter of honor? Perhaps you will accept an amendment to your offer... say a fifty - fifty split?"

Myra smiled in agreement.

Frank applauded.

#

Myra's lessons began with one hour a week squeezed in between Stacy's numerous obligations. At those initial meetings, he tested her talent by having her study well-known performances of roles from famous plays. He then had her prepare and perform the same roles.

"I'm purposely assigning you roles you've seen performed before, not for you to mimic, but for you to study. Later you can decide what the best interpretation is. I'm not asking that you necessarily come up with your own unique interpretation, but that you learn to understand the character. Once you feel as he feels, you will speak as he would speak, gesture as he would gesture, and act as he would act. Afterwards, if you should see a particular performance that you believe demonstrates that which you know to be true, then mimic, but not before."

As the weeks passed, her strengths and weaknesses became apparent with the strengths far outweighing the weaknesses. He surprised her by increasing her individual lessons to several hours each week. Gradually he winnowed out her latent talent and sought new ways to discover the sum of her hidden abilities.

In time, he decided she needed a greater understanding of the universal traits that link average lifestyles, so he sent her into the street with assignments to locate and interact with particular types of people: mail carriers, retail managers, garbage collectors, helicopter pilots, assembly line workers, door-to-door sales people, construction workers, bus boys, and computer programmers.

"I want you to read what they read, eat what they eat, talk about what they talk about."

As he spoke, his right hand worked a litany of knuckle popping. It reminded her of someone counting a rosary. First he cracked his thumb by squeezing it in his fist, then one by one he popped each finger, from the index down to the little finger, by pressing down on it with his thumb, then he would start all over again. He would repeat it several times - continuing the process long after each knuckle had quit making noise.

"You must do what they do, in order to know what they are. Your task is to learn what they laugh at and why; what makes them cry and why. What makes their life similar to their peers at work, and similar to people all over the country; all over the world. Finally, find out how they are different, and if those differences are ends in themselves, or if they are natural. The trick is learning universality the same as you learn individuality. An actor is a sociologist first and a psychologist second."

"After you have ferreted out the universals, and have clearly attached them to your character; there is one step left, and this is the hardest: imprinting the individual's will. This is the crucial difference between a good actor and a great actor. Between one who will be typecast, and if the public likes the type, become a star; and one who will go on to wear diverse roles and master his craft. The difference is one stamps his own will on the character he plays. The other searches until he finds the will belonging to the character, and stamps it on himself. Marion Michael Morrison has played one role his entire life - that of John Wayne. The only thing that changed was the situation. On the other hand there is Dustin Hoffman, a young man worth watching, and one whose training I can take no credit for."

"Knowledge of universals begins at home, Myra. One of the unfortunate drawbacks to your upbringing in a wealthy family is that you never had to learn the various coping mechanisms of the common man. When you add up those mechanisms of daily survival; they equal the sum of an individual's traits. Their severity varies by degrees depending on how far a man must go to maintain his self-esteem against the backdrop of what society considers success; and how much he subscribes to those notions of society. You can observe those degrees by looking at various levels of social strata. However, you must consider that while social strata are primarily based on wealth and position, some people living at its fringes are affected by attitude. Look, for example, at a salesman in a luxury car showroom. To be successful, his wealthy customers must be able to relate to him. He ensures that by projecting an attitude that leads them to believe he is their peer. It's the ability to capture an attitude that makes a great actor."

"I want you to learn how a garbage collector finds pride in his work. I want you to learn the similarities in flying a helicopter, and screwing in the same bolt six hundred times a day on an assembly line. I want you to learn how a salesman musters up the fortitude to keep going after fifteen doors in a row have been slammed in his face. When you've done that, then go out and learn how they all spend their free time."

"A man labels himself by his work, 'I'm an accountant. I'm a policeman,' but that is the obvious facet of his life. What else identifies him? You must find out what he believes in. Watch what he does, not what he says. Actions speak louder than words. You can learn what a man believes by what he eats, how he brushes his teeth, and whether he farts in front of his wife. Keep in mind, however, that people change roles or personas for each differing area of their lives. They behave one way at work; and one way at home; another way at church; and another at the beach. You must find what connects his various behaviors together, as well as, why he becomes different people at different times. The actor must learn this about his character and apply it in his interpretation. When you read your lines, you must think: why would this person do such-and-such? When you can comprehend his motivation, you will know the essence of your character. By understanding this you will perform an incomparable role."

Once during a class, Frank stated, "Go out and find people like your character and observe."

A student then asked, "But what if there aren't people like our characters? What if our characters are written larger than normal life?"

It was the closest Myra ever saw him come to anger in his teacher-role. He said, "The only character I can imagine you not being able to observe would be an alien from outer space. The author of the character, however, would still be an earthling and he could only have drawn from his own experience, and that is within the observable context of this planet."

Needless to say, Myra never saw that student perform in a *Stacy Production.*

"An actor is like a private investigator of the mind. He delves deep to uncover the background of his character, the so-called skeletons in the closet. He searches for the psyche, the motivation, of the character he will portray."

"Finally, Myra, the actor is a philosopher grasping the values by which his character lives. The combined effect is that the actor understands both the inner root that makes his character unique and the outer shell with which the audience can empathize."

One day she came to his office as the cleaning woman - he didn't recognize her. On another day, at his favorite restaurant, he didn't notice that she was his waitress. She even pan handled a dollar from him on the street without gaining so much as a glint of acknowledgment from his eye. With that as encouragement, she faced him one-on-one as a securities broker; he noticed, but was impressed.

It wasn't long before she became his primary student. When he was on the road, she accompanied him. To studios and location sets, to his classes, to review movies and plays, to his auditions, he took her everywhere. Every moment was a teaching experience, as he frequently pointed out elements that she needed to improve her craft. Yet, through it all, their relationship remained unvaryingly and completely business-like. A professional distance stood so solidly between them that it felt like a wall to Myra. Frank was so correct with her, in an industry beset with rumors of director's couch auditions, that his very lack of interest created seeds of desire in Myra.

#

During this hectic period, Myra was thrown into a haphazard intimacy with Frank Stacy. It allowed her an acquaintance with him that no one else ever had. It was only an acquaintance, however, and she often felt as if she were some sort of clinical observer as she watched him move into and out of the various roles that comprised his life. Before her eyes, she witnessed literal transmutations as he moved from teacher, to producer, to director. He became so immersed in each different facet of his life, she found herself forgetting all but the one of the moment.

When he was on a set, he was the director down to consummate detail. His attention was never divided. Seldom did he have to make multiple takes. Filming ran as smoothly as a well-disciplined ship, yet without compromising artistic integrity. He guided the set as if his mind were possessed by a single concept.

It was exhilarating to observe Frank as the dictatorial captain at work. After the camera assistant slapped the clapperboard to begin a scene, Frank would call, "Action!" then using a pencil like an orchestra conductor's baton he would count three silent beats before the actors were allowed to begin performing. Then, until the last line was spoken, he would sit in his canvas chair tracing the scar along his hairline with the pencil's eraser. By the end of the day, the constant nervous action forced a two-inch strip of hair to stand on end. It looked like a cowlick on his forehead, and Myra could tell from fifty paces if he'd been directing.

The pencil, Myra came to notice, was an extension of his hand while he was on any set. With the completion of the scene he would rise from his seat and again lift the pencil to signal three beats before yelling, "Cut!"

Myra asked him the purpose of those beginning and ending beats and he said, "Primarily to give me more film to work with when editing, but the beginning beats also take the edge off the adrenalin rush actors get from the smack of the clapperboard. They don't have to begin at the end of the third beat, only when they're ready. The beats remind them of this and they relax enough to give me a superior performance."

When he was back in the front office, with the production breakdown board in front of him, he could discuss the scene-by-scene layout of a filming schedule with such complete abandon of the thought that he was personally directing it, that his investors would often ask:

"But aren't you going to be directing?"

A quizzical look would form on his face, as if he didn't understand the question. Then the parentheses around his mouth would smooth out, and he would answer, "Who else?"

She seemed satisfied to remain just an acquaintance, as she followed and observed him switch from director to producer to teacher, but on rare occasions in demonstrative instruction he became an actor, her satiation changed to desire. His acting was art. He was *the* mentor. Whenever she witnessed him act, it was in stunned acquiescence. On each such occasion, she found she had to sit or grasp hold of something; her mind would not allow her to observe his transformations and support her legs at the same time. She interpreted the chills running through her body not as admiration, but as love.

He could so absorb a role that the character became a real living person. It was not merely the speaking, or the reacting, but the simplest of gestures. When he angled his head to listen, or drew back his lip to speak, one knew immediately that that was the only way it ought ever have been done.

Without arrogance Frank knew the impact his acting had on his students; because of this he refused to ever demonstrate a role for an actor performing in one of his films. Instead, he used his favorite teaching technique; he asked questions. Questions that always ran in a series.

The method was Socratic, however, many would argue that it was hypnotic. He spoke softly, and to the student being probed, his questions actually soothed, as he gently pried from them the relevant traits composing their characters. It was because the answers came from the students that they would be enacted realistically. As his students became actors, they continued to use the method on themselves: in effect a type of self-hypnosis.

One night Myra encountered a drawback to Frank's method, but she remained tight-lipped as they rushed to the hospital. An actress, performing the role of a depressed woman, became so entrenched in the emotions of her character that she was nearly successful in a suicide attempt at home the day after her last performance. Frank sat up late with the woman, reassuring, still the mentor, as he explained to her, "The trick is to step into and out of a role as easily as you climb on a bicycle and ride. When you're finished riding - you park it."

Seldom did his method have such side effects; and because it worked, Frank would continue to use it. Myra again had occasion to wonder about the long term effects of his method as she witnessed his questioning of a bit player. He did not merely ask the actor: "Why would your character mug this man?" Instead he said: "Since the author is vague about your character's description and motives, it does not mean you should become a generic stereotype of a street bandit. Instead you are allowed artistic license to determine motive, and thus the characterization of your role. Remember, just like real people all characters have their own stories whether or not the author bothered to write it down. Sometimes it's up to you to find it."

"How do you find it? Begin with what you do know. The man you mug is walking through a deserted alley. Do muggers usually sit and wait in deserted alleys?" ... "That's correct, no they wouldn't, not if they intend to do any real business. So, why are you in that alley?" ... "Yes that question will take a little more information to answer. Let's look at what else we do know. You carry a hand gun, but do we know the caliber?" ... "No? Then consider this, career muggers tend to use large caliber pistols that resemble hand-held elephant guns. Gun size alone quickly intimidates victims into turning over their valuables. Are you a career mugger?" ... "You don't know, however, we might be able to determine that from your lines. As in whether you let the gun do most of your talking. Does what you say carry more weight than the gun?" ... "Yes? Then we may assume a small gun. Does a small gun imply a relatively inexperienced mugger?" ... "Yes, I would think so, too. Does your inexperience also explain the location you choose to do your mugging?" ... "Excellent! As you answer these questions and others you will enable yourself to determine why your character became a mugger. Understanding his needs and desires will dictate your actions. Is it out of desperation for money? Is it for the excitement? Is it because your character is too stupid to do anything else, or because he thinks he's too smart to be bothered with a job?"

"You need to do research, and study actual muggers for this role. Go to the jail; interview some that were caught. On the day we film, I want you to feel the adrenalin, the fear, and the excitement you would feel if you were actually mugging someone. You should be so prepared, that after this film, you could take up a little mugging as a side line." The class laughed as Stacy continued, "Approaching your role in this manner will make you an excellent actor; and it will give you the type of satisfaction you previously thought you could only attain from a leading role. Then once you've earned that coveted leading role, I guarantee it will be an experience far beyond anything you could have imagined. I can also guarantee that if you consistently follow this method throughout your career you will never be type cast."

There was another student who took Frank's advice a little too far, and Frank was awakened in the middle of the night to bail him out of jail for confessing to a crime he did not commit.

"What the hell were you trying to do?" Frank demanded as they walked out of the police station.

The boy burst into tears as he said, "I wanted to feel the reality of an interrogation, so I wouldn't stereotype my character. I wanted you to be proud of me at rehearsal. I wanted my scene to be a single take."

Frank put his arm around the boy's quaking shoulders, and told him, "I'll have my lawyers straighten everything out in the morning."

The boy went on to leading Stacy roles. Of his leading performers, those who could not be type cast, each could attribute his success directly to the fear of stereotyping Frank instilled in his students.

Frank Stacy couldn't be type cast either, thought Myra, or rather he wouldn't be. After eleven months, she still could not name the essence of Frank Stacy. He was clearly unique, yet he lacked something. At the same time she could see him as many things and as nothing at all. He absorbed his life roles with a wholeness of attention that would shame a Zen Buddhist, yet she couldn't find the very thing he insisted his own students learn first about any one of their characters. The thread that connected all aspects of the personality. The individual stamp. The taproot that grew deep and shot downward; it was the root that held each man upright: those burning individual desires that make life worth living; it was the root of empathy one man feels for another.

It was the little things she noticed. Little things he didn't have. A sense of humor for one. He could teach comedy; he could subtly add it to his films, but she seldom saw him laugh. His apartment was another. It was sparse save for the very necessities of living. Bare white walls rose high in stark contrast to hard oak plank flooring. There were no pictures, and of the few pieces of furniture, each was plain and poignantly picked by function. He did not even display the mementos of his achievements. He had won two *Oscars* yet she had never seen them, neither in his apartment nor in his office. Lastly, she was aware of his love life - it was a role that did not exist. At least after nearly seven months of constant one-on-one contact, she could say he had no romantic life. What hurt was how easily he ignored all her hints. Most men drooled with their eyes at first sight of her, and the more confident of these would express, in varying degrees, their passionate desires. Frank never drooled, and it drove her nuts.

It was his acting ability that truly kept her on edge. Whenever he took to the stage, she was in awe, and her heart ached with passion. One evening they were in his apartment drinking coffee. Together they took up all the chairs he had for his dining room table. It was the end of an unusually busy day, she watched him add a last notation to the hand written script of *Resurgent Man*, then close it. When he put down his pencil, she closed the script she was studying. Myra had waited for this opportunity. He was tired and she was guessing he was in between roles. The lines around his mouth were smooth, and his hands were lying still on the table. She decided it was an opportune time to ask him a question that had smoldered in her mind for weeks.

"Frank, why don't you ever take a role in your films; why do you only perform for your students?"

"Because I'm only interested in creating the films," he answered. "I can act only because I need to teach others what I want. Without competent actors, I could not achieve my goals."

"But, still, you're so good; you ought to be performing. Others directors do." she pursued, while wondering: "What is he now: teacher, or director?" Yet his knuckles remained silent, and the pencil lay out of reach.

"Others are actors first - film makers second. I'm a film maker." Yet the lines that usually formed about his mouth when he was in his producer-mode were absent. "Acting is a craft. Film making is an art."

She couldn't place the answer, it was out of character. It wasn't from any of the characteristic sets she'd been able to inventory. It also made her angry. "I beg to disagree. Acting *is* an art."

"Look at film making," he argued, "like you would a symphony. The music's composer is the artist; the musicians the craftsmen; the conductor the foreman. Or look at a beautiful building. The architect is the artist, the builders: the plumbers, carpenters, and electricians are the boys in the band, the actors."

"Frank, I could consider the film maker in the same way you consider the orchestra conductor. Unless the film maker is writing all his own stuff. Do you do all your own writing?"

"Very little actually; but you must consider the interpretation. Pigments and canvass do not make a painting art. The painter must interpret his subject. Film is my canvass and actors are my pigments."

"And I say acting is an interpretation in the same way. You are the one who made me believe that acting could be more than a craft. That I had to first understand my character's motives, then to literally become that person in my mind. Thus every movement I make, even a twitch or a jerk, is a fluid expression. The idea of art is to create an image of the subject from a media different from the subject itself, to bring out specific qualities you want someone else to see as you do. My body is the canvas and the pigments, and my mind is the artist."

He smiled in satisfaction, and said, "Perhaps; when I watch you, I do see art; but art is a stylized version of an abstract - it's still the writer who creates it. Art is a conceptual thing. The actor merely brings it to life. Acting may approach art, but it will never be art."

Something about his smile made her react. She thought she was seeing an aspect of him that didn't fit any of his usual patterns. She felt she was just about to grasp who he was. "Frank, maybe you are human."

"What do you mean?"

"This is the first time we've talked. Not the talking we do when you're teaching, but just simple talk. An expression of values; a chance to grasp each other's essence. After all you've taught me, I've never been able to figure your inner workings. I think, however, I may be getting a glimpse."

"And what did you see?"

"I don't know yet."

"What made you think you couldn't discover my essence? If anything, I'd say I'm much more obvious than anyone else."

"Sure it's obvious that you have clearly defined roles, it's as if you have separate personalities, but I can't find the motive behind it."

"I merely try to be the best I can at what I do."

"And you've succeeded at becoming the best, but still there's more to it than that."

"Not that I can see."

"Or will see."

"Myra, what do you want?"

"I want you to take me to bed. Can't you see I've fallen in love with you?"

His face seemed to blank out. Several seconds passed. Seconds that felt like hours. She looked into his eyes searching for a response, but there was none. Nothing reflected from his blank eyes.

Finally, he spoke. "Yes, I can see it now,... but it's just an infatuation - not love. Once you've acquired an acting ability greater than mine, and you will, your feelings will pass."

"No!" she insisted. "It's not an infatuation."

She moved from her chair, and sat at his knees. She kissed his hand, then the inside of his elbow. Her hand traced the length of his arm to caress his neck and the back of his head. At first he resisted, but when she kissed his neck, his body began to respond. She pressed her mouth to his, and his arms enveloped her in an involuntary embrace. His mouth began exploring her body. Myra was ecstatic, but something about the way he moved felt mechanical; but before she could really think about it, he relaxed and continued his inventory of her scent, and the texture of her skin. His study reached a feverish momentum as his tongue touched the cleavage of her chest, and he tore her blouse away exposing her breasts. She threw her head back, smiling in exultation as he drew her nipple into his mouth.

Later as she lay in his arms in his bed, she said, "You don't love me."

"No." He answered.

She started crying, and said, "You will. I'll learn what drives you. I'll find out who you are."

"When you do, you won't love me." His accent sounded slightly different. It was another glimpse, and caused her sobs to stop.

She said, "What did you say?"

He didn't answer. She looked into his face only to find it blank again. She was frightened.

#

Although Frank reluctantly became her lover, a role she was only able to coax out at night, little else in their relationship changed. She remained his constant companion, and her lessons continued unabated. The time had come, he told her, to do some work on stage.

"You've demonstrated success with pantomime. You can now convey with silence, using your body as your only tool, what would ordinarily have to be spoken. It's the very ability that made great actors during the days of the silent motion picture. Your next step is to add speech while reducing to a nuance those same silent actions. All this really boils down to is that your body must match your words to make sense to the audience. The best place for doing that is in the live theater."

"It is the theater where one really learns to act. Being live-on-stage means you have a room full of critics. Your audience reacts scene-by-scene, line-by-line to how well you perform, and whether they boo you. You will learn to fine-tune your character into a believable, realistic person they can relate to, even fantasy characters, or larger-than-life characters. I contend that the only actors who are ready for film, are those who have mastered the stage. You will have to show me that you can master the stage before I will cast you in my films. It's time we find that out."

Her first stage role as a Frank Stacy Student was Roxane in Edmond Rostand's *Cyrano de Bergerac*. She found herself wishing she could be playing Cyrano, and Frank noticed her distraction.

"Where is your mind? I've never seen you perform so poorly."

"Roxane is such an airhead that I'm afraid I've been coveting the leading role."

"It shows. Now get into character and stay there. There will be plenty of leads for you in the future."

"Not like this one."

"Perhaps not," he conceded.

Her second role was the lead. She played Karen Andre in Ayn Rand's *Night of January 16th*. This court room drama ended each night with a verdict pronounced by members of a jury selected from the audience. Because the jurors' decision could differ, the play had two endings. This made Myra feel there were actually two different characters, so she played the role differently every other night. Myra subtly altered the character as she interpreted how Karen would act if she were guilty one night then on the next night if she were innocent. Myra was then able to predict with flawless accuracy the verdict of each night's jury. Frank was the only one to notice, but not before several performances. He congratulated her on her ability, but warned her that she was toying with the author's intentions.

After that run, Frank insisted that she only accept roles from new plays. Roles where she would set the standards. Roles where she would have to be her own role model.

#

It was on the set of *Resurgent Man* that she again noticed a change in Frank. As usual he held Morning-Conference when he and his first assistant director reviewed the dailies along with the production manager, cinematographer, sound mixer, and gaffer; a usually noisy, busy, cheerful meeting with suggestions flying from all corners of the room to fine-tune what most would say was already in harmony. The meetings for *Resurgent Man*, however, were somewhat subdued, yet there was a strong undercurrent of excitement most had never recalled. More notable, Myra thought, was that after the call sheet for the day was read Frank gave very little direction in addition to the instructions he had originally written out during pre-production. However, at the end of each meeting he always gave the same little speech.

"Remember, the effect I'm seeking is to make the audience feel they are watching a documentary, filmed not by man, but by a disinterested god."

This concept excited the camera crew, but for everyone else it evoked a sense of foreboding. To the actors, he gave absolutely no direction. Although he never told anyone how to perform once they left his classes, he always gave his actors general instructions to keep them mindful of the camera's point of view. On this set he did not even do that. Subjects of documentaries are seldom supposed to be aware of the camera Frank reminded Myra.

She would sit beside him aware that he was watching more than directing. He was letting the story evolve in front of the camera. It was so out of character for his controlling nature, she was compelled to ask why.

"That's the way it has to be done for this story."

"That's no explanation."

"Shhhh!" he bade her silence.

She leaned back and watched him. After a few minutes she spoke again.

"You're searching for something." she stated, not asked.

He looked at her in astonishment and answered, "Yes."

"What?" she asked.

"I'm not sure."

Her eyes fell on the hand-written copy of the script. It was clutched in both his hands; and she realized, with a start, that his pencil was not in his hand, but was shoved behind his ear.

"Where did you get this story?" she asked.

"I don't know. It was rolled up in my jacket pocket when I arrived in Hollywood. I thought it was the most fantastic thing I'd ever read, and decided I had to produce it one day."

"Did the author put it in your jacket?"

"I couldn't say. When I decided to go forward with it, I tried to find the author, but he wasn't listed with the *Screen Writers Guild.* I then checked with the *Library of Congress,* but it wasn't copyrighted. So, I hired a detective. He told me that the only Jackson Paine Franklin he could locate was dead, and had been for years and years. I'm sure if there's another one, I'll hear from him just as soon as this picture hits the theaters."

"Where were you before you came to Hollywood?"

"Shhhhh! Too many questions. Watch the set."

She was not the only one to notice changes in Frank. One of the scenes depicted an act of physical violence. In the past Frank had always softened these types of scenes by using long shots, high speed, and smoked lenses, but in this one he did not. A producer-admirer was on location the following day; he was invited to join the crew chiefs in the *Cinemobile* as the dailies of that scene were reviewed. He witnessed a scene shot in slow motion close-up with some of the goriest blood-letting special effects ever employed.

"My God, Frank!" he implored. "This is brutal; this isn't you. This is worse than Sam Peckinpaw's brand of gore."

Frank smiled. "Apparently, what I was seeking to accomplish is working."

As the man left, he whispered to Myra, "If he can do that, I don't see why he refuses to make war pictures."

Myra just shrugged, and wondered what he would think when he saw the trailer for *Resurgent Man*. It had already been sent to theaters as a preview of coming attractions, and it didn't even contain a hint that cruel and ruthless violence was integral to the theme.

#

After the completion of *Resurgent Man,* Frank cast her in the lead of his next motion picture; her lessons were over. *The Tangled Web* signaled the beginning of a brilliant career. Myra Mason's performance was excellent, and her name became a household word overnight. She was even nominated for Best Actress.

Following her nomination, as if to crown her own achievement, she moved into Frank's apartment. She accomplished this feat by using the same aggressive behavior she had used first in getting her acting lessons, and later in beguiling the recalcitrant Frank into becoming her lover. Their living together came as a surprise to no one in the entertainment community, except perhaps Frank.

When she received her *Academy Award*, Myra learned from the *Academy of Motion Picture Arts and Sciences* that Frank had never picked up his two *Oscars*. This struck her as odd at first, but was later convinced that it was perfectly in character for the overworked and Spartan-living Frank. He was too preoccupied to be bothered with the frilly tributes of life. Much later she would change her mind and think otherwise. Meanwhile, she persuaded the Academy to allow her to bring home all three, and she displayed them as part of her efforts of making his townhouse feel like a home, or at least: lived in.

Myra's mastery marked a new era for *Stacy Productions* as Frank cast her as leading actress in film after film. It was during the production of her fourth picture that Myra managed to marry Frank. She knew he still didn't love her, but she had caused him to take on two new roles: lover and husband. He performed them perfectly. The former was rare and sweet, but the latter was so indifferent it made her cry. He was attentive, he was supportive, but damn it, she thought, he was mimicking a role suitable only for TV.

#

Myra made Stacy movies for five years during which time she stretched her ability to encompass greater and greater challenges. Then suddenly her career peaked before she did. It came about gradually as motion pictures that were perfect for her seemed to pass her by. She couldn't believe there were any insidious motives behind her decline, because both her talent and her popularity were still on the rise, but Frank began giving her fewer parts and worse yet: less demanding ones. It wasn’t until a year or more after he quit casting her entirely that she noticed the chasm between them had been forged by her desire to know her husband better. She blamed herself for not learning to understand his desires, but she could never discover what those desires were, and the more she tried the more distant he became.

The distancing of their relationship first began at home. His behavior became more and more stilted, and she found she could cajole him into bed less and less. Although it took years for him to gradually extinguish his role as lover and then director, he immediately terminated his relationship as teacher on the day after their honeymoon. When she asked him why, he would only say that she had learned all that he could teach. Somehow she felt he was lying, but no one could ever prove that with Frank. One of his favorite classroom gimmicks, one which he used to demonstrate the extraordinary will necessary to become a great actor, was to hook himself up to a polygraph machine. After calibrating it, he would sit in the chair and tell obvious lies. The students stood by in awe as the arm drawing the graph held steady. Then he would reverse himself by telling glaring truths, while the lie detector's arm swung erratically from side to side.

When she finally left the Stacy stable; and Frank was no longer her teacher, or director, he began showing her a little more attention at home, but they were no longer lovers. Their relationship reached its pinnacle when they began living together. Myra ended up taking roles with other producers, and as was the case with all Stacy drop-outs, her name was billed with the addendum: FORMER STACY STAR.

CHAPTER EIGHT

The breaking of dawn sent beams of sunshine through the open vents of the Venetian blinds, laying stripes of light across the face of Frank Stacy. Waking, he sat up on the sofa he'd been sleeping on and looked about the strange room. He didn't know where he was, but his mouth felt like a dust bowl, and his head hurt like hell. He saw a nearly empty whiskey on the coffee table, and his stomach turned.

"No wonder," he thought.

Frank seldom drank, and when he did, he only drank one glass of wine. He rubbed his aching head, and his fingers found the stitches on the back of his scalp, and he remembered.

Scenes of his last memory flew through his mind. Myra tricked him into a day away from the office. He was diving, showing off in his back yard pool, then nothing. He could remember nothing after that. He looked around the room, but he couldn't place it. "Zack!" he called out. No answer. "Myra!" he cried. Again, no answer.

His fingers rose to rub his chin in contemplation, as he tried to make sense of his whereabouts. At first he didn't notice, but after a few moments his fingers stopped their unconscious movement with the discovery of a face full of heavy whiskers.

"Jesus, I haven't shaved in days," he said aloud as he pulled on his cheek to note the length of the hair. "Zack! Myra! Anyone, home?"

Behind the sofa was a dining area and a small kitchen. To the right of the kitchen was an open door through which he could see the bathroom. Beside the bathroom he saw a closed door. He walked over and pushed it open. A man was asleep in the bed.

"Hey, wake up," he said, shaking the man.

The man rolled over and opened his eyes to a squint. "Morning, Eugene. Why don't you help yourself to some breakfast? I don't feel like getting up yet."

"Eugene?" Frank said in a bewildered tone.

"Oh, shit," Hooper said, sitting up and instantly awake. "Don't tell me. You're Frank Stacy; and you don't know where you are."

Frank responded with angry sarcasm, "You seem to be keenly apprised of the situation. Perhaps you'll do me the favor of filling me in."

"Pal, you sure keep things interesting," Hooper said, pulling on his robe. "Come on; let's go to the kitchen and make some coffee. I'll need some hangover cure to get me through this one."

Frank pushed Hooper back onto the bed, and yelled, "I want to know, now!"

Hooper jumped up and yelled right back into Frank's face, "Cool your jets, Buddy, or get out. This is my house, and you're here at my hospitality."

They stood face to face, staring into each other's eyes. Finally, Frank softened and spoke, "I'm sorry. It's the shock of disorientation."

"It's okay." Hooper extended his hand. "By the way, my name is Hooper Johnson."

"I know that name; you're an actor."

"I, at least, think so. Now, let's get that coffee."

In the kitchen, Hooper handed Frank the newspaper with the story of his disappearance from the hospital. While he made the coffee, he told Frank what had happened the previous day, what he knew from what Eugene told him, and how he ended up in Hooper's apartment.

When he finished Frank said, "I can't say that I remember any of what happened, but somehow, while you were speaking I had a deja vu-like feeling."

"You need to call your wife."

"I know. I need a few minutes to sort everything out."

"Like what?"

"Like how did my brain, manufacture Eugene Eastly?"

"Because that's who you are. I told you, it's Eugene Eastly who has amnesia, when he thinks he's Frank Stacy."

"That's absurd," Frank said dismissively. "I'm not from Georgia; I'm from New York, and my name has never been anything but Frank Stacy."

"Frank, your acting skills are unmatched, you're capable of being anyone. Can't you imagine the possibility that you've buried Eugene under a chosen personality?"

Frank ignored him. His eyes became unfocused as he stared in thought toward the wall which held the poster of Myra. Hooper followed Frank's glance and when his eyes reached Myra's photograph he felt a twisting ache in his gut. He knew what it was; it was more than longing, it was envy, pure and simple.

After a lengthy pause Stacy said, "Wait a minute. I believe I've got it. I can't remember for sure, but I'm fairly certain Eugene Eastly was the name of a character from a screenplay I seriously considered."

"Frank, you're covering up the truth." Hooper pleaded. "Can't you see what you're doing? You're rationalizing, and you're stretching at that. Can't you consider the possibility, especially after all that happened to you while your memory was completely gone, that you may be someone other than Frank Stacy?"

"No," Frank responded with a studied look in his eye, "I'm not the one that's rationalizing, you are. More likely you're romanticizing. You think it's a good story. It makes you feel good to believe that a country boy gets amnesia; and causes him to become a success. What you don't realize is that it's highly unlikely that the person you described, an ignorant redneck, could achieve what I've achieved. No, I'm sure now, Eugene Eastly was a character I studied closely from a screenplay I once considered for production."

"Which screenplay?"

Frank shrugged, "I've reviewed thousands. Look, I appreciate all the help you've given me. Let me do something for you."

"It's not necessary."

"Then let me put it this way. I want to buy your silence. My problems are personal, and I don't wish to see them on the cover of the *National Enquirer*."

"I don't want your money. Your secret is safe with me."

"Then at least let me help you in your acting career."

"No thanks, I prefer Eugene, you're too much of a hard ass."

"Suit yourself."

"Tell you what, though, I'll take a rain check. I might like to meet you again, if you and Eugene ever get your act together." Hooper chuckled at his pun, and added, "Hey, get it - Get your act together? I don't think that term has ever been more appropriately used."

Frank scowled and said, "May I use your phone?"

Hooper nodded.

"Myra, it's Frank. I'm okay. ... I'm in L.A. ... Yes, I'll tell you all about it when I get home. ... I'll charter a flight out. ... Don't worry, I'm fine now. Listen, I need you to call Chester and have him call a press conference. ... Right, and tell him to keep it simple - we'll elaborate later. ... Thanks dear. ... Good bye."

After calling a local clothier to deliver a suit to Hooper's address, he chartered a plane and booked a limousine. Then he asked Hooper if he might freshen up in his bathroom. Hooper nodded again.

As he was changing he found the name and address of the trucker in the pocket of the sweatsuit. Beside the name was the notation: $40. He asked Hooper what it was. Hooper didn't know. Frank put the slip of paper into his suit pocket.

Two hours after waking, Frank left for the airport in his rented limousine. No trace of Eugene Eastly remained.

Hooper stood despondently in front of his television and looked down at the video cassettes they never got a chance to watch. He was going to miss Eugene. He had looked forward to working with him in *Runaway Grandparents*. He picked up the cassettes to return them; he wanted nothing more to do with Frank Stacy that day.

At the video store while he was waiting for his deposit, he watched the clerk put the cassettes back on the rack. He saw a title he did not recognize and asked the clerk, "What is *Resurgent Man*?"

The clerk replied, "It's Frank Stacy's bomb. Kind of an art piece."

"Art piece?"

"Yeah, compared to the rest of his stuff. Art piece, think piece, whatever you want to call it. It was a box office dud. Although it's done well in the cult market, and in video, so he probably didn't take the financial bath, the critics predicted."

"What's it about?"

"Why don't you rent it and find out?"

"No, I don't think so. I'm a little burned out on Stacy after last night."

"Completely different; totally unlike anything else he's done before - you really ought to try it."

"Okay, what the hell."

CHAPTER NINE

Hooper put the cassette into his VCR and poured the remaining *Jack Daniel's* into a tall glass. He didn't ask himself whether the alcohol was supposed to numb his annoyance with Frank, or his sense of loss over Eugene; he just wanted to dull the ache. He turned up the glass and swallowed deeply, then sat back to watch the movie.

Hooper observed that the opening credits were typically, conspicuously simple:

FRANK STACY
presents
RESURGENT MAN
screenplay by Jackson Paine Franklin

Predictably the director's intentional omission evoked Hooper's anticipation. Almost instantly he began wondering who the performers would be. It was a response critics claimed distracted the audience, but Stacy knew better - it subtly induced rapt attention. It was a masterful gimmick focusing the viewer on each actor's performance. Hooper, no different than the average movie-goer, didn't even notice the manipulation - like everyone else, he just wondered whether he would recognize the performers before the closing credits.

Suddenly, the next credit shocked the actor into sitting upright:

MYRA MASON
EXECUTIVE PRODUCER

"Executive Producer! How can that be," he cried out, and snatched up the video-cassette jacket. He read the copyright date; it had been made before *The Tangled Web* - Myra's first picture. It was just a hunch, but the struggling actor couldn't help wondering if financing *Resurgent Man* had anything to do with her becoming a *Stacy* actress. Hooper glanced at the poster on the wall, he knew he didn't really know anything, but somehow he felt a little bit closer to his goal.

As Myra's name faded, he turned his attention back to the movie. His expectations of experiencing something different from Frank Stacy grew. He watched the opening shots of a lush, almost tropical location, and for a fleeting moment Hooper wondered where it was filmed - then before he knew it he was absorbed in the story.

The child actors impressed Hooper, but the story unfolded slowly and he found it a little dry. He cared mildly about the children, and the eventual disposition of the fat ranger somewhat aroused his curiosity, but all in all he found himself just a little bored as the first act concluded.

He yawned and stretched his legs as he began to wonder just what the point of this movie was.

"Come on, Frank," he muttered to screen, "the kids are cute, but please pick up the pace."

He drained the glass of sour mash, then put his hands behind his head. He was ready for sleep in the event the picture continued in the same vein.

RESURGENT MAN

ACT TWO

SCENE TWENTY-TWO. FOUR YEARS LATER. EXTERIOR. DAY. HIGH SCHOOL.

A battered blue pick-up truck carrying a huge metal box pulls into the school parking lot. Two young women climb out of the passenger door, and enter the school building. One is tall with straight pale blonde hair, the other slightly shorter with dark curly hair. The truck continues to the other side of the parking lot, and stops. Jumping out of the cab is a tall broad shouldered boy with a sun-burnished face topped by short cropped sun-lightened hair. He moves with simple assurance as he unties the rope holding down the metal box. Muscles ripple underneath his T-shirt.

Entering from left is Jimmy wearing a football letter jacket. He is no longer fat but stocky instead. His red crew-cut hair is butch-waxed in front. Beside him is a slender boy in a plaid shirt and pleated trousers with long dark blonde hair combed and oiled into a ducktail.

Jimmy: "Hey, Billy; what the hell is that?"

Billy (turns): "Oh, hi Jimmy, (nods) hi Clark. It's a tank for hauling fish. I built it in shop out of some old air-conditioning equipment I found at the dump. Unfortunately, it sprang a leak so I've got to put a better weld on it."

Jimmy (flippant): "What the hell do you need that for?"

Billy (turns back and drops gate on back of truck): "For carrying trout."

Jimmy: "Oh, is that what you do for old man Simpson - haul fish?"

Billy: "I don't work for Mr. Simpson."

Jimmy: "But I see you over there all the time. I just figured you worked for him."

Billy: "Nope."

Jimmy (demands): "Then who do you work for?"

CUT TO: Billy easily tossing the rope around the back of the tank.

Billy: "Gods of the Pond, Trout Farm."

CUT TO: Jimmy and Clark.

Jimmy (shrugs): "Never heard of 'em."

CLARK:

(Nudges Jimmy) "Ask him."

Jimmy: "Say Billy, we wanted to ask you a question."

CUT TO: Billy sitting on the edge of the tailgate with his back to the tank. His arms are tight against his ribs and in each hand he grips the two ends of the rope that he has wrapped around the tank. He looks up at the two boys as his biceps bulge then leans forward. The huge tank lifts off the bed of the truck.

Billy: "Ask away, but you're gonna have to follow me to the metal shop if you want an answer."

Billy walks toward the school, leaving the two boys behind him.
Clark (gasps): "Jesus Christ, Billy what does that thing weigh?"
Billy (grunts): "About two hundred pounds."

Jimmy runs around to the front of Billy.
Jimmy: "What we wanted to ask you was--"

Billy keeps walking and Jimmy can't finish his question. He runs again to stand in front of Billy, but before he can speak Billy is past him again. He tries once more, but this time he tries walking backward. He trips. When he stands up, he shrugs and runs to catch up with Billy, this time grabbing the back of the tank to help Billy carry it.

CUT TO: MASTER SHOT: INTERIOR. DAY. HIGH SCHOOL METAL SHOP.

SOUNDTRACK: BACKGROUND MUSIC. *How Can I Be Sure* by The Young Rascals.

Billy sets the tank down on a large table, and leans back against it.
Billy (exhales and smiles): "Whew! So, what terribly urgent question does the captain of the football team and the senior class president need to ask me?"
Jimmy: "It's like this, buddy, me and Clark were talking about who we wanted to take to Homecoming, and the conversation led around to you and how you hang out with the two best lookin' girls in the whole school. Well, we wanted to know which one you were taking, because one of us could then ask the other."

CUT TO: CLOSE-UP Billy as his face turns red as if embarrassed for ONE BEAT. Then all color drains from his face entirely. His eyes twitch left and then right with the look of a cornered animal that doesn't know which way to turn.

#

Hooper was interested. He sat up and leaned toward the TV screen. As the change of emotion crossed the actor's face, Hooper roared, "Wow! What is going through your mind, Billy. Man! What a performance. This is incredible. Damn, Frank Stacy, this is what makes you the greatest."

#

Billy: "I hadn't really planned on going."
Clark: "Aren't you going steady with one of them? I mean that's what everybody says, but nobody knows which one."
Billy: "Do you mean have I asked one of them to go steady?"
Jimmy: "Oh, come on Billy, don't act dumb."
Billy (looks down at the scar on his wrist): "No, I've never asked one of them to go steady."

#

Hooper yelled at the TV "Jesus Christ, Billy! What are you thinking?"

#

Jimmy: "Buddy, if you're not going with either one of them, would you mind fixing both of us up."

CUT TO: Billy dropping from the table to stand on the floor. His shoulders square as if in anticipation of a burden.

Billy: "Look guys, I'm not a match-maker, if you want to ask them out - then ask. It's their decision."

CUT TO: Jimmy and Clark who both look nonplused. They look at each other, then over toward Billy, then back at each other. Finally Jimmy punches Clark in the ribs.

Jimmy: "All right! What the hell are we waiting for?"

The camera dollies back to enlarge the MASTER SHOT as Jimmy and Clark walk toward the door, and Billy sits back down.

CUT TO: CLOSE-UP of Billy. His eyes are locked and unfocused. Volume of SOUNDTRACK increases.

CUT TO: SOFT FOCUS CLOSE-UP of Jeannine.

CUT TO: SOFT FOCUS CLOSE-UP of Cassandra.

CUT TO: Billy with tearing eyes.

SOUNDTRACK STOPS.

CUT TO: Jimmy and Clark as they get to the door.

Jimmy (whispering): "I told you he was a homo, didn't I?"

FADE.

SCENE TWENTY-THREE. MASTER SHOT. INTERIOR. DAY. HIGH SCHOOL HALLWAY.

A tall, slender girl carrying a heavy stack of books is walking down a hallway crowded with students. She has thick white-blond hair that hangs nearly to her waist. Her eyes are crystal blue, her lips ruby red and her skin milky smooth. She walks with brisk, light steps that cause the pleats of her plaid skirt to bounce and the youthful breasts underneath her emerald green cashmere sweater to quiver. She exudes a bright-eyed confidence that has the promise of maturity. She has a fresh, happy-with-the-world, happy-with-herself-look; the kind one expects to see on teenagers working in suburban hamburger franchises. She smiles and greets several students, until she stops at a locker. Jimmy walks up behind her as she pulls the locker door open.

Jimmy: "Hi, Cassy."

CUT TO: Cassandra turning around and smiling.

Cassandra: "Hi, Jimmy." (She turns back to her locker.)

CUT TO: Jimmy.

Jimmy: "Say Cassy..."

CUT TO: MASTER SHOT as Cassy turns back around.

Cassandra: "Say what Jimmy?"

Jimmy: "Uh,... how would you like to go to the Homecoming Dance with me?"

Cassandra: "I can't, Jimmy, but thank you for asking."

PAUSE ONE BEAT as Jimmy gives an exaggerated hurt look. She responds to the gesture by saying: "Of course, I'm awfully flattered to be asked by the football captain, but why aren't you taking one of the cheerleaders?"

Jimmy: "Well, you're so much prettier than any of the cheerleaders, and I wanted to ask you first."

Cassandra (gives Jimmy a patronizing smile): "Why thank you, Jimmy."

Jimmy (patronizes in return): "How come you never went out for cheerleading?"

Cassandra: "I guess I've been busy trying to grow up too fast. At least that's what my mother always tells me."

Jimmy: "So, do you already have a date for the dance?"
Cassandra: "No."
Jimmy: "Then how come you can't go with me?"
Cassandra (closes the locker and turns to leave): "Because I've got a steady boyfriend, Jimmy, and I don't think he'd appreciate it."
Jimmy (voices disbelief): "You do!" (BEAT) "Who?"

CUT TO: Cassy walking down the hall, out of earshot.

SCENE TWENTY-FOUR. MASTER SHOT: INTERIOR. DAY. HIGH SCHOOL HALLWAY.

In front of classroom. A bell rings and students explode out the door like birdshot from a scattergun. The front runner is a girl, whose dark, swarthy, earthy sort of beauty would seem more natural if she were an Indian or Gypsy princess. Glistening black unruly curls cascade to the tops of her shoulder. Large velvety black eyes sit in sultry shadow above rounded cheeks and full lips. Her skirt is rebelliously short exposing long dark legs moving unhurriedly but with determination. Bursting from the classroom door behind her, pushing fellow students out of the way like buckshot from a second "just in case" barrel is Jimmy. He keeps pushing until he catches up to her.
Jimmy: "Jeannine, did you get my note?'
Jeannine (without slowing down): "You know I did."
Jimmy: "Well?"
Jeannine: "Are you kidding? You haven't said ten words to me in five years; why should I take an invitation like yours seriously?"
Jimmy: "But, I am serious. I think you're a beautiful girl, and I want to take you to the dance."
Jeannine: "You mean, you want to be seen with a beautiful girl at the dance."
Jimmy: "And, what's wrong with that?"
Jeannine: "Jesus, Jimmy, don't you think people ought to have something in common first? Give it up, you'd be bored on a date with me."
Jimmy: "Never!"

Jeannine: "Why don't you stick with the brain-dead living that you usually make out with? That way you can cop a free feel and it won't even be noticed."
Jimmy: "That's what I like about you Jeannine, you're feisty."
Jeannine: "OOOh, that's a mighty big word for a jock, Jimmy. Better be careful - you don't want to overload your brain cells before Friday night's game."
Jimmy: "Oh, come on, why not go with me? You haven't been asked yet, have you?"
Jeannine (exasperated): "Beats the hell out of me, but as a matter of fact; yes. I've been asked several times already. If it's any consolation Jimmy, they were all as senseless as you."
Jimmy: "Does that mean you haven't accepted one yet?"
Jeannine: "At least you get wiser with time, Bonehead. Speaking of which, why don't you let your hair grow out? No one should know you have that many freckles on your scalp. You know Jimmy, a little hair, and you'd be a good lookin' fellow."
Jimmy: "I must be getting somewhere; you're stooping to flattery. So how 'bout it? You goin' to the dance with me?"

Jeannine stops sharply and looks Jimmy straight in the face.

Jeannine: "Jimmy, you want to buy an elevator pass?"
Jimmy: "There's no elevator here; that trick only works on eighth graders. Do you think I'm stupid?"
Jeannine (starts walking again): "Reverse ditto, that's my answer to your last question."

CUT TO: OVER-THE-SHOULDER SHOT as Jimmy walking behind Jeannine, speaks to her back.

Jimmy: "Oh, come on give me one good reason."
Jeannine (in high pitched, mock, bimbo voice): "Gee Jimmy, that's the night I wash my hair."

CUT TO: MASTER SHOT as Jimmy catches back up.

Jimmy: "Serious reason."
Jeannine (in normal voice): "You won't accept the obvious, why should I believe you'd accept anything else."
Jimmy: "Try me."
Jeannine: "Okay I've got a boyfriend."

Jimmy: "I don't believe it."
Jeannine: "What'd I tell you."
Jimmy: "I've never seen you out with anyone."
Jeannine: "Jimmy, less than a minute ago, I proved, beyond the shadow of a doubt - even to you - that your perception is hopelessly flawed. How can you still expect to depend on your sense of sight?"
Jimmy: "You say some weird things."
Jeannine: "Jimmy, are you trying to flatter me?"
Jimmy: "You know, your friend Cassy is a hell of a lot nicer than you."
Jeannine: "Flattery again. What happened - you strike out with her first?"
Jimmy: "Yeah."
Jeannine: "At least you're honest. So, what was her excuse?"
Jimmy: "Same as yours?"
Jeannine: "I'm sure she didn't tell you it was because you're a Bonehead Jock; she's much too pleasant."
Jimmy: "Nope, she said, she had a boyfriend too."
Jeannine (astonished): "She did?"
Jimmy: "You mean you're her best friend and you don't know?"
Jeannine: "Well, we've never discussed it."
Jimmy: "So, who is your boyfriend?"
Jeannine: "Since your vision is flawed, Jimmy, I guess I'll have to tell you. It's Billy."
Jimmy (laughs): "Billy! Well, you better tell him, because he certainly doesn't know about it. At least he didn't this morning."

Jeannine stops and leans against the wall. Her face no longer amused, but concerned.

Jeannine (softly): "No, he knows." BEAT "He's just being noble."

#

Hooper thought Jeannine looked suddenly more relaxed, and he noticed that as she leaned against the wall she was rubbing the scar on her wrist. A question ripened in his mind. Certain of where the answer was he grabbed the remote control and rewound the tape. He stopped rewinding as Cassy was closing her locker, and Jimmy was asking, "Then, how come you can't go with me?" "Because I've got a steady boyfriend, Jimmy, and I don't think he'd appreciate it." As she turned to go, Hooper saw what he missed before - she was rubbing her wrist. "Eugene - Frank, I don't believe it." He whispered as he punched the button for fast-forward.

When he replayed Jeannine saying, "No, he knows. He's just being noble." Hooper uttered to the screen, "Does he?"

#

Jimmy (snide): "And I suppose Miss Straight-A Cassandra thinks he's her boyfriend too."

Jeannine doesn't answer, but walks slowly away. Her shadowy black eyes focused only inward.

MONTAGE. BACKGROUND MUSIC: *Sweet Pea* by Tommy Roe.

Rapid sequence of shots intercut. First Cassy, then Jeannine, over and over again shaking their heads to boys' gestures that without audible words pantomime invitations to the dance. Clark shows up twice in the sequence. The music fades as the last shot

CUTS TO: SCENE TWENTY-FIVE. MASTER SHOT. INTERIOR. DAY. HIGH SCHOOL HALLWAY. Cassy and Jeannine run into each other in the hall.

#

Hooper felt his body tense up in anticipation of a cat fight between the girls.

#

Jeannine: "Cassy, how many times have you been asked to the dance today?"

Cassandra: "Oh, at least a dozen. You too?"

Jeannine: "Yes."

Cassandra: "What is going on? In all of high school I haven't been asked out this many times."

Jeannine: "It looks like Billy put us on the market - I think you and I need to talk - can you get a library pass for next period?"

Cassandra: "Sure."

Jeannine: "Then I'll meet you there."

DISSOLVE TO: SCENE TWENTY-SIX. MASTER SHOT. INTERIOR. DAY. High school hallway with row of lockers. Billy is opening his locker. When it is open CUT TO: OVER-THE-SHOULDER SHOT. Hanging from the coat hook is a note reading:

The Gods must meet. Today.

CUT TO: Billy tearing down the note, then turning toward the camera. His face is blank.

SLOW DISSOLVE TO FLASHBACK: indicating Billy's memory.

SCENE TWENTY-SEVEN. MASTER SHOT: EXTERIOR. DAY. POND.

The beaver style pond has been replaced by five ponds in a line following the course of the creek. All with concrete dams embedded with country rock blending in with the surrounding craggy outcropping, giving them the appearance of being natural and not man-made. Billy is talking to both Cassandra and Jeannine. All are of their current age.

Billy: "We'll have to drain them periodically, say about twice a year. If we don't, the ponds will fill up with silt that's washed downstream. We can stagger the order in which we drain them, especially since we have to move the fish. The good news is that the silt we remove makes excellent soil, and we might be able to use enough of it to reclaim some of this land and grow our own corn for feeding the fish."

Jeannine: "We're in business now. Cassy, your research is finally going to pay off."

Cassandra: "Our research, and our back-breaking labor."

Jeannine: "It sure didn't take any time to spend all our catfish money on concrete, did it?"

Cassandra: "No, but it sure seemed to take forever to drag enough rocks down here. There were a few times when I thought I was going to die before we thought of using a wheelbarrow."

Jeannine: "Yeah, we were pretty stupid, weren't we?"

Billy (laments): "It feels good to stand back and look at it. I just wish we didn't have to put the hatchery all the way over at Mr. Dillon's. It sure would save a lot of time, if we could build a small shed here."
Cassandra (reassuring): "In nine years, if we keep this up, it will be ours under the homesteading laws, but until then we can't risk a building large enough to be noticed."
Jeannine: "Just think Billy, in nine years we can even build a house here."
Cassandra: "Okay let's quit thinking about the distant future and get on the near future. Billy, which pond do we harvest first."
Billy: "It doesn't work that way. Right now they all contain fingerlings, but as they grow, I'll separate them into ponds by size. Leaving the top one for breeding stock. They grow pretty fast though, we should have our first ready to sell in just a few months."
Jeannine: "I'd say it's time to name our company."
Cassandra: "Oh, I think we should call it Gods of the Pond."
Jeannine: "That's a great idea!. What do you think, Billy?"
Billy: "I like it; it's cool Cassy; it's the same name we swore to when we took our secret oath. But one question: who are the gods of the pond?"
Cassandra (smiles): "Don't you know? The gods of the pond are whoever created it, built it, and have the greatest interest in protecting it."
Billy: "Us."
Jeannine: "Yes, us. The name makes sense. We are the gods."
Billy (raises his wrist and presents his scar to the girls):
"Here's to the gods!"

Jeannine and Cassandra both raise their scars. Jeannine then throws her arms around Billy and Cassy and draws them both into an embrace.

Jeannine (tears run down her cheeks): "You know, this is like the meaning of life... of love."

SLOW DISSOLVE BACK TO SCENE TWENTY-SIX. Billy standing in front of his locker with the note in his hand.

CUT TO: SCENE TWENTY-EIGHT. MASTER SHOT. EXTERIOR. DAY. POND.

Ranger Roy ducks into the woods as he hears an engine running. Billy drives the blue pick-up around the last corner of the logging road and onto the desolate area of tombstone outcropping. He parks and walks down to the water. Along the side of the last and lowest of the five ponds a tent is pitched. Near it is a crackling campfire around which are sitting both Jeannine and Cassandra.

Billy: "What's going on?"

Jeannine gets up silently from where she was sitting by the fire and walks over to Billy. Without saying a word she embraces him and kisses him fully and passionately on the mouth. Billy is apparently stunned. He does not quite return her embrace.

Cassy stands up, and smiles as she observes Billy and Jeannine.

#

As Hooper looked on he muttered aloud, "So, the girls make the decision without leaving scratch marks. Jeannine, the brash one, wins while Cassandra, the mild one, submits to being the good loser and looks on without malice or envy. Bullshit Frank, let's get real. At least Billy looks like he might be uncomfortable with the choice."

But then Hooper gasped as:

#

Jeannine releases Billy, and Cassy takes him into her arms and kisses him every bit as thoroughly as Jeannine.

#

"Jesus," Hooper cried.

#

Jeannine (after Cassy releases Billy): "Have we answered your question?"

Billy (stammering): "I... I don't understand."

Cassandra: "It means you don't have to make a choice."

Billy: "You mean--"

Jeannine: "Unless, of course, you want to."
Billy: "No!"
Jeannine (sighs): "That's what we wanted to hear."
Billy (shakes his head in disbelief; his eyes tear up): "I... I can't believe it. You can't imagine how miserable I've been all day." PAUSE TWO BEATS "I've tried to prepare myself for seeing both of you with other men, but I couldn't do it. My mind refused to accept a life of unrequited love - life without the both of you." BEAT "I feel like I can breathe for the first time all day. You can't imagine how heavy my chest has felt. Oh, (laughs) and now all this fresh air is making me drunk." BEAT (Billy drops on one knee and holds a hand from each girl.) "It's as if I'm in a dream. I have always loved you both. There's no way I could've separated that love in my mind, and today was the first time it occurred to me that I might have to." BEAT "I'm sorry, I didn't know what to do."
Cassandra: "We kind of figured that out - that's why we're here."
Billy (sits all the way down): "I'm really feeling funny, like in here (points to his chest) my guts are boiling hot, while outside I feel chills flowing all over my skin. You see, it's because you two have set me free, free for the first time to say, I love you. I love you, Cassandra and I love you, Jeannine. (Billy jumps up and raises his arms.) "I'm free, I know I'm acting giddy, but I feel lighter than air. Is this relief or joy that I feel? It's neither; and it's both. Suddenly, I feel complete! And, I'm so light-headed right now, I feel like I could float into the stratosphere."

Billy twirls ecstatically as the girls watch in delight, laughing and clapping. Suddenly Billy stops and frowns.
Jeannine: "Billy, what is it?"
Billy (puts his hand against his forehead): "The bubble burst; it was too good to be true. My rational mind just kicked in with an awful thought." (Billy drops to his knees facing them) "Oh, my two loves, don't you see, no one is going to allow us to get away with this."
Cassandra (tenderly): "Billy, we're getting away with a trout farm on public land, why not add bigamy to our list of horrible crimes."
Billy (whispers): "Bigamy."

Jeannine: "What do we care what anyone thinks, there isn't a thing they can do. Our lives belong to us."
Cassandra: "Let us do the worrying for awhile. You've been so noble, that tonight is just for you."
Billy (gestures toward the campsite): "What is all this?"
Jeannine: "This is a promise of our future home here. We decided that you needed a taste of it now, to give you the strength for what we're all going to face in the days to come."
Billy: "Then you have thought out the consequences."
Cassandra and Jeannine: "Yes."

CUT TO: Both girls sitting on either side of Billy with their heads on his shoulders.

Jeannine: "Both of us will go as your dates to the Homecoming Dance," BEAT "and no excuses. Cassy's mother has already agreed to teach us all how to dance."
Cassandra: "Tonight, we've prepared your bed and your dinner."
Jeannine (blithely): "And each of us will sacrifice our virginity to the gods of the pond."
Billy: "But we are the gods of the pond."
Cassandra: "Bingo!"

CUT TO: an aerial view of the firelight flickering against the Gods of the pond.

CUT IN SOUNDTRACK (*Hold Me, Thrill Me, Kiss Me,* by Mel Carter) as the camera rises higher and higher.

FADE. SOUNDTRACK CONTINUES INTO SCENE TWENTY-NINE. MASTER SHOT: INTERIOR. NIGHT. Dimly lit high school gymnasium decorated with streamers, balloons, and Homecoming banners, while couples in formal dress whirl in dance all over the floor. Through an archway of crepe paper flowers, enter Billy, wearing a tuxedo, with Jeannine holding his right elbow and Cassy holding his left. Both girls are wearing party gowns; full and buoyant and crinoline crisp. Several couples stop dancing to point toward the three as they step onto the floor.

CUT TO: Billy and Jeannine dancing a simple waltz, but adding enough finesse to give them an appearance of grace and skill. Beyond them, on the boundary line of the basketball court, Cassy is standing with her hands clasped in front of her, and a satisfied smile on her face. The couples dancing nearest them do not seem to notice them at all. As the song ends Billy kisses Jeannine, and releases her.

CUT TO: Billy and Cassandra dancing, while Jeannine looks on. One-by-one, the couples nearest them stop dancing to watch until there is a circle of people around them. Billy and Cassy do not seem to notice.

CUT TO: Billy dancing with Jeannine.

CUT TO: Billy dancing with Cassy.

CUT TO: Billy carrying three glasses of punch. Jimmy walks up to him.

Jimmy (winks): "Hey - hey, Billy-boy, and all along I thought you were a fag."

Billy's eyes narrow, but he continues walking.

SOUNDTRACK is playing *Surf City* by Jan and Dean, as Jimmy is left standing alone.

CUT TO: Cassy sitting on the bleachers, when a pretty girl with big blonde curls in a red dress sits next to her.

SUE:
"Hi, Cassy."

Cassandra: "Hi, Sue."
Sue (snide): "What's wrong, Cassy dear, couldn't Jeannine get her own date?"
Cassandra: "Do you realize you're referring to my best friend?"
Sue: "Well, I wouldn't let my best friend kiss my boyfriend."
Cassandra: "He's her boyfriend, too."
Sue: "That doesn't make sense. What happens when you want to get married?"
Cassandra: "What makes you think that's a problem for us?"
Sue: "Then, who gets burned - you or Jeannine?"
Cassandra: "Who says anyone has to get burned?"
Sue: "You mean both of you?"
Cassandra: "Yep."

Sue (disgusted): "Oh, you're sick!"

Sue storms off.

CUT TO: Jeannine standing in the door way passing a cigarette to a girlfriend.

ANGELA:

"Boy, Jeannine, you guys are really making waves tonight. I mean, everybody's saying it's like a real scandal."

Jeannine: "They'll get over it."
Angela: "I don't get it. What are you trying to do, make some kind of statement?"
Jeannine: "Of course we are."
Angela: "What?"
Jeannine: "Isn't it obvious? That we're in love."
Angela: "But all three of you? That can't work."
Jeannine: "Says who?"
Angela: "Oh, Jeannine, I always thought you were so smart, but you're just being stupid."
Jeannine: "That's my prerogative." (Jeannine stubs out the cigarette.) "Gotta go; I've got a boyfriend to dote on."

CUT TO: Sue standing on the bleachers speaking excitedly to several couples in a group.

Sue: "... and Cassy as much as said, both she and Jeannine were going to marry Billy."

Several voices in the group gasp, and at least one person cries, "You're kidding!"

FADE.

SCENE THIRTY. MASTER SHOT: INTERIOR. DAY. HIGH SCHOOL HALLWAY. Billy, Jeannine, and Cassandra are walking together. Ahead of them is a group of five boys and three girls that look like hoods. One boy, who seems to be the kingpin, is wearing jeans and a leather jacket, and slouching against the row of lockers.

KINGPIN:

"Hey, look! Here comes the Mormons."

HOOD #2:
"Yeah, why don't you guys go to Utah where you belong!"

CUT TO: Billy, Jeannine, and Cassy as they come abreast of the hoods.
All Hoods (chanting): "Mor-mon ... Mor-mon ... Mor-mon ..."
Jeannine (turning toward the hoods, yelling): "We don't need to be Mormons to be in love!"

Billy grabs her elbow and leads her away.
Billy (whispers in Jeannine's ear): "Just leave it alone. It'll pass."

DISSOLVE TO SCENE THIRTY-ONE. MASTER SHOT: INTERIOR. CLASSROOM.

Billy is sitting on the front row assiduously taking notes. The teacher, a skinny man in a tweed jacket with a beak-like nose and thin dirty blonde hair stretched and plastered over a balding dome, is writing on the chalkboard.

TEACHER #1:
"... and it all comes back to the basic rule of economics that supply creates its own demand." (He swings dramatically around and bends at his waist to lean toward Billy.) "Of course there are some people who understand this much better than others."

The class burst into laughter, and in the background was a whisper of: "Mor-mon ... Mor-mon ... Mor-mon ..."

CUT TO: SCENE THIRTY-TWO. MASTER SHOT: INTERIOR. Classroom of female students with Jeannine seated in the center. The teacher a woman with dark brown hair wearing a polka-dot apron is lecturing.

TEACHER #2:
"... these simple recipes will help you design weekly menus for you and your future spouse. Remember the house may be considered the man's castle, but the kitchen is the woman's domain."

A girl sitting behind Jeannine stands up.

GIRL #1:
(mock innocence) "Is there anything in this chapter covering men who have to build two kitchens in their castles?"

The teacher's face turns red with embarrassment, but before she can respond Jeannine stands up.
Jeannine: "No, but I know an equation that will determine how many servants, including a cook, a three-income family can hire."
CUT TO: SCENE THIRTY-THREE. MASTER SHOT: INTERIOR. High school hallway with row of lockers. Cassy stops in front of her locker. On it is written in drippy white shoe polish:

MATH TEST
1 + 1 = 3 wrong
1 + 2 = 2 wrong
1 x 2 = 5 probably
grade: F-

CUT TO: SCENE THIRTY-FOUR. MASTER SHOT: INTERIOR. High school girl's restroom. Cassy enters to find Jeannine leaning against the wall pressing a wet paper towel to her forehead.
Cassandra: "Jeannine! What's wrong?"
Jeannine: "Oh, hi Cassy. I... urp." (She belches and puts the towel over her mouth.) "Excuse me, but I've been sick all morning. I keep feeling like I'm going to throw up."
Cassandra: "Maybe you should go to the infirmary."
Jeannine: "That's not such a good idea."
Cassandra: "Why not?"
Jeannine: "Because I've already got a good idea what's wrong with me. I missed my period last month, and I think I must be... urp." (She puts the towel back to her mouth.)
Cassandra (giggles): "Pregnant? Really?"
Jeannine nods with the towel over her mouth.
Cassandra: "That's wonderful! Have you told Billy?"

Jeannine: (shaking her head, while removing towel from her mouth): "I was waiting 'til next month to be sure, but from the way I feel now, it must be a good catch."

Cassandra: "Don't tell him right away, okay?"

Jeannine: "Why not?"

Cassandra: "Wait, because I want to get pregnant with you."

Jeannine: "Are you... urp... crazy? I'm still wondering what I'm going to tell the Commandant when he notices one day at inspection I've got a little pot belly."

Cassandra: "Look at it this way, if both of us have to get married, who can argue with us, if it so happens that we have to marry the same man?"

Jeannine (laughs): "Is that supposed to be logic?"

FADE.

SCENE THIRTY-FIVE. MASTER SHOT: EXTERIOR. DAY. Front door of a restaurant. Parked nearby is the blue pick-up truck with the fish tank in back. Standing in the doorway is a smiling man in a chef's hat who shakes Billy's hand, then hands Cassy a check. As Cassy climbs into pick-up,

CUT TO: Billy running into the Commandant on the sidewalk.

Commandant (averts his face so that he does not have to see Cassy in the truck): "William Brooks."

Billy: "Yes sir?"

Commandant: "Son, my daughter tells me you're quite a businessman, and a hard worker."

Billy: "I try, sir."

Commandant: "William, my daughter has reached the age when I can no longer dictate her behavior, although I must admit that since she has formed an alliance with you..." His words choke off as his eyes involuntarily drift toward Cassy. He forces his eyes back to Billy and continues. "her stature has grown to meet my expectations. Son, I have my reservations... I just want you to know I love my daughter."

Billy: "I love her too, sir."

CUT TO: SCENE THIRTY-SIX. MASTER SHOT: INTERIOR. DAY. Mr. Dillon's living room. Mr. Dillon opens the front door and greets Cassy and Jeannine. Cassy holds up a stringer of trout.
Jeannine: "We brought you a present, Mr. Dillon."
Mr. Dillon: "Um, Umm! Jus' look at those sweet fish. Y'all come on in, I was jus' making some lemonade."

CUT TO: Jeannine and Cassy seated on a sofa as Mr. Dillon serves them lemonade then sits across from them.
Mr. Dillon: "Would y'all be offended by a little fatherly advice?"
Jeannine: "Not from you, Mr. Dillon."
Mr. Dillon: "We've been friends, for a long time. An' I worry about you. I seen you grow up, and seen the way you used to be. It used to be the three of you was like brothers and sisters. Now it's like husband and wives. I jus' want to ask if you know that what you're doing is wrong?"
Cassandra: "Is it wrong to be in love, Mr. Dillon?"
Mr. Dillon: "Nothin' is wrong with love, honey. It's jus' what other folks gonna think."
Jeannine: "We don't care what other people think."
Mr. Dillon: "I reckon I'm not gettin' 'round this the way I mean. It's not what they think; it's what they gonna do. An' it ain't what they gonna do to you two girls. They ain't gonna blame you - they gonna blame Billy. It's Billy you gots to think about."
Cassandra: "That doesn't make sense."
Jeannine: "I don't understand."
Mr. Dillon: "That's cause y'all don't know how pretty you are. If y'all were ugly, it might be diff'rent; but folks is gonna think Billy's got mo' than he should. It's envy that always makes folks so mean."

DISSOLVE TO: SCENE THIRTY-SEVEN. MASTER SHOT: INTERIOR. NIGHT.

Dining room Jeannine's house. Jeannine is standing at attention with her three sisters undergoing the Commandant's inspection. After looking at Jeannine's hands, he speaks.
Commandant: "Girls you all pass inspection tonight. In fact, I've hardly found an evening in months when I needed to send anyone back to the latrine. You have all turned into well dressed, refined

young ladies. Even your grades in school are good. It looks as if discipline is finally paying off." (Pause ONE BEAT looks Jeannine directly in the eyes. Pleads.) "Girls, make me proud of you."

CUT TO: CLOSE-UP of Jeannine as she trembles slightly.

CUT TO: SCENE THIRTY-EIGHT. MASTER SHOT: EXTERIOR. DAY. Billy's house. Billy pulls into the driveway then climbs out of the truck. As he mounts the steps to the porch, his father staggers out the front door with a bottle in his hand.

Billy: "Dad! What are you doing home so early?"

MR. BROOKS:
(angry) "I've been waiting for you, boy."

Billy (wary): "What for, Dad?"

Mr. Brooks (yells): "What for! As if you don't know. You ain't ever been nothing but a problem since the day you was born, and now cause of you and your goddamn reputation I lost my job."

Billy: "Lost your job?"

Mr. Brooks: "Fired! Goddamn it. Fired cause no woman wants to buy shoes from the father of a boy who is so goddamn horny he's gotta be walking around with his pecker in his hand all day lookin' to screw every mother's daughter in town."

Billy (attempts to push past his father): "That's absurd; you probably got fired for drinking on the job."

Mr. Brooks (grabs Billy by the arm): "You hold on there! If you haven't noticed, this is a small town we're living in. You just can't go around like you been doing."

Billy: "Just what have I been doing?"

Mr. Brooks: "Don't get smart with me, you know damn well what I'm talking about. Why the whole goddamn town is buzzing that you're going to marry both those fancy looking girlfriends of yours."

Billy: "That's my business."

Mr. Brooks: "The hell it is. It's disgusting, it's illegal, and it's... it's... goddamn it, boy, you ain't gotta marry both of 'em just cause you're gettin' poontang from both of 'em."

Billy (facetious): "Is that why you always spend your lunch hour over at Linda Sawyer's, cause you ain't gotta marry her?"
Mr. Brooks: "That's it, you son of a bitch! Get your things and get outta my house. Now!"

CUT TO: SCENE THIRTY-NINE. MASTER SHOT: INTERIOR. NIGHT. Kitchen Cassy's house. Cassy enters kitchen where her mother is busy cutting up two chickens.

Cassandra: "Hi, Mom."

Mrs. Sibley puts down her knife and turns slowly toward her daughter.

Mrs. Sibley (gravely and with a look of concern on her face): "Cassy, dear..."

BEAT.

Cassandra: "What is it, Mom?"
Mrs. Sibley: "Dear, I'm worried about you, and I think we should talk. I guess you know I've heard the rumors."
Cassandra: "They're true."
Mrs. Sibley: "I was afraid of that. I've seen the way you three are when you're together."
Cassandra: "Mom, we both love him."
Mrs. Sibley: "Cassy, I'm not going to reproach you; you're old enough to make your own decisions. I just wanted to let you know I support you in whatever choices you make."

Cassy throws her arms around her mother.

Cassandra: "Oh, thank you, Mom. I knew you'd understand."
Mrs. Sibley: "I do. Finding a man who really loves you; and makes you happy is hard to do. I had one once. I'd have done anything to keep him."

FADE.

SCENE FORTY. MASTER SHOT: EXTERIOR. DAY. High school. Streams of people are flowing out of the front door as Billy pulls up in his truck. Cassy and Jeannine break away from the crowd and run to his door.

Cassandra (upset): "Where have you been?"
Jeannine: "When we didn't see you in class, we worried."
Billy: "My father threw me out last night."

Jeannine: "Oh, no! What are you going to do?"
Billy: "I spent the day storing my things with Mr. Simpson. He's going to let me stay in the loft over his store."
Cassandra: "You could have stayed at my house, Mom wouldn't mind."
Billy (laughs): "Are you kidding, with all those brats running around."

CUT TO: CLOSE-UP of both Jeannine and Cassy. Both faces still show worry.

CUT TO: Billy.

Billy: "Come on you guys, brighten up. We've got work to do at the hatchery."

CUT TO: SCENE FORTY-ONE. MASTER SHOT: INTERIOR. DAY. Mr. Dillon's barn. Mr. Dillon, Billy, and Jeannine are standing around a long metal tank full of water, while Cassy skims off surface debris with a net.

Mr. Dillon: "Look at all dem little baby fish! When are y'all going to show me the whole works?"
Jeannine: "We really want to show you, but we've got to keep it a secret for eight years."
Mr. Dillon: "Sounds to me like somebody is homesteading."
Cassandra: "How did you know?"
Mr. Dillon: "I guessed it from putting together some things I overheard you talking about it. I reckon you know you got to put in a house and that somebody's got to be living there?"
Billy: "We know, but it won't start taking effect until we turn eighteen. So we've got a few months to figure out how to put in a house that nobody will discover for seven years."
Mr. Dillon: "What do you mean by a house nobody will discover?"
Cassandra: "You see, Mr. Dillon, we found a flaw in the law that prohibits homesteading. If we can hold it for seven years without being noticed, we can keep it."
Jeannine: "But if someone does find it, say like the Sheriff, or one of the rangers, then they can force us to leave."
Mr. Dillon: "I've got just what you need."
Billy, Cassy, and Jeannine in unison: "What?"

Mr. Dillon: "Plans for underground houses. Let's go inside; I'll show you."
Jeannine: "You two go on, I've got to feed the fish."
Billy: "Okay we'll see you tonight, and tell you all about it."
CUT TO: SCENE FORTY-TWO. MASTER SHOT: EXTERIOR. DAY. POND. Jeannine drives the truck to the end of the logging road, parks, and walks down the path to the ponds. As the ponds swing into her view, she sees Ranger Roy scooping trout out of one of the ponds with a net. She breaks into a run.
Jeannine (yells): "Hey, what do you think you're doing?"
CUT TO: Roy turning around. The blue-white flesh of his enormous stomach is pushing out between the buttons of his armpit-stained shirt.
Roy: "Helpin' myself to a little supper."
CUT TO: Jeannine stopping in front of Roy.
Jeannine: "You can't do that. Those fish belong to us."
CUT TO: MASTER SHOT.
Roy: "You're wrong, girl. This is public land, and anything on it is free for the taking."
Jeannine (tears fill her eyes): "But we worked so..." (She bites her lip.)
Roy dumps out the net. The fish flop on the ground, he stomps their heads to kill them. When they are all dead, he puts them into a cloth sack.
Roy: "You and your friends got a nice little set-up going here. From the top of the hill it don't look like nothing is going on. I reckon that means you already know it's illegal; and the way I see it, if you want to keep it up, you're gonna have to give me a cut of the action."
CUT TO: CLOSE UP of Jeannine's face exhibiting shock. Then,
CUT BACK TO MASTER SHOT.
Roy: "There ain't nothing to be surprised at; I been watching you for years."
Jeannine (mumbles): "You've been watching?"
Roy: "Oh, yeah. I know all about you and that blonde coming down here to sleep with that boy."

Jeannine (gasps): "Oh!"
Roy: "But I sure as hell can't tell what either of you see in that dumb redneck."
Jeannine (indignant): "You've got no right!"
Roy: "Oh, don't I?"

Roy throws the bag of fish to the ground, and walks towards her.
Roy: "I figure I can show a little slut like you a better time than your hick boyfriend."
Jeannine (screams): "You stay away from me!"
Roy (continues toward Jeannine while pulling down his zipper): "If you want to keep your little fish farm, you'll do exactly what I say."

Jeannine backs away, but Roy lunges and grabs her arm.
Jeannine: "Let me go, you fat son of a bitch!"

Jeannine raises her free fist to hit him, but before she can land a blow he grabs her fist and pulls her close. Roy pushes her toward the rock outcropping. He tries to kiss her. His fat jowls stream with sweat. Jeannine resists his kisses by jerking her face back and forth. Her eyes glow in terror.

Roy gives up kissing her, and shoves her to the ground. Standing above her, straddling her, he keeps her pinned with his shoes by standing on both sides of her skirt, he puts both hands underneath his protruding gut and fumbles with his belt buckle.

#

Hooper yelled at the screen, "Dammit, Jeannine. Kick him in the nuts."

#

Roy: "Better act like you love it, bitch, or I'll arrest your boyfriend and put him in jail."
Jeannine (whimpers): "Please, please no." Then she leans back in resignation, forced to accept the inevitable.

Roy finds the buckle and pulls it open, while Jeannine screws her face in disgust and firmly plants her elbows against the rocky earth

beneath her. Roy's pants fly open, and Jeannine arches her back for leverage.
Roy (panting): "Oh yeah, baby, you know what to do, don't you. I can always recognize a slut. Now pull up that skirt."

Jeannine pulls at the top of her skirt without moving her elbows, then suddenly her foot flies straight up into Roy's groin. Roy screams as he falls backward.

#

Hooper cheered. Then slapping his thigh in laughter, he said aloud, "Hey Frank, I guessed that kick in the nuts was coming! Could it be that you're getting predictable?"

#

Roy's shoulder slams against one of the broken tombstone-like rocks. The jagged edge slices through his shirt sleeve leaving a bloody gash. Rubble scatters in a dozen directions as Jeannine scrambles to her feet, and runs away.

CUT TO: CLOSE-UP of Roy as the sound of Jeannine's steps recede in the distance. One bloody arm lies immobile out to his side, with the other arm he stretches futilely across the expanse of his belly attempting to reach and cup his aching crotch.
Roy (yells): "That's it, bitch. It's all over now."

SCENE FORTY-THREE. MASTER SHOT: EXTERIOR. NIGHT. Backside of Simpson's Seafood Market. Cassy and Jeannine run up the metal stair case; their steps clang like a fire alarm. On the second floor is a loft apartment. They beat on the door until Billy opens the door. The light from inside falls on the faces of the girls, both of which are streaked with tears.
Billy: "What's wrong?"
Cassandra: "One of the park rangers found our ponds. He tried to rape Jeannine when she went down to feed the fish."

Billy pulls Jeannine into his arms.
Billy: "Are you hurt?"
Jeannine: "No, but that's the least of it. The Sheriff has arrested Mr. Dillon."

Billy: "Arrested Mr. Dillon! What for?"
Jeannine: "They said, he was illegally homesteading the land where our fish are."
Billy: "But he's not homesteading; we are. Besides, they can't arrest you for it, they can only run you off."
Cassandra: "They think he is, because they found our fish hatchery in his barn, and the reason they arrested him is because we're homesteading on what used to be his land."
Billy: "What's wrong with that?"
Jeannine: "They said it's illegal because he was paid for the land thirty years ago."
Billy: "Then we'll just go down to the Sheriff's office and set them straight."
Cassandra: "We already tried. While you were out on your route, we went to Mr. Dillon's to ask him what to do about the ranger, but when we got there a deputy was already taking him away. He wouldn't tell us what was going on so we followed him to the jail. We finally got the Sheriff to tell us why he was arrested. We tried to tell him he was mistaken, but he wouldn't listen. He said it was out of his hands, that we'd have to tell it to the arraigning judge in the morning."
Jeannine: "They wouldn't even let us in to see him."
Billy: "Then we'll go down there first thing in the morning."
Billy pulls Cassy into his other arm.
Billy: "Would you two like to stay here tonight?"
Cassandra and Jeannine (sobbing into his shoulder): "Yes."
Cassy lifts her face.
Cassandra: "Jeannine, do you want me to have my mother call your house and tell your folks you're staying over with me?"
Jeannine: "No, I think it's time I call home, myself."
FADE.

SCENE FORTY-FOUR. MASTER SHOT: EXTERIOR. DAY. Steps of the county courthouse. Adjoining the courthouse is the Sheriff's office and the jail. Billy, Cassandra, and Jeannine are walking up the steps as a hearse pulls away from the jail. Ranger Roy, his arm in a sling, and a smug look on his face meets them as they reach the door at the top of the courthouse steps.

Roy (smiling): "You're wasting your time. The old nigger croaked in his cell last night. Heart attack."

Jeannine screams.

Billy grabs him by the collar.

Billy: "You bastard!"

Instantly Roy punches Billy in the stomach; the unexpected blow knocks the wind out of him. Then Roy hits Billy in the nose. The pain immobilizes Billy. Then with his meaty fist, Roy slams Billy on the top of his head. The impact knocks him to the ground. Before he can get up, a Deputy runs over.

DEPUTY:
"What's going on here?"

Roy: "These are the accomplices of that old squatter that died last night."

Deputy: "The Sheriff knows all about them. He says no charges will be brought against them because they're minors." (He turns and faces Billy) "Why don't you three beat it. Don't you think killing an old man is enough trouble for one day."

Jeannine wails, and the Deputy walks away. Roy rubs his injured shoulder, and looks directly at the sobbing Jeannine.

Roy: "I ain't done with you, honey."

Roy steps quickly away as Billy jumps to his feet. He stands frustrated and tears begin to flow down his cheeks.

Billy: "I hate this goddamn town."

Billy puts his arms around the girls and solemnly turns them around to descend stairs. Running up the steps is The Commandant. Jeannine (wails loud enough to be heard across the street): "Are you proud of me now, Daddy?" (She falls to her knees as tears flood her cheeks.)

The Commandant grasps Jeannine and lifts her up into his arms. He hugs her fiercely.

Commandant (Mr. Warner): "Yes, baby. I'm proud of you. (BEAT) You've forced me to rethink of lot of my beliefs and prejudices. And, I won't say it was easy, but, yes; I'm very proud of you."
Jeannine (hysterical): "Even if on top of everything else that's wrong, I tell you I'm pregnant?"

CUT TO: Billy's shocked face.

CUT TO: The Commandant holding Jeannine.

Commandant (Mr. Warner): "I already know. Cassy's mother told me everything," (He turns to face Billy) "and I'm proud of the son-in-law you've chosen for me too."
Jeannine (murmurs into his shoulder): "Even if I'm sharing him?"
Commandant (Mr. Warner): "Uh... Yes, but only because of whom you're sharing him with."

Billy takes Jeannine's shoulders in his hands, gently pulling her away from her father's grasp.

Billy: "Mr. Warner?"
Commandant (Mr. Warner): "Yes, William?"
Billy (tears continue down his cheek): "I'm sorry I didn't ask you before, but I didn't think you would understand. Please allow me to ask you now. Will you grant me your daughter's hand in marriage. It will have to be common-law marriage. I'm afraid no other law will recognize our love."
Commandant (Mr. Warner): "Yes, son, I will. You've been a good influence on my rebellious daughter - and don't think I haven't noticed the changes at home."
Jeannine: "Billy, I'm sorry I didn't tell you about being pregnant."
Cassandra: "It's my fault Billy; I asked her to wait. I was afraid if I wasn't pregnant too, that I might lose you."
Billy (pulls Cassy tighter to his chest): "You will never lose me."
Commandant (Mr. Warner): "William." (When Billy looks his way, he points to the receding figure of Ranger Roy.) "If that bastard gets within ten feet of my daughter - you fix his wagon, you hear."
Billy: "Yes, sir!"

CUT TO: SCENE FORTY-FIVE. INTERIOR. Billy's apartment. Mr. Warner, and Mrs. Sibley help their daughters move their belongings inside.

CUT TO: SCENE FORTY-SIX. EXTERIOR. DAY. CEMETERY. Beside an open grave and a shiny silver casket. Billy, Cassandra, and Jeannine, dressed in mourning, stand tearfully as earth clods pound against the casket.

CUT TO: Billy opening the passenger door of the pick-up for Cassy and Jeannine (still dressed in mourning) as a tall black man in a dark suit walks up.

GEORGE SANDERS:

"My name is George Sanders, I was Mr. Dillon's attorney. Allow me to offer condolence; I will miss him too."

Billy: "Thank you." (Billy turns back to the truck.)
George Sanders: "Please wait, I need for you to stop by my office. You see, Mr. Dillon made you his heirs."
Cassandra: "What?"
Billy (angry): "We don't want it. We only wanted him; and... and those... those people..."
George Sanders (hands Cassy his card): "You don't need to make any decisions today. Whenever you're ready, come by and see me."
Cassandra: "Let's go to the pond. I always feel better when I'm there."
Jeannine: "Yes, let's."
Billy (reluctant): "I guess I really ought to check on the fish; I just haven't felt like doing much of anything."
Jeannine: "I wonder if they'll let us sell our fish, now?"
Cassandra (puts her arm around Jeannine): "One bridge at a time, let's cheer up first."

CUT TO: SCENE FORTY-SEVEN. MASTER SHOT: EXTERIOR. DAY. POND.

The truck is parked at the end of the logging road. Billy is holding hands with both girls as they enter the craggy wasteland. All have changed out of mourning. In front of them, sitting on a boulder is Ranger Roy.

Roy (laughs): "I can't believe it! I am one lucky son of a bitch. I hoped I would catch the three of you down here, but I didn't think you'd ever come back."

Billy breaks away from the girls and storms toward Roy.

Billy: "Look here, now. Haven't you caused us enough trouble--"

Roy (interrupts): "No, you look here!"

Roy shoves a piece of paper into Billy's hand.

Billy: "What is this?"

Roy (crosses his arms over his chest in satisfaction): "Just read it."

The girls rush to Billy's side and read along with him.

Cassandra: "It says something about removing easements and improvements from public land."

Jeannine: "What does that mean?"

Cassandra: "I don't know."

Billy: "It's a court order."

Roy (bellows joyfully): "You bet your sweet ass it's a court order. It authorizes me to destroy your fish farm."

Roy immediately ducks behind the rock he was sitting on. Suddenly a ground rumbling explosion knocks the three teenagers into the dirt.

Cassandra (screams): "What are you doing?"

She tries to get on her feet, but Billy pulls her back down and throws his body over both girls as water, rock, blood, mud, and fish pound the ground around them. Seconds pass before it stops. Billy and the girls sit up. All are soaking wet, mud splattered, and blood stained with the grimy remains of their achievement. The girls are crying again as Roy walks up holding a golfer's umbrella over his head. Except for his sweat stained armpits he is dry.

Roy (chuckles): "Jesus, you guys look disgusting; you really should have brought umbrellas."

Cassandra: "You murdered our fish!"

Billy: "You son of a bitch!"

Billy pushes off the ground with his fists curled. He lurches toward Roy. Roy suddenly produces a long barreled revolver with a huge gaping bore and points it in Billy's face.

Roy (menacing): "Just try it, son. I'm dyin' to splatter you in front of these girls' adoring eyes."

Roy pushes past Billy toward the trail. As he passes Jeannine, he winks.

Jeannine (hysterical): "Stay away from me!"

Roy (laughs): "Honey, the way you look right now, I wouldn't touch you if my pole was ten feet long."

He continues laughing as he walks up the trail. As he reaches the turn in the trail, he spins the revolver on his finger western style and slams it neatly into its holster.

Billy pulls the sobbing girls to their feet.

Billy: "Come on, let's get out of here."

Cassandra: "No wait I want to say good-bye to the pond."

FADE.

SCENE FORTY-EIGHT. MASTER SHOT: INTERIOR. NIGHT. Billy's loft apartment. Around a table sit Billy, Cassy, Jeannine, and her father.

Jeannine: "Daddy, we've decided to sell Mr. Dillon's farm and move to Alaska. People who can handle the extreme conditions up there tend to be a lot more tolerant."

Mr. Warner: "But what will you do?"

Jeannine: "What we do best - raise fish."

Cassandra: "There are wonderful opportunities in salmon in Alaska."

Mr. Warner: "I wish you luck. You know I'll miss all of you." (He reaches over and pats Jeannine's belly.) "Here is my perfect excuse for having to come up and visit."

All four laugh.

Billy (sober): "Dad, there's a last piece of business I have to take care of before we can leave."

Mr. Warner: "The fat ranger?"

Billy nods.

Mr. Warner: "What did you have in mind?"

Billy: "I'd like to take a baseball bat to his head."

Mr. Warner: "William, I don't advise that - you could go to jail, if you're caught. Under normal circumstances I would expect a jury to acquit you, but you aren't exactly popular in this town. Nor would I expect a change in venue to create a favorable position for a man with two wives. On the other hand, I don't want that man living in the same town with my two other daughters. I want revenge as much as you, but we've got to go about it in a different way."

FADE TO BLACK as he leans conspiratorially toward the center of the table.

SCENE FORTY-NINE. MASTER SHOT: EXTERIOR. DAY. Outside back of Simpson's Seafood Market. The blue pick-up is parked at the base of the metal staircase, and the bed packed full. Billy and Cassy are tying down a rope. Jeannine is sitting on the bottom step. Jimmy drives up in a Mustang convertible.

Jimmy: "Hey, guys! Have you seen the mob in front of the Ranger station?"

Billy: "No. What's going on?"

Jimmy: "You won't believe it until you see it, but there must be a hundred people trying to get in there. They want that fat ranger, but the Sheriff is blocking the door with his gun drawn."

Cassandra: "What do they want him for?"

Jimmy: "This morning old man Hawkins, the garbage man, found some pretty interesting literature while he was emptying the cans behind the Ranger's cabin. I hear he found a stack of illegal underground sleaze magazines full of artwork depicting grown men raping children and animals."

Jeannine (bites her lip): "That's really disgusting - you must be kidding?"

Jimmy: "I'm serious. Old man Hawkins took the magazines to the Sheriff, and Phona Farnsworth was there complaining about stray dogs digging in her garden when he arrived. Anyway she saw the magazines; and, heck it's probably the biggest thrill she's had in years, but anyway, Phona got right on the phone and wasn't long before the word was all over town. Then before you know it, people started gathering outside the Ranger cabin. Pretty soon they were like a mob. They're saying they're gonna tar and feather the guy."

Cassandra (droll): "No."

Jimmy: "Really, I saw Mr. Pulte with a couple of buckets of tar, and his wife was carrying several pillows. I heard her say that fat ranger has made passes at her several times."
Jeannine (mock wonder): "Really?"
Jimmy: "Yeah, you really oughta go take a look." (He pauses ONE BEAT as he looks at the loaded truck. "Say are you guys moving or something?"
Cassandra: "Yes, to Alaska."
Jimmy: "Jesus, all the way to Alaska; what for?"
Cassandra: "To become masters of our own dominion."
Jimmy (nonplused): "Aren't ya gonna finish school first?"
Billy: "Nope."
Jimmy "Well gee, guys, I'll certainly miss you - who the hell am I going to gossip about now?."
Jeannine (laughs): "I've always said you were an asshole, Jimmy, but at least you're an honest asshole. Too bad we're moving, I could get to like you." (She stands up, walks over, and kisses him on the cheek.) "Come see us sometime. My father will give you the address. We'll probably be good and hungry for a little hometown gossip by the time you get around to it."

Jimmy drives away. DISSOLVE TO:

SCENE FIFTY. MASTER SHOT: INTERIOR. DAY. Inside the cab of the pick-up truck, Billy is behind the wheel, Cassy is in the middle, and Jeannine is riding shotgun.

CUT TO: Crowd outside the ranger station as the blue pick-up drives past.

CUT TO: MASTER SHOT.

Cassandra (academic): "What do you suppose will happen to him?"
Jeannine (angry): "I hope he does get tarred and feathered,"
Billy: "That will never happen. Most likely things will die down; and the town will make him feel so unwelcome he'll leave."
Cassandra: "Then what?"
Billy: "He's an embarrassment to the Parks and Forestry Department, so he'll probably get transferred to some other government agency far far away from here."

Jeannine: "Why don't they fire him?"
Billy: "I suppose they could, but I've never heard of anyone getting fired from a government job. It seems they'd rather hire two additional people to compensate for one bad apple than chuck out the spoilage."
Cassandra: "That doesn't make sense."
Billy: "That's because government doesn't have to run at a profit. Government is like mold growing on a loaf of bread. It keeps spreading until there is no bread left."
Jeannine: "Then what?"
Billy: "If there's no more bread, I guess it consumes itself."
Cassandra: "Ha! Now there's justice for you."

FADE. As the blue pick-up shrinks down the highway.

#

The doorbell rang in Hooper's apartment, and he stopped the VCR. He cursed silently as he walked to the door. He wasn't in the mood to see anyone or do anything except finish watching the movie. He never expected to find himself this involved in any motion picture.

He opened the door; it was Sally. She pushed on in and said, "What's wrong with you? You look like you just got back from another planet. Were you sleeping? Don't tell me you forgot my acting lesson."

CHAPTER TEN

An airport limousine pulled into the circular drive in front of the Stacy's pink Spanish villa. A smartly dressed driver stepped out of the car and opened the passenger door. Frank Stacy climbed out, while Myra Mason, who was just inside the house, flung open the front door.

"Frank!" she cried and dashed down the walk.

He had barely taken a step before Myra reached him. She threw her arms around him, clung to him and pressed her face into his shoulder. Her screen perfect beauty was marred by the reality of her swollen and tear stained cheeks, her bloodshot eyes, and her neglected hair that was pulled back in a pony tail with frazzled loose ends falling out. Her face mirrored her three days of anxiety, and the effect it had on her psyche.

"Oh Frank, I was afraid I'd never see you again. Are you sure you're okay? How does your head feel?" She lifted her black encircled eyes to look into his eyes. Her hands slid across his shoulders, down his arms and clutched his coat sleeves.

"I'm fine, everything's going to be all right." He took hold of her shoulders and pushed her gently away.

"We should go to the doctor's to make sure."

"No, I haven't time."

"But, you need to have those stitches removed."

"That can be done later. Right now, I have got to call the office, and find out where I'm supposed to be today."

"No, Frank, don't go. Please stay home today. You ought to rest."

"I'll be home tonight. We'll have some time then." He pushed her the rest of the way back, forcing her to release her grasp.

She watched as he walked into the house. She knew from his touch and from the look in his eyes that sleep would overtake her long before he would come back home.

Frank called Constance from his desk in the study. He was pleased to find that she had not abandoned the office in his absence.

While she informed him of the appointments he'd missed, he reached into his jacket pocket to find a pen. Because it was the new coat, there wasn't one, but his hand, absent-mindedly searching, fumbled across a piece of paper. He pulled it out. It was the scrap with the trucker's name and number. After hanging up with Constance, he looked at the strange hand writing, then dialed the number out of curiosity.

"Hello, this is Frank Stacy. May I speak to Dan Osborne."

"Did you say, Frank Stacy?"

"Yes, I did."

"Well, I'll be damned. Mister, have I got a bone to pick with you. I don't take to being a guinea pig in anybody's publicity stunt especially when they take me for forty bucks. You should've been paying me--"

"Hey, wait a minute!" Frank interrupted. "Publicity stunt, what are you talking about?"

"Don't act stupid with me, mister. I know all about you now. I've got your little scheme figured out - you ran around the countryside playing like you had amnesia to promote some movie. Well, you fooled me all right, but I think it's pretty low for a rich guy like you to take money from a guy who can barely make ends meet..."

Frank listened carefully, and thought, "Publicity stunt? I can't remember anything - and that's going to cause some serious credibility problems, but... hmm, this publicity stunt thing could just be the answer I'm looking for."

Osborne continued, "...I understand you had to stay in character, or whatever it is you guys call it, but still; you didn't have to accept the money I offered."

"Mister Osborne, you apparently expected to get it back otherwise you wouldn't have written me out a receipt for it."

"I didn't write out nothin'. You did."

Frank froze at the man's statement. If Osborne didn't write it out, Frank thought, then that hand writing belongs to whatever character he had been playing for the last four days. The shock was overwhelming, and his hand began to shake as he looked at it. He had immersed himself into the traits of many characters, but never had his handwriting changed.

Stacy forced himself to recover from the cognitive dissonance the trucker's revelation was causing, and answered, "I'm just testing you Mr. Osborne. I had to make sure you are the same man that I borrowed the money from. Now I'm certain, and I want to return your money along with a hundred dollars interest. In addition to that, because of the great favor you served me; I would also like push some work your way. There's a big need for experienced drivers who can haul heavy equipment to out-of-the-way areas where we shoot on location. You interested?"

"Why... uh, yes sir, Mr. Stacy. Gee, I'm sorry if I was rude before, but you see, this guy told me you was taking advantage of me, and well, it got me pretty riled up, you see. I mean, now I that I know the score and all--"

"It's okay." Frank cut off the man's rambling. "One other thing Mr. Osborne, I'd like you to witness my performance to the press. Do you have any objection to that?"

"Uh, no sir. What is it you want me to do?"

"I'm going to give your name to some reporters. When they call you just tell them exactly what you told me."

Frank hung up, and dialed Constance again.

"Connie, what did Chester give the press?"

"He kept it simple like you requested. I'll read it to you: 'Frank Stacy is no longer missing. He is safe at home, and fully recovered.' Is it okay?"

"Yes, now listen carefully. I want you to pull that script; oh, I can't remember the name, but it's the one about a felon who had amnesia and knew nothing about his criminal past."

"You mean *Accidental Angel*?"

"Yes that's it. I want you to pick up our option on it. Then give the title and a synopsis to Chester, and tell him my amnesia was a pre-production publicity stunt to promote the movie. I want his press release to go as an exclusive to Marcy Breedlove over at *VARIETY*."

"But, Frank, I thought you decided that script didn't merit production?"

"Just listen!" Frank snapped.

Constance gasped, then quickly bit her lip. It was the first time Frank had ever raised his voice to her.

"Have Chester give Ms. Breedlove the name of Dan Osborne as a resource. She can locate him through the Independent Trucker's Exchange out of San Diego."

"Now listen very carefully to this, it's very important. I want you to find out if the primary character in *Accidental Angel* changes his name to Eugene Eastly when he gets amnesia. If he doesn't, get the author on the phone and tell him I want a rewrite. Not a big one, just that the felon must change his name to Eugene Eastly. Got it?"

"Yes."

"Lastly, post our notification that auditions will begin in two weeks."

"Certainly, but what's the rush? This isn't like you."

"I'm not asking for your opinions, just do it. I'll be at the office in an hour."

#

After Frank left the house, Myra wandered listlessly into the study. She thought it silly, but she hoped his presence was still lingering in the room and that she might bask in its radiation. The imprint of his body in the leather chair, stamped by years of sitting behind this desk, invited her to snuggle in and absorb his scent. It was an odor mixed of polished cowhide and the cologne he wore during those early days when she was his student. The smell sent her mind drifting back to happier days when she was Frank's primary interest.

As she contemplated those earlier times her eyes rested trance-like on the desk top. It was the scrap of paper that slowly brought her out of her silent reverie. Several minutes passed before the wadded paper, a crumpled contrast against an empty expanse of polished wood, rose like a distant sail on the ocean to interrupt her hypnotic gaze. Frank was extremely fastidious and never left debris on his desk, and like a white signal flag at night it piqued her curiosity. She picked it up, read it, then read it again. "This isn't Frank's handwriting," she thought, then tucked it in her pocket. She would ask him about it later.

#

Hooper rewound the video-cassette of *Resurgent Man* for the second time. Tears ran down his cheek. While he waited for it to finish, he started writing a letter.

Dear Frank,

I just finished watching Resurgent Man. I'd never seen it before today. I was really moved. I even wept. It was the type of movie Eugene told me he wanted to make. The ending, however, was more tragic than I expected; at least more tragic than I would have expected from Eugene.

I wanted to tell you, now that I've seen Resurgent Man, I'm more convinced than ever that you are Eugene Eastly suffering from amnesia. As I watched the tragedy unfold, I felt that somehow this was the key to your amnesia. I'm assuming, of course, that you authored the script.

Yesterday when Eugene realized he was Frank Stacy, he concluded that smashing his car into that tree in Alabama caused his amnesia. Perhaps it was more than the car crash that caused it. Could it be that your friend Jack, whom you said was traveling with you to Hollywood, died when you wrecked the car? Could this be the darkness in your past that's causing your memory loss?

Please Frank, I ask you as a friend of Eugene - your other half, to seek psychiatric help and get the two of you back together.

Sincerely,
Hooper Johnson

When the letter arrived at his office, Frank frowned at the return address, but he opened the envelope anyway. He winced as he read the last line, then his hand, closing involuntarily, crushed the letter. His hand began to shake, and to control it he shook his fist in the air, and said, "Goddamn you, Hooper Johnson."

Suddenly he felt a headache coming on.

"Why?" he thought. "Why is this preposterous thing happening to me? I know my own life, and I remember growing up in New York. Yet... this stranger's letter is bothering me?" He shook his head and dropped his hand toward the wastebasket releasing the crumbled paper. It hit the rim and fell to the floor.

Later that afternoon, as Connie was closing the office, the strong pen strokes of the hand written letter beside the empty wastebasket caught her eye. It looked like fan mail, something she seldom bothered with, but seeing the title *Resurgent Man* after so many years caused her to pick it up. It was the film that brought Frank and Myra together. It was the film that cost Connie Frank's love. Not that she ever had it, but before *Resurgent Man,* it always seemed possible.

She recalled that during its filming, that she detected a curious mood difference in her boss. It was a desperate hope, but considering the theme of the picture, she thought perhaps Frank was sending her subliminal signals that he wanted both Myra and her. Frank had demonstrated affection for her, it was more than the affection a boss shows for a secretary, and she knew she had not read him wrong. Unfortunately, she was only able to detect it, when he was working on the producing-end of a project. It was hard to tell if it was real or imagined for they were only the smallest of gestures: a light touch, a gentle word.

"He's only leading me on," she thought. She expected it to quit after the marriage, but it didn't. Connie wished she had been right about the subliminal messages; if he had asked her to, she would have gladly played second fiddle. "As it is" she thought, "I'm playing second fiddle anyway, but without the accolades, or should I say, the benefits."

In actuality, Connie was quite comfortable - exactly where she was, whether her beliefs were true or untrue. She was ready to fight anything or anyone that threatened her little bubble of hope.

After finishing the first paragraph of Hooper's letter, she nearly tossed it back, but she continued. Before she finished the second paragraph, she had to sit down. Memories were flooding her senses.

All the weirdness she had ever ignored came rushing into her consciousness. "No, no..." she cried, but she continued reading.

After she read it in its entirety, then re-read it again, she went to the filing cabinet and pulled out the script for *Resurgent Man*. On the title page she read: A Screenplay by Jackson Paine Franklin. She went back to pull the contract with Franklin. It was missing.

She could not imagine where that contract was. Other than she or Frank, no one ever used the filing cabinet. It must have been misplaced. "Probably Frank," she thought. "When he's in his director-mode, he's such a mess in the office. Why, he can't even run the fax machine."

"Well," she muttered aloud, "there's always a contract; I'll find it."

They had one for every film Frank ever made. A screenplay was a property that had to be purchased. The paperwork had to cover a myriad of details from royalties, such as what to do in the event the film became a mega-hit, and if there were spin-off sequels, television shows and merchandise. She looked under Franklin, and found nothing. She looked under Jackson even Paine, but still nothing. She even looked under Mason, where she found the producer's contract with Myra, but nothing else to do with *Resurgent Man*. Her search continued under a variety of headings and even through the drawers of Frank's desk - yet there was no contract to be found.

If the file was permanently lost, she knew she could still determine what they had paid for the property by cross-checking it against accounts payable. At least she could prove that a contract had once existed. Constance went into the store-room and unstacked dusty boxes until she reached the one marked 1976. The ledger was easy to find; and soon she was running her finger up and down line after line of eye-straining entries. Soon her back was aching from bending over and reading in the poor light of the storeroom. She wished cheap computers had been invented years earlier. An hour later she had flipped through every page and still turned up nothing.

Connie was not beaten yet, she went back to her desk and dialed the *Screen Writer's Guild*. Jackson Paine Franklin would have to be listed with them. Ten minutes later she knew there was no one by that name in the guild's computer files. She asked them to pull their copy of *Resurgent Man* to verify the author's name. The girl on the other end of the line said that would take several weeks. Connie said she would wait. She hung up the phone and looked down at the crumpled letter on her desk and whispered, "Goddamn you Hooper - whoever the hell you are - you don't know anything."

#

A few days later when Connie answered the phone, a man asking to speak to Frank said his name was Hooper Johnson. It sounded familiar, and she felt a pit form in her stomach.

She buzzed Frank, and told him who was on the line. She was grateful to hear his brusque response. It was the same irritated edge that had developed since his return, but it was the first time she enjoyed hearing it. He stated, in no uncertain terms, he was not interested in speaking to that man now or ever. She was to tell Johnson to leave them alone and never call again. When she hung up, she opened her purse and glanced at the crumpled letter she had saved from the trash. Her suspicion was confirmed, the name was the same. "This Hooper Johnson is a problem," she thought. She then willed herself to never allow him to bother her boss again.

Connie, however, was becoming upset by her boss's behavior. He was working harder than ever. A twelve hour day for him was no more unusual than anyone else working eight, but now he was driving himself eighteen hours every day. She found herself feeling guilty when she left before he did. She did not know if it was the extra hours, but his temper, which prior to the pool accident she had never seen, was now the single element uniting all his activities. The frequency with which his anger surfaced increased daily. He snapped at actors, crew members, and investors. He even yelled at his editor, whose brilliant splicing created the demanding effects Frank expected, and easily made him one of the most important people on the *Stacy* team. She wished she could do something, but she was afraid. All she could do was hope everything would work out in time. Her loyalty was uncompromising, but she felt she had let him down. It was her fault Frank had the diving accident. If she had never allowed Myra to talk her into manipulating his schedule, Frank would be fine today. She felt shame, and toward Myra, she felt hatred.

Hooper Johnson was undaunted when he found he could not get past Frank Stacy's secretary. Getting nowhere fast was a fact of life in Hollywood. Hearing the word no was but one of the many ways an actor paid his dues. This time, however, his persistence stemmed from his feeling for Eugene. There was something about that kid that would not allow Johnson to let go. The problem was Frank, who did not want help. Frank made the best movies in the world, but Hooper could only imagine the kind of movies a sincere kid like Eugene could make with Frank's help. That single thought drove Hooper to action. There was only one problem: he had to keep his plans for Frank Stacy separate from his thoughts and desires about Mrs. Frank Stacy.

On Monday morning, July 20th, Hooper received his call to report for shooting *Runaway Grandparents*. When he arrived on the set early the next day, there were reporters with cameras and microphones swarming as thick as flies in a stable. Every one of them wanted a scoop of dirt on Frank Stacy auditioning for a bit part. Anybody could have given lines in front of a camera that day.

Stacy was notorious for eluding the press. This was an opportunity to learn something about him from people other than his own tight-lipped crew and performers. It was said that Frank was so alert to snooping reporters, that he could smell one fraudulently auditioning for his classes. The truth was that any journalist talented enough to make it into Frank's classes never bothered to return and write about their undercover investigation - they remained with Frank as actors.

Michael, the first assistant director, floated from one microphone to another saying, "How could we have recognized him; he's Frank Stacy. His performance was absolutely flawless, and to think it was actually two performances at the same time. Simply everyone that day thought he was a Stacy Student, but who would have known he was the real McCoy. He's so convincing, he could fool his own mother."

The director only needed Johnson for two days. The first day he spent twelve hours and seven takes in dirty clothes slurping soup-colored water from a bowl at a mission hall table. Meanwhile, the star, a recalcitrant grandmother, now bag-lady, was given stern advice by the nun in charge. On his second day, he sat on a curb swigging tea from a whiskey bottle wrapped in a brown paper sack, while a camera in front of him tracked the action behind him. It was a classic gold digging courtship. Hooper wouldn't see it until it was on the screen, but upstage was the leading lady, who was being wooed by a wino, who wanted nothing more from the results of his amour than a chance to earn the price of a drink.

It was a stupid and depressing story that attempted to illuminate the plight of the homeless with a mix of compassion and humor. In the end, it was a cheap attempt to make some dough by tapping into the national zeitgeist. Hooper didn't care what the motive was as long as he got paid his eight hundred bucks.

The next day, with some cash in his pockets, and some time on his hands, he decided he would try to get to Frank through Myra.

As he drove to Fresno, Johnson questioned his motives: "Did Eugene really impress me all that much, or is it the mystery that's so intriguing?"

It was clear that Frank was not going to talk to him about his past. And, from what he'd been able to dig up in the library, Frank had demonstrated prescience in carefully guarding his past from the press. Which probably also explained why he chose to live in and operate his business from Fresno, an agriculture-based city just out of the reach of LA's influence. All anyone seemed to know about Frank was his directorial reputation. No one really knew him, except possibly Myra Mason. Surely, she had seen some questionable aspects of his life to make her wonder.

The picture of Myra in his head caused a twinge in his loins, and he questioned his motives even more. "Am I really doing this because of my fondness for Eugene?" he mused out loud. "Can I even say that I'm just pursuing my curiosity about Frank's mysterious past? Or should I just admit that in reality this is all about that promise I made myself back in that Galveston movie house nine years ago? Truthfully, I don't even know myself."

The phone number was unlisted, and their Fresno home was walled like a fortress, so he called Myra's agent. As he expected, the agent had never heard of him, but Hooper asked him to please tell her that he was the man who found Frank. The agent, who mostly represented Stacy actors called Frank first. He was quickly and sternly instructed that Myra was not to be bothered. Hooper met the same luck when he left her a message at the S.A.G. office.

Next he spent several long and fruitless days parked in front of the Stacy's house. He hoped to catch Myra coming or going, but whenever it looked like there might be some activity by the gate, a police car would cruise by and tell him to move on. The frustration of waiting was beginning to get to him. He was just about ready to conclude that getting an audience with the President of the United States was easier than seeing Myra Mason off the screen, when he got a break. He was reading *VARIETY* magazine, and saw the audition notice for *Accidental Angel*.

After reading the synopsis of the movie provided below the notice, he cried gleefully aloud, "Ha! Frank, your little shell is finally beginning to crack, and that complicated mind of yours is trying desperately to repair it. But, I've got news for you, Humpty Dumpty - it ain't gonna work!"

When he arrived at the studio, he was surprised at how few people were waiting. Usually an open audition packed the people in. One could count on long lines, hours of waiting, and without an agent - a slim chance at being noticed. It was when he signed in that he learned why so few were trying out. The receptionist looked at him and asked, "Have you ever studied under Mr. Stacy?"

"No," he answered.

"Then you're wasting your time," she told him.

"I'll take my chances," he answered.

"Then I'll need to see your resume."

Hooper had not come prepared to actually audition, so he had not brought one of his glossy, black and white, eight-by-ten headshots with his list of achievements typed on back. He did, however, have a photocopy of it in his wallet. He pulled out the sweat-moistened copy, unfolded it, then dropped it on the desk. The girl reacted with disgust, grimacing as she lifted his crease marked likeness. Hooper ignored the slight and walked on past, into the sound stage.

Once inside, he stayed in the shadows out of the eye of Frank Stacy. From his dark vantage point, Hooper scanned the room for Myra. From what he remembered reading, she was his constant companion during auditions, filming, and nearly everything else. What he did not know was that his information was ancient, it was more than five years old and predated their marriage. Myra was not there; Hooper would be facing Frank, himself, once again.

The studio buzzed with hushed voices between the readings, and politely quieted when someone took his turn on the stage. Murmurs of approval or disapproval moved through the small crowd at the finish of each audition. Frank would tap his pencil against his clipboard for silence. In front of center stage was a video-tape recorder, and on Frank's signal the camera operator filmed instant screen tests.

Johnson observed how relaxed and candid Stacy was during the auditions. He spoke fondly to his students when he gave them lines to read. There was no intimidation here, only encouragement. Hooper couldn't help but admire Frank Stacy; he really was the best. There was no doubt he had earned the right to sit in that chair and direct the talents of others. This was Frank Stacy's world, yet the irony of it all was that it was Eugene Eastly's dream that put him here. Eugene was not here to enjoy it; and as far as Hooper was concerned, Eugene was getting ripped off.

Over an hour had passed and Johnson still had not seen Myra when the assistant called his name.

Stacy shot out of his seat, and demanded angrily, "Who did you call?"

Hooper was instantly energized by the unveiled emotion in Frank's voice. He answered for the assistant, speaking evenly and deliberately, "He called Hooper Johnson."

Immediately following the sound of Johnson's voice was a sharp report as the pencil in Frank's hand snapped. The director's perpetual prop clattered to the floor in two pieces as he stared at the interloper coming down the aisle.

Hooper stepped up onto the brightly lit stage and turned toward the seats. He could see Frank's face reddening before him and hardening into an ugly grimace. He realized his presence was violently upsetting the man; and that it was Frank's enormous control that kept him from exploding on the spot. Both men knew that legally, Stacy had no choice but to let Johnson audition.

Nevertheless, Hooper was amazed at the power the film giant was giving him by allowing him to see any emotion at all. His intention had not been to audition, but now he felt an unusual energy flowing through his body. It was the energy he felt on stage during the last performance of a long running play - when you do it for your own memory of it - when you milk the audience for every emotion you've learned you can evoke. That was the kind of energy he felt, but not quite. It was the energy he felt during a lucky-streak when he played poker - when it does not matter what you are dealt - you will win - because you will it. It's only half because you believe it, the rest is because who you're playing believes it. It was the energy he felt when he was shooting pool, or throwing darts, or bowling - when you finally find the right stroke - and can't miss. Then every time you get another pocket, or bulls-eye, or strike, it reinforces your confidence, but at the same time reminds you of how fragile it is, and you pray it will last one more turn. That was the kind of energy Hooper Johnson felt as he accepted the pages from the script girl.

"Mr. Johnson," Stacy inquired sarcastically, "I thought you weren't interested in any of my productions?"

"I changed my mind."

"Well, I've changed my mind as well. Your audition will be judged on the same merit as anyone else who comes here today. You'll receive no favors. Now, what part are you auditioning for?"

With only an instant to decide, he stared directly into Stacy's eyes and answered with conviction, "The lead."

A unified gasp arose from isolated voices spread around the darkened corners of the studio. It was unheard of - a non-student earning a lead, much less even auditioning for it. Frank stared back at Hooper for several heartbeats, while the rest of the room stood silent as a crypt, then said, "Read from page nine, lines seventeen through thirty-seven."

The room murmured as a whole. Frank picked up a pencil fragment from the floor, and tapped for silence.

Hooper read once through the lines, then paused and looked at Frank.

Frank, accepting that as Johnson's signal he was ready, gave him no more time and yelled, "Action."

Hooper couldn't believe the lines he'd been assigned. He closed his eyes. In his mind he pictured Eugene on the night he burst through his front door crying; begging Hooper to help him with his horrible secret. He opened his eyes.

"Aaiiiii!" he screamed.

"Eugene! Wake up, Eugene. Wake up," Frank read.

With a look of terror in his face, Hooper reached out toward the video camera and read, gasping for air, "Oh God... Oh God, Carol, thank you... I was having the nightmare again."

"It's okay honey, you're awake now."

Hooper was shaking as he continued, "No, it's not; you don't understand. I was hungry; no it was worse - I was starving. I was in a store begging the owner for food. He laughed at me, and told me to get out. Then I... I couldn't control myself." Hooper's voice rose in pitch. "I was grabbing him by the collar, and pushing a pistol into his nose. His sneering grin turned to terror, and then I... started laughing." Frank leaned forward as he noticed a slight change in Hooper's intonation. He had added just a hint of hysteria to his voice. "I told him I'd take what I wanted. Then it happened, just like always. He pulled away from me, and my finger clamped down on the trigger. His head exploded. It was an accident, I tell you. I didn't mean to pull the trigger. Oh, God, blood was everywhere... my hands... my face."

"It's okay now." Frank read in tones of reassurance, while out of anyone's sight, he was steadily making the knuckle cracking motion over and over. The pencil fragment was once again on the floor.

"No, it's not!" Hooper swept the script to his side, and dropped his face a fraction of an inch to expose the tears running down his cheeks. "No, it's not okay... because... because somehow I know it's true."

Hooper closed the script. The studio remained silent; not even the gentlest whisper could be heard. Then with the passion of a Marine Corps barber, Frank barked, "Next."

Hooper left the studio. His lucky streak was over.

#

As he was walking toward the parking lot a Mercedes convertible drove past him and parked in front of the studio entrance. The woman driving removed her scarf and sunglasses, and Hooper recognized Myra Mason. She got out and lifted a thermos and a basket from the back. Hooper felt the familiar twinge in his loins, but this time it was followed by butterflies in his gut. It was amazing that he could feel nervous about anything after standing up to Frank Stacy on his own turf, but he was. He had to force himself to walk over to her car.

"Miss Mason?" he called when he was within speaking distance.

She glanced over her shoulder, and said, "Sorry, no autographs today." Then she added cheerfully, "I've got to feed my husband." She hurried past him into the studio.

Hooper knew he could not speak to Myra inside, so he leaned up against her car and waited. He did not have to wait long. Fifteen minutes later she came back out of the door. The look on her face surprised him; no longer was it reflecting the cheerfulness he had seen before; instead he saw an aura of despondence.

"Miss Mason." he said jumping up from the hood of her car.

Looking up toward the voice she said, "What are you still doing here?"

"I was waiting for you."

"What made you think I'd be right out?"

"I didn't. I was prepared to wait all day."

"For an autograph, that's ridiculous; you could've written me, and received a signed photo."

"I'm not here for an autograph. You said that."

She gave him a hard glance and said, "Do I need to call a guard?"

"I wish you wouldn't. I've been trying to get in touch with you for some time. You see, I'm the man who helped your husband when he didn't know who he was."

"You're that truck driver?"

"No, I'm the fellow who gave him a place to sleep."

"Frank never mentioned you. Anyway your business is with him not with me. You can catch him inside. Good day." She pulled open the car door.

"Miss Mason, Frank isn't interested in talking to me. That's why I need to speak with you."

"Then you're certainly not going to get anywhere with me." she replied as she turned the key.

"Miss Mason, please wait. I want to talk with you about Eugene."

"Oh, that's simple," she answered while putting the car in reverse. "Eugene is the main character of his newest movie. Frank was playing Eugene as a publicity stunt."

"Look," Hooper insisted, as he walked beside the moving car, "I know he wasn't playing. I know he truly believed he was Eugene, and I know something else - you believe it too."

"Then you should be decent enough to keep that knowledge to yourself." She shifted into drive.

"But, there's more."

Myra ignored him, and hit the accelerator.

Hooper yelled after her, "Eugene was Frank's name when he was a child!"

The tires squealed as she hit the brakes.

She turned and stared at Hooper.

"It's true." he cried.

She backed the car up, and ordered, "Get in."

#

Johnson had briefly given Myra his background and how he came to take up with Eugene. He'd just begun to elaborate on his theory when she told him, "I'm not sure I can accept this."

"Then just consider the facts."

They were sitting in a private alcove of a restaurant isolated from the general public both by its location and its prices. The dining area was a series of small segmented rooms; each a study in the comfort and luxury taken for granted by the very wealthy, and nearly unknown by ordinary men. The total concept was designed to cater to the rich and famous when they did not wish to be recognized.

Myra found herself impressed with Hooper's acclimation to surroundings that were obviously beyond his means. It did not occur to her that he was acting.

"What facts?" she asked. "I'm not aware of any so called, facts."

When he first got into the car with her, he was disturbed by the pain he saw in her face, but now he was witnessing the resiliency which made her a superb actress. Her eyes were now focused in cheerful interest, an ability denoting the underlying strength that enabled her to handle a variety of situations. "Here," he thought, "is the quality that makes successful acting."

"First off," he answered, "Frank sincerely believed he was Eugene Eastly for four days. Second, as Eugene, he was twenty years behind on his history."

"Your first so-called fact I can maybe accept, but the second, well, you don't know Frank. If you had ever seen him acting, you would understand. He's like a chameleon, or better yet, he's the sea god, Proteus, changing his shape at will. You just can't know this, but when Frank puts on a role, he doesn't leave anything out."

"Not anything! Come on, no actor is that thorough."

"All the way down to the way he buttons a shirt; I tell you - you just don't know him."

"And I suppose he's ambidextrous when it comes to using a pencil?"

"Whether he's actually ambidextrous or not you'll believe he--" Suddenly, she paused. She didn't know why, but for a brief instant her mind pictured the little scrap of paper she found on Frank's desk the day he returned. However, before the thought could fully register, Hooper was taking advantage of her pause to ask another question.

"If you're so convinced, then why were you willing to listen to me?"

"Because you mentioned Frank's childhood, something Frank has never told me about. I know nothing of his life prior to his arrival in Hollywood."

"Okay let's change the subject. What can you tell me about *Resurgent Man*?"

Myra looked at Hooper with renewed interest, and asked, "Why?"

Hooper noticed the change, and asked, "I see I'm asking the right question. Why is that?"

"During the filming, Frank was a little different from his normal self... from his directing persona. Really it was just a feeling. Now, you tell me."

"Same as you, it's just a feeling."

"What do you want to know?"

"Did Frank write it?"

"No."

"Oh."

"What's wrong?" She asked while noting the sound of disappointment in his voice.

"I had this theory that somehow, that story, was the key to Frank's past, but it was contingent on Frank having written it. Like maybe something from his unconscious came through the pen while he wrote it."

"It's funny that you said pen instead of typewriter."

"Whatever."

"But, it is significant. The original screenplay that Frank worked from was written by hand. Screenplays are never submitted unless they're typed. I thought it so odd, I even asked him where he came across it. And, this is really weird; he said didn't know. He told me he found it among his belongings when he arrived in Hollywood.

Now if Frank had told you his name was Jackson Paine Franklin then your theory might make some sense."

"Jackson? That's it! Eugene told me that he and a friend named Jack left Georgia together to come out here and make movies. That must be who wrote the screenplay."

"Now that you mention it, I remember Frank asking where Jack was right after he woke up from his diving accident."

"My theory might also explain where Jack is."

"But you said, your theory depended on Frank having written *Resurgent Man*."

"Yes, I know, but it might still make sense. I thought of it right after I finished watching the movie for the second time. I know there's no reason why it should have occurred to me, but it was the tragic ending that made me think that perhaps Jack died when Eugene wrecked the car. If that's true, then Eugene felt responsible for Jack's death, and his guilt caused the amnesia, not the crash."

"I believe you."

"Why?"

"I've got your proof. When I asked Frank where he got the script, he told me it wasn't registered. He hired a detective to find the author. The report came back that the only Jackson Franklin he could locate was dead and without heirs."

"That's kind of flimsy for proof."

"One other thing, when Frank woke up from his accident, he thought he was waking up from a car crash."

"And that's when he asked you where Jack was?"

"Yes."

"Then I *am* right."

Myra sat back to absorb all the new information she received. She sipped her cocktail; played with the straw; then stared at Hooper and studied his face. Hooper felt his heart rate increase as the minutes passed before she spoke.

"All right, Hooper, what makes you so interested?"

Hooper averted his eyes for a second, while he recovered control over his hidden emotions, then answered, "It's simple really. I liked Eugene. No offense to you, but I don't particularly care for Frank."

"Most people never get a chance to be around him long enough to get to know him, much less have the time to get to like him," she replied defensively.

Hooper shrugged, "I suppose you're right; I'm certainly one of those people."

"Oh, Hooper, what should I do?" she uttered with exasperation.

"Ideally, you should get him into a psychiatrist's office."

"That's out of the question. I'm trying to save my marriage not ruin it."

"I don't understand?" Hooper's heart jumped at the revelation.

Myra paused briefly, then said, "I don't know why I should tell you this, but we're estranged. Our relationship was dissipating long before the accident. Now it's even worse. I'm afraid anything as threatening as that would finish us."

"I was kind of counting on you."

"I'm sorry, but believe me, I've been trying to break through these walls of his for years. I've always known something was odd about him, so I pushed him to open up. I guess I pushed too far. The harder I pushed, the more distance he put between us. I never see him anymore. When he's in Fresno, he spends all his time at the office, and if I'm not working, I rattle around that big house like an idiot. When he's here in L.A., he never calls. So, I come down here and rattle around the condo. Every day I bring him lunch, and hope--"

"And, he runs you off?"

"No, he never runs me off, but he doesn't offer me that special attention anymore. He tells me I've learned all that he can teach me. I'm his equal as an actor."

"I've seen your work; I can believe it."

"You're both wrong, no one can match him."

"You really love him don't you?" The question came involuntarily out of his mouth. He found he was holding his breath when she answered.

"Yes, but I've never been able to win his love."

Hooper almost sighed as he felt the relief her words gave him, yet despite that he couldn't stop the next words from rolling involuntarily off his tongue. "That's not your fault; he's incomplete. You can see that now. Can't you?" Yet, inside his head, his conscience screamed back, "NO! Stop! Not this way."

"I suppose," she answered.

"Isn't there anything you can do?"

Myra paused in thought. After a moment she said, "Well, there is Zack."

"Zack?"

"Zachary Lowell Reid."

"The shipping heir?"

"Yes."

"What can he do?"

"I'm not sure, but he's Frank's best friend - only friend."

"I can't imagine those two together."

"Not many can. It's odd, Frank who's always so serious about his work, and free-wheeling Zack, the world-famous playboy who has no ambition beyond having a good time. But, when Frank gets together with Zack, he forgets all about work. When he's with Zack, he doesn't seem to be playing any of his roles."

"Playing roles? What are you talking about?"

"That's what I meant when I said earlier that I've always known here was something a little odd about Frank. He separates all the aspects of his life. I mean totally - cleanly. When he's being Frank the director, that's all he is; that he's also an actor or a teacher is completely out of his mind."

"You mean like multiple personalities?"

"No, he's aware of his other roles; it's just that he doesn't allow them to overlap except where absolutely necessary. In fact, it was almost simultaneous with our marriage that he quit being my teacher. He couldn't seem to combine both roles, and still perform them to the perfection he demands of himself."

"But everyone is like that."

"Yes, but not to the degree which Frank takes it."

"That's too weird; you must be imagining it."

"I know I'm not, yet I'm probably the only person who's ever been close enough to him to notice. Most people are only involved with Frank in one area of his life. With the exception of his students, but then the only other role they see him is as director, and that has its own natural distance."

"His secretary must have noticed."

"Yes, I suppose she has, but ever since the accident she has been very curt with me. I don't think she'll be much help."

"So, tell me, how is he different with Zack?"

"Actually, I'm not quite sure, because I can never get close enough. You see, if I'm around, Frank becomes Frank-the-dutiful-husband. I have only been able to observe them from a distance. But, when Frank is with Zack, he's relaxed; it's as if his body belongs to him for the first time. The intensity and concentration disappears from his face, and his whole body becomes as languid as a resting cat. It's ridiculous, but they play like a couple of kids. They act silly, and seem to be oblivious to the world around them. I've always hoped that he would stay that way after Zack left, and be that way with me, but he never does."

"What makes you think Zack can help?"

"I don't know that he can, but I feel like Frank becomes a human being when he is with Zack."

"It sounds like Frank is more like Eugene when he's with Zack."

"I couldn't say, but maybe Zack can talk him into going to a psychiatrist."

"If Zack believes you."

CHAPTER ELEVEN

Zack hesitated before the opaque glass door. As his eyes focused on the cobalt blue letters that spelled *Stacy Productions*, he recalled his surprise of last night when Myra appeared at the door of his San Francisco home. However, he had been more surprised at what she had to say. It made sense though; he couldn't help notice how Frank's personality would alter whenever she would join them. It was almost as if his face changed, but he had never considered it any of his business. Now Myra had asked him to make it his business; she said he was the only one who might be able to get through to him. "You're the only person around whom he doesn't take on one of his work personalities. Yes that even includes me; to him, I only represent more work." He thought it was ironic that they had met under the opposite circumstances. His uncle Ralph had introduced them in hopes that some of Frank's hard work and determination might rub off on him.

#

Ralph Smurling looked across his desk at the twenty-one year old son of his late brother-in-law. Zachary, he thought, is a smart boy, an attractive boy; what makes him so lazy? Those strong shoulders along with his height might have made him a tribal warrior some centuries ago. No, it's not his father's money that's spoiled him, it's his easy intelligence and looks. It's that quick wit and sly grin that's given him everything in life with no money down.

"Zack, I asked you down here today to offer you a little direction. Since your father is no longer around to do it, I thought you might not take offense if I made a few suggestions. Let me start by asking you this: why haven't you taken a place in the family business?"

"Uncle Ralph, not many people know this or would even guess it, but Father hated his work. He had none of Grandfather's Phoenician blood. He ran the shipping line because of the guilt Grandfather impressed upon him. Until I was sixteen, I assumed and dreaded that I would have to do the same. Then on the day he died, Father told me a secret. How he wished he could have dumped the whole goddamn company and gone canoeing up the Amazon or snow skiing in the Alps. He encouraged me not to make the mistake he did. He said he didn't expect me to learn the business unless that was what I wanted to do. Go out and enjoy life, he told me, follow your own dreams, and quite frankly, Uncle Ralph, that is exactly what I am doing."

"Your father did not mean for you to do nothing with your life."

"But you're wrong, I'm doing plenty with my life."

"A constant party is not a life."

"Those are your values Uncle, not mine."

"Would you just sample it, my life that is?"

"How?"

"There's a young man who started working for me at the beginning of the summer. He wants to be a director. I don't usually take on apprentices, but his persistence was remarkable. He's good too; he won't need me very long. In my entire career I've never seen anyone learn quite as fast, but he works too hard. I never see him take any time off. I'm thinking the two of you might complement each other."

"How's that?"

"I'm hoping that while you're teaching him how to relax and enjoy life, you might acquire some of his work ethic."

#

The rain had stopped pounding on the head of the boy who walked along the empty highway. Steam rose from the blacktop. As he inhaled, the odor of ozone entered his nostrils. The metallic scent reminded him of the taste of a cold iron pipe when you put your tongue on it. It was one of those odd taste memories that people acquire and catalogue when they're kids, when they don't mind putting their tongues on things adults would think strange or gross.

The boy walked on as if in a daze; he did not know why he was walking or where. He stopped and read a sign which told him he was on Highway 10 in Alabama, and that he was facing west. That he was in Alabama was meaningless to him, that he was on

Highway 10 was meaningless too, but that he was facing west struck a chord and he continued walking.

He was not a somnambulist, but walking along Highway 10 in Alabama at night along the long stretches of empty land that seemingly leads nowhere does tend to make one feel as if he were in an effluvial dream. His skull felt full, and his feet felt light, as he marched west toward a destination he could not conceive.

Eventually the sun rose to bake dry his clothes, and awaken insects to buzz annoyingly about his head. Occasionally, a truck zoomed by blowing hot air and a mixed scent of rubber, oil, and tar up his nose. About noon a trucker stopped and offered a ride. He climbed in the cab and stiffly faced out the windshield.

"Going far?" the trucker asked.

"Just going west." the boy answered.

"I'm going as far as Jackson, Mississippi."

"Jackson," the boy repeated. The name struck another chord. It told him nothing, but it was familiar, so he smiled and said, "Jackson, yes, that's where I'm going."

As they continued down the road the boy watched the trucker's driving skills with interest. The trucker noticed.

"Ever drive a truck?" he asked.

"No, but I'm sure I can."

"What's your name?"

The boy hesitated; it was only a second or two, but it occurred to him that he did not know his name. He was not particularly bothered by this lack of knowledge, but the truck driver was glaring at him, waiting, and he felt an obligation to comply. What was the name of that town? He thought. No, too obvious. It came out, "Ja... uh... Joe."

The trucker furrowed his forehead, but said only, "Mine's Eric."

After a while, they stopped at a diner, and the trucker bought him lunch. Throughout the meal the boy watched the short order cook intently. The trucker noticed this too.

"I suppose you also think you can cook as fast as that guy?"

"Uh, huh." the boy answered confidently.

Hours later, the trucker let him off outside Jackson, and the boy walked the last mile down Highway 18. His stomach rumbled at the sight of a neon sign indicating a diner. When he opened the door the place was busy with people. A harried woman, working alone behind the counter yelled in greeting, "Hi, be with you in a sec. Want coffee?"

He smiled and said, "You need a fast cook, don't you?"

She laughed and said, "No kidding."

Without asking, he walked around the counter, picked up the flipper, and started working on the orders lined up on a wire over the griddle. Without comment the harried woman picked up the dishes as he completed them and served them to starving customers.

Two hours later when the dinner-rush subsided, she asked, "You're a godsend. How long you been a cook?"

He shrugged, "As far back as I can remember."

"What's your name?"

He still didn't know. He thought a second, as he recalled the trucker's disbelieving brow, and figured he needed something better, then answered, "John... John Smith."

"Suit yourself." she said in disbelief. "I'm Agnes."

At dawn he promised to return the following night, and set off to find a place to sleep. Nestled in a hay loft he woke to the sound of an engine chugging. He looked down to see a farmer start a tractor. He watched carefully. He did not know who he was or what he could do, but he had found that if he observed something closely, he was able to learn quickly. Even though he did not know who he was, he found the mystery of it exciting.

Back at the diner that night, after the evening rush, Agnes turned up the volume on a TV set attached to the wall. The boy turned his attention to it, and was suddenly mesmerized by the movie on the tiny screen. He did not know its title was *The Gods Of Autumn*, but the picture struck another chord, and the melody in his mind began to take shape. He still could not hum it, but he did know one word to the song: West. He had to move on.

Agnes noticed him watching and said, "Good picture, I've seen it before."

The boy turned away from the TV and said, "I've got to go. I'm sorry I can't work for you anymore."

"What's wrong?" she cried.

"I've got to go west. Jackson isn't my destination after all." He tossed his apron on the counter and headed for the door.

"Wait, you've got some money coming," Agnes called, but he was already gone.

He hitched a ride that took him down Highway 80, but dropped him short of Shreveport, Louisiana. Walking west again, he saw a tractor like the one he saw in Jackson. His stomach was talking so he veered toward it, and knocked at the farmhouse door.

A man clad in overalls answered, and the boy jabbed his thumb over his shoulder toward the tractor and asked, "Sir, would you swap me some supper, if I do some plowing for you?"

"Past plowing time, son, but the weeds do need to be turned under. Can you hold a straight course?"

"Yes, sir."

"Good, then it's a deal. What's your name?"

The boy hesitated to use John Smith again, then remembered a motel sign he liked. "The name's Benbow..." But he could not think of a first name to go with it.

The old man cupped his ear. "How's that?"

He thought of one. "I said, Ben Bowen, sir."

Then he was driving a tractor; trying to hold it steady between rows of soybean. It was harder than he thought, but he was doing it. The old farmer told Ben Bowen he did a good job, and invited him to stay on a while, but the road was calling him and the sun setting in the west was nagging him. He stayed the night, long enough for a needed bath and breakfast in the morning.

Then he flagged down another trucker.

"I don't usually pick up riders," the driver said, "but I'm about to fall asleep. I figure a little conversation will keep me awake."

"If you want to get some sleep, I can drive this rig."

"Haw! You're just a kid."

"Am not! I'm twenty-one." the boy insisted, although he had no idea how old he really was. "Why don't you let me prove it, then when you're satisfied you can climb in the back and sleep."

The trucker looked at the boy from underneath his heavy eyelids and said, "Okay, we'll give it a go."

The boy ground the first gear and the trucker's jaw puckered as the big rig lurched forward, but by second gear he was shifting smoothly and the trucker's face relaxed.

"What's your name?"

"Mack, just like the truck." he answered confidently.

The trucker climbed in the back and said, "Wake me when you get to Dallas."

It was dark in Dallas when they pulled into the truck depot next to the train yard. The boy bid the driver goodbye and wandered toward the tracks. He found a train pointed west and climbed inside an open boxcar and fell asleep. A sharp pain in his foot woke him, and he looked up at the burly shape of the yard detective. Without a word the big man picked him up by his jacket collar and tossed him out. The boy did not stop to argue. He ran. Several hours later exhaustion forced him to stop. During his run he'd lost his sense of direction, and finally collapsed in a drainage ditch along the side of a noisy road. He was hot and sweaty and pulled off his jacket, rolled it up and lay his head against it. The jacket crackled as the weight of his head leaned into it. He sat back up and squeezed the jacket. Paper was inside the lining. There was no zipper to open the lining; it was permanently sewed in, but there was a pocket. He stuck his hand inside. The bottom of the pocket was ripped and he could feel the cool sheets of paper. He had to roll up the sheets a few at a time to get them out. Finally, he had them all, and by the passing headlights he was able to sort them by number. The first page read:

RESURGENT MAN

Original Screenplay by Jackson Paine Franklin

That's why the name Jackson was familiar. He thought. This must be my name. A dull chord sounded in his mind, as he read the name again. Then out loud he cried, "That's it; my name is Jack." The dull chord struck again, louder, sending pain through his head. He said, "Jack," over and over, and each time the dull thud came until he felt the throbbing pain of a migraine headache caused him to stop. He fell asleep whispering, "My name is not Jack."

The morning sun woke him, and when he stood he saw a road sign which told him he was standing beside Highway 287 West. He re-rolled the manuscript and replaced it in the jacket pocket. He stuck out his thumb and walked backwards to face the cars heading west.

Highway 287 faded into Highway 66, and New Mexico faded into Arizona. Behind him suns would rise and in front of him they would set. The rides he caught were good, they took him farther west, and they were educational. One driver, his Brooklyn accent strong, talked long about his childhood in New York City. The boy hung onto every word and every intonation, because each passing day had taught him that acting was his sole defense mechanism for survival.

July 2, 1967 was hot and sweaty along Highway 66 when a traveling salesman pulled over for the boy holding out his thumb. It was his sixth week of walking and hitching, but the boy was unaware of the passage of time. The asphalt stretching out behind was a time-line depicting the content of his memory. The hills had turned to plains and the plains to desert, and from where he stood it looked like the desert would soon turn to mountains. He chose not to think beyond the road because he found it caused him pain. At first he had been excited by the mystery of not knowing, but whenever he tried to solve it, a sharp pain shot through his head. So he let it be, and his life on the road comprised the entirety of his consciousness. Walking with his thumb out, sleeping in abandoned barns, washing up in streams, and working when he could bluff his way into a job. The jobs had grown scarce as he had had to grow wary. In one town a sheriff tried to arrest him for vagrancy when he told the wrong man he was a brick mason. He could have done the work; he'd seen it done before. The problem arose when he couldn't identify a tool to hand the man who had asked for it by name. The man's brother was the sheriff, but the boy ran faster. When he found work - he ate out; when he didn't - he ate outside, often from the garbage cans of roadside diners. All along he kept moving. West was only a direction, not a destination, but it remained focused in his mind as his sole, albeit vague, motive force.

"Where ya headin'?" asked the traveling salesman whose chubby close-shave reddened cheeks instantly broke into a sweat as he pushed open the door.

"West."

"California?" the heavy man inquired as he loosened his necktie against the arid air pouring in through the open car door.

The question sparked a latent memory in the boy's mind. It was another chord, so he nodded as he climbed into the passenger seat.

"Seeking your fortune or seeing the country?"

"I guess seeking my fortune," the boy answered with a sample of the Brooklyn accent he'd learned.

"Then don't get into sales, ‘cause you'll end up seeing the country instead. It gets awful lonesome hauling up and down these highways, and every town begins to look like every other one until..." he prattled on and on. The salesman's hunger for simple conversation was starved by a daily diet of sales pitches.

The blasting air conditioner made the boy cold so he unfolded the jacket he'd carried over a thousand miles. Once again he glanced at the rolled up stack of papers poking out of the inside pocket. His life, despite being in constant motion, was actually in a comfortable stasis. Deep within him, he felt it was what he needed, but that stack rolled up in his jacket pocket interfered with his comfort, yet he couldn't throw it away.

"So what are ya going to California for? You wanna be a movie star?" his boring benefactor behind the wheel jested.

The word 'movie' struck another chord of familiarity, but it did not hurt in his head. The boy looked down at the stack of papers and read: Screenplay. He answered, "Well, something to do with the movies."

"Good luck, but I can tell you this; you won't find much work of any kind out there. Hey, I've got an L.A. newspaper here somewhere." He reached into the backseat. "Here it is. About a week old, but you can look through the want-ads and see for yourself what I'm talking about."

As he opened the newspaper, his eyes fell on a picture of Ralph Smurling. The chords strung together and played the melody, and an entire section of his mind ripped open and poured out memory. Memory of things about movies.

"Oh, look!" he exclaimed, "This is the man I'm going to work for."

The salesman glanced at the picture and read the caption. "Yeah, does he know it yet?"

"No."

"Well, if you want it bad enough I reckon you will. At least that's what they keep telling me at all those motivational seminars the company makes me go to. What's your name kid, I'll have to keep a look out for it whenever I'm in L.A.."

His blood went cold; it was the question he'd learned to dread along the road. It didn't matter who he encountered, or how well he did a job, no name he ever gave satisfied belief. In the past several weeks he'd been Joe, and John, and Ben, and Steve. Fred, Mack, Sven, and Vinnie. Tom, Tim, Tony, but he always got that look. The one that said, "You're lying." Hell, he'd lied about many things lately, successfully lied: where he was from, where he'd worked before, but when it came to his name his voice betrayed him. He looked again at the name on the manuscript, the name that caused the pain, but he had heard the melody, and maybe...

"I said, what's your name?"

"It's uh," he looked down again and cringed. He couldn't say the whole name maybe just the last name. "Frank... lin... uh..."

"Frank Lynn, hmmm, so you're using the old double first name as a stage pseudonym. I don't know about that Lynn part, though, you shouldn't use a girl's name. What you need is two men's first names. A good strong sounding name like John Wayne. I'll bet you didn't know he changed his name from a girl's name. His name used to be Marion."

When the boy, now comfortably calling himself Frank, arrived at Nordwick Studio, at the end of the second week in July of 1967, he was promptly turned away by the guard. Without the proper credentials he would not be allowed to enter.

"Sorry son, that's the rules. If I let every star-struck kid in who wanted to get into the movies, nobody would get any work done."

"Then would you tell me when the next studio tour is?"

"Look kid, this ain't Universal or MGM; there aren't any tours."

Frank looked down at his feet as he scuffed one shoe against the concrete. "If I just stay here by the gate, will you introduce me to Mr. Smurling when he comes out?"

"No loitering." He pointed to a sign.

Frank's eyes followed the direction indicated by the guard's finger, but beyond the sign his glance fell on the high chain link fence topped with three strands of barbed wire.

The guard noticed his contemplative pause and looked to see what was gathering Frank's attention. Sternly, he said, "And don't go getting any ideas about climbing that fence, either. It's rigged with an electronic monitor so sensitive that an alarm goes off if anything heavier than a bird so much as touches it. If I catch you around that fence, I'll call the cops so fast it'll make your head spin. You got that?"

"Yes, sir," he muttered and turned away.

Frank's next attempt was at Smurling's office. The receptionist told him, "I'm sorry, but Mr. Smurling is a busy man. He won't accept an appointment like this."

"Maybe he would see me if I caught him early when he first comes in?"

"I don't think so. He's seldom here when he's shooting. Nor does he keep regular hours when he's not; I doubt you would ever just catch him. May I make a suggestion?"

Frank nodded.

"Why don't you enroll in one of the colleges that offer classes in film? That's where most people get started these days."

"I'm not most people, thank you," he answered and walked out the door.

Frank was walking along the sidewalk toward the entrance to the studio desperately trying to think of a scheme to get in when he saw a man exiting the gate on foot. The man was wearing a green coverall, and over his shoulder was slung a tool belt. He was heading in Frank's direction.

Stopping, Frank waited until the man was within a few feet of where he stood. "Hi," Frank offered with an infectious smile. "You work for that studio?"

"Nope, just freelance and piece work."

"Piece work?" Frank asked as he fell into step with the man.

"Yup, it ain't like workin' for one of the big studios where they'll keep a plumber on full time."

"Why not?"

"Just ain't a whole lotta call for running water on these small sets."

"But, still it must be really neat working around all those movie stars and all. So, what kind of stuff do you do?"

The man was eager to talk, and Frank gently pumped him for information. While he spoke, Frank observed the man closely. He noticed the man favored his right leg with a slight limp, and parted his hair on the left side. His left thumb was hooked through the tool belt buckle to keep it from sliding off his shoulder. The man's accent, Frank surmised, was a nasal twang from the Great Lakes.

A few blocks later they parted. "Say, what's your name?" Frank asked.

"Jeff Terry."

"See ya 'round, Jeff."

Jeff waved with a mock salute, his right forefinger touching the outer edge of his eyebrow. Frank added the wave to his inventory.

Frank now knew what he was going to attempt, but he needed props, and props cost money. Not a lot of money, a few dollars would do. He walked into a pawn shop, but the man wasn't interested in his cheap watch or his rumpled jacket. Turning toward the door to leave he shoved his hands down his pockets in dejection. Against his finger tips he felt something metallic. He pulled out a gold Saint Christopher medal, on a gold chain. What luck, he thought, and turned back to the pawn shop proprietor.

"The chain's broken," the man said, then flipping the medallion over he read out loud, "ALL MY LOVE, STACIE. Say are you sure you want to part with this?"

Frank nodded.

"Let's see, eighteen carat and pretty heavy. I'll give you twenty-three dollars."

Later, in a *Sears* department store, Frank bought a green coverall, a leather tool belt, a monkey wrench, a pipe cutter, a pair of pliers, and a tube of pipe dope. After he paid the cashier, he slipped on the coveralls. Then thanking her, he bid goodbye with a mock salute. She watched him as he left. It struck her as odd, that she had not noticed his limp when he came in.

After washing the coveralls in a coin laundry, he spent the night sleeping behind a hedge of boxwoods in front of a bank one block from Nordwick Studio. He rose as night faded to a pre-dawn light, and brushed the dirt off his sleep-wrinkled coveralls. He stopped in a gas station bathroom and carefully combed his hair with a part on the left. He was ready to enter the studio.

He hooked his left thumb through the buckle of the tool belt that rode on his shoulder like a saddle. The handle of the monkey wrench slapped his upper arm in time with the scuffing sound made by the leather of his right shoe.

The guard stepped out of the gatehouse. It was the same man who ran him off the day before. Frank kept to the center of the drive. He hoped the shadow light of dawn along with the distance to the gatehouse would distort his face just enough to allow the guard's imagination to correct the errors.

"Morning Jeff, I see they got you up early." It worked.

"Yup, new schedule on that rotten shower scene over in Four. They gotta have water by ten." Frank continued his pace.

"Stop by and have some coffee on your way out."

"Will do." He raised his right hand and touched his forefinger to the outer edge of his eyebrow. He made it; Frank the method actor was born.

It took him half an hour, but Frank finally found the right sound stage. Inside it was dark and deserted, but by eight o'clock it would be bustling with people. Smurling's chair was behind the cameras; Frank could not resist sitting in it. He dropped his tool belt on the floor, and took in the set from the director's vantage point. It felt good. He imagined himself giving orders to the camera crew.

"Listen up everybody!" he called out loud. "We're going to do a pick-up on scene 37 today. After reviewing yesterday's rushes, I found the scene to be a little tiresome and the way it stands, we're running the risk of relieving the audience's anxiety. We've worked too hard at making them tense and - dammit - I don't want anyone thinking it's a good time to get up and buy popcorn."

"Now since we can't increase the tempo without destroying the relevance of the conversation, we're going to change the point of view. No grumbling; all I need is a single over-the-shoulder shot. Where's the script girl? Cathy! Oh, there you are; I want you to make sure John raises the same shoulder when he stands up as he did yesterday in the master shot."

"Everyone, take your places."

He stood up and put his hand over his eyes as if he were blocking light. "Who's my gaffer?" he called out. Then as if hearing an answer he replied, "Hi Fred, glad to have you aboard. Now what I want you to do is have your best juicer put a square beam of fill-light in the middle of the living room. Have him make it look like sunlight coming through a skylight, and I want dust motes, shiny almost like glitter. Then between the sun beam and John's chair I want a thirty degree plane of light from the floor up that slashes the sunbeam at..." He paused then called out, "Joan how tall are you?" He paused again then said, "Five-foot-six ... Fred, make that slash no higher than four-foot-eight at the center of the beam."

He sat back down then turned in the seat toward the camera crane. It stood black in the darkness like a petrified dinosaur head frozen in the act of struggling to climb out of the tar pits.

"Joe, I want you to drop down and dolly forward so you're looking over John's left shoulder through the sunlight at the door.

When Joan opens that door I want her to look like the vision of an angel to John."

"John, when you see Joan I want you to rise slightly out of your chair. She looks so benevolent through the sun beam that you assume her news can only be good."

"Joan, do not begin your lines until you've passed through the beam. As soon as you've reached the other side, stop."

"Fred, make sure you kill her key light as soon as she enters the sunbeam. Do not replace it when she steps out.

"John, she no longer looks like a shimmering angel. A wedge of moldy darkness covers her face. You drop back into your seat because you realize she's come to drop a bomb."

"Joe, let me know as soon as you have that angle, and we'll do a quick rehearsal to get the marks on the floor before we go for a take."

Frank jerked around in the chair to face the sound of clapping hands behind him.

"Excellent performance," said the source of the clapping. "Too bad I don't have a script with a role for a director."

Ralph Smurling walked into Frank's view. Frank leaped guiltily from the chair. The director's eyes moved from Frank's coveralls to the tools beside his feet. "You didn't need to come down today. I told the office I didn't need water in the fountain until Friday, or did you come down in hopes of auditioning?"

"I'm not an actor Mr. Smurling."

"Could have fooled me."

"I want to be a director sir. I came down here because you're the best."

"Then you're not a plumber? Do you realize I can have you arrested?"

A faceless man spoke in Frank's memory. "You're gonna learn this trade, boy, if I have to beat it into to you."

Frank said, "I actually am a plumber, and I can make your fountain work, sir."

Smurling stepped a little closer to Frank, and studied his face. "Son, you're not old enough to be a plumber."

"I'm twenty-one," he insisted, then offered, "Mr. Smurling if I can fix your fountain, and I'll do it for free, will you let me just hang around and watch. I can learn from observation."

Ralph studied the boy again then said, "Okay, but if you can't fix it - I call the cops."

"It's a deal then?" Frank said, offering his hand.

Smurling looked into Frank's eyes, then for a reason he could not explain took his hand. "It's a deal."

Ralph led Frank to the fountain then left. Quickly Frank searched for the main water pipes. Then he found copper tubing and a valve. When he bought the tools he didn't have enough money to get a tape measure so used a length of string he found on the floor. His hands deftly took to the task of measuring the distance then cutting the tubing. After beveling the edges, he fastened the valve. In less than thirty minutes he finished, and turned the fountain on.

Smurling looked up from his papers when he heard the water. The boy was standing in front of his accomplishment.

"Looks like you win."

"Only if I can prove to you that I'll be a good assistant."

"We'll see. What's your name, son?"

"Frank."

"Frank what?"

Frank paused, the name Frank had worked, but was Jackson a proper last name. A dull ache ebbed at the back of his skull and a gold medallion glittered in his brain. His body shivered in response. He heard the pawn broker reading, "ALL MY LOVE, STACIE," then asking, "Are you sure you want to part with this?" As he stood there facing the director, he thought that maybe he should not part with all of it, so sealing into his name a root to his past he answered, "Frank Stacy, sir."

"Well, Mr. Frank Stacy, you pull up a chair here beside me, and I don't want to hear a peep out of you all day."

"Yes, sir."

Frank sat quietly all that day. The next day Ralph began to send Frank on errands. He was impressed with how ready he was to tackle any task. He asked pertinent questions, and showed an innate insight into the making of motion pictures.

Toward the end of the week, he noticed Frank had not changed his clothes, and his nose told him it had been a while since the boy had bathed. He had written off to youth, the amazing number of doughnuts and cups of coffee the boy would consume each morning until one afternoon a few days later, the Key Grip told him that Frank was spending his nights sleeping behind the prop chest. When he confronted Frank about it, Frank admitted that he had not been out of the sound stage since he entered. He said he was afraid the guard would not let him back in. Ralph looked at the smudged and determined face, and said, "Son, it's time I put you on the payroll." That evening he found Frank a room in a boarding house. The next morning he sent his administrative assistant, Constance Barnes to take him clothes shopping.

#

Thirteen men tumbled out of a ragged sailboat. Staggering through the surf they each dropped to their knees upon reaching the beach. In front of them, twenty-two people held their breath as three massive cameras slowly sank deeper into the soft sand. They were filming the final take of *Baker's Dozen*. Max Sanders as Baker, with hair and clothing drenched, his ripped shirt flapping in the artificial wind, grasped a handful of sand, raised his fist, and cried, "Home!"

Ralph Smurling stood up, and yelled into his megaphone, "Cut and wrap."

The crowd of onlookers applauded. The actors and crew hugged and cheered.

A tall, sun bronzed man with blonde hair sauntered up to the director's chair. "Hello, Uncle Ralph."

"Hello, Zachary. It's about time you came around."

"Actually, I came to surf, but I thought it might be amusing to watch you work, so I came here instead of my usual spot."

Turning to Frank, Ralph said, "Zachary, this is the young man I've been wanting you to meet. Frank Stacy meet my insolent nephew, Zachary Reid."

Frank nodded, and Zack said, "Frank, do you surf?"

Frank shook his head, and Zack said, "Then come along; it looks to me like you're all done for the day."

Replying, Frank began, "I'm sure it would be fun, but there's still a whole lot that I need to--"

"Go on, I'll take care of everything." Ralph interrupted.

"But--"

Ralph looked him square in the face and said sternly, "That's an order!" Then a little lighter, added, "And, if you're not hung over when you show up for work tomorrow morning - you're fired."

Smurling laughed inwardly as he watched Frank force himself to relax. It was as if he needed permission not to work.

Zack said, "Come on Frank, it's time for you to become the master of a new dominion."

Suddenly, Smurling noticed a real change come over Frank. Frank turned and faced Zack, and as he did his whole body went from controlled rigidity to fluid expectation. The serious expression he had come to take for granted was now one of eager excitement. It was exactly what one would expect from a boy.

"Whadda ya wanna do today, Jack?"

"That's Zack, and if you're going to be a Californian, then you're going to have to conquer surfing."

"What are we waiting for? Let's go."

Ralph watched as they walked away. He could no longer hear them over the surf, but he could see they were both talking. He felt curiously aware that he'd just witnessed something important, but what, he could not say.

The next day, Frank showed up for work, early as usual. Smurling observed him working as hard as ever, and asking the same tough-to-answer questions. His focus on becoming a motion picture director was not in the slightest deterred by his day of decadence with Zachary.

Frank's diligence was unnerving to Ralph. He would carry out the tasks of Smurling's productions during the day, then devote his nights to study. The only time he took off was to sleep.

Whenever one of the big motion picture cameras became available, and the opportunity coincided with some free moments from his work, Frank would sit behind it and look through the lens at a single object, or a person if he could talk them into it. He would view his subject from every imaginable angle, and he would do it for hours on end. Smurling was never able to deduce how he did it, but Frank was able to induce union crane operators and lighting engineers to assist him in his lengthy vigils behind the camera. He was not even polite. Frank sat behind that camera and barked orders: pan right - pan left, lights up - lights down, tilt camera up - tilt camera down. But what he found most shocking was when he overheard performers asking Frank if he would like them to stay. From the director to the best boy his evolving talent had them all mesmerized.

Smurling concluded that Frank was going to work himself to death before he would ever get to make his first movie. Several weeks had passed since the day he introduced him to Zachary on the beach, and he was forced to assume his effort of bringing them together was a waste of time. Then unexpectedly, late one morning, he saw Frank leave the office without a word. He looked out his window and watched him climb into Zachary's Jaguar. He did not see him again until the next morning. Then every other week or so, Zachary would show up, at the office, on the set, or on location, and Frank would disappear, abandoning whatever work he was involved in. This new spontaneous irresponsibility in Frank irritated the hell out of him. Then one morning as cast and crew were waiting on location, and while he had to cajole nervous investors over schedule delays and cost overruns he asked Frank to review the previous day's film for him. When he was finally able to enter the projection room, he found it empty and the dailies flapping in the projector. He was mad enough to fire Frank, but then he remembered it was his own fault for introducing him to Zachary.

#

Zack was not sure what it was he was supposed to do, so he decided it was easiest to be himself. Either the opportunity would present itself, or it would not. He pushed open the door.

Connie looked up, and smiled. She liked to see Zack, and today was no different.

His long legs and great strides easily carried him to the front of her desk where he bowed deeply and said, "Zachary Lowell Reid."

"Do you have an appointment?" she asked with mock gravitas while suppressing the emerging giggle Zack's presence always demanded.

He whirled to her side of the desk and dropped to one knee, then pressing her hand to his lips he replied, "I have no appointment; it was merely an excuse to," then sweeping his hand in a gesture indicating the office, "seduce you away from all of this."

"And what about your wife?"

"But, my love, a man of my means needs many wives to help squander all the idle wealth."

"I think, sir, you've been watching *Resurgent Man* again. I shall have to decline."

"Why?"

"If I ever go after a married man, it's going to be for one who builds fortunes, not squanders them." As she spoke, her eyes involuntarily moved toward the closed door of Frank's office.

"Forsooth!" he cried, rising up from the floor. "Your eyes, my dear, revealeth a dark secret."

Connie said nothing, and Zack saw fear replace the humor in her eyes. Fear that he would betray her slip.

"Connie, don't look at me that way." He said seriously. "Am I the type who tells?"

She shook her head.

"So, tell me, is anyone in with the major domo?"

"No," she answered smiling again.

"Good, by the way, you may as well cancel the rest of his appointments for the day." he said while turning the door's knob.

As he entered the office, Frank was on the phone saying, "for the next few weeks. Call my secretary..." Frank looked up to see who had arrived, and then finished, "...in the morning, and she will schedule you."

When he hung up, Zack said, "You've just performed your last act of work for the day."

"Oh, yeah?"

"Yeah, for the rest of the day you're going with me to the club where maybe we'll play tennis, but definitely we'll buy drinks for women who are not our wives."

"Then what will we do with them?"

"Send them home horny and frustrated to their unexpecting and unprepared husbands."

"And is there a name for this activity?"

"Charity."

"Charity! I'll have to ask the Junior League about this."

"But you can't, June is this year's President."

"Then we'll have to go water skiing instead."

"But, I planned the day around getting drunk."

"That's fine because I've finally figured out what that extra thong on the back of ski is for."

"What?"

"It's designed to hold a bottle of beer until you're up out of the water."

"Are you sure?"

"What else could it be for?"

"Then what the hell are we waiting for!"

"Nothing. Let's go."

Half a case of beer, and a full case of first degree sunburn later, Zack and Frank were watching the sun set from the patio of a lakeside tavern.

Stretching, Zack exclaimed, "Unh! What a day; I've strained every muscle in my body. Do you realize we haven't cut loose since the day of your accident?"

"Yeah. Thanks. You showed up just in time too. I needed a break, I was beginning to get stressed out."

"Stress? You? Why you thrive on stress."

Frank pushed his seat back and stood up. "Zack, I believe it's time to go on down to the club, and buy drinks for those women you mentioned."

"Not yet, I'm too tired. Besides, I want to hear more about your being stressed out."

"It's not important. Let's go."

"It sounds like somebody is trying to change the subject." Zack sing-songed.

Zack saw Frank's eyes flash, and then focus into a hard stare. It was barely perceptible, but Zack could see a slight shift in Frank's face. Then in a voice Zack had never heard before, Frank asked, "Since when have our conversations ever remained on a single subject?"

"You're the one who brought it up. And, you've got to admit your behavior has been a little weird lately."

"I suggest you drop it; our friendship can't support meddling."

"If concern is meddling, then I'm guilty. Why don't you want to talk about it?"

"Because there's nothing to talk about."

"No? You get banged on the head, then you disappear for three days during which time you try out for an extra's part in a low budget movie, and you expect me to believe that's nothing!"

"Zack, that accident afforded me an opportunity to put on an excellent act as a publicity stunt for my new movie. It's as simple as that. Now, can you leave it alone?"

"A publicity stunt? Don't forget I was there. And c'mon, when does Frank Stacy need to resort to publicity stunts. No, I'm not buying it, and neither does Myra..." He gasped in response to his slip.

"Myra! What does she have to do with this?" Frank yelled. Zack had never seen him like this before.

"She's concerned, Frank. Your publicity stunt story has too many holes in it. She merely wants you to consider the alternative."

"There's nothing to consider! And I'll thank you to leave Myra's insecurities to me."

"Myra's insecurities?"

"Yes. If you must know all about my marital problems, Myra has just the sort of grasping, clinging personality that would invent the absurd idea that I am someone else."

"Frank, calling Myra insecure is what's absurd."

"What would you know? You don't live with her."

"I won't believe that a woman who's achieved what she's achieved can feel inferior. What I can believe is denial when I hear it. Why don't you see what a psychiatrist has to say? No one ever has to know about it."

"That's it! I don't have to listen to this," Frank snatched his car keys off the table. "One other thing; stay away from my wife!"

Myra sat pensively by the door. Three hours ago Zack called to admit his failure. She was wondering whether Frank would come home at all when she heard a car in the driveway.

When she opened the door it was not Frank's car, but one of the neighborhood security cars. The two officers were walking a staggering drunk Frank toward the door.

"We found him passed out on the steering wheel about a block down the road, Miss Mason. He wasn't in a wreck; the car was parked. There was an empty bottle of *Jack Daniel's* on the seat beside him, I guess he just fell asleep."

"Thank you, gentlemen," she said taking Frank's elbow.

When she closed the door, Frank aroused and pulled away from her grip. "You bitch!" he cried, then with the last of his conscious energy he swung his hand and slapped her face.

The pain shot through to the back of her head, but Myra did not make a sound. She stood face to face with Frank while biting her lip to keep it from trembling. The only reaction he could read was the look of horror in her eyes. He started to raise his hand again, but the movement caused him to lose his balance and he collapsed onto the floor.

Myra woke Sara, her maid, and together they carried him to bed. After dismissing Sara, she undressed Frank, now completely unconscious, then climbed into bed. She fell asleep sobbing on his shoulder.

CHAPTER TWELVE

It was dark when Hooper entered his apartment, but from across the room he could see the message light flashing on his telephone answering machine. When he turned it on, he heard:

"Mr. Johnson, this is Frank Stacy. After careful consideration, I've chosen you for the lead in *Accidental Angel*. Ordinarily, I do not cast anyone who I've not personally trained, but in view of your ability, and your appearance, I've made an exception. However, your acting does have some rough edges which will need to be worked out before we can begin production, therefore I will expect you to attend my classes for the next few weeks. Call my secretary... in the morning, and she will schedule you."

Hooper was stunned. He said aloud, "I can't believe it. I got the lead in a Frank Stacy picture." He replayed the message four times. Finally, he was convinced. He was so excited he started dancing about the room singing: "I got the lead. I got the lead. I got the lead in a Frank Sta-cee. Yippee!"

When he was finally able to settle down, he had a sobering thought, "Is Frank trying to buy me off?" Then he thought of *Resurgent Man*, and decided that the man behind that film would never compromise. "Just maybe," he hoped, "this film which is supposed to cover-up his past, will, in the end, make him face it."

#

Eugene felt a warm body beside him. He opened his eyes. He was in bed and beside him was the woman from the pool, and he remembered. A shudder ran through his body as he climbed quietly out of the bed. There were so many things he did not know, and it scared him. As he glanced out the window toward the pool, he thought, whatever he'd become he'd done more than well by Ellaville standards. He had to learn who he was and whether he wanted to have anything more to do with it. He opened the door to the hall, but before stepping out, he realized he could not go snooping around the house half naked. There was a closet, surely it must have clothes that fit him. After all, it was his house.

Myra woke to see Frank, standing in boxer shorts, sifting through their bedroom closet. Glancing at the clock she saw that it was 10:30 in the morning. Her surprise at the hour was checked by the pressure of the pillow against her swollen cheek. What she felt as distress when she went to bed was now anger. After pushing herself up into a sitting position against the pile of pillows, she remarked with irritation, "I don't believe it, Frank; even with a hangover, you've never been this late to work before."

Eugene gasped.

Myra saw Frank freeze as if he'd been caught in an act of larceny. The instant passed and his body thawed with a slump. As he turned toward her, she thought it odd to see him postured with his chin against his chest, and his hands clasped in front of his groin. It passed through her mind that perhaps he was expressing his guilt for hitting her. She was about to tell him the soreness in her mouth would not be satisfied by an act, when he muttered:

"Sorry ma'am, I didn't mean to wake you, I was just looking for some clothes to put on."

Myra caught her breath; her reproach was stilled by the sound of the southern accent. Knowing the answer, she still had to ask, "Eugene?"

"Yes, ma'am." He raised his head, but on seeing her rosy nipples through the material of her negligee he dropped his eyes back to the floor.

"Where are you going?"

"Nowhere; ain't no place for me to go. I just figured I'd try to find out who I'd become."

"I'd like to help you." She climbed out of the bed.

He couldn't help but watch as she walked across the room to the intercom on the wall. He'd never seen such a beautiful woman, nor one quite as naked. Her sheer pink gown had the cut of a man's shirt and thin pin-stripes that encouraged the eye to follow every curve from her neck down to her ankles. His survey stopped as his eyes worked their way back up to the four blue-black stripes across her left cheek. She flipped the switch and he heard her ask someone named Sara to serve coffee and pastry in the solarium in ten minutes.

"Eugene, there's a robe you can wear hanging inside the closet door. After we eat, I'll go through the wardrobe with you."

His eyes focused on her breasts as she walked toward him, but he quickly averted them when he noticed she knew where he was looking.

She said, "It's okay Eugene, whether you remember it or not, we are married."

He looked up to her face, as water started forming in his eyes. "But, I don't even know your name."

"It's Myra," she answered as she took the robe off its hook. Then helping him put it on, she added, "I know you're frightened; I would be too, but I want you to feel you can trust me." After she finished tying the belt she slid her arms around his waist, and kissed him lightly on his chest. "Eugene, I will help you remember. You don't know this, but I've been trying to meet you for eleven years."

"What do you mean?"

She removed her arms from around his waist and took her own robe from the closet door. "Frank Stacy has never been able to love me because you've been missing."

"I don't understand."

"I didn't either until recently, but whenever Frank buried you in his subconscious he lost the primary part of his identity."

"How can you know that?"

"Let's go downstairs; I'll explain over breakfast."

When they entered the solarium, Sara was setting the table. As the two sat down, the parallel bruises above Myra's delicate jawbone attracted her attention. Her eyes narrowed to hateful slits, and she slammed the silverware down in front of Eugene.

The noise drew Myra out of her reverie of studying Eugene's face, and she snapped her attention toward Sara. Realizing Sara was merely exhibiting loyalty to her, she refrained from reproach and said, "Sara, Frank doesn't remember last night. He has amnesia again."

Sara gasped, then stared at Eugene.

"Sara, I'd like you to meet Eugene Eastly."

Sara nodded hesitantly to him.

"And Sara, please be patient with him when he asks you questions that don't seem to make sense. Also when you've finished serving; please call Connie and tell her Frank is sick and will not be in today. Do not explain what is wrong; that will remain our secret for now."

"Yes ma'am."

When Sara left the room, Eugene pointed to Myra's face and asked, "Did I do that?"

"Frank did it, Eugene, not you. Though, I suppose I was asking for it. I got his best friend to ask him to go see a psychiatrist."

"Do you want me to go?"

"That's up to you. I won't make the same mistake twice."

"Then I'll wait. You mentioned my best friend; who is he?"

"Zack Reid."

"Zack?" he asked excitedly. "Is that a stage name? Did he change it from Jack?"

Two thoughts collided in her mind. One was an image of Eugene's horror stricken face as it must have been at seeing his friend Jack dead in the car beside him. The other was a question: Did Frank substitute Zack for Jack? She looked at Eugene's face, and knew she could not tell him Jack was dead. She shook her head and answered. "No, Zack's always been Zack. You met him several weeks ago when you woke up beside the pool."

"Several weeks," he muttered. "I was wondering how long it had been, but I was afraid to ask; I didn't know if it had been a day or years. I don't remember too much from that first day."

"Do you remember Hooper Johnson?"

"Yes. You know Hooper?"

"Yes, Hooper came to me after you became Frank again. It was Hooper who persuaded me that you actually existed."

"What do you mean by, 'actually existed?'"

"Eugene, I should explain first that Frank is the world's greatest living actor--"

"Actor? But, I thought I was supposed to be a director."

"You are. The best, but you also became the best actor in order to train your own performers. When you, Frank that is, studied a role, he would spend hours determining all the basic motivations and passions driving that character until he actually seemed to be that person. A talent so remarkable that he could actually fool people who knew him."

"So what does that have to do with my existence?"

"When Frank returned home after being you for three days, he told me that Eugene Eastly was the name of a character he'd studied. He explained that the trauma of the accident caused that part of his memory which held all of his studies into the character of Eugene Eastly to temporarily replace his memory of being himself."

"Jesus! And Hooper didn't believe that, huh?"

"No, he didn't."

"Does all this have something to do with what you were going to say before about the primary part of my identity?"

"Not your identity, Frank's identity. You are that primary part. I've only just figured that out, but I always knew something was missing. You see, Frank taught me that to really absorb the character of a role you are playing you must fully understand his most fundamental desires, and then you must make them your own. By doing so you make the individual traits of your character realistic to the audience, no matter how much larger than life the author drew them. But, even following his own theories, whenever I studied Frank, I could never determine what his fundamental desires were. The more I tried, the more his life seemed to be a caricature of things he was supposed to be. You see, I thought it was because of his great acting abilities that his own individual characteristics appeared as stereotypes."

"But that doesn't make sense. Isn't making movies his main desire? It's mine. It seems it should be his."

"No, it's more philosophical than that. It's why you want to make movies. As Frank would say, it's a question of values."

"I don't understand what you mean by stereotypes?"

"It's just that whenever Frank was directing I felt like he was acting, yet when he was acting I never felt like he was. What made me wonder about it in the first place, was that I noticed he seemed to lack the natural ease of transition normal people have in moving from one walk of life to another. With him it's always immediate like flipping on a light switch. With Frank, everything is black and white," giggling, she added, "except his movies."

"Myra, I don't understand what you're saying or what happened to me, but I need to know. There are so many questions I want to ask... I just don't know where to start."

"Eugene, there are many questions that I want to ask you, too. You see, Frank would never tell me about his youth. He would only say things like: I grew up in New York City, all normal childhood diseases, nothing spectacular, nothing out of the ordinary."

"But, I grew up in Georgia."

"I know."

"I want to know everything, but more than anything I want to see some of my movies. God, I feel weird saying that."

"Eventually, you won't. Come on, let's take our coffee to the projection room."

#

Hooper dialed the number for *Stacy Productions* again. He had called a moment before, but somehow the connection was broken right after he stated his name to Frank's secretary. When she picked up again he said, "Hi, it's me again, we were cut off."

She did not answer, he heard only a click, and then the dial tone. "That's weird," he thought, and dialed again. Again, the phone clicked off as soon as he spoke. He called the operator. When he explained what had happened, her best offer was to report the problem. Not satisfied he dialed one more time. The results remained the same. He looked at his watch; it was ten o'clock. He decided he would have to drive up to Fresno, but in the back of his mind he sensed a problem.

He was not wrong. Four hours later, he pushed open the smoked glass door labeled *Stacy Productions*, and presented an effusive smile to the woman behind the desk.

Connie looked up to see the tall man with broad shoulders and curly brown hair entering her office. She could not resist returning the smile to the man with the sparkling green eyes.

"Hi, my name is Hooper Johnson. Frank told me to get the schedule for my acting lessons from you."

He was amazed by the instantaneous transformation on her face. The smile with which she greeted his entrance disappeared as if it were erased by his voice. The scowl replacing it made him think of a cornered animal.

"Mr. Stacy warned me about you, Mr. Johnson. That trick will not work. He is not interested in seeing you."

Hooper was stunned. He said, "Miss... I'm sorry I don't know your name."

"Barnes. Now if you don't mind, would you please go? You're not welcome in this office." She turned her attention to some papers on her desk.

"Miss Barnes, yesterday I received a message on my answering machine from Mr. Stacy. He informed me that I was chosen for the lead in *Accidental Angel*. He also instructed me to report to you for my acting lessons. If he has failed to tell you this, would you please ask him now?" He nodded toward the closed door behind her.

She looked up and responded sternly. "Mr. Johnson, that is the most absurd story I have ever heard. I'm surprised you would even attempt it, as I'm sure you're well aware that Mr. Stacy only selects his performers from his own students. I think it's time for you to leave."

Hooper was angry. "Just ask him."

"I can't do that. Mr. Stacy is not in today."

"Where is he?"

"None of your business. Now will you leave, or do I have to call building security?"

Hooper stared at her in the vain attempt that with his eyes he could force her to act. She did; she picked up the phone. When he heard her ask for security, he turned and left.

He stopped at a pay phone in the lobby and called the *Screen Actors Guild*. He asked for the address of the *Frank Stacy Acting School*. Ten minutes later he pulled into the parking lot of a converted wedding chapel two blocks from Stacy's office. Tacked on the door he found a notice reading: 'All Classes Canceled Until Further Notice.'

Not satisfied, he walked across the street to use another pay phone. He dialed Frank's home phone. Sara answered the phone. Not familiar with Hooper's name she checked her list of people authorized by Frank or Myra to call them at home. At first she did not see the name, but along the column of the page she read in Frank's jagged handwriting: 'Hooper Johnson - DO NOT accept any calls!'

"I'm sorry Mr. Johnson, but Mr. Stacy prefers that you do not call here. Please do not call again. Thank you." She hung up.

Hooper threw the receiver against the phone. As he turned away, he stamped his foot against the sidewalk. He punched the air with his fist as a futile gesture to the thought burning in his brain: Frank Stacy had purposely given him false hopes as some sort of sick revenge for attending, and then participating in the *Accidental Angel* auditions.

He jerked open the car door, but an indistinct thought nagging the back of his brain caused him to pause before getting in. In front of him, flapping in the wind like a semaphore was the paper notice tacked to the door of the former chapel. It caught his attention and forced the doubt to crystallize in his mind: "Why would Frank cancel all his classes?"

He already knew the impossibility of getting into the Stacy estate, so he went back to the phone. When Sara answered, he said, "Wait, don't hang up. Please just listen. If Frank should decide he does want to speak to me - I'll be at the *Vintner Inn* tonight. Tomorrow I'll be back in L.A.. Thank you.

She hung up.

#

As the closing credits for *The Tangled Web* scrolled up the screen, Eugene, sitting in the dark beside Myra, exclaimed when he saw her name, "Wow, that was you - you played Lydia. I didn't even recognize you. It's funny but the whole time I was watching I kept thinking that the real Lydia must have been playing herself because no one could have been so comfortable in the role as she. I don't know that I could ever imagine you playing another role."

Myra took his hand in hers and with her other hand stroked his arm. "Eugene, you don't know how happy it makes me to hear you say that, but I have done so much more. I want you to see it all: your work and mine. Shall we watch another?"

The morning passed into afternoon as they watched *Blackmarket Trader*, then *Furnace Of Hephaestus*.

"Can you sit through another?" Myra asked.

"Three is enough for one sitting, but tell me, are all of them like these?" He pulled his hand away from her.

"What do you mean?"

"I mean are the plots of all Stacy movies so shallow? Don't any have any more message to them than simply to stroke common emotions? Do they all depend so heavily on fast paced action? Don't get me wrong, they're quite entertaining, but it's all technique with no depth to the story line. In fact, I noticed some techniques I had thought of back home; it's reassuring to see there are some connections between Frank and me."

"Of course, Eugene you have to keep in mind that they're geared toward turning a profit, but can't you find anything artistic about them?

"Sure, the acting."

"You find the acting artistic?" She asked in surprise. She was thinking of Frank's opinion that acting was merely a trade.

"Sure, the characters are all perfectly developed, and the lines are delivered so convincingly that you forget you're watching a movie. Like an idea sculpted in flesh, only I regret seeing ideas that only prick the surface of the skin."

Hearing Eugene's words served as a refreshing contrast to Frank's rigidity.

Then he added, "Of course that goes back to the intensive training all the actors have been given."

All she could say was, "Oh."

"What I'm asking is hasn't he made any meaningful pictures, anything that's philosophical? Political? Something to make you angry instead of feeling good when you leave the theater. Something to make the world change." Eugene demanded as visions of Jack passed through his thoughts.

His questions exhilarated her interest. This was a human being talking - not an actor, a robot. He was asking the very questions she, herself, had always wondered about. Why hadn't Frank stretched himself beyond the popular genres? She recalled her first meeting with Frank; it had looked then like that would be his next direction. She remembered his words, "This picture will be an attempt to experiment deeper with my artistic credo." Unfortunately, it never really developed. Whenever she asked herself why, she always found herself thinking that it was something missing in his character - that essential essence she could never uncover. She started to mention *Resurgent Man,* but decided not to. She was afraid that if she mentioned the title, he would recall the accident which killed Jack and suppress again, perhaps forever, the human identity of Frank Stacy.

"Not even one?" he asked.

A connection she had never before made formed in her mind. "It's funny that that should be important to you, because what I said before about you being the primary part of Frank's identity will answer your question. You see, Frank is a kind of workaholic. Worse than George Gershwin ever was, who literally worked himself to an early death. Frank makes one movie after another without a break. His projects are sometimes lined up for years to come. It's as if he can't find satisfaction. Maybe that's the connection - he wants to make movies meaningful to Eugene, but since you haven't been around it could not be done. It even explains to me why he wouldn't pick up his *Oscars*."

"*Academy Awards*, really? More than one?" Eugene asked with astonishment.

"Two. Best Picture and Best Director," she answered while wondering if he heard what she had said about Frank.

"Really, where are they? I'd like to see them."

"They're in the study."

"I should have assumed as much from all that Hooper said." he said, as he rose from his chair. "Say, can we have Hooper over some time?"

"Sure. Whenever you like." She stood to follow him to the study. She could feel the change in his demeanor, and as for herself, she was more than a little emotionally drained. Since he was already changing the subject, she chose to follow his lead in winding things down.

"Do you have any more questions," she asked as she watched him fondle the *Oscars*, "or should we think about dinner?"

"No dinner for me." He yawned and stretched his arms. "I'm going to take a nap. All that whiskey Frank put into me last night is beginning to take its toll."

"Don't!" Myra screamed, grabbing his arm.

"Jesus!" he cried in alarm at her clutching. "What's wrong?"

"Eugene, I'm frightened; please, don't go to sleep. I'm afraid you won't come back."

He pondered the thought for a moment then answered, "Okay, then why don't we invite Hooper over for dinner?"

"So soon? Don't you want to wait a few days?"

"It's like you said, I may not have but tonight, and he's the only friend I have until I find Jack."

"Eugene, I'm your friend. I was hoping you would spend the evening alone with me. There are so many things I want us to talk about." To be as persuasive as possible she spoke in a voice suitable to a screen sex goddess, but even as the words passed her lips she knew it was the wrong approach.

"Myra, you belong to Frank; and I'm not Frank."

"But you are. Can't you see that I desperately want the chance to know you?" she begged.

"Myra, please forgive me, but I need time. Time to become reacquainted with my own identity. Don't you realize it's more than what I've done as Frank that I don't know - I've lost twenty years. It's like I've traveled twenty years into the future. History has been made that I'm unfamiliar with, and inventions. Until the other day I didn't even know how common and compact nuclear reactors had become, or--"

"What?" she interrupted. The emotional upheaval she was trying to suppress made it difficult to deal with the variety of things Eugene seemed able to express.

"You know, like the ones they put in ovens now."

"Eugene what are you talking about?" she held her voice low, but inside she was near hysteria.

"Come on, there's one in the kitchen here or don't you ever cook? Surely your car must be powered by one, if a tiny oven can be."

It dawned on her what he was speaking of and she relaxed. "Are you talking about the microwave oven?"

"I don't know what it's called. I just saw one in a diner and when I asked a guy how it worked he said it was 'nuked'."

Myra burst into laughter; a hard, cathartic laughter that released all the anxiety she'd been feeling. "Oh, Eugene you do have a lot to learn. Those ovens don't run on nuclear energy, but I couldn't tell you how they do work, and as far as I know nuclear reactors still take up an area equivalent to a city block."

"So you see?"

"Yes, Eugene I do, but I still want you to want me. It's something I've been trying to win for eleven years."

"Eleven years," he muttered shaking his head. "Myra, I know I'm supposed to be older than you, but to me I'm just out of high school, and you're as old as my teachers. I understand you want Frank to love you, but I can't even imagine being Frank although somehow I am. Gee, Myra, I'm embarrassed to admit it, but I don't even know about sex. My girlfriend back home probably would've taught me if I hadn't been so busy thinking about movies. That's another thing - I don't know what happened to her. I guess Jack married her."

"Your girlfriend?" Myra asked anxiously.

Eugene did not seem to notice the emotion in her voice and answered eagerly, "Yes, Stacie Rogers."

"Why would Jack marry your girlfriend?"

"Oh that's easy, but you'll probably think it's bad. Me and Jack were both in love with Stacie, but she couldn't choose between us. But that didn't bother us, since me and Jack are such good friends we were both going to marry her."

Images from the movie that got her into Frank's office slammed in front of her eyes, "But that's... that's from..." She couldn't force herself to say *Resurgent Man*.

"I told you, you wouldn't understand, most people can't."

"But was she in love with both of you?"

"Of course she was. The three of us used to go everywhere together. There were many warm spring days when we picnicked out in the fields of Jack's farm. Jack and me would stretch out on the blanket and watch the clouds, and while Jack talked, I would imagine the clouds were great gods fighting, and Stacie was always sitting between us running her fingers through our hair. We would take long walks in the woods because that was the only place we knew to go where the three of us could hold hands without being stared at. Jack was the only one of us who could drive, and he--"

"Only Jack had a car?" she asked thinking of Eugene's car wreck in Alabama.

"Well no, actually it was an old blue pick-up truck. Then later on both me and Stacie got cars, but until then Jack used to drive me to other towns so I wouldn't miss any new movies, and Stacie always came along. She couldn't bear to be away from us."

"But, you never slept with her?" she asked, although she really did not want to know the details.

"No, but on occasion she would sneak out and spend the night with Jack, but they never had sex, we were all saving ourselves for the day we married. But, she kissed wonderfully. Her lips felt so soft. And, I would imagine that when my tongue touched hers it would be like tasting the freshest sweetest drink in the world."

"She never spent the night with you?"

"She couldn't, because I lived at home."

"And Jack didn't?"

"Jack was an orphan; he lived all by himself on a farm he inherited."

Still incredulous at the similarity to *Resurgent Man*, but also jealous of another woman, she asked, "She didn't mind marrying both of you, even though it's... it's different?"

"No, Stacie loved me just as much as she loved Jack. We were the best of friends."

Something about the way he spoke made her question whether it was really true. It wasn't insistence; he was too calm, but something, she couldn't put her finger on it made her wonder, and her curiosity made her ask more questions. "Where do you think Stacie is now?"

"Well, she could be in Alaska, or out here somewhere."

"Alaska?" she asked, but thought, *Resurgent Man* again.

"Yeah that's where Jack wanted to live."

"Why would they be out here?"

"I'm hoping they're still waiting for me."

"After twenty years?"

"I keep forgetting it's so long, in my mind it was only a week since I last saw them."

"You don't think she's still in Georgia?" Myra asked carefully.

"I suppose she could be, that is, if Jack went back home. I'm glad you're so interested. I hope you understand the way I feel, and that you'll even help me find them."

"Sure," she offered reluctantly, then trying to imagine what this girl now a woman looked like, she asked, "Eugene, how old is Stacie?"

"She's two years older than me; same age as Jack."

Myra found that odd. Two years to someone her age made little difference, but for a teenager two years were like light-years. What nineteen year old girl would be seriously interested in a boy two years her junior, especially when she had another boyfriend her own age. Suddenly, she had a horrible thought: what if the three friends did not have the relationship Eugene said they did? What if it was just Jack and Stacie? Could Eugene have been so jealous of

Jack that he killed him? Maybe not murdered him outright, but purposely caused the accident which killed him. It was too dreadful to think about, but as Frank's past was becoming uncovered, she had to know.

"Frank... uh, I mean Eugene, why don't you go on and call Hooper. I need to be alone for a few minutes." She waited until he was out of the room before she started crying.

She locked the study door before pulling the telephone directory out of Frank's desk. After a few minutes of deliberation, she decided she could not tell one detective agency from the next, and chose the one with the largest ad. Her instructions to the man were simple. Find Stacie Rogers. Last known address: somewhere around Ellaville, Georgia, twenty years ago. No, she would not give him her name, this case has to be absolutely confidential, and to insure it, she would pay him cash in advance.

Eugene, meanwhile, found Sara and asked where he kept his personal directory. When he did not see a listing for Hooper he asked her, "Do I have any other directories - I don't see Hooper's number in this one."

"Well, I'll be," she muttered to herself, then louder she answered Eugene, "He called earlier. He's staying at the Vintner - I'll look up the number."

When Hooper picked up the phone Eugene said, "Hey, Hooper it's Eugene. Why don't you come over to my house for dinner tonight?"

"Holy shit!" Hooper gasped. "That sure explains everything."

CHAPTER THIRTEEN

Sara admitted Hooper to the house without words. As she was walking him through the hallway to the living room, Myra intercepted them in front of the study.

"Please step inside Mr. Johnson, I would like to have a word with you in private."

"Good evening, Miss Mason," he answered as he entered the room.

Without greeting him, she turned to Sara and said, "Thank you, Sara. That will be all for now."

After closing the door she turned and faced Hooper, "Mr. Johnson, I will be brief. I do not want Eugene to have a relapse. In his current state of mind, he is receptive toward discovering who he has become, and considering Frank's attitude, I would like to preserve that. Therefore I am asking you not to bring up *Resurgent Man*."

He could not understand her curt and formal behavior toward him, but he noticed her composure was much better, although more controlled, than the last time he had seen her. His composure was also well controlled despite the fact he was standing face-to-face with Myra Mason in her home, but this he attributed to his excitement in learning Eugene was back. He answered, "I don't see why not. If he sees the picture, it may help him to remember."

"And it may result in his recalling that he caused Jack's death, and it's too soon to risk it."

"Then you should make haste in getting him to a shrink."

"No psychiatrists!" she yelled angrily.

"But I thought--"

"You thought! I'll show you what your thinking got me." She walked briskly to the other side of the room, and stopped at a small cherrywood bar. "Come over here."

She picked up a towel then poured the clear contents from a crystal decanter on to it. Putting the wet towel to her face she dragged it across her left cheek with a grimace. As Hooper watched the swift movement of her delicate hand, he saw the layers of make-up disappear from her face to expose four parallel bruises. "This is what I got for trying to get Frank to a psychiatrist."

He could not help but smile at her sense for the dramatic. Seeing his grin Myra demanded, "What do you find so amusing?"

"Not this," he answered soberly while gently touching her jaw with his fingers. "This is only what you think you got; actually what you got was Eugene."

"I guess you're right," she said softly and smiled. The warmth she felt from his fingertips was reassuring. She looked longingly at his strong shoulder, and considered leaning against it, but she suddenly remembered that Eugene preferred this man's company to her own, and she stepped back quickly, leaving his hand stretched stupidly in the air.

Her shoulders bent forward offensively, her eyes narrowed, and she barked, "One other thing, mister. Why didn't you tell me the other day that you auditioned for *Accidental Angel*? You told me you were waiting to see me."

"I was."

"Then why did you crash his audition?"

"Auditions are open to all."

"By law, yes, but you know he only chooses his students. What were you trying to do; make him angry? That's no way to help him."

"Actually, considering the script, I couldn't resist."

"I trust you're now satisfied that it was a waste of time."

"Oh, but it wasn't. I achieved something even you couldn't without first being his student. Frank Stacy gave me the lead."

"I don't believe it!" she snapped.

Despite her words, Hooper could see that she was stunned. He said, “Unfortunately for me, I'm afraid no one will believe it until Eugene recovers Frank's memory. Apparently he became Eugene again before he could tell anyone else."

"What do you mean?"

"He called while I was out yesterday. On my answering machine he offered me the part and instructed me to call his secretary for details, but when I spoke to her she didn't know anything about it."

"He was with Zack yesterday. I want to hear that message; I can verify if it was his voice."

"Too late, I never dreamed I would need it for evidence, I reset the answering machine, and another caller has since recorded over it."

"No proof, huh?"

"Are you calling me a liar?"

"No, but I forbid you to discuss this with Eugene."

"I'll do what I think best. I don't intend on sacrificing a career opportunity like this."

"I wish I could throw you out of here!"

"Look, I'm not going to jeopardize your husband's sanity."

"Make sure you don't, and I'll get you all the parts you can handle in a year."

"I'm not interested in your help. I've never asked anyone's help; I'll make it in this industry by my own ability or not at all."

She was surprised by his statement, and found herself looking at him a little closer. "Hmm, I'm surprised it's Eugene you like and not Frank." Then she walked to the door and said, "I'm going upstairs to put my face back on. You'll find Eugene down the hall."

#

Eugene was sitting on the sofa with his attention intent upon the television when Hooper entered the room.

"Hey buddy, how's it going?"

"Hooper!" he cried jumping up. Then with his hand outstretched he rushed over to meet him in the middle of the room. "Boy, it's good to see you again. How about a drink? I got Sara to send out for some *Jack Daniel's* for you. You know television sure has changed. I've been observing how they're-- Hey, I forgot to ask you, have you shot *Runaway Grandparents* yet?"

"Slow down, Eugene, we've got all night," he said, but in his mind he was thinking he ought to make it a short evening. Eugene made Frank's forty year old body seem just like a kid's, and in response he found himself reacting like a big brother. He had a feeling that his presence might serve only to distract Eugene from ever remembering the past twenty years.

During the afternoon Eugene had become obsessed with watching TV, and much to Hooper's chagrin did not turn it off when he arrived. Later, as the evening progressed to dinner Eugene asked that the television follow them. Both Myra and Hooper complained, but he insisted that it served as an instant history lesson and also prompted questions he needed to ask.

Hooper was amazed that Eugene was able to divide his attention between him and the various shows being aired, and still talk constantly. However, he took no surprise when Eugene commented that the censors had certainly relaxed in regard to sex and language, nor was he impressed with Eugene's observation that TV story lines had advanced beyond the single plot structure, but were still stupid compared to the theater - such an observation one would expect from the seed of Frank Stacy. What did shock him, though, as he, with a little help from Myra, brought him up to date on famous facts, was Eugene's lack of awe with the 1969 landing on the moon. "Aw, come on, Hooper, the way they were shooting rockets in the air one of them had to hit the moon sooner or later."

Regardless of his insight, Eugene's maturity was still that of a teenager. Both Myra and Hooper turned red with embarrassment while Sara was clearing the dinner dishes. Eugene looked up at her as she picked up his plate and asked, "Sara, is *Hazel*, the maid, your favorite TV show?" Sara just ignored him, but when she served dessert, Eugene's portion was significantly smaller than the others.

After dinner Eugene was flipping the pages of *TV Guide* when he said, "Hooper, here's the perfect indictment of television's progress: *Star Trek, Perry Mason, Leave it to Beaver, Andy Griffith Show, Bewitched, The Addams Family, Beverly Hillbillies, The Honeymooners, Twilight Zone.*"

"I don't follow you."

"These programs are twenty years out of production and they're competing successfully against current programs running in prime time."

"That's because TV hit its absolute low during the 1970's, so don't feel like you've missed all that much. But it won't stay that way much longer. The competition from the cable and video markets is forcing regular TV to get better. It won't be too long before the airwaves are completely deregulated."

"Cable and video markets?"

Hooper sighed. He was beginning to weary of having to explain things to Eugene he should already know. Twenty years of knowledge was locked away, somewhere, in his head. As he went on to describe cable and video he began to wonder why Myra was so pensive. He'd been helplessly aware of it all evening as he tried to get her to participate more in the evening's history lesson. Finally giving up, he concluded it must be her fear of not knowing which direction Eugene/Frank would go next.

However, giving up wasn't enough; he found that whenever Myra didn't approve of the direction the conversation was going, she would change the subject. When Eugene asked Hooper if he'd gotten any new parts, he glanced at Myra and saw her eyes narrow in warning. So he lied, and answered in the negative. Her tension was contagious and Hooper wished that she'd just go to bed so he could relax, but she was staked out and prepared to wait until Hooper left first. Between her protectiveness and Eugene's childishness, he was beginning to feel she was the mother, not the wife. The awkwardness of the situation increased his anxiety to the point that the second he saw Eugene yawn, he jumped up and suggested it was time for him to go, but when Eugene insisted he sleep over, he resigned himself to the inevitable. As he walked upstairs, he added a silent footnote to his agreement of staying over: to leave before the others got up in the morning. He simply wasn't prepared to face Frank in his own house should it be him to awaken instead of Eugene.

Inside the guest bedroom, he undressed and went into the bathroom to wash up. When he came out, the door to the hall was open and Myra was leaning against the frame. The look on her face told him that this visit was not a social call. If he could have interpreted it, he would have read a mixture of hate, and pleading in her eyes, but her late night invasion of his privacy occluded his perception and only served to synthesize his anger.

Forgetting his nakedness, and his attraction toward the woman in front of him, he threw the towel he was drying his face on to the floor and strode with restrained fury across the room to confront her. Mad at her chaperone-like behavior all evening, but also mad at himself for not knowing how to deal with Eugene, he was unable to keep the edge of irritation out of his voice as he jabbed his finger and said, "Miss Mason, you've been putting distance between Eugene and me all night as if I were a virus you had to protect him from. Just what the hell is it that you find threatening about me?"

"You are a threat, Mr. Johnson. He's gone to bed now, and not to our room. He refuses to sleep with me. All goddamn day he's been distant. I'll grant that he doesn't know me, but every gesture I've made to get acquainted he's rejected. All he could talk about was you. How you're his only friend!"

Hooper could see the tears forming in her eyes.

She added quietly, "Now that he's gone to sleep, I'm afraid he'll wake up as Frank; and at the same time, I'm afraid that he won't."

"I'm sorry," he said, putting his hand on her shoulder.

She pressed her head against his chest and his arms moved to embrace her.

She sobbed, "Hooper, I'm afraid. I know I'm guilty of rushing things, but I've been waiting eleven years to get through to Frank."

"We both have to be patient, but not to the extent of doing nothing. We must take action."

"But what?"

He placed his hand around the back of her head, and pulled it back to force her to face him. "You know what. We have to get him to see a psychiatrist."

"But what if he refuses... like Frank did?"

"Then we had better show him *Resurgent Man*."

"But... but what if that causes Frank to come back?"

"Even if it does, Eugene will return again later, and again and again as long as we keep confronting Frank with his existence. If Zack can cause Eugene to come out, you can too. It's too late for

Frank to turn back to the last twenty years. The stone that will cause the avalanche has already been pushed over the edge."

Her arms tightened about him. It was not a kiss he felt that caused signals of pleasure to dart up and down the inside of his thighs, but the gentle pressure of her lips as she leaned for support against his shoulders. "Hooper, I'm glad you're here. I'm going to need you through all this."

As he looked down at the talented and beautiful actress he had admired for years, he realized he did want her to need him, but not like this. To win her in a time of vulnerability would not reward him the prize he wanted. Frank and Eugene must be brought together, so that he could compete not just fairly, but completely for the woman in his arms. Uniting the severed mind of the world's greatest movie maker would be but the first goal he would have to score in a lengthy game. It was from this revelation, from this conceptualization of desire and its direction, that the sensations in his thighs penetrated his groin and awakened him to his nakedness.

"Oh, my God!" he cried, pushing Myra back and looking down at himself.

As he ran into the bathroom Myra laughed and said, "Oh, Hooper, I didn't notice either."

"Well, you certainly know how to flatter a guy," he called out from behind the bathroom door.

"Oh, don't take it personally; after hookers and nurses, no one has to look at more naked men than actresses."

"Myra."

"Yes?"

"Go to bed!"

"Good night, Hooper."

CHAPTER FOURTEEN

In the morning Sara greeted Myra's waking by presenting her with two notes. One from Hooper explaining he left at dawn because he did not think it wise for him to be there if Eugene should wake as Frank. The other was from Eugene, informing her he had gone to Frank's office. On finishing the note from Eugene, she looked at the clock; it was nearly a quarter after ten.

"Sara, do you know when he left?"

"About eight, ma'am."

"Oh no, poor Connie!" she cried; recalling that Frank's secretary knew nothing of Frank's condition. "Why didn't you tell me?"

"I thought he was being Mr. Stacy again, ma'am. He sure looked it in his suit and leaving at the usual time and all. I didn't see the note until a few minutes ago when I went in to clean."

"Oh well, no chance to warn her now. I guess I'd better call and see how she's making out."

#

When Eugene entered the office vestibule Constance leaped to her feet and said, "Oh Frank, I was so worried when you didn't come in yesterday. Sara called, but she wouldn't tell me anything; I was afraid you'd gotten hurt while you were skiing with Zack."

She couldn't understand why he just stood there and stared without answering. Finally, he said, "What is your name?"

"What?"

"Are you my secretary?"

"Frank!" she cried in bewilderment.

"My name is Eugene Eastly, although I understand most people around here know me as Frank Stacy. The fact is I have no memory of being Mr. Stacy. If you're his secretary, I'm going to need your help."

Now Constance was the one staring. She recognized the name. It was the name he used on his publicity stunt. The same name he instructed her to have the author of *Accidental Angel* use for the main character, but why was he using it now. Sure, she had seen him acting before, and always convincingly, but never had she seen him mix a role into his business life.

She opened her mouth to speak when suddenly she remembered the words from that letter she had found; the one from that Hooper Johnson who'd been annoying Frank: 'once Eugene realized that he was also Frank Stacy, he concluded that smashing his car into that tree in Alabama caused his amnesia.' That letter she realized had to have been written before Frank asked her to have the changes made to *Accidental Angel*.

"You seem stunned, surely you knew?"

She shook her head, then muttered, "I don't think I can handle this."

Her head was bowed now, but he could see the glisten of water filling her eyes.

"You are Frank Stacy's secretary?" he asked again.

She nodded.

"Then I need you. I need your help."

His plea seemed to lessen the gloom she was feeling. It came only as a glimmer of hope, but perhaps this would be the way to get the man she had secretly loved for years. After all, she thought, he was asking for her help, not Myra's.

"My name is Constance; you usually call me Connie."

"Thank you, Connie. I guess we should start with you going over my normal routine."

"You don't really have a normal routine, except your acting classes which you teach every Monday, Wednesday, and Friday unless you're out of town on location. Your--"

"You'd better cancel those classes until further notice. I'm afraid I don't know the first thing about acting."

Connie gasped. She would have been less surprised to hear the Pope confessing he knew nothing about Christianity. "But, Frank, how can you--"

"It's not Frank; it's Eugene. I can because I have to; I don't know what Frank knew. You've got to remember that."

"I'll try, but it won't be easy. Eugene, please don't take offense, but don't you think it would be wise for you to go by the name most people know you by?"

"I'm not trying to hide anything."

"I can understand that you want to be honest, but if word gets around about your not remembering anything, it could be disastrous."

"I don't see your point."

"If people hear that you think you're someone else, they'll think you're crazy--"

"Is that what you think?" he demanded.

There was only a hint of anger in his voice, but she knew her answer was crucial to the future of their relationship. She paused to carefully pick her words. "I'll admit that I don't understand what you're going through; however in the past seventeen years, I've been through a lot with you and am willing to go through a lot more."

Eugene said nothing, so she continued.

"I'm thinking of those tough early years when you were unproven as a solo director and investors wouldn't even give us an interview. We budgeted your first films on a shoestring; a tattered and knotted shoestring at that. I followed you when you left R.S.P. despite everyone who told me it was a losing gamble; I knew it wasn't. During that first film I hung right in when everyone else was ready to give up. There was the point when both of us racked up our credit cards to the limit to get just one more day's production costs."

"Those were the days that made you what you are: the best. You had to dig deep and draw on every bit of ingenuity you could muster simply to survive. Since you couldn't afford but a single take for each scene, you rehearsed your performers until they were ready to pass out. Since you couldn't get well known performers to work under such conditions, you had to hire inexperienced ones. Although you saved money by taking those inexperienced non-union performers, you still had to work harder because you had to train them perfectly so there would be no mistakes when you were finally ready to run those precious feet of film through your camera.

There's one weekend in particular I'll never forget; it was the one when you walked every square foot of a park you'd selected for a location shot. You never uttered a word except to thank me when I brought you coffee and doughnuts, and for 48 hours I stayed awake with you while you struggled until you knew exactly where the action would take place and the how cameras had to be placed to capture it."

"Now I'm thinking, if it gets spread around that you're crazy, then investors are going to become shy again. If that happens, you'll be ruined. We won't be able to do what we did before because production costs are enormously higher than when we started."

Eugene paused before answering.

Connie could see from his face that he was carefully weighing the consequences in his mind. How much he actually understood, if what he told her earlier was true, she could not tell.

His hesitation ended with a smile, but it was a smile of submission - of compromise. "I'm beginning to see your point. Call me Frank."

"Thank you, Frank."

He walked across the office as if taking it in at a glance, then walked back toward her desk. She thought she noticed a slight swagger to his gait, as he asked her, "Now where were we?"

His behavior was curious; in a small way it made her think of a young heir to a great business coming in to take over without having a bit of knowledge as to its function, but arrogantly attending to it as if he were born to know how. In the back of her mind she was torn between hoping it was merely an act that required her to humor him for a while, yet at the same time praying it was an opportunity to take him from Myra.

"You were asking me to cancel your classes," she told him, "however, I've already taken care of that since you were missing yesterday."

"Good. I'm almost afraid to ask, but am I in the middle of a production schedule right now?"

"Surprisingly no, since usually you tend to overlap schedules from one production to the next. You just finished negotiating the distribution rights for *Moon Colony* last week. You were brilliant; no one has ever seen you close a contract so fast and concede so little. Then that same afternoon you began preparation on the production schedule for-- Oh!" she gasped in sudden understanding.

"What?"

"It's true!"

"What's true?"

"That you really don't remember."

"I told you--" his voice rose angrily, but she cut him off.

"Wait, don't get mad. Please realize this transformation of yours is a little difficult for me to grasp, but I see now. When you decided to produce *Accidental Angel* instead of *Highway Robbery*, it didn't make sense to me, but it does now. You rejected *Accidental Angel* two years ago; you said the plot was too sluggish to interest your regular investors, and you wouldn't take the responsibility for speculators who would lose money by investing strictly on the strength of your name."

"So what made me change my mind?"

"*Accidental Angel* is about a criminal who gets amnesia then because he can't remember his past he is able to become a good person. When Frank told me to pick up our option on ANGEL, he told me to have the author change the name of the criminal to Eugene Eastly."

"No!" Eugene screamed.

"Wait," Connie cried, "you don't understand. Frank did it for the same reason I told you that you should go by the name of Frank and not Eugene - so no one will think you're crazy. Frank told everybody that his three days of amnesia was a publicity stunt for ANGEL. He picked up a movie he did not believe in, to cover up the truth, and you have got to go along with it for one reason. To save your reputation."

"But that means going forward with this *Accidental Angel* picture!"

"That's right."

"But I can't!"

"Don't you understand what I just told you? You have to."

"Connie, there's nothing I'd rather do than direct a movie... it's... it's just that I don't know enough to fake it."

"Don't worry about that; your assistants know what you want. You can lean on them, and of course I'll be right there beside you."

"Are you sure that'll work?"

"Of course it will," she said warmly as she tenderly placed her hand on his shoulder.

"I suppose we can give it a try, but what if I never regain my memory? I'm still going have to learn how to direct, and who can we ask to teach Frank Stacy?"

"Don't worry about that now."

"I'm sorry, but I have to; besides, I have a different idea. What I'd rather do is hire the greatest director I know of, that is, if he's still alive. You've probably never heard of him; no one else I've asked has, but he's the man I wanted to study under before I had the accident. His name is Smurling."

Connie gasped, and said, "Ralph?"

"You know him?" Eugene asked excitedly.

Connie just stared at him.

Eugene couldn't fathom the blank look in her eyes. "Well?" he demanded.

She turned her eyes back to him, and said, "Sorry, that was just one shock too many for one day. Frank," she said steadily, "you and I met while working at *Ralph Smurling Productions*."

"You mean I've already worked for Smurling," he mused.

Connie watched his face, and from the strained lines at the corners of his eyes, she could tell he was trying desperately to dredge up memories that ought to be there.

He shook his head as if giving up, and said, "Since he already knows me, Mr. Smurling should be perfect. Is he still alive?"

"Yes, he's still alive." Her voice was soft, almost a whisper.

"That's great! Why don't you call him right now and make us an appointment?"

"Frank," she cried, "you know I can't!"

"What!" he cried back.

"Oh God, Frank, I don't know how much more of this I can handle."

"Handle what?" he cried again.

With her face turned down to hide the tears, she shook her head slowly back and forth. "I'm sorry Frank, I keep forgetting. I know you're depending on me to tell you everything, but what we did to Ralph Smurling was one of those things a person would rather not think about."

"What did I do?"

"You ruined him."

"Ruined him! How?"

"Frank, it wasn't intentional on your part, but the results were the same. I've more reason to feel guilty than you do. You see, Frank, Ralph asked you to direct a war movie he was producing. It was considered a great script; it was about a combat squadron of sharpshooters who by themselves killed an entire regiment of Japanese during World War II, but you turned it down. Which, by the way, stunned the hell out of everyone because you were the whiz kid who couldn't get enough. Ralph then insisted you do it, because his investors were backing him only so long as you directed. Again you refused, and all you would say was that you would not make war movies. Then Ralph got angry and told you to make the movie or get out. You shook your head, and walked out; and following right behind you went half of Smurling's staff. Oh, we thought you were being so noble for holding to your principles, although none of us really understood them until about year or two later when the anti-Viet Nam War movement became mainstream."

"Ralph's investors, of course pulled out, but at the same time they put out the word that you were a bad risk. It was one of the reasons we had such a hard time in the beginning. It was also what caused most of the people who followed you from R.S.P. to leave shortly thereafter. You couldn't afford to pay them like Ralph had. Of those who followed, I'm the only one left."

"And Smurling?"

"Ralph never made another movie, apparently he gambled everything he had on the pre-production costs of that picture. It forced him to retire."

"Oh no," he said sadly. He dropped into the chair beside her desk. His shoulders slumped in grief, and he asked, "What is he living on?"

"His wife is an heir of a shipping company and they live off of her trust fund. He still lives comfortably."

Eugene stared vacantly at Connie as he sorted the new information in his mind. Connie held his eyes silently. After a few minutes, he rose and began exploring the austerely decorated rooms designed not as a showplace but a working office. His own workspace, while behind closed doors was but a crude metal desk topped with an old black telephone and an ancient intercom. Cracked and peeling gray paint coated several dented filing cabinets along the wall behind the desk. The chair behind the desk, a model of efficiency designed to keep its occupant comfortable for long periods, stood in sharp contrast to the two torn and lumpy upholstered chairs on the opposite side. The message was obvious: no one was expected to get too comfortable while Frank was working. Against the far wall was a tattered couch that must have been purchased from the same thrift shop as the upholstered chairs. Eugene guessed it opened into a sleeper when he noticed the corner of a bed sheet hanging underneath. An open door beside the couch revealed a bathroom.

The hallway running from his office door to the cutting room was a maze of clutter. He had to squeeze by stacks of dusty spools, film cans, and boxes. After negotiating his way through, he pulled open the tightly sealed door and was surprised to see the walls and floor were as white and clean as a hospital operating room. There were no windows and one wall was lined with shelves stacked heavily with film cans. The table he saw against the wall was the finest German engineered editing machine money could buy. There were three screens for multiple viewing, and on an engraved panel he read that it offered the capacity of four sound heads, although he was not sure what that meant he guessed correctly that it referred to the number of sound tracks that could be run at the same time. The only chair in the room was the twin to the one in his office. Next to the editing machine was a heavy vinyl box on wheels which took him several minutes to figure out how to open. Finally after pressing a recessed button the lid rose up with a soft hiss, and he saw several strips of film suspended inside. He reached out to pick up the strip nearest him when something in the back of his mind keyed a memory he did not know he had and caused his hand to freeze. It told him not to touch the celluloid, itself, only the protective leader tagged to the head of the strip. Gently, he lifted the film by the yellow-white leader on which was written: *MOON COLONY*, 3:14, Alien close-up. The frames reminded him of something from the TV show *Star Trek*. He replaced the strip. When he turned back to the door, he saw another table with several spools on either end and two rectangular holes cut into the surface on either side of a machine that reminded him of the belt grinder his father kept in their basement. Hanging from the rectangular holes were white bags that looked like laundry hampers. It took him several minutes before he figured out that it was a soundtrack synchronizing table. He remembered having read about them from the books Jack brought him. He wistfully wished he knew how to work it, but none of Frank's useful memories were forthcoming.

From the cutting room he returned to the reception area, and saw a door across from the Connie's desk that he had not noticed before. Opening it, he was shocked to see a long dark mahogany table, with thickly padded, high back, leather swivel chairs surrounded by walls garishly covered with movie posters and awards. Compared with the streamlined integrity of the rest of the office this room seemed fatuous and out of place. Turning toward Connie he asked, "What's this?"

"That's where we skin the suckers," Connie giggled.

"Do what?"

"It's the Conference Room. In your own words Frank: All this circus crap is simply to keep the investors impressed until they've signed the check."

Eugene laughed. Then after a moment's pause said, "Connie, I've made a decision, I'm going to call Smurling anyway. I didn't have anything to do with his downfall; and from the way you tell it, neither did Frank, but first I'd like you to get me the script for *Accidental Angel*, then show me where I keep my files on it."

During his tour of the office Connie had quietly hoped Frank's personality would re-emerge, but at the same time she recalled how irritable he had become. Frank had been frightened, and his short temper and harsh words were the outward reflection of that fear. Eugene, however, was not afraid; even though he did not have Frank's knowledge, he was pressing forward to save Frank's career. She could not help admire the courage he was demonstrating.

After he finished reading the script, Eugene picked up the file Connie had placed on his desk. The first page contained Frank's casting notes, and Eugene was hurt to learn his friend Hooper had not mentioned the great news that Frank had selected him for the lead. It was surely his first leading role; his first big break. He took no surprise when he read Myra's name as the female lead. From the movies he'd watched so far, she was always Frank's leading lady. However, he was curious why *Accidental Angel* did not dominate the previous evening's conversation, why it had not even been mentioned. Thinking about it, he concluded they must have assumed it would not be produced until Eugene once again became Frank. Eugene, however, had no intentions of going back to sleep for another twenty years, he punched a button on the intercom.

The intercom did not respond, so he tried another button; again he failed. After a few more tries he gave up and walked into the reception area. Connie was on the phone.

"Connie," he interrupted, "when you finish with that call, I want you to call my house and get Hooper Johnson on the phone."

Connie gasped and covered the mouthpiece. "Hooper Johnson is at your house? But I thought you didn't want to have anything to do with him."

"That doesn't make sense Connie. Why would I have given him the lead in *Accidental Angel*?"

Again she gasped. "Then it's true. Oh no! Yesterday, I threw him out of here. Frank, you never told me."

He looked at her curiously, not understanding why Frank would not like Hooper, but all that was history as far as he was concerned, so he said, "Now you know. Let me know when you have him on the phone."

"I have your wife on the phone now. I'll ask her to put Mr. Johnson on."

A moment later she turned back to tell him Hooper had already left.

Eugene then said he would like to speak with Myra, and asked Connie to transfer the call to his office.

When he picked the phone up, Myra said, "Eugene, why didn't you wake me and let me know where you were going?"

"Because I didn't imagine you'd approve. And, I need to figure out who I am on my own."

"I'm sorry if I made you feel that way. I promise I'll give you all the space you need."

"Myra as long as you're on the phone I might as well tell you now that I'm going to go ahead and produce *Accidental Angel*."

"But, how?" she asked. It was obvious from her voice that she was startled.

"Myra I wasn't ignorant when I left Georgia," he answered tensely. "However, I'm planning on getting some help. And, if what I've heard about Frank's teaching method is true, then I shouldn't need to do all that much directing anyway."

"*Resurgent Man* again," she mumbled, thinking of how little directing he did during its filming.

"What?" he asked.

Realizing her blunder, she quickly said, "Oh, nothing, but what about Hooper, you've never trained him?"

"I believe in Hooper, and apparently Frank did, too. If he needs any help, you'll be there to coach him."

"I'll be there? What makes you think I'll be there?"

"Haven't you read the script? Your role is the wife of the lead."

"My role?" She asked incredulously, then as if the answer popped into her head, she asked, "Eugene did you choose me for that part?"

"No, Frank did."

"I can't believe it; Frank hasn't used me in years."

"What are you talking about? What about all those films we watched?"

"Never mind, Eugene. When do rehearsals begin?"

"I don't know yet. Connie will let you know as soon as we've figured it all out."

After hanging up, he impotently punched the intercom buttons again. Giving up, he went back out to the reception area and said, "Connie bring me Smurling's number, and then show me how this damn intercom works."

A few minutes later he was dialing.

"Hello, Mr. Smurling, my name is Eugene Eastly, and I would like to talk to you about directing a motion picture for me. ... Yes, sir, I realize you're retired, but you see I love your movies, especially *The Unyielding* and *Gods Of Autumn*, in fact I even used a similar title for a screenplay I wrote. ... No, sir, that's not the one I have in mind. ... The reason sir, I'm asking you is because I had hoped once to become your student. ... Oh, about twenty years ago, but, I was in this car accident which prevented me from meeting you. ... No, I wasn't paralyzed or anything like that, but the thing is sir, you've already met me, only I don't recall it. It's like this, Mr. Smurling, you know me as Frank Stacy."

Hearing only Ralph's steady breathing on the other end of the phone, Eugene waited patiently for a response.

Smurling compiled in his mind all the images he had of Frank Stacy. The day they met, and the hesitation Frank had before giving his last name. The next picture he visualized was seeing Frank as the young dynamo on the sound stage, controlling precisely though rigidly every task he was assigned. Then the day he introduced him to Zack, and the sudden way in which his whole body seemed to relax. Later there were the days of spontaneous irresponsibility whenever Zack showed up that angered him to no end. He chuckled softly at his idea that Zack would ever grow up. He had given up on Zack, but had made Frank his partner. Then he recalled the day Frank left him. He'd never seen Frank get so stiff and act so irrationally. In hindsight, now that the anger of that day was long forgotten, he realized he should have discussed the script with Frank first. Who would have thought a war story, any story for that matter, would have mattered to the boy who wanted to do nothing but make movies, any movie. He'd heard about Frank's three days of amnesia, and of course the follow-up story explaining it as a publicity stunt. At the time he figured Frank must finally be getting bored of making movies, if it took stunts to keep him amused. Now this phone call.

"What did you say your name was?"

"It's Eugene Eastly, sir, but I'm continuing to use Frank's name professionally. I imagine you can understand why."

"Eugene, I'll help you make your picture."

"You sure you don't mind?"

"No, in fact I'm flattered, and I don't mind telling you I miss the excitement of a busy production schedule."

"I’m sorry Frank destroyed your career, sir."

"Think nothing of it, Eugene. I'm responsible for the destruction of my career."

"Thank you, sir, and please if you will, call me Frank from now on."

"Certainly, Frank, and Frank..."

"Yes, sir?"

"Call me Ralph."

"Ralph, one last thing, have you forgiven Constance?"

He hesitated, then said, "Yes."

"Good, then I'll have her get back in touch with you regarding the details."

#

Myra hung up the phone, and turned to Sara who was making the bed.

"Sara, he's going to try and make a movie. I've got to stop him; he doesn't know anything about making movies."

Sara turned from her work and raised an eyebrow in disbelief, but Myra didn't notice.

Myra continued, "But I couldn't say anything over the phone. I'm so afraid, of putting pressure on him, of causing him to become Frank again. He'll make a fool of himself; I just don't know what to do."

Sara's face was bitter. Wrinkles radiated from her pursed lips to display her disapproval; she couldn't understand why Myra had stayed with Frank as long as she had, especially as common as Hollywood divorces were. To her, Frank had always been strange, and worse: unloving. She looked as if she were ready to spit when she said, "If you're asking me, I'd have him committed. He's crazier than a Pentecostal talking in tongues. In the nuthouse - that's where he belongs."

Myra's face brightened. "No Sara; locking him up is not the answer. Frank could act his way out of a situation like that. I wouldn't even try; hell, Frank could turn it around so fast I'd likely be the one to end up getting locked away. No, that's not the answer, but it is time for me to get some professional help. I should have done it long ago."

#

The heavy oak door in the quiet carpeted hall of the medical building bore a small brass sign which read: Dr. Samuel Garcia, Psychiatrist.

Sammy Garcia and Myra Mason were childhood friends. Their parents sent them Monday through Friday to the same private school; a choice their wealth and position dictated. On Sunday they saw each other in the Episcopal Church built uptown by tithes that had the quality of dues. Every summer they went boating, played tennis, rode horses, and took golf lessons from the country club pro. They grew up precisely as privileged children were expected to. Sammy never dated Myra, although at one point she had expressed interest. Sammy said their type of friendship lent itself only to platonic love; she thought that meant he was gay, but her timing coincided with his declaring his major in college as Philosophy, and at that moment he was caught up in the pretension of becoming a neo-modern ascetic. Nevertheless, he remained intelligent and witty, and that was enough for her. Later on, he shifted out of his asexual phase and made some noises about dating her, but by then she had become interested in someone else, so they remained buddies. Then as the years passed, differing professions and ideas more than distance separated them, and their current relationship was summed up by a Christmas card greeting once a year. Like the links of a chain sweeping backward year after year, those cards were all that was left to connect their past to the present.

She pushed open the door to his office hoping that he was smart enough to answer her troubling questions. Of one thing she was certain, that he would be discreet enough to keep them confidential.

After whispering her name, Dr. Garcia's receptionist walked Myra quickly and silently across lush carpet, by magazine-laden Victorian furniture, and past fur-collared dowagers through a door into Sammy's private office. After a few minutes of dry kisses, long-lost-friend hugs, and Sammy's effusive gushing about his oldest friend becoming famous, Myra interrupted and said, "Sammy, save the cocktail party talk for later, right now I need help."

Sammy gave her a hurt look, but rebounded by saying, "My apologies, dear. Will this be a couch session, or shall we just chat across the desk?"

"Across the desk will be fine. I'm not crazy yet, but if I don't get some professional answers to my husband's behavior, I will be."

"Then there is something to those *National Enquirer* stories after all?" He chuckled as he took his chair behind the desk.

Myra smiled as she sat across from him. "Those stories are the cover-up, but what I'd like to do is start at the beginning, and give you what I've observed over the years."

As she thought about where to begin, she noticed a tray of cigarettes on his desk, and picked one up. "I'm not really a smoker, but boy, could I use one of these right now."

Sammy passed her a lighter, and she lit the cigarette. Then while she spoke, she tapped it nervously against the ashtray in a rhythm of anxiety. It was difficult to explain behavior she herself did not understand, behavior others never saw, and what she felt at times must be her imagination. Slowly and carefully she depicted Frank, the man with interchangeable roles. Roles that never overlapped even though each was closely related.

"Can you see what I'm trying to show you - that it's the way he separates each area of his life so completely?"

"Myra, are you suggesting multiple personalities?"

"No, it's not like *The Three Faces Of Eve*, he's still the same person, although it does seem as if it's only his body that's carried over from one role to the next. Do you know anything about Zen masters?"

He nodded.

"I don't know much, but from what I've heard it's part of their discipline to completely immerse themselves into a single concept. Frank is like that. When he's directing, he has absolutely no thoughts of production, you know like the business end of film making. For instance, there was one time when some investors showed up on the set and in between takes, wanted to discuss distribution, and I swear he looked at them like he'd never seen them before. They never saw it, but I noticed a slight shudder in his body. Immediately afterwards his eyes sparkled with recognition, and he asked them to repeat the question."

"It sounds to me like he just concentrates very well, and those men broke his concentration causing him to be momentarily disoriented."

"Yes, it's like that but more so. You see, he's always like that. It's like he's maybe on the verge of having multiple personalities."

Sammy's years of experience worked as a barometer gauged to detect false alarms. Over the years he'd dealt with all types of hypochondriacs, and what his profession called *psych-you-chondriacs*, a person bent on labeling themselves, their friends and their families with mental problems that simply were not there. For these special cases he liked to use what he called *verbal shock therapy*. Uncertain where Myra was coming from, he decided to give her a dose.

"That's good enough for me. I'll diagnose him as schizophrenic, and if you'll sign the papers now, we can get him committed tonight for observation."

"No! He's not crazy."

"How can you be sure?"

"I know the difference. Crazy people, when they talk to you, either won't look you in the eyes or they look too intently into your eyes. Frank is neither evasive nor does he stare. When you talk with him he looks at you normally."

"Ah ha, I see," he said almost sarcastically, but it was enough for Myra's Stacy-trained perception to catch.

"No, you don't see." she insisted. "It's not as if he's afraid, and it's not as if he tries to bore into you to read in meaning beyond what you have said. If you'd ever studied under him, you'd understand. When he was teaching me, I was amazed at how well he could determine motivating traits of various characters. I feel like he lost his own true motivation somewhere while he was perfecting his ability to assume those of other people."

"I'm still incredulous; you'll have to do better to convince me. What else?"

She went on to explain Frank's curious child-like relationship with Zack, and how her own stilted relationship with him seemed to mirror a television situation comedy."

"It sounds to me," Sammy began when she finished. "like Frank's relationship with Zack is perfectly normal, and that you are suffering from jealousy. Perhaps your marriage is faulty simply because the two of you are incompatible."

"I can't accept that, and besides, I haven't even gotten to the part about his amnesia yet."

"Now, wait a minute. I thought that was supposed to be a publicity gag."

"That's what Frank wants the world to believe, but a month ago he had a diving accident, and when he came to he thought he'd been knocked unconscious in an automobile accident in Alabama in 1967, and that his name was Eugene Eastly."

"That was when he was supposedly on his publicity gag?"

"Yes, it lasted for three days then he was okay again."

"How did he explain what happened?"

Myra first had to explain Frank's acting ability before she could make Sammy understand how she initially believed Frank's theory that his injured brain had simply used the wrong memory cells when the numbing effect of the concussion had worn off. Cells containing his studies of a character, not a real person by the name of Eugene.

"So, you can see why it seemed natural that I would accept it."

"Well, I've come across too many strange things in my career to deny the possibility of anything. However, I've never heard of anything like that before."

"But, Sammy, Frank wasn't suffering from amnesia or from becoming a character he studied. It's Eugene Eastly who has had amnesia for twenty years."

"How do you come to that conclusion?"

"I'm not really certain, but ..." Myra went on to give him the theory she and Hooper had come up with: how Eugene's friend Jack must have died in the car wreck, and how it was Eugene's guilt that caused him to forget his past.

"That all sounds pretty flimsy for evidence," Sammy said, "but if true then Eugene is suffering what we call a dissociative hysterical neurosis."

"A what?"

"That's psychological word-salad for amnesia caused by a mind too immature to deal with an unpleasant or threatening situation. In the case you describe, it would be called a fugue state. The fugue reaction can be likened to an animal's instinct to flee from danger, but for people flight implies cowardice, and his problem is compounded with the human emotion of guilt. He cannot resolve it consciously so he makes an unconscious decision to forget the problem and thus the guilt, then he is able to run away from it. For many people, the fugue state, which is often characterized by compulsive wandering, is a symbolic substitute for suicide."

"That's it! Eugene was unable to deal with causing the death of his friend, so he forgot about it and wandered away. Then changed his name to Frank Stacy."

"No, I don't think so; in that circumstance he would most probably have repressed only the memory of Jack, not everything else, but I still find that too difficult to buy. For Frank Stacy to have achieved the success he has had, and to have the ability to read people the way you have described, he would have to have a good deal of psychological maturity. Because of that I can't see him being unable to accept Jack's death. However, I could be wrong."

"But what else could explain it?"

"Sometimes that takes years of therapy."

"Years!" she cried.

"Hold on; don't get upset. I said years to uncover the cause. Fugue states usually clear up spontaneously, and if not, can be accelerated under hypnosis or sodium pentothal. All you have to do is bring Frank in. If he is in a fugue, then the prognosis is good because of the three days during which he had memories from his repressed past."

"But, Sammy, Frank thinks he's Eugene again, right now, and he doesn't remember anything about Frank Stacy."

"Oh, I see."

"Is that worse?"

"No, but it's rare. We still do the same thing, though. Can you bring him in?"

"I don't know."

"What is he doing right now?"

She laughed helplessly, and said, "He's trying to make a movie, without knowing the first thing about it."

"Excellent!"

"Are you kidding? He'll make a fool of himself!"

"Maybe, but he's doing exactly what he needs to be doing. By facing what he cannot remember, he may force a gradual, if not spontaneous, recollection of the repressed memory. However, try to get him in; we may be able to save him some embarrassment."

"What if I can't get him in? I mean, what if he suddenly becomes Frank again and still doesn't remember being Eugene. I tried once before and I got a knuckle sandwich for my efforts."

Sammy burst into laughter, and cried out, "Knuckle Sandwich! Come on Myra, no one, not even a star like you can seriously use silly Hollywood metaphors like that." Myra blushed and he answered her question. "If he should return as Frank without the Eugene memories, I suggest you don't push him. With a history of fugue, he could change identities and flee again if the stress or family pressure gets too great. I wouldn't worry about that, though. You can't cross a bridge before you get to it. Just keep me apprised of any new development."

#

Dusk had passed, and night blanketed the foyer where Myra sat apprehensively waiting for her husband to come through the door. She did not know who to expect. Would it be Frank, or would it be Eugene? Was it too soon to hope for the miracle Dr. Garcia spoke of?

Sara's heels tapped across the stone floor as she entered the darkened room to turn on the lights. Once the entryway was illuminated, she could see Myra's huddled figure on the settee with her feet on the bench and her arms pulling her legs against her chest. To Sara she looked like a pitiful little girl as she rocked back and forth with her cheek supported against her knees. Although she wanted to say something, seeing Myra's watery green eyes, wide with anticipation, stopped her. Sara walked away shaking her head, and mused over her reasons for ever coming to California. At least, she thought, life in her Midwest hometown was simple.

Myra snapped her head up as she heard a car pull into the gravel circle outside. She had just gotten to her feet when Eugene burst in.

"I can't believe it!" he cried in excitement.

"What?" she asked brightly; the enthusiasm in his voice instantly lifted her spirits.

"I just can't get over that I'm going to make a movie with Ralph Smurling. It's what I always dreamed of doing."

"But I thought--"

"Oh, I know all about that, but it's been straightened out. He's going to be here Monday, and hopefully by Friday we'll have the production schedule worked out. Get ready either way because rehearsals begin on the 24th. I've already booked time at Nordwick starting September 1st."

"Eugene, don't you think you're rushing things a little?"

"Not at all. I'm doing what I'd always dreamed of doing, and because Frank has made so many movies it's almost systemized. For me it's simply a matter of following the routine."

"Eugene, you and Frank are the same person - you've got to start thinking that way."

Eugene scowled, "I know that's what you want, but since I have no memory of ever being Frank Stacy, I don't have any sympathy for him. All I know is that I've got to get on with my own life. My only concern with Frank is to finish making the movie he started. But please understand, I'm going to let production as well as direction follow Frank's course, only because I intend to learn what I can from his famous technique."

"Then it's not really yours."

"Maybe not, but I may find a way to put my personal touch on it."

"Eugene, Frank's knowledge is your knowledge. You can have both. I tried to explain to you yesterday, how I could always tell something was missing from Frank. I know what it is now, because I see it in you. You're excited, and in eleven years I never saw Frank get excited about making a movie. He just made them."

"Then what's the problem?"

"I don't care whether you have Smurling or not; whether you lean on Connie and the assistant directors, whether you depend on the training the performers have had. Dammit, you still need Frank's knowledge, and his expertise to make this picture. You can have it, too. All you have to do is see a friend of mine. He can bring it back for you."

"What kind of friend?" he asked suspiciously.

Hesitantly, she answered, "He's a psychiatrist."

"No!"

"You don't understand. You can have both."

"I won't take that risk. I've lost twenty years of my life, and dammit, I'm going to make a movie!"

"You're acting like a child."

"Maybe I am, but I'm going to fulfill my dream just in case Frank takes over again. This may be my only chance."

"But you are Frank Stacy; can't you even try to understand that?"

"I don't want to talk about it anymore!" he screamed.

The high pitch of his voice was distressing, and she feared the stress she was causing might make matters worse. It might cause Frank to come back without Eugene, or worse. She feared both could end up being buried forever under a new fugue.

"I'm sorry," she said softly. "Would you just think about seeing the psychiatrist? He's an old friend of mine, and I trust him."

He looked into her pleading eyes, and relaxed. "I'll think about it, but not until we've finished filming *Accidental Angel*. Fair enough?"

She nodded.

CHAPTER FIFTEEN

Angel Flies High

** * * * ACCIDENTAL ANGEL - - PG-13. Yes, that's four stars for Frank Stacy's latest, but if you're an addict of the Stacy school of 'Jump Start' movie-making you're in for a disappointment. There are no automobile chase scenes, no laser toting aliens, and no raging disasters. Instead, expect a refreshing new idea without a shred of recycled storyline.*

The ACCIDENTAL ANGEL is Gene Eastly a middle-age book keeper, family man, and leader in the community. He is plagued with nightmares in which he murders a grocery store clerk, until one day while in the waiting room of a dentist's office, he picks up an out-of-date news magazine and reads about an unsolved murder. The face of the victim is the same one from his nightmares.

The real thrill is the gut wrenching dialogue between Gene and his wife as he confesses his discovery, and how he intends to resolve it. Gene is played by, (yes, I know I'm not supposed to tell, but the surprise this time is a brand new actor for the Stacy stable) unknown, Hooper Johnson. Opposite Johnson, in her first Stacy flick in over five years, is Myra Mason. Expect Academy Award nominations for Best Movie, Best Actress, and Best Actor.

#

Monday morning Connie looked up from her desk to see a grayer, heavier, Ralph Smurling than she remembered. As he entered the office, she was surprised to see a healthy happy glow in his face; she had expected him to be gaunt and bitter, but considering the past, she was still afraid to be familiar with him.

"Good morning, Mr. Smurling. Mr. Stacy is expecting you. Please walk on in."

"Connie, seventeen years is a long time - plenty of time to forget. You needn't be formal with me; I could never blame you for following that young whirlwind. Hell, I'd have done the same thing myself, and don't think I never noticed the sparkle in your eyes every time he was near you."

"Oh!" she gasped.

Smurling chuckled as he walked into Frank's office.

He flopped into the chair across the desk from Eugene, and said, "Young man, before we start hashing over that script let's get acquainted. The first time we met you were awful tight lipped about your background, but you had such an intrinsic grasp of directing I never really thought about it. Now I'm curious. Curious to know about Eugene Eastly the plumber, who went on to become the world's best director, and then forgot all about it."

"I'm not a plumber, sir. My father's the plumber. Do you know him?"

"No I don't, but he must have taught you, because you slipped into my studio in the guise of a local plumber who part-timed it as a grip. I was on the verge of calling the cops when you said you could do the work. I said prove it, and well, the rest is history. So tell me about this father of yours. Was he in some way connected with the theater?"

"No, my father never had anything to do with theater. In fact, I believe he was about as far removed from the entertainment business as a man could get. He would even taunt me and call me queer-boy and homo just because I was interested in the movies."

"Surely you exaggerate?" Smurling prodded.

"Not at all, my father's a bastard, or rather was. I don't know if he's still around; and I don't care. I never wanted to be a plumber, but he made me learn it. If I didn't, he'd beat me; and sometimes if I learned too quickly he'd beat me anyway. It was so bad that on Saturdays I had to sneak off to see the new movie that came to the town theater. Unfortunately, it didn't take him long to figure out where I went and he would wait for me outside. After the show, I knew if I took the wrong exit I was going to get a whipping as soon as I stepped outside, right there on the sidewalk in front of God and everybody. He wouldn't even let me read about it. If he found any books I had on film making, he'd tear them up - even if they belonged to the library."

"What about your mother?"

"I don't think my mother ever had a mind of her own; she just parroted Dad. I always hoped to get through to her some day. She liked to watch movies, so I thought she would understand, but she never did. I remember one Sunday afternoon I was watching your picture *Gods Of Autumn*. It's still my favorite movie."

"Yes, you mentioned it the other day. I believe you said you had *Gods Of Autumn* in mind when you titled a screenplay you wrote."

"Yes, *Gods Of The Pond*. I'd intended for it to be the first movie I would make, but I want to wait until I find Jack, since he inspired me to write it."

Eugene did not interpret the look of recognition that crossed Smurling's face. Although, Frank and Ralph had had their falling out, Ralph couldn't help but follow the skyrocketing career of the man he got started. He recognized the name from *Resurgent Man,* but the cause of his surprise was learning Eugene was unaware of it having been produced.

"You were going to tell me about a Sunday afternoon you recalled."

"Yes, I was watching the movie for about the hundredth time on TV, but each time I'd always see something new..."

#

Spring is hot in southern Georgia; sticky, sweaty hot, and sometimes hotter than summer in most of the rest of the country. It was in cut-off jeans, and a t-shirt that Eugene Eastly watched *Gods Of Autumn* on the spring day he recalled to Ralph Smurling. Lying belly-down on the floor where the room was coolest, he stretched his body cat-like to find comfort on the balding carpet. Rattling behind him, on a ring-stained coffee table, was a dusty, black enameled, oscillating fan his mother had purchased before the second world war. As it stirred the warm air, dust woolies flapped gently from the finger guard: ragged streamers trying desperately to prove the old fan's worth. One bent blade sang, "ting-a-ting-ting", in a metal-against-metal, frame-whacking-racket. It forced Eugene to press his face closer to the round screen of the old TV just to hear the words.

His mother, red faced and moist with a wooden mixing spoon in her hand, walked into the living room from the kitchen. As she stood over him, Eugene could smell the steamy reek, of fatback and overcooked vegetables that perpetually scented her faded cotton gingham. It was a flavor endemic to Southerners, savoring a sense of security, home, and a mother's love; it was carved into the genetic stone of their being. Eugene loved it.

"Eugene, what are you doin'? Don't you hear your father callin' you? Eugene!"

"Yes, ma'am?"

"Your father needs you to help him."

"But, Ma; I'm studyin'."

"You ain't studyin'; you're watchin' TV! Now get along."

"But I am studyin' - look at this scene: the technique, the lighting, it's... it's incredible. This is the kind of movie I'm going to make."

She grabbed his ear and pulled him up while saying, "Enough of this foolishness. You get out there and help your father. Now!"

He pushed open the screen door, and shooed flies drawn by the odors of cooking. The front yard looked more like a junk yard with mounds of rusting pipe, two broken washing machines, a car up on blocks, a tub, three sinks, and a toilet with no tank. Small dirt clouds rose about his ankles as his bare feet slapped patches of powdery baked red earth among the mottled and yellowing, rain-starved grass.

Jim Eastly, in greasy overalls, had his head underneath the hood of his work van as Eugene reluctantly approached.

"Dad, can't I help you work on the truck later?"

"No."

"But, Dad--"

"Hand me that crescent wrench over there."

"But, Dad," he pleaded as he handed him the wrench. "I'm watching this movie, and it's real important to me."

"I know what you're watchin', and I seen it a million times. I can tell you anything you want to know about it. Now, get me a screwdriver."

"Can you tell me whether Smurling used a hand held camera with a wide angle lens, or was the camera mounted on tracks when he followed Lorna Bennelli down--"

"Don't get smart-ass with me boy! Here, hold back on this hose so's I can loosen this bolt."

An hour passed and the matter of seeing the movie became moot. Eugene resigned himself to a day of sweating over a hot engine, and roasting under a blazing sun. Soon he was as black with grease as his father, while despite his desires, he was acquiring insight into human nature as well as automobile repair.

His son's silent stoicism, was not lost on Jim Eastly, who was determined to impress his will on Eugene. So, he began to lecture him.

"Boy, sooner or later you're gonna have to learn how to make a living and now's a good a time as any. You're gonna need a trade someday so you might as well learn mine. Cause sure as shit draws flies, ain't nobody else gonna teach you for free."

"But Dad I'm going to make movies."

"That's nonsense. You're gonna be a plumber, just like me. Ain't nothing wrong with it, and it's a good livin'."

As Jim climbed into the cab to start the engine, Eugene wondered about that good living. He knew his father made money, but he also knew his father was real friendly with the local bootleggers. Jim Eastly had a taste for the good stuff too. He wouldn't drink the local brew. He had to have store bought whiskey, and in a dry county, the good stuff came dear. Then as soon as he was good and liquored up - he knew better than to go home; Charlene Eastly would start whining and complaining which irritated the hell out of him - he was off to visit the local whorehouse hidden down that back road off of Highway 240. Why it was hidden he couldn't say, because in a county of less than four thousand people, everybody knew about it. If there was any money left after he treated himself to whiskey and women, he must have been hiding it, because he sure never spent any on the family. Eugene wore clothes until his knees and elbows wore through, and shoes until his feet either hurt or popped out. His mother could stand some new clothes herself, but it was her teeth that desperately needed attention. It pained Eugene to look at her mouth and he cursed his father for not giving her money to see the dentist.

Once the engine was running, Jim got back under the hood and pulled a rubber coated cable out of the side of the engine block. Then holding the end of the cable toward Eugene he said, "Stick your finger in this hole."

"In what hole?"

Pointing at the end of the cable, he said, "This one."

"Why?"

"Don't ask stupid questions, just do it!"

Eugene did as he was told, and poked his finger into the hole.

"Yeow!" he screamed. A bolt of electricity surged up his finger and through his body knocking him flat on his back while his father laughed and smacked his palm against the fender of the van in glee.

It was only a moment before Eugene recovered, and he yelled, "Hey, why'd you do that to me?"

"So you'll know what not to do. Now hand me that ratchet."

#

Ralph leaned toward Eugene and said, "It sounds like your father was a sadist."

"I don't know that word," Eugene responded.

"Well, let's say the word sadist describes your father. It makes me wonder how you got away enough to study filming at all."

"Oh, that was easy. My best friend Jack was an orphan; that is until his mother died when he was fifteen years old, and he found out who she was. Anyway he inherited a small farm from her, so he moved there, and that's where I used to go."

"And you're expecting Jack to come out here to California so you can produce *Gods Of The Pond*?"

"No, he's out here already. We left Georgia together, only we got separated and I don't know where he is."

"Would he have gone back?"

"No. Well, maybe, but just to pick up our fiancée."

Ralph found Eugene's self-disclosure a little disconcerting, and decided he'd rather talk with Zack before he listened to any more.

He shifted the conversation back to business where it should have been all along.

"I see. Well Frank, what do you say we tackle that script? We've got a lot of preparation to do if we want to make that start date you're projecting, but if we can pull it off, we could possibly be ready for a Christmas release."

"Sure, Ralph, but before we get started, there's one thing I'd like to change. Frank changed the name of leading character to Eugene Eastly, to cover up my waking up for three days last month. I understand the importance of continuing the charade, it's just that seeing my name like that bothers me. I'd like to shorten Eugene to Gene, and leave everything else the same. I don't identify with the name Gene, so it will make me feel better."

"Suits me."

#

Accidental Angel was Hooper Johnson's big break. The leading role he had longed for, wished for, and worked for was actually going to take place. Therefore, it was not without anticipation that he awaited the arrival of the big day when he would finally get to show his stuff in front of the rolling cameras.

Thrills did not exist for Hooper that could match the thrill of acting. However, it was during his early years that he made the pain of his yearning worse by forcing himself to discover this fact about himself the hard way. It was by pursuing substitutes, in the wake of each of his failures to grasp the elusive acting career he so desired, that he finally felt the true depth of his passion. It was only by occasionally walking away from acting that he learned he could not live without it.

Hooper initially felt the thrill as a teenager when he landed a role in a high school comedy. Discovering first what made the audience react, then fine tuning it night after night, until through his performance, he could control the crowd in front of him. It was like a virus that would infect him for life. Finding out his body could be used as an instrument to evoke emotions from the souls of perfect strangers was a knowledge - a power - he would never again be able to resist. Eventually, it became more; his passion to affect others grew to include what he could create out of himself. He recognized the segments of his own life as roles in themselves, and worked to uncover the roots of his own desires in order to give completeness to a self-confidence that was only beginning to mature. For three years he dominated his high school theater, and his popularity among the students soared. Unfortunately, high school was the end to his easy life as an actor. His family could not afford to send him to college, so he left his modest Ohio home for the rigors of New York City.

The days of being the funniest kid in class were over. Wisecracking comments in the back of the room and imitating his teacher's voices and gestures were no longer considered talent enough to get him recognition. He was competing against trained acting students in the city where the phrase *survival of the fittest* carries more clawing-uphill credence than in the jungle where the concept was first conceived. His cool reserve was shattered at his first audition when he was asked politely to leave; the director did not respond like his teachers had to his flippant answers.

His cocky self-assurance would have gotten anyone else thrown out, but Hooper was big. Six feet four inches, one hundred ninety-five pounds was slightly intimidating. He looked more the football player than actor, and topping his wide shoulders was the face of a British Isles mixed breed. Curly red-brown hair framed his hazel eyes, but it was a trace of Cherokee Indian from his mother's side that lifted his cheekbones, and streamlined what would have been an Irish-potato nose. Big as he was, he felt like a midget as he walked out the stage door with the fresh streaks of a tongue lashing still burning red on his face.

He was not stupid; he took his lumps and learned quickly. He was aware of what he was up against, and that he could not afford formal training. Instead, the city became his classroom; and his teachers: the people around him acting out their lives in their natural habitat. He took his acting lessons in the bar where he worked nights, on the subways during rush hours, and on sidewalks uptown and downtown, but never in Greenwich Village where he felt no one was ever themselves.

Behind the bar it was easy; his customers, who always wanted to talk about themselves, or to reveal personal secrets, made studying their gestures simple for Hooper. Sometimes he would get carried away and it would cost him a tip when a cocktail patron noticed he was being mimicked. By the end of the night his tip jar was only half as important as how well he did at guessing people's professions by their traits.

He was especially amused by the subway trains. When riding those bumpy, jerky, brain-rattling cars, he lovingly named moving monkey houses. He would hang from the hand grips and ape intriguing individuals around him, all the while wondering what thoughts passed behind the eyes of vacant stares.

Working at night gave him his days to attend auditions, and after each one, on his way home, he would pick out a person on the sidewalk to follow. Then during the course of a few blocks he would fall into step with them while trying to discern additional quirks he could try on for size. His free afternoons were spent walking back and forth in his tiny room reciting lines from play after play, continuously growing more and more comfortable in newer and broader characters.

Persistence may have paid off with the directors, if they could only remember his face, but he always auditioned in character, thus never looking the same. His efforts of improving his ability were appreciated off-Broadway for small roles in all too often short-running productions, but on Broadway he never received a part. Rumors of theater-politics, nepotism, and mishpacha only, passed among disgruntled auditioners leaving the theaters, but he wouldn't listen, and for five years he never missed a Broadway audition.

It was in his fifth year, after the closing of a sixteen week run in a repertory theater, the longest for both him and the theater, where he enjoyed a leading role, that the pain of emptiness first hit him. The weeks of rehearsal and preparation, the camaraderie with the cast, the feeding energy of a grateful audience night after night, was abruptly over. The final cast party on closing night was tearful as actors and actresses, who had leaned on each other as reinforcement to stay in character for four months, realized the relationships they had established would never again be the same. They said their good-byes while promising to see each other often, but knowing they would resume their natural characters on leaving. People who had felt bonds as close as those of childhood would tomorrow be competing against each other for newer greater roles.

From this ending, Hooper was fortified with a sustaining energy left to him like a residual payment, a royalty from his four months of performing. Rising early the next morning, he hit the audition trail. A month passed, and the payments stopped. The pain of loss felt from a successful ending that had worked as inspiration, now worked against him. It was just pain. Three months passed, and his home-grown persistence was waning. After six months the pain was gone, but with it went his self-assurance. His hunger for the food that could only be fed by an audience had turned to starvation. Six months lean, he chose margarine because butter wasn't available, and moved to Key West, Florida.

It began as a vacation, in a warm place where the art-inclined could mingle and tell lies, but the clear waters beckoned and he learned to scuba dive. The new knowledge excited him and he took it, reveled in it, and because of it, landed a job diving for an off-shore oil drilling company. The sensation he felt as he swam through shark infested waters renewed his soul, and it took nearly two years before he remembered he was an actor. It happened on an evening of shore-leave from the oil rig platforms where he bunked six weeks at a time in the middle of the Gulf of Mexico. He'd agreed to take a fellow worker's sister out to a movie in Galveston. The picture was a grainy sixth generation copy of *The Tangled Web*, but it was clear enough for Hooper's first sight of Myra Mason. He sat unmoving to the end. The intense feeling he experienced kept him glued to his seat through all the closing credits until the screen was blank.

When the lights came on his date asked impatiently, "Ready?"

Looking up as if he didn't recall where he was, he said, "Huh?"

"You look like you're in another world. Are you smitten by that actress's face?"

"No, her acting," he whispered.

"Oh, she was wonderful, wasn't she?"

"She's good," he said as he stood.

"Good! She's more than good; she's the best there is," the girl stated as she followed him up the aisle.

Hooper whirled around and, as if Myra, herself, were there offering challenge, he jabbed his finger toward the screen and said, "That's where I belong, then you'll know who's the best there is."

He turned and walked out the door.

When the girl caught up to him, he was waiting beside her car.

"How 'bout dropping me off at the bus station?" he asked her.

"Bus station? But you've got to be back at the dock by midnight."

"Just tell your brother to sell my gear. I'll call him first chance and give him my forwarding address."

Back on the acting trail he decided to work his way west toward the ultimate goal, the guaranty of getting decent parts: Hollywood stardom. He performed in college plays, summer stock, and local TV ads, and even received a part in a play at the Guthrie Theater in Minnesota. He also waited tables, framed houses, and spread manure, because it paid the bills supporting his passion; and on occasion it covered the price of a ticket to see a Frank Stacy movie starring Myra Mason.

Once, Hooper had a satisfying summer performing beneath the stars in Santa Fe, but the arctic breath of winter whistled down through the Rocky Mountains and closed the season of Theater in the Park early, leaving him undiscovered by recruiting agents who would have attended the last scheduled shows. With no indoor parts emerging to replace the thrill of the amphitheater, he hitched a ride to the ski town of Taos before the pain could start. He hoped that bracing wind and splashing snow powder would burn his cheeks as he sped down the mountainside. He prayed for ersatz excitement that would fill the cleft hacked in his soul by those mysterious forces that once again forced him off the stage. It worked, so he remained through the thaw.

He spent a year with no acting success in Hollywood before hiding in Utah hang-gliding, but that too was fruitless. Sailing in the sky, wafting in the wind, and tacking into tufts of rising air above the Utah ranges offered him his usual physical placebo to acting, but it also gave him too much time to think about it, and before long he was bellowing Shakespeare to the echoing canyons below. At age thirty-one he went back to Hollywood to pay his dues; he was tired of trading the thrill of contentment for empty excitement.

In five years in Hollywood, he'd played many extras, and a handful of parts with a line or two, but as hard as he tried he couldn't land a role significant enough to gain recognition. He did some live theater, when he could get parts. Again, he never missed auditions, only this time not on the energy of youthful confidence, but on an energy-radiating determination that came from a solid core deep inside his sense of life. Part of it was learning to relax while waiting in line, thus not wasting energy trying to stay up until it was necessary. Instead he created a mental image of a panoramic portfolio in front of him from which he only needed to pull the correct file when called on.

Avoiding jobs that could take his mind away from his goal, he took only entertainment related work. He did not care if it was digging ditches on an outdoor set, or sweeping the aisles of a playhouse at midnight. Most of these jobs were temporary, and they kept him in enough cash to cover his needs; a modest living for a patient man.

On Monday, August 17, 1987 Hooper received his script for *Accidental Angel* via courier. After signing the driver's receipt, he quickly pulled the booklet from the heavy envelope. Excitement flowed through his being as he turned back the cover, but as he viewed the first page he was struck by the second name on the list of principle players: Myra Mason. He had not anticipated this; this made everything different. It was one thing for Myra to watch his performance, but for her to be interacting with his performance meant the duel with Frank for her hand had to begin sooner than he'd figured. He wanted Myra, and he'd intended to win her by the only standard either of them measured: acting ability, but he had not planned on the stage for *Accidental Angel* to become the arena for that contest.

Hooper felt that Frank was playing with fire when he chose to produce *Accidental Angel;* and since he had been selected as the lead, he intended to make this production the catalyst that united the mind of Frank and Eugene. That done, he would put his *Stacy*-credit in his resume and use it in the coming years to get roles where he would give Myra-winning performances. His original plan, an idea conceived on the night he received Frank's message on his telephone answering machine, now had to be scrapped; to play his role in that manner against Myra as the supporting-lead would destroy his acting credibility in her eyes - even if she understood his motives.

Being chosen for the leading role had been difficult for him to accept seriously. There was no question that he was excited; this role would get him the recognition he craved, but a twinge of guilt nagged him whenever he considered the reason he was given the role. Frank was not around to assure him it was granted for ability. But, to even consider asking Frank such a question caused a pain he did not want to acknowledge. Perhaps self-doubt was his unnamed guilt, but in rationalizing his lack of respect for the role, he tried to persuade himself that Frank gave it to him as a mouth-zippering blackmail payment.

Unwilling to accept the role of a blackmailer, Hooper's original intention was to take the pay-off, then turn it back around, and use it to extort from Frank an admission that he was Eugene Eastly. It would have been easy, simply by molding his character the same way he had for the audition: after the boy he met on the set for *Runaway Grandparents*. Now, however, there was no reason to do that, Frank was not around, just the boy... and Myra.

He picked up the phone and dialed Sally's number.

When she picked up, he said, "Sally, it's Hooper; I need some help. ... I've been given the lead of a lifetime and it's got to be right, but I've only a few weeks to prepare. Do you remember my telling you how I heard about a new system for learning lines I wanted to try? ... Good, will you have some time in a week? ... I know a week is a long time when there's a short deadline, but I've got to do some crucial research into character-type first. ... It's not because of the deadline that I want to experiment with the new system; it's, it's something else entirely. ... I'll drop the script off this afternoon, so you can get prepared ... no, seven days is not really enough time to do the character research I would like either, but it will have to do. ... Thanks, I'll see you this afternoon. Bye."

Hooper had three weeks to turn the paper character, Gene Eastly, into a living person using his body. The author's synopsis stated that Gene, a successful C.P.A., in his early forties, was happily married with two children, and currently a city council member. Gene's success in accounting gave him the recognition he needed to get elected to the city council. Once there his budgeting miracles saved the town money, enabled them to cut taxes which in turn encouraged new business to move in, thus raising the standard of living for everyone. This made him very popular in the town and gained him the attention of his political party who began encouraging him to run for Congress. Gene, however, has a skeleton in his closet: a past he cannot remember. A dismal criminal past conveniently veiled by amnesia.

During his first week, Hooper needed to rough out the generalities of each of those roles before he could begin to add any individualism. Because time was limited, he decided to concentrate on those areas in which he had the least experience: accounting and city management.

The accounting part presented no difficulty; he had friends in the business who gladly allowed him to tag along for a day or two. Persuading members of a local city council to grant in-depth interviews, however, was not as easy, but with the weight of Frank Stacy's name behind him, he finally got in the door.

Cup after cup of coffee was used to concentrate the material he needed to cover in those seven days, and at the end of the week with his brain feeling stuffed, he phoned Sally and cried, "Ready or not, here I come."

Sally sat on her sofa with the script open in her lap, and asked Hooper, "When you did your research did you keep in mind the amnesia angle?"

"I did more than that; I read up on it, and I've got a new name for it. In Gene's case, because he changes his name and crosses the state, it's called a fugue."

"Fugue?"

"Yeah, it comes from the Latin word for flight. It's a psychogenic form of amnesia that functions as a defense mechanism. A fugue is a response against pain caused by highly emotional memories. My character not only forgot his crime, but also fled his hometown where he committed it."

"I should've known you'd be thorough. Shall we begin?"

"Yes. Now what I want you to do is read until you reach my first line then stop. Here's the twist. This will be the first time I have heard those lines. Nor, have I read any of my lines yet."

"You haven't looked at the script! You haven't started learning your lines?"

"No. And, I don't want you to tell me what they are. The purpose of this is for me to take what I have learned in my research, along with what the author has allowed my character to know up to the point you stop speaking, and then to react as my character would to the last line you read."

"React? React how?"

"By saying what I think and feel given the circumstances."

"Then what?"

"Then you tell me the actual line and I see how close I came to it. Thus I'll see if I'm connecting with the author's intentions. Then you read the next line, and I react again, and so on throughout the whole script."

"Is this what Frank Stacy has been teaching you?"

"No. Frank isn't going to teach me."

"But I thought--"

"I know; he only uses his own handicraft, but this time he's doing it differently."

"Wow, I always knew you were good, Hooper, but if Frank Stacy doesn't think you need training, well... Wow!"

Hooper shrugged guiltily in the knowledge that Frank had indeed intended for him to attend his classes so that he could be imprinted with the *Stacy* style. He didn't bother mentioning to Sally that he had been spared by the timely arrival of Eugene.

#

The phone rang and Hooper bolted upright in bed. He glanced around the room until he was able to shake off enough of his dreams of Gene Eastly, C.P.A., repentant murderer, and amnesiac, to remember where he was, and who he was, then he picked up the phone. As he croaked a hello, he heard Myra's voice.

"Hooper, did I wake you?"

"Uh, yeah; sort of."

"I just wanted to ask if you have read your script yet?"

"Of course I have."

"Then we need to talk."

"Of course we do; we have to rehearse."

"No, I mean about the other thing."

"What does that have to do with the script?" he asked suspiciously, thinking of his previous intentions.

"Well doesn't it make you think of something?"

"Myra it's too early in the morning to talk in riddles. Would you please get to the point?"

"Boy, do you wake up grumpy," she answered testily then added, "and for your information it's already afternoon."

"I'm sorry. What does it make you think of?"

"Do you think that by producing *Accidental Angel,* Frank is confessing guilt?"

"I don't see the connection."

"It's a subconscious confession for killing Jack."

"That doesn't make sense. If you had said it was a subconscious confession of being in a specific state of amnesia, I'd agree with you because I already believe that's the case, but how can you see a connection between an accidental death and murder?"

"Oh, I'm sorry; I forgot I haven't told you yet. My mind has been working a million miles an hour. I've been to see a psychiatrist, and I've even hired a detective to find Eugene's girlfriend from Georgia."

"You what?"

"Yes, you see, Eugene told me that he and Jack had a mutual girlfriend, who loved them equally, however--"

"*Resurgent Man.*" Hooper said, interrupting.

"Yes. However, I suspect the girl loved only Jack. I'm betting Eugene wrote *Resurgent Man* to persuade her that she could love them both, but I fear it didn't work and Eugene caused the car accident on purpose..."

"Wait a minute; slow down. Eugene didn't write it - Jack did."

"But maybe he did. Eugene commented the other day before you came over that he had many ideas for screenplays. If he didn't write it, it ruins my theory. Anyway, you were the one who planted that idea in my mind in the first place."

"That's pretty weak, but for the sake of argument let's say he did write it, but I can't imagine him writing it to persuade her to love the both of them, not with the way the last scene ended."

"Hooper, you're forgetting the closing, the end which depicted that the idea the three lovers were living out would go on anyway. And, the first to carry it on would be two males with one female. The resurgence of their belief that men must live as they see fit."

"You don't need to explain the movie to me. I understood it, although I'm more inclined to call the closing redeeming rather than resurgent, but let's get back on track. What the hell did Eugene say to make you think he killed Jack?"

"Well, it wasn't so much what he said; mostly it's intuition."

"Something had to stimulate your intuition; what was it?"

"At the time of this supposed threesome, Eugene was in his teens; figure somewhere between fourteen and sixteen since we don't know how long the relationship had been going on. Both Jack and the girl were two years older. Now you might not understand this, but for a teenage girl a younger boy is simply out of the question."

"I'll buy that. What else?"

"It was something I learned from the psychiatrist. Sammy, he's an old friend of mine, told me that what I described is called a fugue."

"Yes, I found that out myself."

"Anyway, he said that a man with Frank's achievements would necessarily have to have the psychological maturity to deal with an accidental death."

"So what does that mean - that he doesn't believe Frank is in a fugue?"

"It means he doesn't accept the car accident as its cause, which is what makes me think it may have been murder."

"And what did the shrink think?"

"I don't really feel he believed much of what I said. He thinks it's more marital incompatibility than anything else."

"That's what you get for going to an *I'm Okay - You're Groovy* Hollywood psychiatrist. So, tell me about your detective."

"I haven't heard anything yet, but then he doesn't have a whole lot to go on. It's been twenty years, and Stacie Rogers of Ellaville, Georgia, could now be Stacie New-Married-Name of Anywhere, U.S.A."

"Her name is Stacie? Hmmm. Jack and Stacie, huh. Now what was Jack's last name uh,..."

"Jackson Paine Franklin."

"Jackson Paine Franklin and Stacie Rogers, Franklin and Stacie, Franklin Stacie, how about that? You know you might have something with that intuition of yours. That *menage a trois* must have been awfully damn important in Eugene's mind if he named himself for those two after he lost his memory."

"Oh," Myra gasped, "I never connected those names before."

"Hon, you're dealing with pure brilliance here," Hooper said lightheartedly.

Myra didn't hear his cheerfulness, and to Hooper's surprise lashed out at him, "You damn well better be brilliant. I can't believe you're going to perform in a Frank Stacy production with no training whatsoever; why, it was a year of rigorous training before I got my first chance."

"Hold on, I don't need to listen to insults. It's not as if I know nothing of acting. Don't forget, Frank did choose me on the basis of my audition."

"And it may have been on the basis of a bribe since you know too much."

"Myra, I'm not going to get angry. I'm going to write off your insults to the fact that you're nervous about Eugene trying to direct a film, but you don't have to worry, he's got that Smurling fellow to help him out. From the old movies I've seen that were Smurling's, I'd say Eugene made a competent choice."

"Yeah, and Frank Stacy will wind up in the same state of obscurity Ralph Smurling found himself in for the last seventeen years."

"Myra, I understand your fear and your frustration, but you've got to put your anxiety aside. Eugene needs your help."

Myra was silent and Hooper heard only the soft sounds of her breath over the phone. He longed for the day when Frank was normal, and he could challenge the famous director's hold over this woman.

"I'm sorry, Hooper," she finally answered. "It's just between hiring the detective, talking to the psychiatrist, my husband disappearing, and a stranger taking his place, who may turn out to be a murderer, I am a little on edge. Add to that, Connie doing her level best to drive a wedge between Frank and me, and finally to top everything off, we're running on an accelerated production schedule - it's just too much!" Myra was crying, "I'm sorry Hooper, you're the only one I can talk to; you're the only one who understands, and I yelled at you. I'm sorry."

"Enough apologies already," he said cheerily. "You should be happy you're going to be working again. Don't tell me Frank's system has spoiled you, so what if everything isn't perfect; where's your acting spirit? Break a leg, lady." Then added in a baritone, announcer's voice, "The show must go on." He paused, then said, "Hurry up would ya, and laugh or groan or something, so I can quit using dumb clichés."

#

"That's another thing," she said to Hooper as they were waiting to do their walk through on the set, "I don't understand why Frank cast me in this role. Not only hasn't he cast me in years, I didn't even audition."

"Does Myra Mason need to audition?" he asked.

"Hooper Johnson, I've auditioned for every role I've ever played in my entire life. And, Frank has always insisted that every part be auditioned for."

"Don't you think you can do it?"

"Don't be ridiculous, it's actually a very easy role."

"That's what you think," thought Hooper, "because the performance I'll be giving will demand the best of your ability in return." He said instead, "I envy your camera awareness. That's the one area I know I'm deficient in."

"That's what the crew is for. They won't let you blow it."

"I appreciate the confidence. Speaking of which, you seem a lot calmer today than you were on the phone last week."

"I'm on the job; it's my acting spirit that you worried was absent. It always returns as soon as I see the lights. You're right Hooper, I'm a trouper." She giggled at her rhyme, then added, "But you've got to admit it is a little weird for Frank to cast the way he did this time."

"I guess," Hooper said, softly. He was beginning to feel a little overwhelmed.

"Come on, there's Frank," Myra said, taking his elbow.

"Frank?" whispered Hooper as he looked across the room and saw the man sitting behind the lights in the same pose as the man who auditioned him. "You mean he's back?"

"No," Myra whispered back. "I should've told you. Eugene is using Frank's name for practical reasons."

"Whew! That's good; I wasn't quite ready for that." However, as he looked back across the room to the man in the canvas chair, he could only imagine Frank Stacy, and a thought popped into his head. "Maybe Frank cast us this way to purposely throw Myra and me together." But, he immediately replaced that thought with, "Nah, that's just wishful thinking compounded by an attack of the butterflies. Come on Hooper, old boy, break a leg, yourself."

#

As Hooper and Myra approached the directors' chairs, Frank turned away from his conference and winked at Hooper. Behind the boyish grin on Frank's face, Hooper once again recognized Eugene. Myra whispered that the meeting was of all the film crew chiefs, and began naming off the cinematographer, mixer, gaffer, and head grip.

"You know I've hardly seen Eugene in the past two weeks. He's been sleeping at the office."

"Why is that?" Hooper whispered back.

"I don't know; I don't think Connie has been giving him my messages."

"You want me to ask him? He takes all my calls. In fact, Connie, who three weeks ago was my mortal enemy, is now my best friend."

"No, that's all right. He talks to you because you're his friend; he hasn't decided where I figure into his life, so he's avoiding me, and Connie's only too happy to comply."

"She's certainly the archetype of the loyal secretary."

"You mean she's in love with Frank. No, don't give me that funny look. I can tell when a woman is jealous, and she's been jealous of me for eleven years."

"So why is she suddenly so friendly with me?"

"Because you're important to Eugene, and to her that's seems a way to his heart."

"Oh."

"But, none of that matters now, because now that we're in L.A. he's working out of the condo, and he can't avoid me. Of course Connie is living there also, along with Ralph Smurling."

"Sounds like a circus."

Myra laughed, "It would be if we didn't have the top three floors of the high-rise. As it is we have more than enough room for several guests without people getting on each other's nerves."

“Why so much space?”

“Frank uses the first floor as an office when he's shooting in L.A., and I use the rest for entertaining prospective producers.”

When they were within hearing range of the conference, Smurling looked up and called cheerily out to them.

"Hey, you two, I'll bet you're wondering why you got your call when the sets aren't even finished yet?"

Hooper shrugged, and said, "As a matter of fact I was."

"It's this simple; you remember how I explained that we're on a super-tight time and money budget?"

Hooper nodded.

Ralph continued, speaking rapidly, "That means production has to be super-speedy. So while you're getting your beauty sleep, the Grip Department will be finishing the sets for the next day's shooting. Shooting by the way begins tomorrow. Today Wardrobe will be fitting you, and then you'll go to Make-Up. After which the Focus Operator will walk you through the set and tape your marks on the floor, while at the same time the Gaffer will set each of your key lights. You guys will have to get whatever rehearsing you need to do between you, in your spare moments." He paused then added in a serious tone of voice, "Frank wants this to be a one rehearsal - one take. That means FUBARs get printed. Let's avoid 'em."

He turned back to the department heads, and said, "Gentlemen."

They all rose, and headed off to their duties. Hooper looked at Myra and whispered, "What does FUBAR mean?"

"It used to mean: Fouled Up Beyond All Recognition, however, I believe the F-word has been updated to meet current standards."

Hooper added, "Geez, he's a regular hard ass isn't he."

"Not at all; you just didn't look at his eyes."

"Look at his eyes? I was too busy listening to his words."

"Oh, come on Hooper, didn't you see that gleam? He's as happy as kid who just found his lost dog. He's working again; don't you get it?"

"Maybe, but I still heard 'one take,' and maybe that's not scary to you, but it's enough to make me nervous."

"It has to be this way," Myra dropped her voice to a hush. A bearded cableman, who looked more like a truck driver in his cobalt blue, *Stacy Productions* T-shirt began hanging microphone wires near them. Whispering, she continued, "The problem is: certain investors have already put up money for future films Frank already scheduled. This one was not scheduled, nor has it been properly financed."

It was only by chance that Myra found this out. Several days had passed since she'd seen or even heard from Eugene. Connie accepted her messages, but no one ever called her back. Her anxiety level was rising exponentially with each passing day while she spent her time alone in the confines of the sprawling Spanish villa with only Sara and the work of memorizing her lines to keep her company. When only ten days remained before they were to leave Fresno, and the peaceful San Joaquin Valley for the crowds of L.A., she had enough. She wasn't going to be ignored any longer.

Myra pushed open the frosted glass door with the cobalt blue letters of *Stacy Productions*, and started to walk straight for Frank's office. Connie leaped from behind her desk, and bodily barred Myra's way.

"What do you think you're doing?" Connie demanded.

"I haven't spoken to my husband in days. I came to see what Eugene's problem with calling me is, and to see how he's progressing."

"There is no Eugene, only Frank."

"Frank's back?" Myra gasped. "Is he both of them? Have the memories blended?" She whispered hopefully, thinking of what Sammy had told her.

"No, it's still Eugene, but Myra, we must all call him Frank. I think you can understand that."

Myra imagined the reaction it would cause if she called him Eugene in front of his students. "Yes..., yes I can. Now please step aside."

"No, Myra; you know the rules: no performers in the office during Schedule Planning. That rule has included you since you finished your training and it still holds."

"Circumstances are clearly different now. I asked you to step aside."

Connie braced her arm against the door frame, and with the propriety of an owner to a trespasser said, "No."

"Out of my way, bitch!" Myra hissed. "Don't think I'm unaware of your husband-stealing motives."

Connie gasped as the shock of truth caused her arm to drop to her side. Myra reached past her and grabbed the door knob, but before she could turn it - it turned by itself, and the door swung away from her hand to reveal a smiling Zachary Lowell Reid.

"Why hello, Myra. I've just had the pleasure of meeting Frank's alter ego."

Connie put her forefinger to her lips and said, "Shhhh!"

"Don't be silly Constance, my love, there's no one around to hear me."

Connie blushed and awkwardly clasped her still extended finger with her other hand and pulled it down to her breast as if it didn't know how to move on its own.

Behind Zack, Myra could see Ralph and Eugene standing beside Frank's desk. Then looking back to Zack she noticed he was dressed in a suit and holding a brief case. "Gee, Zack, what's going on? You look... you look different."

Zack laughed. "You mean I look odd. Not too many people ever catch me in the act of doing business."

"Doing business?"

"Yes, Uncle Ralph, here," he swung his thumb over his shoulder to point, "invited me over to invest some of my idle inheritance into Frank's new movie."

"I don't understand." Myra said. "Why now? Why never before? And what about all of Frank's usual investors; where are they?"

"Whoa, whoa, who-o-a Myra!" cried Zack gleefully while Eugene and Ralph joined him at the door. "One at a time. First because he needed it, and second because I'd never been asked before. As to the other investors..." He shrugged and turned to Ralph.

"Myra," Ralph began, "why don't we all go back inside and sit down."

#

"... to sum it up, Frank's production schedule is booked for the next two years, with financial commitments already earmarked for specific films. Frank's current project is supposed to be *Highway Robbery* which will be followed by *Dream Car*. Frank gave himself, and subsequently us, some extra time by completing in one day the negotiations for *Moon Colony*'s distribution rights which should have taken weeks. We're guessing he figured his *Highway Robbery* investors would accept a reasonable delay. All in all that still doesn't leave us much time."

When Ralph finished, Myra looked at Zack and said sarcastically, "And Zachary here is picking up the whole tab for *Frank's Folly*, excuse me, I mean *Accidental Angel*?"

"No, he's merely matching Frank's own investment."

"But that would take everything Frank has - no, it would take more. Not even Frank can accurately predict all the below-the-line costs. Why the studio rent alone for a single day over schedule could throw the whole budget into the red. How--"

"Connie's worked it out," interrupted Eugene. "Tell her Connie."

Connie gave Myra a smile of superiority before she began, "I've figured out a way to juggle the books, so to speak. Kind of robbing Peter to pay Paul. I've taken a little bit from each of the deposits our regular investors have made toward our future productions, which of course I'll replace after--"

Myra interrupted, "That's illegal! And, if it's a flop; Frank could go to jail."

"Not Frank - me. Frank is investing every cent he's got. The least I can do is gamble a few years of my freedom for him." Connie leaned back with a smug look on her face.

Myra said, "You needn't worry. If that should happen, I'll pick up the difference. I have my own money. In fact, I'll help you even further; you can forego my salary. That should help keep your above-the-line costs down a little. Then you can pay me a percentage out of net, if there is any."

"Myra, Connie has uh... I - I mean, we already decided to do that," stuttered Eugene.

"You did?" Myra's eyes narrowed as she looked from him to Connie.

"And Hooper, too." Eugene added. "He said he didn't mind, considering that a leading role in one of my pictures would help his career so much, he would consider it payment in itself."

In some way Myra didn't like the way she heard the words 'my pictures' pass Eugene's lips. It was the way he was behaving - without any of Frank's business authority or maturity; Frank would have said, 'my pictures' and an aura of confidence would fill the room. It surprised her, but she was feeling some resentment toward him, and at the same time she was certain it had nothing to do with jealousy over the way he was hanging on to Connie's apron strings.

The Wardrobe Manager signaled for them to follow, and Myra said to Hooper, "This is it; as soon as I slip on the wedding band she gives me, I'll be Mrs. Gene Eastly, mother of two, and wife of a prominent public accountant. From that point forward I'll expect you to call me Carol, or honey, or whatever endearment Gene would use. Don't expect me to respond to anything else until the end of shooting, because that's who I'll be, and I will have no other husband in mind but you. Playing the wife of an amnesiac ought to be the easiest role I've ever had."

"I'll call you Carol, but don't expect me to follow your example and stay in character constantly. It's not my style."

Myra took his elbow to lead him toward the dressing rooms as she shook her head and said, "And you think you can perform to Frank Stacy's standards."

Hooper pulled his elbow from her grasp, and turned her around to face him. "And another thing - don't expect my complete performance until the cameras are rolling, but I'll give you this warning: when they do roll don't count on this to remain your easiest role - you'd better be prepared to react to an unexpected performance."

"What are you alluding to? Our sex scene? Ha! Hooper, who do you think you are? Valentino?" She turned and walked on to Wardrobe.

Hooper's face burned with embarrassment. He wished he had kept his mouth shut. Not only did she misinterpret his challenge, but she came uncomfortably close to naming his desire before he had a chance to prove his worth. To calm his nerves, he hung back before going on to wardrobe, and took a few deep breaths.

"In-two-three," he counted to himself while inhaling. "Out-two-three," he exhaled. He repeated the procedure several times in an attempt to clear his mind. He began to feel the tension leave his muscles. He smiled and nodded at several of the crew members as they busied themselves about the set, but none returned the greeting, and all of them gave him wide berth whenever their tasks brought them in his direction. Feeling the tension returning, Hooper stamped off in disgust toward Wardrobe.

When he entered the room, Myra was gone. The costumer stood up from her sewing machine without a word and began taking his measurements. Hooper's attempts at conversation were met with silent hostility. Her deft hand snapped the tape around his waist and along his inseam as if she were cracking a whip.

CHAPTER SIXTEEN

As he relaxed on the plane carrying him to Hollywood, Eugene had a few moments to stop and think about Jack. Production planning for *Accidental Angel* had not allowed him much time for any diversions including catching up on all the events and inventions he'd missed in twenty years. He still couldn't remember all the Presidents that served between Johnson and Reagan, although he did remember the one that came from a town twelve miles from his home. When he did have spare time he tried calling *Directory Assistance* to see if Jack was listed in L.A.; he'd also tried Anchorage and Fairbanks, Alaska, and finally Ellaville, Georgia, but he had no luck. He found it curious how all his new friends seemed to shy away whenever he asked them to help.

As he looked out the window to enjoy the sights of his very first flight, he wondered what happened to his copy of *Gods Of The Pond*. He'd looked through his files at home and at the office, but in that mass of paperwork he did not see his title listed. He wondered whether Jack still had a copy, and if not, or if he never found Jack, if he would be able to rewrite it. As the jet passed over the quilted patterns of fields and pastures, he thought back to the day when he first read the manuscript to Jack and Stacie, now over twenty years past, yet to him only a few weeks. It was in the shade of their favorite tree in the middle of Jack's pasture on the little knoll that rose like a big bump in the grass, or maybe it was an ancient Indian burial mound. He was tickled when Stacie recognized herself, but he was overjoyed when she said that was exactly how she wanted the three of them to live when they moved to Alaska. It was a happy story, the first of a series that would bring about Jack's dream of an independent country in Alaska. Perhaps, he thought, it could still happen.

With Ralph Smurling's arrival in town, Eugene's life became a roller-coaster. His thoughts of Jack were forced to take a back seat as Connie ushered in and out of his office: set designers, studio representatives, and filming equipment rental agents. He was even too busy for his secret fear: going to sleep one night - forever, and Frank waking up instead. The work was thrilling even if he had little input. He understood nearly all they told him, after all, he had spent his youth reading up for a movie-making career. For the most part though, he found himself merely along for the ride as Ralph and Connie took care of the details Frank had blanked out on. Meanwhile, he was learning from his idol, *the* Ralph Smurling, and it was wonderful to bask in the great director's presence. He had no inkling that Smurling was disappointed in him.

Ralph kept that to himself. He was surprised at finding that Eugene was little more than a passive observer. He was nothing of the aggressive young man he'd met twenty years earlier. There was in Eugene none of the innate directing ability Frank had demonstrated within his first few days. He seemed only to want to learn by watching.

"The old Frank," thought Ralph, "wanted nothing less than for me to get the hell out of his way so that he could get his own hands-on experience."

The only positive difference he could name was that Eugene seemed genuinely happy, an emotion he never really saw in Frank except when he was with Zack. While the whole situation was strange, all in all; Ralph did not mind, he was just plain happy to be working again. He did not even care if the picture flopped, a possibility he believed inevitable.

It was as the airplane taxied down the runway that Ralph's showmanship rose out of retirement and enabled him to purge his mind of morose thoughts, even if they were legitimate concerns.

He ran them through his mind one last time: "An unknown actor in the leading role. Who the hell is this Hooper Johnson, anyway? He's had no screen test; he doesn't even have an agent. A secretary working as Production Manager. I don't care if it is Connie with all her years in the business, it's not the same. Oh, and if the time factor alone isn't enough. Never in my entire career have I ever had to put a picture together on such short notice. All of which is accentuated by the secrecy surrounding this weird problem of Frank's."

"What the hell," he said aloud, "the show must go on."

#

As she stepped out of the limo in front of Frank's condo building, Connie clutched a leather briefcase tightly to her breast. Inside was the original manuscript of *Resurgent Man*. She did not know why, but she suspected it held the key to unlocking Frank's heart. Her only clue was that it was written by Jack, the same Jack, Eugene was always talking about. But Jack was dead, and Eugene did not know it. She wondered how it would affect him, but it scared her to be the one to tell. "Let Myra do it," she thought, "she's already had her chance with Frank and blown it."

When Myra greeted them at the door, Connie smiled too cordially, but her smile warmed to happiness as Sara led her to her room. They passed what were apparently separate bedrooms for Frank and Myra. It was a fact she had long suspected, but now that she knew, she took an oath. She dropped her briefcase on the bed and facing the wall separating her bed from Frank's, and quietly said, "I promise you, Myra Mason, that before *Accidental Angel* is finished it will be on my door that Frank knocks."

#

By the time Connie got back downstairs, Ralph and Eugene were busy at work in the office. She was thankful of the condo's design. All the bedrooms were on the third floor, while the kitchen and living areas were on the second, she felt such a set up was perfect for discouraging Myra from bothering them on the first floor, which was reserved for the Front Office whenever Frank shot in Hollywood.

When she entered the room, Ralph was bent over at the waist, facing the wall across from Frank's desk. His broad bottom spread the vent in the back of his suit jacket. He was attaching the strip of cardboard that designated the final scene of ANGEL to the production breakdown board mounted on the wall. The doorbell rang loudly, and masked the grunt Smurling uttered as he straightened up. Connie started to back out of the doorway she had just entered.

Ralph chugged toward her and said, "That's all right Connie, I'll get it."

Left alone with Eugene, she walked behind his chair. This was one of the rare moments she longed for, had vowed to take advantage of, and like a silk net over an elusive butterfly, she placed her hands tenderly on his shoulders. "Have you finished working out the shooting sequence?"

Eugene did not consciously notice the amatorial tone of her voice, but he did shift comfortably under her touch. He pointed across the desk to where Ralph had been standing a moment before.

"Yes, we'll begin with all the Accounting office scenes. Then we go on to the library scene while the Accounting office set is converted to the Town Council headquarters. The set for the Library will be broken down for the Dentist's office, and with the completion of that shot, we'll be able use all the space for the house sets. It will take the grips two days to complete the house, so we'll be shooting the nightmare during that time. The first shots in the house will be the dining room scene, while the living room and bedroom are finished. The last set will be the victim's home for which there'll be no additional construction. We'll only need to redecorate the original living room."

"Excellent!" she cried, "You're really picking this up fast."

"You really think so?"

"Yes," she lied.

Ralph came back into the room with a large manila envelope in his hand. Eugene asked "Are those our permits for the location shots?"

"Yes," Ralph answered, "that was Express Courier at the door."

"Is there any legal work we lack at this point?" Eugene asked.

Connie purposely did not remove her hand from Frank's shoulder when Ralph returned. Eugene did not shrug her off. She squeezed him once then let go, while answering his question, "Yes, we still haven't gotten the children's contracts or their release forms signed yet, but we have an appointment with the parents day after tomorrow."

"Good!" responded Ralph. "Then I say it's time we go over to Nordwick to see how the carpenters are doing."

#

The camera assistant, a young man in his early twenties, stood in front of Hooper with the open slate in his hand while the focus operator checked the camera lens one last time. Beside that camera was a smaller camera for video-tape, which gave Frank Stacy an instant idea of how the day's filming was turning out. When Smurling yelled, "Roll," the assistant called out, "Accidental Angel, scene two, take one." Then, leaning his body back slightly, so the slate was only inches from Hooper's face, he slapped the arm down with a crack that made Hooper wince. Hooper started to turn and say something, but Smurling yelled, "Action," and Hooper's body automatically became that of Gene Eastly's.

The opening scene of *Accidental Angel* is a luxurious office. A young, and pretty receptionist answers the phone, "Gene Eastly, C.P.A.". The camera cuts to an inner office, then pans showing a man, forty or so years of age, in a conservative grey suit sitting behind a large mahogany desk. In front of the desk sits another man, this one dressed in a stylish blue suit.

The camera cuts to an over-the-shoulder shot, from behind the man in grey as the man in blue speaks.

"Gene," he says gesturing with a stapled stack of papers, "I can't get over how much money I made this year, and I owe it all to your suggestions. You know, instead of an accountant, you ought to be a business consultant."

Cut to over-the-blue-suited-shoulder as Gene answers, "Lou, what do you think I've been doing for the last ten years?"

Cut back to master shot showing side view of both men laughing.

"Well, I'm not supposed to tell," Lou began, "but because of all the miracles you've performed for the town's treasury, there will be a little surprise for you after the town council meeting this week."

"Miracles, what miracles? All I've done is the job I was elected to do."

"No sirree, Councilman Eastly, those were miracles. First you balanced the town's operating budget. Then by giving us efficient ways to run the town you were able to show us how to lower taxes. Lower taxes have encouraged the growth of new business, and those new businesses have created new jobs. Why the entire standard of living in Somerville has increased since you took office."

"Okay then Councilman Manning, what's the surprise?"

Lou standing said, "That, old boy, you'll have to wait for."

The men shake hands and Lou exits.

The scene dissolves to Gene stepping out of his office while flipping off the light. The master shot includes a secretary. She's an attractive girl with a fresh-scrubbed, small town look about her.

Gene says, "It's five o'clock Cathy; quitting time."

"Oh, I didn't notice," she says smiling, then turns off her typewriter, and picks up her purse.

That scene fades to black and then Gene enters the front door of his home. Two well dressed children, boy and girl, ages seven and eight respectively, run to greet him, and he catches both of them in his arms.

They cry out happily, "Daddy! Daddy!"

He kisses them both and asks, "How was school today?"

Both answer at once, reciting detailed events of the day, and Gene seems to hear both their answers.

He lets them slide back to the floor as an attractive woman enters the expensively furnished living room. She's wearing a crisp stylish dress, high heeled pumps, and a string of pearls around her neck. They clasp hands and kiss, then the woman asks, "How was your day, dear?"

"Same old, same old," he answers jokingly.

He drops his attaché case on a chair as an olive skinned maid walks in and says, "Señor Eastly, you jus' in time fo' dinner. I feex your favorite chicken."

The scene fades gradually as the camera pans around and around the table while the family eats. Joyous music masks their words and voices, their cheery faces say it all in the brightly and warmly lighted dining room.

The brightness fades to black, and the new scene opens in a gloomy light. The camera is hand held; its lens is covered with a fog filter. The camera moves up and down aisles in a grocery store. The view gives the effect of tunnel vision and every object seems to have an eerie halo. The background music is played in bass tones with a steadily rising heartbeat tempo.

The camera tilts up and holds on a shelf of bread, the shot is canted or lopsided to give the subjective sense of a person who is mentally off balance. It then zooms in on a single loaf. When the perspective widens again the loaf is on the checkout counter behind which stands a man with his hand out, gesturing for payment. The man is about thirty-five years old, and balding. He wears dark, large-framed glasses.

No money enters his open palm, so he picks up the loaf of bread, and starts laughing. With his other hand he points toward himself, and then toward the camera. The exaggerated modulation of his mouth makes it possible to read the words on his lips as he says, "Me Give You?" He laughs some more, it too is exaggerated. Then he points toward the door, and again his lips can be read as he orders, "Get out." Suddenly, the barrel of a revolver in pressed against his nose, and he is no longer laughing. That frame is frozen for three heart beats, then the man's face explodes into red. The music stops, the picture fades to black, and the music is replaced by a man screaming.

The darkness fades as Carol is shaking Gene in their dimly but warmly lit bedroom.

"Aaiiiii!" Gene is the source of the scream.

"Gene! Gene, wake up! Gene!"

He stops screaming, and gasping says, "Oh God... oh God, Carol, thank you; I was having the nightmare again."

Carol pulled the shaking Gene into her arms, and said, "It's okay honey; you're awake now."

"No, it's not; you don't understand. I was hungry; no starving. I was in a store begging the owner for food. He laughed at me, and told me to get out. Then I... I couldn't control myself. I was grabbing him by the collar, and pushing a pistol into his nose. His sneering grin turned to terror, and then I started laughing. I told him I'd take what I wanted. Then it happened, just like always, he pulled away, and my finger clamped down on the trigger. His head exploded. It was an accident, I didn't mean to pull the trigger. Oh God, blood was everywhere... my hands... my face."

"It's okay now," Carol reassured.

"No, it's not! It's not... because... because somehow I know it's true."

The scene fades as Carol rocks Gene's head against her breast.

#

Hooper opened his eyes when he heard the knock on his dressing room door.

"Come in," he yelled to the door.

Myra entered the room as he was sitting up on the cot.

"Were you sleeping?" she inquired.

"No, just resting," he answered, then asked, "What are you doing here today?"

"I came to watch you."

"I thought this was a closed set."

"Did you think that would apply to me?"

"Not really, but still I didn't expect you to come around until you received your call."

"And you didn't expect me to come watch you after you practically challenged me to do so."

Hooper stood up as if for emphasis, and said, "That was a demand, not a challenge; it was not to entice you to come and watch, but to prepare you to put your best ability against mine when both of us are on stage together."

"A demand! Ha! I witnessed your so called ability today, and frankly there's little to anticipate. I'll admit you're better than I expected, but then it doesn't take a genius to shuffle papers in an office, give a little dictation, and then smooth talk a few clients about tax shelters."

"Stick around... " he paused, then added contemptuously, "Carol. Today we're doing the library scene and I have very few lines to lean on. Everything I have to convey to the audience will have to come from here," he pointed to his head, "and here," he jabbed his thumb against his chest.

"You're right, *darling,*" she sneered the endearment, "that will be something to see. I find it hard to imagine how anyone of your size, with your football player's build, can portray genuine fear."

"I love an audience," he said sarcastically as he sat back down on the cot.

Myra pulled open the door to leave, and added before walking out the door, "The real test will be tomorrow when I watch your scene in the dentist's waiting room. Not only will I be interested in your enactment of controlled fear, but how it compares to what you do today."

"The dailies look good, Frank," Ralph said to Eugene as the lights in the screening room came on. "Say, Connie, how about getting us some more coffee."

"Ralph, do you usually ask your Production Manager to fetch coffee?"

Irritation crossed Ralph's face and he said, "Connie, think of me as a ship's captain. I don't care how you delegate the orders once you get them, just as long as they get done."

"Yes, sir," she muttered, as she got up from her seat.

When she was out of hearing range, he said, "Frank, there are too many prima donnas in this industry. You've got to be a hard ass if you want to get anything done."

"But Connie..."

"Is no different. It's gotta go all the way down the line, because the buck stops with you. You know this is really funny, me telling you this. It's as if I'm finally having to give you the lessons I expected to have to give you twenty years ago, but which you didn't want." Then mentally he added, "or need."

It made Eugene uncomfortable whenever Smurling waxed about the past, so to change the subject, he said, "I've been studying some editing effects and I was thinking it would be fun to use a few wipes, you know when the upcoming scene pushes the current one off the screen, instead of intercutting and fading all the time."

"Frank, we aren't filming a weekly episode of *Batman*. A wipe is not sophisticated enough for anything but TV; as a punctuation mark, it's much too strong. The object is to avoid anything that reminds your audience they're watching a movie."

"Oh," Eugene replied sheepishly, then to change the subject one more time, he said, "So the dailies are good, huh?"

"Yeah, but that's to be expected. This script is about as complicated as TV situation comedy, or worse, a soap opera. The real work will be in the cutting room, that is, if your actors come through for you. If they don't, it really won't matter what we do when we sit down to the editing machine."

"But I thought that was why we shot so many extra feet, so we would be able to weed out the errors."

"Son, once you've synched up the sound to the picture there's little more you can do at the *Movieola* with a spool of bad acting."

"Then we've got nothing to worry about, Frank Stacy's actors are the best."

"You're forgetting that wild card we have out there."

"But Frank picked Hooper himself."

"Pardon me if this offends you, but Frank picked Hooper on the last day he was reported to be himself; a day, mind you, spent in a drunken stupor. The next day he was you, and I have to wonder how much influence you must have had on his decision, especially since you insisted we keep him."

"Hooper will come through."

"He damn well better."

#

When the camera assistant stepped in front of him to open the hinge on the blackboard slate, Hooper reached out and gave him a shove that made him take three steps forward to catch his balance. The boy turned around, his eyes glaring, and Hooper admonished, "You try to clip my nose one more time, kid, and I'll take you out to the parking lot and teach you some real slap-stick."

The assistant's eyes fell on Hooper's huge fists, then without stepping back he turned around to call the scene and take.

"Bob, you're going to have to reinvest twenty-two percent of that profit back into R&D if you want to keep your current tax status." Gene Eastly has his hand on the shoulder of the man he is speaking to as they walk out of his private office into the reception area.

"Gene, I'm not sure that's enough, Zena's on to something hot right now, and keeps asking for more capital. I'm thinking maybe I ought to go public."

"You ought not rush into anything like that. You're about to the end of your fiscal year. Let's wait until then; we'll re-examine the books, and see how far along Zena is. Going public simply doesn't have all the advantages it appears to when the sole object is capital consumption."

"I didn't get where I am today by being hasty; we can talk about it later," Bob says, as he extends his hand.

"Until then," Gene accepts the handshake.

Gene then turns back to his office, and the camera cuts to a close up of Cathy, his secretary. "Mr. Eastly, it's one o'clock. The town council meets in thirty minutes."

Cut to a close-up of Gene. "Oh, thank you, I'd about forgotten."

Cut back to the master shot as he walks to a coat tree, and picks off a hat.

"See you later," he says while tipping the hat to Cathy."

Cut back to close up of Cathy. "Good luck."

Cut back to close up of Gene. "Good luck for what? It's just a council meeting."

Back to Cathy, giggling. "I'm not supposed to tell."

Cut to master shot as Gene walks to exit. "Gee, am I the only one in town, who doesn't know?"

Fade to black.

The scene opens on the council meeting in progress. Around an oval table sit nine men and three women. The Chairman with a gavel in front of him, sits at the head of the table. Cigarettes smolder in ashtrays, and cups of half finished coffee are in front of most members. Each has a stack of papers in front of him. The master shot gives the subjective view of someone sitting at the opposite end of the table from the Chairman.

Chairman says, "Motion to approve the new appointment for police chief carries. Is there any more new business?"

Pan to man on right who asks, "Shouldn't we decide on imposing zoning restrictions for the northeast quadrant?"

Chairman raps his gavel, and says, "Mr. Quinn, you're out of order. Procedure must be followed if any of us hope to get to the end of this meeting. You know you must first request the floor; then you must phrase your question as a motion."

Mr. Quinn says, "Sorry, may I have the floor?"

The Chairman replies, "Mr. Quinn has the floor."

Mr. Quinn proposes, "I move we impose zoning restrictions for the northeast quadrant of Somerville as surveyed in the official city map."

A woman across from him says, "I second the motion."

Gene stands up and says, "Mr. Chairman, the floor."

The Chairman answers, "The Chair recognizes Mr. Eastly."

Gene says, "I move to table the motion."

"Second," adds Lou who is sitting next to him, who also, says, "and I move we adjourn."

"Second," says another man.

"Hey!" cries out Mr. Quinn. "That's out of order we have to vote on tabling first."

The Chairman raps his gavel, and says, "No, Mr. Quinn, you are. A motion to adjourn is always in order. Do I hear a call for the vote?"

"Call," one of the women answers.

"All in favor?" asks the Chairman.

"Aye!" resounds the majority.

The Chairman raps his gavel and says, "Carries. This meeting is hereby adjourned until next week: same time - same place. Good, now we can get on with some real business. Anna, why don't you ask those gentlemen in the foyer to come on in? Gene, don't you move."

Three men, enter the room behind Anna while the rest of the council members make room for them around the table.

When the three are settled, the Chairman continues, "Gene Eastly, I would like you to meet Oscar Dubois, Larry McIntosh, and Craig Emerson."

"Pleasure," states Gene as he shakes each of their hands across the table.

"Gene," continues the Chairman, "Oscar here, is state *Republicrat* Chairman; Larry and Craig are his assistants. Oscar, I'll turn the floor over to you."

Oscar chuckles and says, "I trust everyone in the room is a registered *Republicrat*?"

Lou laughs and says, "In this state are you kidding? I didn't think there was anything else."

Everyone laughs.

Oscar continues, "Gene, we're here today because of your remarkable reputation."

Cut to Gene nodding curiously.

Cut back to Oscar. "The state party has been watching you, and we want you to run for Congress--"

"Yippee!" interrupts Lou.

All the council members jump up from their seat and rush to slap Gene on the back. "Congratulations." "All right, old boy!" "Congratulations."

Gene stands up and says, "Gee, I don't know what to say."

Oscar says, "Say yes. You'll be a shoe-in. Everybody in this district knows who you are, and what you've done for the town. Once you get to Washington and make a little noise for a term or two, we can start grooming you for the Governor's seat. Then you can do some real good for the state."

"Aren't you moving a little fast?" asks Gene.

"Not at all," Oscar responds, "you're just too modest."

Gene's face is a picture of joy, tears form in his eyes.

"So, what's your answer?" asks Oscar.

Cut to close-up of Gene's happy face, "I..."

Insert the end of Gene's nightmare, the point where the pistol goes off in the grocery store cashiers face.

Cut back to close up of Gene's face, now suddenly distraught. "I'll have to think about it," he answers gasping.

Cut to master.

"Ho! Ho! The surprise was too much for him," cries Lou with glee.

Oscar slaps him on the back and says, "You let us know; there's plenty of time, yet."

Fade to black.

The scene opens in the middle of Gene's nightmare.

The grocer's bloody face dissolves into Gene gasping in bed and Carol waking to the noise.

"Gene? Gene, what is it?" Carol asks.

"It... it was the nightmare again."

Carol puts her arms around him and says, "Oh no, not again. That's twice in one week. It's been so long since you've had it that I was hoping you were over it, that it wouldn't come back."

"Why," whispers Gene, "why must it seem so real."

"It must be your excitement about the nomination."

"But that doesn't explain why it came back the other night."

"Try to sleep honey; there's an explanation and we'll find it."

"That's what I'm afraid of."

Fade to black.

Gene is unrolling a cinnamon-raisin bun on his plate in the bright, sunny, happy world of his dining room. Beatriz, the maid, is pouring him more coffee. The children are struggling to find a prize in the bottom of a cereal box. Carol is tapping the shell of a soft boiled egg.

"You're looking well rested this morning," Carol says to Gene.

"Only because I passed the night without my dream."

"Good," she says while toasting him with her orange juice. "May last night set a precedent for the rest of your life."

"Thank you Carol, but I've been thinking; maybe I've been having that dream because I'm somehow feeling guilty about the wonderful life I have."

"Nonsense, honey. You have absolutely nothing to feel guilty about. You earn your living, and do public service as well. You give to charity, and you don't kick dogs. What more could anyone ask?"

"I don't know, but I can feel it within me - some kind of unnamed guilt."

"Dear, you're just too hard on yourself, those nightmares probably have a simple explanation; Beatriz's cooking for instance."

Cut to close-up of Beatriz's face. First her eyes widen in surprise; then they squint in anger as she says, "They is no-ting wrong with my cooking!"

Gene laughs and says, "Nothing except that I eat too much of it."

Cut to Gene getting up from the table.

"Well, I'm off to work."

He bends over and kisses Carol.

"Don't forget your appointment with the dentist," she reminds him.

Dissolve to Dentist's Office.

Gene enters the reception area and rings a bell beside a smoked glass window which is opened by a pretty girl, about age eighteen, dressed in white, and very pregnant. Her protruding stomach keeps her from sitting very close to the edge of her desk.

She says, "Good morning Councilman, and congratulations."

"Thank you," answers Gene. He then adds, "Boy, gossip sure travels fast around here."

She says in return, "What else is there to do in a small town."

"I can think of at least one other thing," Gene answers slyly while glancing obviously toward her belly.

They both laugh; then the girl says, "Make yourself comfortable. Dr. Baine will be busy for a few more minutes."

In the background the whirring sound of the dentist's drill can be heard. Gene winces at the sound, and the receptionist giggles.

After Gene sits down, he sorts through the stacks of magazines on one of the tables.

Gene looks up toward the receptionist, and says, "Looks like you guys never throw magazines away."

She answers, "Yeah, some are even over ten years old. I love to look at the automobile ads. Those old cars look so funny; they're so big."

Gene laughs and leans back as he finally selects one to read.

To the girl he says, "I see what you mean. Here's one almost fifteen years old."

Camera cuts to over-the-shoulder to direct audience attention on the pages. After flipping past several pages, he stops on an article headlined: ***Unsolved Crimes***. He reads briefly then turns the page. His hands start shaking as the audience sees a photograph of a familiar face.

Cut to close-up of Gene expressing horror.

Insert of Gene's nightmare showing Grocer's face.

Cut to magazine photograph. Now include the caption which reads: Milton Barrow, grocer murdered for $16.43. Killer never found.

Cut to close-up of Gene, then dolly back to give full frontal length as Gene stands, shaking. As the camera moves backward, the audience sees the horror in Gene's face transform to fear.

Cut to master as Gene walks rapidly to the door. To the receptionist whose back is turned, he stutters. "Uh, t-tell, Dr. Baine, I'll have to reschedule. I... I just remembered a previous engagement."

As the receptionist is turning to face him, she is saying, "Oh, you're not going to let a little drill noise scare you now..."

But Gene is gone before she completes the sentence.

Looking bewildered at the door swinging closed she finishes, "...are you?"

Cut to Gene inside a car driving. Tears are in his eyes. Cut to outside car to show where Gene is driving. This is followed by a series of shots intercut to rapidly denote the passage of time. Gene inside the car looking frantic, to a cut outside the car showing another road, or highway Gene is taking. Gene obviously has no apparent destination in mind. Finally cut to Gene inside car as he slows to a stop. He is hyperventilating, and takes a minute to slow down his breathing. He then opens door. Cut to facade of Library.

Cut to inside Library. Master shot as Gene goes from card catalog, then to disappear down an aisle, then returning with yellowing newspapers. Cut to Gene sitting in front of a microfilm projector, intently reading.

Cut away to telephone ringing in Gene's home. Carol answers.

"No, he's not here, Cathy. ... What do you mean he never returned from the dentist? Did you call there?"

Cut to Cathy looking worried, as she answers, "The girl said he left without ever seeing the dentist. ... Sure, I'll call you as soon as I hear from him. ... I hope so, too. Good bye."

Cut back to Gene sitting in front of microfilm projector. He is shaking his head with his palm pressed against his face. Spread about the table are several open yellowed newspapers. He looks up toward the ceiling, his face is red, his eyes swollen and bloodshot. He opens his mouth, and a sticky string of saliva hangs from his top lip as he quietly cries out, "Oh God!"

Cut to Gene, jacket draped over his arm, tie missing, and shirt unbuttoned three times. He is carrying a bottle of whiskey, and a box the size of a large book wrapped in brown paper. He enters his front door.

#

Myra pushed open Hooper's door without knocking, then stepped halfway inside.

Hooper looked up from his cot, taunted, "Well Carol, hello. I can see that you're completely in character now. Otherwise why would you assume you could just walk into my room, unless you really believed you were my wife?"

"You don't have to do that anymore."

"Do what?"

"Call me Carol. I only asked you to do that for your sake anyway."

"My sake?"

"Yes, I thought you needed every advantage possible to help you create your character. Now I see that I was wrong."

"What is this?"

"An apology, if you'll accept it." She said, then entered the room with a huge bouquet of roses, and placed it on the counter."

"Flowers? You're bringing me flowers?"

"A peace offering. And, because a dressing room just doesn't look right unless it has some flowers." She turned from the counter to face him, and asked, "Will you please accept my apology?"

"I accept."

Myra sat on the edge of the cot, and said, "You're good, certainly good enough to be in any Frank Stacy picture. I'm sorry for having insulted your ability. Actually, I'm ashamed; I don't usually make judgments without any evidence."

Hooper propped himself up on his elbow, and with a broad grin said, "Enough already! I'm appeased."

Smiling gently Myra said, "I'm glad."

Hooper then frowned and said, "I'll be glad when the rest of the cast and crew come to the same judgment. I've never experienced such a lack of respect and courtesy in my life. I always thought Stacy's gang consisted of real professionals."

"Give them time. You haven't had to pay the same dues they've paid; they don't understand. I didn't, but as you can see, I've come around."

Neither said anything for several seconds while Hooper's frown softened back into a smile.

It occurred to Hooper that if Myra was behaving in accordance with the rules of propriety, she ought to be leaving at that moment, but, he also thought, proper etiquette would never have allowed her to sit so close to him while he was lying in bed. He put his hand on her wrist and said, "Thank you, Myra."

Sensing the change in atmosphere, Myra looked around the room, and then asked, "What are you doing here today? You don't shoot again until day after tomorrow."

Hooper chuckled as he said, "I guess it's just that I'm still excited about actually having my name on a dressing room door. Besides, I haven't any better place to be; and this mobile home has more food and drink stocked in it than I could use in a month."

Myra laughed and said, "Hooper, you're a neophyte after all."

Hooper squeezed her wrist, and asked, "Would you care to go for some dinner?"

Myra paused briefly before answering, "No, I want to get back to the house; I'm hoping Eugene will get in early tonight."

She stood up, walked to the door, stopped and turned back to face him, "I'll see you Thursday, I trust you'll be as good as you were yesterday because it'll be me and you, kiddo."

Hooper leaned back against the pillow and put his hands behind his head, "Expect better."

Myra raised a doubting eyebrow to him, but said nothing.

Hooper laughed and she walked out of the room.

As she walked over to her car, she noticed she was feeling a little odd, a little lightheaded. "Am I getting sick?" she thought, but as she started driving the music on her stereo seemed to sound better than usual. For some reason driving seemed to be a pleasure, as if somehow she had suddenly become more competent behind the wheel. Then it occurred to her: she was happy.

"I'm happy," she giggled out loud.

She inhaled deeply, as if some weight had been removed from her shoulders. "Gee, I haven't felt this good in weeks." Then she thought, "No, years."

Shortly after Myra arrived home, she made her daily call to the detective, and he had her answer. Tracing Stacie Rogers had taken so long because she had married under the name Smith, and finding the right Smith out of hundreds took time. Currently, she lived with her husband and five children on a farm in Marion County, the next county west of Ellaville. The detective gave Myra an address and a phone number. Myra's urge was to fly out to Georgia immediately, but since she was in the middle of filming *Accidental Angel*, she did the next best thing. Phoning from home presented the risk that Eugene might walk in, or later see the call recorded on the long-distance bill, so she bought two rolls of quarters and found a comfortable phone booth.

"Hello, may I speak to Stacie," Myra asked the woman who answered.

"This is she," answered Stacie. Her high octave voice rang melodiously with an accent so pure and sweet; it sounded like a caricature to Myra's non-Southern ear.

"Stacie, my name is Myra Mason; I'm calling..."

"The movie actress?"

"Yes."

"Well, I'll be."

"I'm calling because of my husband."

"Eugene?" she asked.

Myra was startled. "You know that?"

"Oh, yes. How could I forget little Eugene? I recognize his picture all the time, although I'm probably the only one around here that does."

"The only one?"

"Well, his Daddy did, but nobody'd believe him when he went around telling everyone that Frank Stacy the movie director was his son, and I didn't say nothin' 'cause he was always so mean to Eugene. I didn't think he deserved the recognition. So, what may I do for you?"

"Stacie, it's like this: Frank, I mean Eugene, doesn't like to talk about his past, and I wanted to ask you some questions - it's important - he's having some problems."

"I'm sorry to hear he's not doin' well. What would you like to know?"

"I guess I mostly want to know about Jack."

"Jack's dead," she said bluntly.

"I was afraid of that, could you tell me how he died?"

"I'd rather not. If that's what Eugene don't like to talk about, then I can understand. It's still pretty painful to me too - even after all these years."

"Could you just tell me this: was Eugene in any way responsible?"

Stacie did not answer right away. As each second of her pausing passed, Myra's fear grew. When she finally spoke, the soprano lilt of her drawl had deepened to melancholy. It was a question, not an answer she had, "Why? What did he say to make you think that?"

"It wasn't anything he said; it's just that Frank is having some emotional problems - part of which is - he thinks Jack is still alive."

"My goodness!"

"I'm only guessing, which is why I called you, but is Frank having this fantasy because he's responsible for Jack dying?"

Her voice was on the edge of tears. "I don't like to think about it."

"Then it was his fault?"

"Miss Mason, you don't understand; Eugene adored Jack. Maybe his sense of loss is the reason he's blaming himself. I can understand his pain; I've often wondered myself whether I could have, or should have stopped him. It wasn't Eugene's fault, it was Jack's own fault."

The vagary of Stacie's answer did little to assuage Myra's fears. At best it told her the auto crash was an accident, at worst that Stacie had no idea that Eugene perceived Jack as a rival and would kill to get her. Only hope held her spirits aloft.

"Is he having some serious problems?" Stacie asked.

"Yes, but it's probably best that I don't discuss them; please, however, accept that your answer comes as a relief to me."

"I will."

"Thank you. Would it be too much for me to ask you to tell me what Jack was like? You see, Eugene talks about him all the time, but what he says often seems distorted."

"I thought you said he never talks about the past?"

"He never did until recently, and it's not so much what he says about what Jack was like, but what he and Jack will do together in the future."

"Oh, my."

"So, could you tell me about him, just a little?"

"Well, I suppose. Jack was... Jack was carefree; he loved to play. I guess the one picture of him that has remained strongest in my memory is from a picnic we took up to the hill in his back pasture. He climbed up this one old tree that was there all by itself. Whenever I think of him, I see him hanging upside down from a branch in that tree just acting as silly as he could. Jack had another side though; he was a dreamer, who had ideas of faraway places, and how things ought to be. He was my one love."

"Your one love! What about your husband?"

"It's not the same. Don's a good man, but I could never again have the feelings I once had for Jack."

"What about the way you felt for Eugene?"

"Eugene! Oh that's silly; he was just a kid. Jack and I used to call him our puppy because he was always tagging along behind us."

"But he said--"

"Eugene was just infatuated, that's all."

"But how could you let him think...?"

"I felt sorry for him; his daddy was so cruel."

"Do his parents still live out there?"

"No, they're dead."

"Did Fran... uh, Eugene ever ask you to join him in California?"

"Sort of, right after Jack was killed. He asked me to marry him, and go away with him, but it was just his way of consoling me."

Myra gasped at learning Eugene returned Georgia to see her after the car accident.

"Miss Mason, it was nothing. You aren't jealous of a childhood infatuation are you? I hope that's not why you're calling."

"No," she said, quickly, then to cover her surprise she said, "I was curious if his identification with Jack would go that far; I'm afraid the answer, even though I anticipated it, startled me. What I'm really trying to learn is what kind of role model Jack was to Eugene. May I ask if it was true that you were going to Alaska with Jack?"

"He told you about that too?"

"Yes."

"I guess I would have. I loved Jack so much, I would have gone with him to the moon. Jack was an idealist. Oh, he spoke so beautifully - so passionately; I would have died for him, just to let him speak for another minute. It's hard to imagine today that I used to feel like that. It makes me wonder if I would still do it today? I don't know. I don't even know if I would go to Alaska. Today I've become so practical. Don's a very practical man, and we've got five demanding children. Together they dull the cutting edge of every vision Jack ever gave me. My life today makes the way I used to be, seem but a dream. The kind of dream when you wake up you can't remember the details, only the mood."

"You mean you never think of the things you and Jack used to think anymore?"

"It's not so much that I don't think it anymore - it's just who's got the time?"

"Is it really just the time?"

"No, it's just as you get older, you feel more vulnerable. I remember Jack once said: 'Courage is easy for the young because they believe they're immortal; and it's easy for the old because after a full life, they've nothing to lose; but courage for those in middle life is admirable, because they've lived just long enough to be intimidated by their vulnerability.'"

"Jack sounds as if he were very wise."

"Jack was living in the wrong time."

"Let me ask you this: did you like the way Eugene made Jack's screenplay?"

"Screenplay! What screenplay?"

"Why, *Resurgent Man*."

"Jack wrote that?"

"Yes."

"That's funny - I never saw Jack writing anything - it was always Eugene who was doing all the writing."

"But you did see it?"

"Yes, it made me cry, and afterward I was sick in bed for a week."

"Oh, my. What made you sick?"

"I don't want to talk about it."

#

"Cut!" Ralph called out.

The cameraman stopped the camera then looked with anticipation toward Smurling.

Ralph hesitated, then leaned over to Eugene and whispered, "Frank, did you like it?"

"Yes," he answered.

"Then you need to tell them."

A wide grin of pride swept Eugene's face. He whispered excitedly, "Really?"

Smurling nodded.

Eugene turned to the cameraman and yelled, "Print it!"

The cameraman muttered, "About time." Then began running out the rest of the film, while his assistant prepared to remove the roll.

Zack had become a regular sight around the sound stage. He could always be found sitting quietly behind the directors, silently observing the proceedings. It was a producer's privilege, and in his finely tailored suits, he even looked the part.

Smurling, however, found it perplexing that his happy-go-lucky nephew had maintained such a steadfast interest in the production of *Accidental Angel*. When Eugene got up to retrieve the film from the cameraman, Ralph turned in his chair to speak to Zack.

"Zachary, you've been so serious lately. This is unlike you. Have you suddenly decided after all these years that you would like to work in this field?"

"No, Uncle Ralph. I'm no more aroused by the making of motion pictures than I've ever been."

"I'm sorry to hear that."

Zack shrugged and said nothing.

Smurling looked his nephew's face over in search of an answer before he asked, "I'm puzzled Zack; what is it that you find so absorbing here every day?"

Nodding toward Eugene, Zack answered, "I've lost my closest friend. This Frank doesn't even know who I am, but one day he may wake up and need me."

Smurling muttered angrily, "The real Frank Stacy never needed anyone."

"That's where you're wrong Uncle Ralph. Frank has always needed people. Take Constance for example; she's been his right arm for years, even if he never acknowledged it, and in some strange way, Frank Stacy also needed me. Right now I'm feeling pretty guilty for having betrayed him. If I hadn't tried to help Myra push him into a psychiatrist's care, he'd be fine right now."

"You're kidding yourself, Zack. You witnessed the evidence yourself the day he had the diving accident. The man has a serious problem, and nothing you did aggravated it."

"I don't know. Right now all I can truly identify is my own sense of loss."

"I admire your loyalty, son."

"Thanks."

Eugene handed the film canister to Connie.

"Connie, I want you to get this on over to the lab." As he spoke, he wrote out his instructions on a scrap of paper. "Make sure they understand this is a rush job. I need an answer print tonight, so we can check the special effects. Ask them to send it back on reels, not on cores. I know it costs more, but we're in a hurry. If you'll take over some of our own cans for them to return it in, we can make up some of the expense. Order four dupes, because we'll be using this nightmare scene several times. Make sure they know the ASA speed it was shot at, and that we used both diffusion and fog filters, I don't want them thinking they need to lighten the picture."

"Anything else?" Connie smiled; she was impressed with how much he sounded like the regular Frank at that moment.

"Oh, yeah," he answered, "just one other thing. I've been told we can't assume this lab will remember to print everything on single perforated stock, so you better remind them. Boy, I hope we don't have to reshoot any of this."

"Do you want the sound track on this print?"

"No. We're not going to use today's recording until we add the echo in the sound booth."

"Okay. I should be back in an hour."

"That won't be necessary. You go ahead and take the rest of the day off. I'll see you back at the house tonight, or in the morning if I'm late."

Connie's face dropped. Her interpretation of Eugene's response was simple, if not puerile: he was beginning to not need her.

Back at the condo, after dropping off the film, Connie found herself alone, except for Sara who was busy at her own tasks in the kitchen. Bored, she went up to her room to lie down, but she was too restless to sleep. After a few minutes of staring at the ceiling, she remembered the script to *Resurgent Man*. Flipping through the pages, she tried to develop a plan, or even an idea of how to use Jack as an approach to reach Frank. Nothing was forthcoming, but something about the handwritten manuscript bothered her, which was odd. She'd looked at it dozens of times without feeling that way. It was the familiar way the "L"s were looped. In fact, she'd seen them recently. Tracing through her mind the past few days she tried to recall what she'd read that looked similar. With a gasp she remembered. It was from the instructions Frank had given her for the film processing lab. She leapt from the bed, and took the scrap of paper from her purse. It was the same. Not just the "L"s, but all the letters. It dawned on her, Jack never wrote it. At best he may have collaborated, but Eugene wrote it.

Now she could formulate a plan. It would be easy. The next time Eugene spoke of the movies he and Jack were to make, she would ask if they ever wrote one together. Jack had been some kind of philosopher to Eugene, at least that was the way it sounded whenever Eugene talked about him. From there it would be simple, she would show him the movie. She knew he hadn't seen it because Myra had warned her not to mention it. Now she understood why. Myra was going to attempt to take Jack's place and win Frank's love once and for all, but now that she knew the secret, she would beat Myra at her own game. First, she would have to learn what values this Jack used to possess. Connie stretched out on the bed and began reading *Resurgent Man* as if she were preparing for a final exam.

#

Cut to Carol as Gene enters the living room. Worry is clouding her face. She holds out her arms in such a manner that her body language implies not only her concerned questions, but also the offer of the same secure embrace she might give an injured child.

She cries, "Oh, Gene, I've been so worried. Cathy called and said you never returned to the office, and that you left the dentist without--"

She abruptly stops speaking. Cut to the whiskey bottle in his hand. Cut back to Carol's face registering shock.

Cut to Gene silently crossing living room to enter dining room.

Cut to master shot of dimly lit dining room as Gene drops a brown paper wrapped box onto table then removes a crystal glass from china cabinet. He pours a generous slug of whiskey into the glass then sits down. He does not drink, instead he contemplates the glass, turning it around and around in his hand.

Carol follows him, then sits across from him on the same side of the table and asks, "Gene what is wrong? I've never seen you like this. You're scaring me."

Cut to close up of Gene. He asks, "Are the children in bed?"

Cut to close up of Carol nodding.

Cut back to Gene. Slowly and quietly he begins to speak. "I made an important discovery this morning. Then I had to make a decision that will affect all our lives - mine, yours, and the children's. Afterwards I spent the afternoon coming to terms with--"

Cut to Carol interrupting, "What discovery?"

Cut back to master. With one hand Gene pushes to her the magazine already opened to the page with the grocer's picture; his other hand tightly clutches the whiskey glass. He speaks over swallowed tears, "I discovered the source of my nightmare."

Carol reads, and then looks up cautiously. Her eyes water and her mouth moves in agonized contortions as she says, "What are you saying? That you..." She can't finish.

Gene finishes for her, "...killed him." Gene's face is a picture of tautly controlled anxiety, as he continues, "I never knew I killed a man; that is I didn't remember it, until I saw this picture. Apparently, it was such a shock to my mind that I went into a psychotic amnesia. I even changed my real name without knowing it, but I remembered it today. Carol, I was born Stanley Whisenant."

Cut to Carol standing, and screaming, "No! No! It can't be so... you're mistaken. It's the stress of running for Congress that's making you believe this."

"Carol, quiet! You'll wake the children."

Carol is sobbing heavily and the tears are running into her open quivering mouth.

"It's true," Gene explains, but his suppressed will causes the words to fall into the staccato rhythm of an overly rehearsed speech. "Carol, it has all come back to me... I spent several hours today in the library reading all the recorded accounts of the crime... At some point during my reading, enough material entered my brain to erase whatever mental block was keeping me from remembering."

Carol asks while trying to control her tears, "D-did... did you find out if the authorities were looking for St-Stanley... for you?"

He utters with chagrin, "They apparently had no clues as to who to look for."

Carol, unaware of the shame in his answer, sighs in relief; and says, "Oh, thank God."

Gene says to her sternly, "Carol this is not the end of it."

She moans softly, "I know; you'll have to drop out of the campaign. If any nosy journalist finds out you've changed your name, it will be hard to explain."

"It's more than that, Carol... much more."

Carol notices his conscience-stricken voice now, and demands against her own reasoning ability, "What do you mean?"

"I committed a crime. I must atone for it."

"But no one knows you did, and if we don't tell - no one ever will." Carol argues as if she spoke with perfect logic, then suddenly a questioning look crosses her face, and she cries, "Oh, no! You didn't tell anyone else did you?"

"No, not yet."

Carol sighs.

"Carol, you don't understand, just because no one knows doesn't make it right."

"Yes I do understand!" She holds the magazine picture up to him and says, "This happened over fifteen years ago. You are a good man, a respected man; you're no longer the man who committed this."

"It doesn't matter that I'm no longer the type of man capable of committing such a crime; it happened." He takes the magazine from her and points to the man's picture and says, "There's nothing I can do to make peace with this man; it's irreparable, but he was not the only victim. He had a wife, who is still around. A wife whom I've learned is nearly destitute because my crime. She deserves restitution."

Carol whispers, "What are you going to do?"

Gene pushes away the still full glass of whiskey, and pulls the brown paper wrapped box toward him. "I thought about this very carefully," he begins in a tortured broken voice. "I'm going to liquidate all my assets, except for the house which I'm going to put in your name. It comes to a sizable amount when converted to cash. Half I'll put into a trust fund for you and the children. Then I'll take the other half and anonymously set up another trust fund for the victim's wife."

Carol looks relieved; crying happily, she gets up and hugs Gene while saying, "That's fair; you are a good man. I should have trusted that you would know the right thing to do, but you don't have to set up a trust fund for us."

Gene gently pushes her away, and says, "That's not all of it, Carol."

"What do you mean? What more can you do?"

"I've got to offer her restitution for her husband's death, not merely for what he was worth financially."

Carol's face is white with fear; she is trembling as she watches Gene tear open the brown paper wrapped box with the precision of an automaton.

Cut to close up of the box as Gene removes a nickel plated revolver.

Cut to Carol gasping.

Cut to close up of Gene as he says, "I've got to offer her my life."

Cut to Carol screaming, "No! No! No!"

Gene implores, "Carol, please, the children."

Carol ignores him, grabs him by the shirt and yells, "That's crazy. You can't do this. You belong to me, to the children."

Gene grabs her hands, pries them loose, and then continues to hold them firmly. His eyes struggle for composure as he pleads, "Carol, you're not making this easy for me."

He guides her back to her chair and forces her to sit down. He then drops to his knees, still holding her wrists, and continues, "Please help me, Carol. I've got to do this thing. I'm going to see her and offer three choices: one, she can turn me over to the police to whom I'll plead guilty, or two, she can order my death which I will grant by my own hand--"

Carol leaps up and tries to free herself from his grip.

Gene tightens his hold, and pulls her close to his face as he finishes, "Please Carol, I need you to listen. My third offer will be to indenture myself to her for the rest of my life. Carol you must understand; this is the only power I have to bring about justice. You know the type of man I am; and you know my values insist that it be this way."

Carol drops to the floor, and Gene releases his grasp. Carol puts her arms around his knees and cries.

Fade to black.

"Cut and print!" Eugene yelled.

Hooper reached down and helped Myra to her feet. Still sobbing she put her arms around his shoulders, and whispered, "You were right; you're remarkable."

"You were pretty remarkable yourself," he said as he returned her embrace.

She pressed her wet eyes to his shoulder, and said, "It was only because of your performance. I couldn't have responded as well with anyone else."

Hooper wondered if that included Frank Stacy, as her body continued to shake in his arms. He hugged her lightly once more and said, "Thank you." Then he slid his arm around her back and led her off the stage. After finding her a chair, he told her he was going to rest. As he walked away to his dressing room, he could not see the gleam of admiration in Myra's eyes that followed him out of the room.

Connie, however, did see it. She smiled and looked over at Eugene who was busy in conversation with Ralph. If Eugene noticed at all, he did not seem to care. That made it all the better for her; she had no competition except for Jack, a boy who had been dead over twenty years. A boy Eugene admired for his cool independence. The same self reliance that had marked the career of Frank Stacy, and the reason she had fallen in love with him. Maybe she did not share the same self confidence, but she knew how to appreciate it. It would be her understanding of his character that would eventually gain her the title she wanted: Mrs. Frank Stacy.

The current Mrs. Frank Stacy sat quietly alone where Hooper had left her. Inside her body the emotion of the performance gradually subsided. In its place she felt a relaxing energy while visions of Hooper seemed to dominate her mind. Like the first time she saw him, when she thought he was an autograph hound outside the audition hall. She recalled his perception, and that he was the first to understand what was really happening to Frank. There was also the evening back in Fresno, when she called him into the study and despite her attack, he stood up to her and offered his gentle understanding. Then later on that evening, when it was so funny that neither of them noticed his nakedness. She tried to picture what he looked like, and then remembered that she would get a second chance in just a few more hours. Their bedroom scenes were coming up next. She could not believe the implications of what she was thinking. It caused her eyes to move to Eugene, and the sight of his body made her think of Frank. Eleven years with Frank, and never during that time did she have the sense of joy she was feeling now. It was almost impossible to imagine that anyone could be better than Frank, but after today's filming she had to admit, despite Eugene's presence in Frank's body, Hooper was the better actor. Hooper's acting contained the passion of a man who could enjoy life. Frank could never stop working long enough to enjoy life. Then it occurred to her: it was *because* Frank lacked a sense of self that he could act as well as he could. It was because he was constantly seeking his identity and because he could not find it. Frank's ability was an accident. All he had done was capitalize on his coping devices.

She could now admit that it was more than his acting ability that attracted her to Hooper; Hooper was more of a man. A man she could love; already loved, she thought. As she recognized her emotion, she suddenly realized she never did love Frank. It was her youthful admiration of his ability that she had interpreted as love. Now, in her maturity, she knew the difference. She wondered if she had a chance with Hooper.

Her eyes wandered further across the sound stage to where the visitors sat. A wave of jealousy passed over her as she saw the girl to whom Hooper had given the pass that allowed her onto the closed set. The girl's name was Sally, and Myra knew they had studied acting together, but she did not know if they were lovers. The thought alone caused her pain. Her only relief was her observation that Hooper had only once gone over to speak to her. That, she tried to convince herself, was not the way lovers behaved.

Myra stood up and stretched. She decided she needed to rest a little. She wanted to be ready for a love scene that was going to require every bit of her talent, and every bit of her ingenuity as well.

"Action!" called out Eugene.

Gene is sitting on the edge of the bed unbuttoning his shirt. The bedroom is dimly lit by a single lamp burning a low wattage bulb. Behind him is a partially opened door with bright light radiating around the cracks. Water can be heard running inside.

The water stops running and Carol's voice is heard from behind the door. She speaks calm and evenly as she asks, "When are you leaving to see Mrs. Barrow?"

Gene answers, as he removes his shirt, "I have a number of loose ends I need to tie up here before I leave."

"The trust funds?" Carol asks.

"Yes that, and I need to take care of a few of my clients' needs before I go. I should have everything taken care of in a week, and then I'll take the first train to Salina."

"The train? Why aren't you flying?"

Gene stands to remove his pants as he answers, "Because I can't carry the gun onto the plane."

Several seconds of silence pass. Then Carol says lightly, "Yeah, I guess no one cares if a train gets hijacked."

Gene, down to his boxer shorts, hangs his pants in the closet, and then as he turns back toward the bed, the light goes off in the bathroom. Carol enters the room dressed in a sexy negligee. Having applied fresh make-up, she is stunningly beautiful.

She says in a low sultry voice, "I guess that gives me a week to remind you just how valuable your life is."

Gene responds angrily, "Carol, can't you realize--"

Interrupting him, she says in the same voice, "I'm going to make sure you realize your life is worth living; that it is something you have earned and clearly have a right to."

"Not until justice has been served."

Carol puts her arms around his neck, and while kissing his chest says, "Still I am going to do everything I can to make you hesitant."

Gene pushes her away, but she struggles to get nearer. He takes her wrists in his hands and holds her back, but she drops to her knees and kisses his thighs. "Carol stop! This is not appropriate."

In between kisses she says, "This is the most appropriate thing I have ever done in my entire life. I have lived a life of leisure among the best circles in town. I have had the pleasure of being in love with and being loved by the most wonderful man in the world, and right now I'm going to do my whorish best to save him from himself."

Gene flops onto the bed in a sitting position without releasing his grip on Carol's forearms. Carol continues to kiss his legs passionately as he pleads, "Please Carol; try to understand. I have values by which I have lived the majority of my life, and morals that define my life. Can't you see that I must keep them in order? Have I not imparted any of them to you and the children?"

Carol looks up and says, "Maybe you have your values in the wrong order."

She starts kissing his boxer shorts. Gene releases her hands and presses his own hands in his face as he begins to cry. "Carol, you know I love you, but what would that love mean if I allowed a crime of the magnitude I committed to go unpunished?"

With her hands now free she runs her fingers up the sides of his chest in gentle caressing touches. She says, "What meaning would my love for you have, if I did not try to stop you? You are my greatest value."

He lies back onto the bed and rolls his shoulders over, turning his still covered face away from her. His body shakes in silent sobs, and his knees pull in slightly until he is in a semi-fetal position. Several minutes pass as Carol continues to kiss and stroke him until he begins to respond. Gene's body unfolds slowly as he cannot help but become aroused by Carol's persistence. Finally, he pulls her face up to his and kisses her. Carol returns it passionately while enveloping his body with hers.

In a voice still wet with tears, he whispers, "Carol, I love you. I can't imagine a life without you, but I can't imagine a life with you as long as I leave this unresolved."

Carol does not answer, but instead she releases her embrace and slides down his body to remove his boxer shorts. She then straddles his hips while pulling loose the bow at the top of her negligee. The shimmering fabric falls away exposing her breasts, and she reaches between her legs.

Hooper is shocked, but quivers only slightly out of character as Myra actually does grasp his soft penis then strokes it gently to erection. No one on the set notices, not even the camera crew. Myra's costume, the silk negligee, was draped perfectly over their hips to cover her impromptu addition to the scene.

Carol begins rocking gently on top of Gene. She leans back and her face lifts up with pride. The camera cuts to a close up to show a single tear trickling down the side of her cheek, as she proclaims, "Gene, I love you so much, I want to burn the memory of it into your mind so that whatever place your convictions force you to go, my love will always remain alive inside of you."

The camera dollies back as Carol's lovemaking increases in momentum. Gene's hands grasp her thighs as if he's holding on to a runaway horse.

Carol arches her back further in the agony of a final exultation. She looks Olympian in her key light as even greater tears flow down the sides of her uplifted cheeks. Then toward the unseen heavens above, she cries out, "This is your restitution, Gene Eastly. You are not an accidental angel. You have earned your place in heaven. The goddess of justice may be blind, but she would not have given you this life unless you deserved it."

Cut to close up of Gene. His facial features are distorted in pain. The normal wrinkles around his eyes are deeper, becoming tiny ravines for the tears to run. He cries, "Oh Carol, did that goddess send you to ensure that my punishment is indeed deserving, by forcing me to give you up."

Carol collapses on top of him and whimpers, "Oh God, I'm failing."

Eugene yelled, "Cut!"

Hooper whispered to Myra, who remained lying on top of him, "What the hell do you think you were doing? Trying to keep me in character, or yourself?"

She smiled and whispered back to him, "I love you, Hooper Johnson."

Hooper glared angrily at her and said, "Get off of me Miss Mason, the scene is over."

Myra was stunned; she couldn't move. Not only had her character's plan to stop her husband fail, but her own plan to let Hooper know how she felt failed. Hooper impatiently pushed her off, and then snatched his robe from the waiting assistant. He stormed toward his dressing room.

Myra pulled the sheet up to her face and cried into it. The script girl leaned over the edge of the bed with Myra's robe in hand, and asked, "Miss Mason, are you okay?"

Realizing she was not alone, Myra looked up and smiled, "Yes, yes, I'm okay. It's just a little difficult to come back down from a performance like that, but thank you for asking."

She slid off the bed and allowed the girl to help her into her robe.

Berating herself for her stupidity, she moped back to the trailer lot. When she opened the door to her dressing room, she found Connie sitting on her cot, a leather briefcase was in her lap.

"What are you doing here?" she demanded.

Connie smiled and said, "How about an apology for starters?"

Myra scowled, and said angrily, "Apologize to you for what?"

"You misunderstand; I want to apologize to you."

Myra looked a little surprised and asked, "For what?"

"For the cool way I've been behaving toward you. I think you know why. I've always hated you for taking Frank from me, but now I can see you're giving him up."

"What do you mean, giving him up?"

"I've noticed you don't care for Frank anymore. Believe me; it's easy to tell. For the past several days you haven't tried to get between Frank and me when we're at the condo. You're no longer hanging around the office or the set to constantly make sure Eugene is handling everything all right. The way I see it, you've left him to sink or swim."

"Connie, I don't have to listen to this. I intend to stand by my husband until he's well. Is that clear?"

Connie smiled; she thought Myra must be tired because her answer was neither shrewd nor veiled. Myra as much as said she intended to leave Frank; it was everything she wanted to hear. Still she wanted to confirm it, and decided to force the issue into the open. She asked, "Almost, I just have one other question. Are you going to want Frank back when he's himself again?"

"Connie, I don't think this conversation is appropriate."

"Then what about Hooper?"

"What are you asking?"

"Myra, I'm not blind. I see how you look at him. I suspect you're in love with him."

"That's none of your business."

Connie smiled again. Myra did not even attempt a denial. "That's true, but I want us to be allies."

"Allies!"

"Yes, I want Frank; that's no secret to you - never has been, but now you're interested in another man. I know you won't release Frank to me until he's well, so I want to help make him well. At the same time, I know you want Hooper, but you won't feel free to have him until you've seen that Frank is better."

Myra sighed and finally sat down. She studied Connie's face for several moments. It was, she decided, no longer the face of an enemy, and said, "Okay Connie, we'll be allies. I'm glad you love Frank; he's going to need someone."

"Thank you."

Myra leaned over and opened her refrigerator. She removed a bottle of wine. "Would you care for a glass of wine?"

"Please."

After pouring two glasses she said, "It's kind of nice to feel I can let my hair down with you Connie. I imagine at one time we might have become friends if it hadn't been for Frank. I know it was you who kept that office running, and I also know you had to have noticed Frank's weirdness even before I did. It's surprising that either one of us could fall in love with a man of such tightly controlled emotions."

"You mean how he focuses on one thing or another, but can't or won't concern himself with two things at once?"

"Yes! Connie, I'll bet we could really compare notes. But first I ought to tell you that I've discovered that what I felt for Frank all these years was not love. I guess that evens the score; He never even pretended to love me. I don't believe he can love, but Eugene can, and that's why we have to get them together."

For the next hour Myra told Connie of what she'd learned from the psychiatrist, and how it was important to get Eugene to see him. Connie then showed Myra the instructions written out for the film lab, and asked her if she recognized the handwriting. Myra thought the even-lettered, juvenile-ish script did look familiar. She rummaged through her purse and pulled out the scrap of paper that had the trucker's name and address on it. It was the same.

"I found this on Frank's desk at home right after he came back from his disappearance. I was curious about it at the time, but I forgot all about it. I guess it must be Eugene's writing."

Connie nodded.

"So what's the significance?" Myra asked.

"Look at this." Connie opened the briefcase so Myra could see the original *Resurgent Man* manuscript.

Myra gasped and said, "So, Eugene did write it."

"You already suspected it?"

She told Connie of her conversation with Stacie Rogers Smith. How Stacie was unaware of Jack ever having written anything. She did not, however, mention her other suspicion: that Eugene killed Jack because Stacie loved Jack and not him.

Connie said Eugene had mentioned both he and Jack were Stacie's lovers, and it was because of the similarity to the storyline of *Resurgent Man* that she had hoped to gain from the manuscript some insight into winning Frank's love.

"Has it helped you any?" Myra asked.

"I was hoping to learn from it what Eugene admired about Jack, and then try to become his substitute, but that was when I thought Jack wrote it. When I discovered it was actually written by Eugene, I wasn't sure whether it was about Jack's ideals."

"I believe you can assume it is," Myra said, then went on to tell her what Stacie had told her about Jack.

"I would guess that the way Frank translated Jack's wisdom for himself is in his integrity toward film making, except that it doesn't particularly show up in the screenplays he chooses. I've always felt they were rather banal considering his talent. I shouldn't complain though; it was how he could take an ordinary story, full of predictable platitudes, and use his craft - his art - to turn it into something larger than life, that attracted me to him in the first place. I believe the reason I'm able to operate the office efficiently is because I modeled myself after Frank. I suppose that makes me a third generation interpretation of Jack. Frank, though, has never acknowledged what I do for him. Oh, he does now that he is Eugene, but Eugene seldom demonstrates Frank's talent. Do you think Frank will finally notice after this production is over and your psychiatrist friend puts him back together?"

"I hope so; I wish you luck."

"I wish the same for you."

"Thanks Connie, it looks like I'm going to need it. The way things are going, it looks like I'm going to end up walking away from this production without any men in my life. The damnedest thing is that I've been doing some of the best work I've ever done."

"Are you talking about the way Hooper walked off the set?"

"You saw?"

"Yes, I must admit I've been spying on you two. What happened?"

"I told him I loved him, and he got angry."

"You know it might be that he's a little intimidated. After all, you do have one of the biggest names in the business."

"I don't think so; he's too confident to be threatened by my achievements. It was my fault; I was unprofessional."

"From what I've seen, Myra, it's more than your acting he's watching. Maybe you ought to go see him."

"Thanks Connie, I will."

Myra knocked on Hooper's door. When she entered he was sitting in front of his mirror. To her reflection he asked, "What do you want?"

Myra stood awkwardly behind him trying to keep eye contact in the mirror. "You know that was our last scene together."

Hooper nodded.

She put her hand on his shoulder, and felt a slight flinch. "Well... I'm going to miss working with you."

He remained silent.

She put her other hand on his other shoulder and said, "Hooper, all I can think of is throwing my arms around you and kissing you, but you're being so cold. I don't understand. I thought you were interested in me; the way you've looked at me, spoken to me, touched me."

"That was part of the performance," he said.

"I'm talking off stage Hooper, and don't try to tell me you were doing it to stay in character because you've already told me you don't need that. Besides, it's been going on since before you were chosen to play Gene."

Hooper did not answer.

Myra was getting exasperated. "Dammit Hooper, tell me what's wrong?"

"How about you're married."

"Bullshit! Same reasons as before, I already know you like me - want me."

Hooper turned around and faced her. "Okay I admit it; I like you, and want you, but I don't want to hear, 'I love you' from Carol Eastly. I want to hear it from Myra Mason when she's no longer in character."

"I don't believe I'm hearing this," she cried. "I gave the most brilliant performance of my life, and you missed it. I purposely wanted you to be aware that I was not completely immersed in my character. That I could be both Carol to Gene, and myself to you. Perhaps it wasn't particularly professional, but I liked the symbolism of letting you know how I felt while we were both in the place that is most important to us: the stage."

"I do like it; it's poetic, and it wasn't completely lost on me. However, until Frank and Eugene are united, I'm going to find it difficult to accept that you're not on the rebound."

"Why you son of a bitch!" Myra cried, and then turned and jerked open the door, but before leaving she turned back again and added, "Boy, was I ever stupid to fall in love with you; but even worse I was a fool to try and defend it." She whirled around and stormed down the pavement.

Hooper leapt from his chair to go after her. His face was burning in embarrassment. He could not believe how stupid and foolish he had been. He should have known that someone with Myra's self assurance, who could have the courage to do what she did that day on stage, would never be on the rebound.

He stepped onto the pavement facing the direction of Myra's retreat, but a moving figure from behind him caught the corner his eye. He turned to see Eugene staring at him, and looking a bit dumbfounded.

"Did you hear all that?" Hooper asked.

Eugene nodded.

"Then I may as well admit that I'm guilty of trying to steal your wife."

"Why do you suppose I cast her with you in the first place?"

Hooper literally stumbled when he heard the voice. The accent was distinctly northern. "Frank?" he asked, but the man said nothing. Then leaning closer to him he asked, "Am I hearing you correctly?"

"Hear what correctly?" asked a southern voice that clearly belonged to Eugene.

Hooper shook his head to clear his brain, and stared without answering.

Eugene slapped his back and said in his cheery Southern twang, "Hey, hey buddy, that was some performance you gave today. Hooper you are something else. You know that?"

"Uh, thanks," Hooper mumbled.

"Say, I was looking for Connie. You seen her anywhere?"

Hooper shook his head.

"If you see her, send her my way. I tell ya, I couldn't make it without that girl."

Eugene headed on down the row of trailers, and Hooper wandered slowly behind him. Was his mind playing tricks on him, he wondered, or did Frank Stacy actually speak to him. By the time he reached Myra's dressing room, she was gone. For the day he was told.

#

Gene awakens as his two children are climbing on the bed. Carol is not in the bed.

His son, with baseball mitt in hand, says, "Daddy can we play catch today?"

Competing for Gene's attention, his daughter pushes in front of the boy and holds up a book as she says, "Daddy, I need you to help me with my math homework. My teacher says you know more about math than anybody else in town, and that I should be doing better."

The boy starts pulling his arm and insisting, "Come on Daddy, get up. Let's play some catch."

Gene looks over his children's heads and the camera pans to show that he is looking at Carol who is peering into the room through the crack in the door.

Cut back to Gene who is standing now with an arm around each child as he says toward the door, "You're trying to make this as hard as possible, aren't you?"

Cut to Carol pushing open the door. "I'll use whatever it takes."

Cut to Gene's son. He proclaims to Carol, "Nothing's too hard for my Daddy!"

Cut to Gene's face wincing. Fade.

Gene hangs his hat on the coat tree, and then says to Cathy, who is sitting at her desk. "Morning Cathy; please pull and bring into my office the files for *Dunford Software, Fant's Youth Hostel, Frankel's Fast Deliveries, Kahn's Komedy Shop, Liston Marina, Mustakis Gym, Patrick Tile & Bath, Stone's Stationary, Tony Lea Tours*, and *Vonn's Fly & Tackle*."

Cathy scribbles the names rapidly. When he finishes, she says, "My goodness! That's everything due for month end. Why so soon, are you planning to hit the campaign trail already?"

Gene says, "As soon as you're finished, please get Mr. Oscar Dubois on the phone for me."

Gene enters his office and pulls the door closed.

Cut to Cathy looking bewildered. She then turns and gives a questioning look to the receptionist who shrugs in response.

Dissolve to Cathy placing a large stack of manila folders on Gene's desk, and saying as she nods toward the phone, "Mr. Dubois is on line one."

Gene thanks her then waits until she has left the room to pick up the phone.

Cut to Cathy with her ear pressed to Gene's door to listen.

Cut back to Gene saying into the phone, "Oscar, I've given the nomination a lot of thought, and I'm afraid I'm going to have to decline. ... My reasons? Well, you know that saying about a man rising to the level of his incompetence? ... Let's just say, I have a feeling that if I become a Congressman, I'll reach that level. ..."

Cut to inside the train station. In front of a train car Gene kisses the kids. His son is dressed in a suit, and his daughter is wearing what might be an Easter dress. Gene hugs Carol as if he'll never see her again. He then releases her, and with a look of pain and resignation on his face, he disappears into the train.

Cut to the train pulling out. Gene waves from the window to Carol and the children. As soon as they can no longer see him, Carol takes the children by the hand, and rushes away.

Cut to outside the train station. Carol hurries the children into the car.

Cut to Carol driving very fast, passing other cars, and speeding through yellow traffic lights. She follows a sign for the Somerville airport.

Cut to Carol at the ticket counter with a wad of cash in her hand. She is saying to a female reservationist who is holding some tickets in her hand, "Yes, I know it's about to leave. Could you please just call the boarding gate? I have no luggage and I'll run all the way; they won't have to wait more than a couple of minutes. Please! It's an emergency."

The reservationist picks up the phone. Carol slaps the cash on the counter while snatching the tickets from the woman's hand. She then grabs her children's hands and cries, "Run, quick now, like a bunny!"

The camera follows their retreating backs briefly then cuts to the boarding gate as they arrive panting. A smiling flight attendant says, "You must be Mrs. Eastly."

Carol nods.

The flight attendant adds, "You can relax now, Mrs. Eastly. You and your children are going to make your flight to Salina."

Cut to a jet lifting off.

Cut to Carol hailing a cab outside an airport.

Inside the cab she gives the driver an address.

Cut to Carol and the children climbing out of the cab in front of a quaint, one-story brick house. Carol says to the driver, "Please wait."

They walk to the front door, and Carol squats down to face the children, and says, "Cindy, Danny, I want you to listen very carefully. We're going inside to see a lady we've never met before. I need you to be on your very best behavior. I want you to do this for your father. Do you understand?"

They nod.

She stands up and knocks on the door.

A woman in her early fifties, wearing a day dress and an apron, opens the door. She looks down at the well dressed children then back up to Carol. She smiles and says, "Hello."

"Mrs. Barrow?" Carol asks.

"Yes," the woman answers.

Carol smiles and says, "Hi, my name is Carol Eastly. These are my children, Cindy and Danny."

"I'm pleased to meet you."

"Mrs. Barrow, may we come in and talk with you?"

She looks at Carol suspiciously and asks, "Are you Christian Witnesses?"

"No ma'am, nor am I selling anything, or collecting donations for charity."

She smiles again, steps inside so they may enter and says, "I suppose it's okay, you seem like nice people." Then chuckling she says, "That is as long as you're not here to rob me."

"Oh, no ma'am!" Carol cries.

"Come on in. I'm not really worried about robbers; I'm prepared." As she speaks, she reveals to Carol a small automatic pistol in her apron pocket.

Carol gasps and begins to fall, but catches herself against the doorjamb.

"My goodness, honey," says Mrs. Barrow, "I didn't mean to scare you. I was only showing off."

Carol recovering says, "I guess I'm just not used to seeing guns."

The woman chuckles and turns into the house.

Cut to close up of Carol, looking frightened as she whispers to herself, "Oh Gene, she's got a gun. If you confess first, you may never get to make your offer for justice."

Cut to inside the living room as Carol settles the children into chairs then sits across from Mrs. Barrow.

"Mrs. Barrow, I know our meeting like this seems odd, but later today you're going to meet my husband, and I know he will not bother to tell you much about himself. He does not know I'm here, and I'm sure he would not have allowed it, but what he has to tell you should not be heard without knowing what kind of man he is."

"I'm going to meet your husband? My, my, this is so mysterious." She then pauses as if something has just occurred to her. She then says, "Oh, I get it. This is some kind of sales technique. The wife comes and warms me up, and then the husband comes and gives the pitch."

"I promise you Mrs. Barrow, this is not a sales technique."

Impatiently, she responds, "Then I don't understand why you're here."

"I'm here to tell you about my husband."

Mrs. Barrow grows more annoyed. "You said that already, and I'm sufficiently curious. Please get on with what you want to say."

Carol's voice has the quality of a plea as she says, "I'm sorry Mrs. Barrow, my coming to you will probably be the most important thing I've ever done in my entire life, and I'm afraid I don't know quite how to begin."

Mrs. Barrow softens slightly. "I can't imagine that talking to me could possibly be as important as you say."

"But it is! You see I love my husband very much. Oh, that's not what I wanted to say."

In the manner of a school teacher prodding a reluctant oral report, Mrs. Barrow says, "Perhaps it would be easier if you began by telling me why your husband is interested in seeing me."

"I can't."

"Why not?"

"That's his business with you, and if I told, I'd be betraying him more than I already am."

"Are you trying to warn me of something?"

"No... I mean yes. I'm trying to warn you of my husband's goodness."

Mrs. Barrow says gently, "Honey, are you in some way afraid I might take advantage of your husband's goodness?"

Carol starts to speak but pauses and blinks tears from her eyes.

Mrs. Barrow leans forward slightly as she notices, and says, "Is that it?"

Carol answers with tears clogging her voice, "Y-yes, but I didn't want to be so obvious. This is a lot harder than I thought it would be. I want to somehow tell you how good he is, but to say he's a good accountant, or husband or father doesn't really do it. He--"

Danny, impatient at maintaining his very best behavior, interrupts, "He's the greatest Daddy in the whole world and he's going to be in Congress, too!"

"Wait a minute," Mrs. Barrow says in a tone of realization. "You said your name is Eastly right?"

Carol nods.

"Are you from Somerville?"

Carol nods again.

"Then your husband must be Gene Eastly."

Nervously Carol says, "Y-yes."

"Oh, I've heard about your husband. He's the accountant who saved Somerville from bankruptcy, and now the bigwigs down at the capitol want him in Washington. I read in the newspaper how he convinced all those big companies to build their new plants up there. A lot of people in your section of the state are indebted to your husband, Mrs. Eastly, including my nephew, who was unemployed for a year. He has a good job now, because of your husband. You're a lucky woman Mrs. Eastly, your husband has a fine reputation."

Carol answers weakly, "Yes he does."

"I'll bet I know why you're here. My name is on the membership list of the *Republicrat Party*, and your husband is coming by for a campaign contribution. Well, you tell your husband he can save himself a trip; I'll write the check today." Mrs. Barrow stands up and says, "I'll get my check book."

Carol cries, "No, that's not it! Gene has declined the nomination."

"What?" Mrs. Barrow asks in surprise. Then as she is sitting back down, says, "I'm afraid I'm quite confused."

"I'm sorry, Mrs. Barrow. I should have foreseen that my coming here would leave you in a quandary, but my husband is going to visit you for an entirely different reason than you might guess. I came because I want you to know that he is more than a politician. It's other people, people who know what kind of man he is, that want him to become a politician. When he gets here, you'll find out why he cannot be one. I came to you because I want to help Gene, and because I love him more than life itself."

Carol pauses and wipes her eyes.

Cut to Mrs. Barrow staring silently.

Cut back to Carol as she continues. "Mrs. Barrow, I guess what I want to tell you is that Gene's the kind of man who never lets his wife forget he loves her, yet gives her room to pursue her own interests. He's nurturing when I need it, and he always seems to know when."

"He's dependable; you never have to doubt his word. If he makes a commitment, he will do everything within his power to fulfill it. If you're a friend in need, he's always available. You don't even have to be a friend. He's the type of guy that will pull over and help a stranger stranded on the side of the road with car trouble."

"It's hard to explain something that should be experienced. I wish I could give you my mind for a day just so you could feel as I do. You see, Gene has had a good life, yet he knows how to appreciate what he's had. I... I'm the one who will attest that he's earned it. I guess that's what I want you to know."

Carol looks to her children, then adds, "He's also a father who cares about his children, who'll play with them and help them study. He has not only taught them right from wrong, but has given them strong values to live by. He... he has even done that for me."

"That's all Mrs. Barrow." Carol stands. "Thank you for allowing me to speak to you today. Children, it's time to go."

At the door, Carol says, "One last thing, Mrs. Barrow. I would consider it a great favor if you wouldn't mention to my husband that I was here."

Mrs. Barrow nods. The camera pans to follow Carol and the children walking to the cab.

Cut from the cab pulling away from the curb to Mrs. Barrow shaking her head with a puzzled look on her face.

Cut to inside the cab as Carol instructs the driver, "Please take us to the nearest car rental agency."

Fade to black.

Carol and the children are sitting inside a parked car with tinted windows. Carol is behind the steering wheel sipping coffee from a styrofoam cup, and staring out the windshield. The children are in the back seat.

Danny asks, "When will Daddy be here?"

Carol answers, "I don't know darling. His train arrived an hour ago. It could be any minute."

She looks over the seat at him and adds, "Finish your *Egg McMuffin*."

"I don't want it," he whines.

"Then draw in your coloring book, like your sister."

"She's got all the good colors."

"Danny, there are plenty of colors and she can only use one at a time. Try to be good; we may be here a long time."

Cut to Cindy pointing and shouting, "Look Mommy, here comes another car and it's going real slow."

Cut to car driving down the street towards the camera. After a moment, Gene can be seen inside.

Cut to Carol. "It's your father, now be quiet. We don't want him to know we're here."

Cut to Gene climbing out of the car with his attaché case in hand. The camera pans as he walks up to the door and knocks. Mrs. Barrow opens the door, and then allows him to enter.

Cut to outside Carol's car looking in from the back as Carol says, "Keep your fingers crossed. This will be the longest wait of our lives."

Cut to inside Mrs. Barrow's house.

"What may I do for you, Mr. Eastly?" Mrs. Barrow asks as they sit down.

"Mrs. Barrow, what I've come to tell you will upset you. However, before I say anything else, there's something I want to give you."

Gene raises the lid of his attaché case in his lap so Mrs. Barrow cannot see into it.

Cut to over-the-shoulder shot. Camera peers down into Gene's attaché case as he slides some papers out from under his nickel plated revolver. When the papers are removed the magazine article with Mr. Barrow's picture can be seen. The lid drops down, and the camera cuts back to master shot of Gene handing the papers to Mrs. Barrow.

"Mrs. Barrow, this is a trust fund I have set up for you. It will pay you a monthly dividend or upon your instructions the trustees will grant you the entire sum of the principal any time you wish."

"My goodness!" she cries. "This is over a million dollars. Have I won a sweepstakes or something?"

Cut to close up of Gene. His eyes are downcast as he begins speaking, but slowly he forces his eyes up to meet those of Mrs. Barrow. "It's not a prize, and I want you to understand that it is in no way a bribe. It is not something you have earned, but it is something you deserve."

"Mr. Eastly, you're as baffling as your--" she cuts herself off with gasp before she says the word, "wife".

"Pardon me?" he asks while leaning forward as if to catch the rest of whatever it was she was going to say.

"It's nothing. Please go on."

Her blunder does not affect him, and he continues, "Mrs. Barrow, I've suffered the same nightmare off and on for over a decade. A nightmare that was apparently the key to a memory loss I've had for the same length of time. Until last week, I did not understand the dream, that is, until by a stroke of chance I discovered an article from an old magazine."

He reaches into the attaché case.

"Mrs. Barrow, I have spent many hours trying to think of a gentle way to tell this, but there just isn't one. I'm afraid I'll have to be blunt. In my dream I kill a man. When I saw this article I knew it was not just a dream."

Gene hands her the magazine and says, "My memory has returned to me, Mrs. Barrow." Then as he sees that she has seen her husband's picture, he adds, "I'm the man who murdered your husband."

She gasps as she drops the magazine. For a moment she wavers in her seat then recovers to leap out of the chair. The trust fund papers fall from her lap and scatter on the floor. She points a shaking finger at him, and cries, "You... that's what this is all about. I don't believe it... you, you killed Milton?" She pauses only an instant, for the knowledge to penetrate, then screams, "You killed my Milt!"

The camera dollies for a close up of her hand as it slides into her apron pocket, but she does not withdraw her hand. The camera dollies back again and pans to show that Gene is standing also. His head is hanging down in shame. The camera moves back even further, and Mrs. Barrow can be seen contemplating him, as tears run down her cheek.

She pulls her hand out of the pocket, then holds it with her other hand. Looking down at her shaking hand, she asks, "Why... why did you come here? Why are you giving me money? You said it wasn't a bribe. You were safe; no one knew who killed Milton."

Gene raises his head. "I came because justice needs to be served. For the past fifteen years, I've been able to live a life that did not rightfully belong to me. My brain, in a primitive form of self preservation, gave me amnesia, and allowed me to get away with murder. Then I finally remembered my crime, but during the lengthy passage of time until I recalled my past, I matured and acquired a sense of honor, and that sense of honor demands I offer you restitution. The money I'm giving you is only part of what I owe you."

"Owe me!" she cries indignantly.

"You have a right to be offended, Mrs. Barrow. The greatest debt is to your husband, but unfortunately it's outside my power to repay him. Your husband was not the only victim, Mrs. Barrow. You too were injured by my crime. I took from you your lover, and caused you to suffer untold emotional anguish for years. I'm here because honor demands it. My values are now more important to me than my self-preservation. Maybe I should say, my self-preservation is rooted in my values, and that I cannot live with myself."

"What do you want from me?" Mrs. Barrows cries softly.

"I want you to be my judge and jury. I want you to decide to your satisfaction my fate and my future. On your own, I figure you have only one choice, but I wish to offer you three. Your first choice is that you may turn me over to the police, which is your own option. If you decide to do that, I will surrender myself voluntarily, make a full confession, and plead guilty, thus accepting whatever punishment the state sees fit. However, you may prefer one of the two options I will provide. Since our state does not impose the death penalty, and if you feel that an eye for an eye is the proper service of justice, then I will offer it myself."

Gene sits down and pulls a typed letter from his attaché case and hands it to her. She accepts it motionlessly. Her facial features seem slack and weary. There is little expression in her eyes to show that she is even listening to Gene. All that can be seen is a distant sadness.

"This will be my suicide note. It contains a full confession including how I remembered having committed the crime after fifteen years. Also, for the sake of my children, when they are adults and have the reasoning power to understand, I mention my pecuniary restitution to you, and why my beliefs demand that I take my life."

Gene turns the open attaché case toward her so she can see the gun. "I have already purchased a weapon with which to take my life. I am very serious about this offer. If this is what you wish I will leave here, and shoot myself. I will choose a location where the authorities will quickly find my body, and where no one will be disturbed. In my pocket will be a certified check made out to a local funeral parlor along with instructions for my burial. I've tried to plan everything in advance to spare my wife as much pain as possible. She knows the choices I'm offering you and she will receive a coded telegram from me informing her of my death before the authorities have the chance."

Gene turns the attaché case back around and shuts it. "My final offer is to indenture myself to your service for the rest of my life. This offer implies any meaning you wish to attach to it. At your wish, I will be a laborer, or an object for torture, or your companion. Please understand, I did not come here for forgiveness, but to offer these three choices as the only apology I am able to give. If you need time to think, I'll wait outside, or at my hotel for as long as you wish. My life has belonged to me fifteen years longer than I deserve, it is in your hands now."

Gene rises to his feet. Mrs. Barrow stares blankly at the chair he vacates. The camera pans as he walks slowly across the room. As he opens the door, the camera cuts to Mrs. Barrow. Her face is hard now, and the automatic pistol is in her hand. With a shout she orders, "Get back over here, and sit down. You said there was only one choice I had on my own. Well, you were wrong. I can think of at least one more."

Gene returns slowly as the camera cuts back and forth showing his progress to the chair from three separate angles. The visual effect is that of a long march, the end of which awaits execution.

When he sits down she says, "For fifteen years, I've had to imagine the face of Milt's killer. I always saw him as slimy, scar-faced hood, and now you come in here. You, fresh as apple pie, so clean, so well mannered, and claim you're him. It's difficult to accept Mr. Eastly. I figured it would take someone meaner than my Milt to kill him. Milton was not a nice man, but he was good provider, and in the innocence of my youth I loved him without question. After his death, I thought it was simply because I didn't know how to run a store that my receipts were so much lower than his. I later found out it had nothing to do with my ability. Milt ran a type of extortion racket by employing a local youth gang to force the poor people in the neighborhood to buy a weekly overpriced box of groceries. Without Milt's leadership the gang fell apart, and the neighborhood happily did their shopping in the supermarkets instead of with me."

"Mr. Eastly, if you had come to make this confession fifteen years ago I would have shot you immediately, but as you said earlier, in fifteen years, a person matures a great deal. You obviously have. What were you, one of the thugs my Milton hired? Or were you from a rival gang?"

"No, ma'am. I had run away from an orphanage. Most of my time was spent searching garbage cans for something to eat. It was in a garbage can that I found the gun I used on your husband; it was probably ditched there by some other criminal. When I went into his store, I couldn't bring myself to rob him, so I tried begging a loaf of bread from him. He laughed at me, and as hungry as I was my brain must not have been working... no, that's just an excuse. His laughing made me mad, so I pulled the gun out of my pocket. I told him I would take it anyway, but then the gun went off. That's the last I remember, everything is a blank after that."

"It sounds like your subconscious guilt caused you to become the man you now are. I wonder what type of man you would have become if that gun had not gone off."

She points the pistol at Gene's nose and slides back the hammer. There is no fear in his face.

Mrs. Barrow says, "A twist of fate, Mr. Eastly, caused you to become a good man. Why you're nothing but an accidental angel."

Gene's carefully controlled composure breaks into an expression of surprise.

"What did I say Mr. Eastly?"

"You called me an accidental angel. It's funny because my wife used the same term when she tried to dissuade me from coming to you, except she told me that I wasn't one."

Still pointing the gun at his face, she responds, "It doesn't particularly matter whether it was accidental or not. I can see from your reaction to the barrel of this gun that your offer is sincere. You are clearly willing to accept death, or the police, or indenture yourself to me for life. Do you see now what my other option is? The one you didn't mention?"

"That you can kill me instead of my committing suicide? I don't see how that really changes anything except to put yourself in jeopardy."

"You're wrong, Mr. Eastly." She slowly lowers the pistol's hammer back into place, then puts the gun back into her pocket. "I can forgive you and let you go. I'll accept your trust fund; it's getting harder and harder for me to make a living, and I'm getting old."

"Why are you doing this?"

"Because you are a good man, and you have earned the right to walk away from here."

"I've done nothing here to prove that."

"You've fearlessly satisfied me that your offer is genuine; your wife did the rest."

Gene leaps to his feet and yells, "My wife? What has Carol--"

Mrs. Barrow interrupts him by pulling the gun back out of her pocket. "Get out of here Mr. Eastly, before I change my mind. Go home to your courageous wife who has wisdom where you have only convictions."

The closing credits rise up the screen as Gene steps out the front door. Carol throws open the car door, and begins running toward him. The picture freezes as the two embrace.

"Cut!" Eugene cried out, then added, "I want a rewrite."

"What!" Ralph cried back.

"Yes, everybody gather around I've got a great idea."

The people on the set moved toward the directors hesitantly. The crew, most of whom had been with *Stacy Productions* for years, thought it odd that Frank would request everyone to gather around for a rewrite, but the difference in Frank's behavior had not passed by them unnoticed and their curiosity drove them forward.

Hooper took Margo Erikson, the woman playing Mrs. Barrow, by the elbow and led her over. Margo, a long time *Stacy* veteran, who among other roles played Cassandra's mother in *Resurgent Man,* looked up at Hooper and raised an inquisitive eyebrow.

Myra, who had been avoiding Hooper by sitting in the back with Zack, rose quickly and dove through the crowd like a mother after a drowning child. Zack followed slowly after her.

Ralph whispered almost hysterically, "Frank, that was a perfect take. And, we're out of time. We need to be spending every last minute we have in the cutting room."

Eugene ignored him and said, "Listen up everybody! I'm not thinking about anything major; just a pick-up at the end of this last scene. Hooper, Margo, y'all pay close attention. It goes like this: As Gene is opening the door to leave, Mrs. Barrow makes a last minute decision and tells him she does want him as an indentured servant, but only for one weekend out of every month. This is the gimmick: she doesn't want to take him from Carol, whom she respects and admires. Yet once a month, she wants him as a lover."

Margo is shocked and cries, "Jesus, Frank! What the hell are you trying to do; make this a sequel to *Resurgent Man*?"

"*Resurgent Man*? What's that?" Eugene asked.

A unified gasp rose from the crowd.

Myra, her face turning white in shock, stood frozen behind Eugene.

Hooper left Margo's side and pushed through the crowd until he was standing in front of Eugene. He whispered hoarsely, "Eugene, *Resurgent Man* is a film you made! Margo was in it."

"Oh, shit!" Eugene whispered back. Then speaking louder for the crowd to hear, "Calm down folks, you know how forgetful I get when I'm absorbed in a project."

It seemed to work as several satisfied murmurs flowed through the crowd.

Eugene continuing said, "Margo, let's hold off on the wisecracks; you know I don't like sequels."

"Sorry Frank."

"That's all right. Now, I'd like some input from you on this. How will your character make this final demand?"

"Gee, I couldn't say off hand. I'll have to work on it. You know, determine her motivation in order to get my character in the right frame of mind. Once I've done that, I'll know the right words and actions."

Myra unfroze, and said only loud enough for the nearest ears, "Frank, you've got to consult the writer for a change like this. He's got a contract you know."

Connie, who had been by his side all along, finally came to her senses, grabbed his arm and added, "Frank, this is a discussion for executive staff only, let's take it up back at the condo."

Myra agreed, "Yes, Frank, Connie's right. Let's go home."

Eugene said to Margo, "Thanks, Margo. Work on it for me." Then he looked at the crowd, and yelled, "Okay folks, that's it for today. Everybody is on call for tomorrow."

Ralph said anxiously, "But, Frank... the time."

"Calm down Mr. Smurling. The studio and the equipment are still ours for another day." Then to Connie he asked, "Connie can you get hold of the writer today?"

"Yes."

"Then let's go."

With Myra and Connie on either side of him, Eugene began walking toward the door. Hooper caught up and grabbed Myra's elbow, and said, "I would like to speak to you."

Eugene and Connie continued on as Myra stopped and whispered hotly, "Not now. Can't you see we've got a fucking crisis on our hands?"

Hooper calmly replied, "I can see a crisis finally coming to a head. Eugene is going to want to see *Resurgent Man*."

"Jesus Christ, Hooper! Are you stupid? It will probably make him remember he murdered Jack."

"Take it easy, Myra. First off, you don't know that it was murder. Second, you thought he was making *Accidental Angel* as a subconscious confession of murder, and that the similarity of it to his own past would stimulate his conscious memory, but it hasn't. It could be your theory is wrong. It's time to cross the next bridge."

"I have. I spoke to Stacie Rogers. She confirmed my theory that she was only in love with Jack, but that's not all, she also told me that Eugene came to her after Jack died and asked her to marry him. Obviously, she refused."

"What!"

"It means my theory still stands. I've got to go." Myra turned back to the door.

"I'll see you tonight," Hooper said to her trailing figure, but she didn't answer.

CHAPTER SEVENTEEN

Ralph caught up with Myra, Connie, and Eugene as they were getting settled in the back of the limousine. He climbed in, took a seat beside Eugene, and said, "Frank, you've got to consider the budget. A change like you're asking is going to take more than little pick-up, the impetus for Mrs. Barrow's demand has to be established in an earlier scene."

Eugene responded impatiently, "So we can do an insert of her checking out his body. We'll cut-in right after he enters her house. That makes two short takes tomorrow. No strain on the budget."

"You mean maybe four or five," Smurling argued. "We've got to have reaction shots of Gene and then his answer, and then another take of her acceptance. I don't see how--"

Myra interrupted, "May I make a suggestion?"

"Please," answered Ralph.

She sucked in her breath. She'd made her decision. "Why don't we show *Resurgent Man* to Eugene this evening, then see if he still wants to go ahead with the changes?"

Connie reached across and gave Myra a squeeze on the forearm, and a smile of agreement. Myra returned the smile.

Eugene asked, "Hey, I was gonna ask about that. I thought I'd seen everything Frank made, but I don't remember seeing that title. What's it about?"

"Why that's the one you--" Ralph began, but Myra kicked him in the ankle to interrupt.

She said, "Let's not give him anything to anticipate, and let him enjoy it from the beginning."

#

The four were gathered in the living room around the TV ready to start the VCR when Hooper knocked at the door.

Sara was letting him in as Myra came to the top of the stairs to see who it was.

Hooper saw her and called up, "I still have to speak to you."

Walking down the stairs, she declared dispassionately, "It'll have to wait. The moment of truth is here."

Hooper smiled. "Are you always this dramatic?"

"It's the business I'm in. Remember?"

"Full time?"

"Okay, so I'm guarded. I'm not used to making a fool of myself."

"Neither am I."

When she reached the bottom of the steps, he stepped closer until they were face-to-face, and then disclosed, "I wanted to tell you I acted stupidly in my dressing room the other day."

"Stupidity creates its own punishment."

"I'd rather not live with it."

"You'll inure in time."

"Will you?"

"I already have."

He put his hands around her waist. He could feel her tremble at his touch. "That's bullshit, Miss Mason. You've been searching for me your whole life, and I've... When I first saw you perform, nearly ten years ago, I knew my own search was over. All I had to do was climb the mountain; you were the standard I set for myself to surpass. Then finally I get to meet you, but not under the circumstances I would have wished. You were distressed by Frank's condition, and he was the man who dictated your standards. I could not compete against a man broken in two. I had to be careful; I was afraid of becoming a big brother to you."

"Oh, Hooper, why didn't you say this the other day? Don't you see that Frank would have lost anyway? I wouldn't have compared you to Eugene, only to Frank."

"Don't you think you're premature? What happens when Frank and Eugene are finally united?"

"I didn't fall in love with whoever that man will be. I can't imagine that I could. Frank is a man without emotions of his own and Eugene is a boy with adolescent emotions. What kind of fusion do you think that will make?" Myra laughed, and added, "Hooper, Eugene hasn't even been laid, and Frank..." she finished the sentence without mirth, "Frank never had the capacity to desire it."

"But Frank is brilliant, and Eugene is sensitive and likable, combined they'll be incredible."

"I doubt it. At least not right away. You've got to look at it this way: Frank's value accrual arrested at age seventeen. That he recognizes various values in various people is simply a working knowledge to be used for his films. He never made any his own. If I had to guess why, I would say because his subconscious mind was too busy denying his past. That's why he doesn't make any emotionally impacting movies. *Resurgent Man* was the only one, and only because it was from Eugene. Now that I've seen Eugene direct, and I compare it to the manner in which Frank made *Resurgent Man,* I suspect Eugene must have been close to coming out. It was almost as if Frank's directing ability was put on hold."

Connie came to the top of the stairs and yelled down, "Hey, what's going on down there? We're getting tired of waiting."

"We're on our way," Myra hollered back.

Connie leaned over the rail and saw Hooper. She turned back toward the living room and announced, "Eugene, Hooper is downstairs."

Eugene rushed out into the hall, broadcasting, "All right, Hooper's here." Then turning toward the kitchen, he shouted, "Hey Sara, bring out the *Jack Daniel's*."

When Eugene stepped up to the rail, Hooper started to remove his hands from Myra's waist, but she put her own hands on top of his to hold them down. In a low voice she revealed, "There's one other thing you need to know. Frank never loved me. He even told me he never would."

"That explains the other day."

"Explains what?"

Hooper told her about Frank coming out after she stormed out of his dressing room, and his confessing to having purposely cast them together.

Myra let go of Hooper's hands, and put her hands around his waist. "Hooper, you made me realize I never loved Frank. You were right when you said, I'd been searching for you my whole life. Shall I be blunt?"

"No. It's my turn. I love you, Myra Mason."

"Without doubt?"

"Without doubt."

"Good. Let's go upstairs and watch the movie. I'm going to need your help."

#

Ralph was not in the living room when Hooper and Myra arrived. When Myra asked where he was Connie answered, "He said, he had some work to do, and to call him when Eugene made a decision."

Myra sighed, "It's probably for the best. Let's get started."

Handing Hooper a glass of whiskey, Eugene grinned and asked, "Who're you gonna sit beside, Hooper, me or Myra?"

"I'm remaining neutral; I'm sitting beside Constance."

"The hell you are," chimed Connie, "because I'm sitting by Frank."

Eugene shrugged, gulped his *Jack Daniel's*, flopped onto the sofa, and then pressed the play button on the VCR's remote control.

"Are you in this one, Myra?" he asked while the FBI warning flashed on the screen.

"No, I financed it."

"Make any money?"

"I broke even, barely. This is Frank's only box-office failure."

"Why was that?"

"It was too aesthetic for his usual audience. Now be quiet; it's starting."

Eugene was feeling good, actually more than good, he was feeling confident and satisfied. He was bordering on becoming cocky. It was more than the alcohol he was drinking; it was the experience of making his first film. Certainly Ralph and Connie had prodded and instructed him, but he had made some real decisions on his own. Now he had to sit through some stupid movie Frank made over a decade ago, to satisfy everyone that his latest idea was valid. He wished Margo Erikson could have kept her damn opinions to herself. A sequel to a flop, what kind of crap is that. If anything, he was thinking of a prequel. By adding just a touch of his concept that a man might successfully have more than one lover, *Accidental Angel* could function as a precursor to *Gods Of The Pond,* which he planned on making next.

He thought Myra seemed nervous, but he had grown accustomed to seeing her that way, although she had been better lately. He thought perhaps it was because he had seen her and Hooper together. He decided he ought to give them his approval so they didn't feel the need to sneak around. He chuckled to himself when he considered that he would have to divorce a woman he never married. Letting Myra get away would probably piss off Frank, but he did not care. He felt no loyalty to Frank whatsoever, nor did he intend to let Frank come back.

What he found odd as they all sat in front of the TV, was that Connie seemed anxious too. Not merely odd: disconcerting. Connie was the stabilizing edge to his life - the one person who did not treat him as if he were ill. She was always supportive when he broached an area of film about which he was uncertain. She never instructed him; instead she stroked his vanity by giving subtle suggestions. In many ways, she reminded him of an older version of Jack. It was always Jack who gave him comfort after his father had given him a beating.

The booze was making him talkative, but no one else seemed to want to join in. To Hooper he solicited, "Have you seen this before?"

"Yes, the day after we met on the *Runaway Grandparents* set." Then nodding toward the television he advised, "You might want to watch the credits."

Eugene reluctantly returned his attention to the TV, and as he did he read: screenplay by Jackson Paine Franklin.

"Jack!" he shrieked. "Jack wrote this? Why didn't somebody tell me? Where is he?"

The others exchanged glances, uncertain of how to reply. Finally Myra reported, mixing lies with truth, "I guess we never made the connection that he was your Jack. We don't know where he is; none of us have ever met him."

"There must be some record," he exclaimed.

"We can check on that when we get back to Fresno," Connie promised.

"I can't believe it. Jack came out here after all. Why that son of a gun got into the movies before I did. This is really exciting. I can't wait to see what he wrote."

Eugene settled down, his interest was animated, but as the opening scene progressed it became more so. He leaned forward as he saw the two little boys walking along the stream bed with their stringers of fish. He started squirming in his seat as the one boy left and the other began building a dam. Then with the arrival of the two girls his lips began to move silently. When the girls joined the boy in building the dam, Eugene shot to his feet and screamed, "That son of a bitch stole my screenplay. Jack didn't write this; I did. It's not *Resurgent Man*, it's *Gods Of The Pond*."

Myra rolled her eyes at Hooper in a manner that said, "I told you so." then she picked up the remote control and flipped off the VCR.

Connie said softly, "Frank, can you consider a different possibility?"

Hooper and Myra looked at her with curiosity.

Eugene demanded, "What?"

It could have happened that Jack brought you the screenplay and you didn't remember him, or remember having written the screenplay. Jack probably knew how important the story was to you, as Eugene, and convinced you, as Frank, to produce it. Telling you he wrote it may have been the only way you would accept it."

"Is that the way it happened?"

"I don't know, but knowing Jack for who he is, doesn't it sound probable?"

"Yes... yes it does, but why would he have changed the title."

"I don't know, but I'm sure if he was the one who changed it, it was for your sake."

"Gee, now I'm embarrassed for calling him a son of a bitch. Please don't ever tell him; that is, when we find him."

"We won't."

Myra rolled her eyes toward the ceiling in relief, and Hooper picked up the remote and said, "Shall we finish watching it?"

Eugene replied, "Yes."

The movie continued, and the three who had seen the picture watched the one who had not. Eugene amused himself by reciting the lines as the actors spoke them.

He was amazed at how close the pictures came to what he imagined as he wrote it.

When it got to the scene when Jeannine described her father, Eugene disclosed to his companions, "You're going to see several aspects of my father in this picture; I created three separate characters from him. Billy's father is my old man drunk. Roy, the fat ranger, is my father the womanizer. Finally, Jeannine's father is a caricature of my father being the strict disciplinarian. I never had many friends because whenever they wanted to play, I couldn't because I had ten million chores to do. One kid told me my father was a fascist, and I said, 'yep that's my old man: Daddy-Dictator.' The kid laughed and the name stuck. That's why Jeannine nicknamed her father the Commandant. The Commandant, however, is a corrected image. He evolves into what I always wanted my father to be."

After a while, Eugene ceased reciting lines. Instead, he was humming along with the background music, and switching to each new song with the very first beat. The others assumed it was merely another way in which to show off his foreknowledge. However, they were wrong. Eugene had become so absorbed in the picture that he was unaware of his activity. It was during the school scenes in which Jeannine and Cassy were receiving countless invitations to the dance that he noticed. Eugene unconsciously shifted from humming to singing in an awful falsetto. His voice rose louder and louder and he rocked back and forth in complete oblivion to the others in the room. Connie caught Myra's glance, and with wrinkled nose, and a grimace on her face, she stuck out her tongue to express her opinion of Eugene's voice. Myra giggled silently in return. It was in an attempt to match the singer's notes that his voice cracked and he stopped. Red-faced with embarrassment he offered, "Sorry y'all, I didn't notice how carried away I was getting."

The others laughed. Eugene, in turn, shrugged off his embarrassment, and grinned along with the mirthful faces. Then as everyone turned their attention back to the picture, Eugene announced, "Hey, y'all wanna hear something funny? All these songs are my favorites, but I didn't write them into the script."

Thinking of the original manuscript back in her room, Connie agreed in astonishment, "That's true."

Myra whispered to Hooper, "How about that as support for my theory?"

"You mean the one about Eugene trying to come out during the filming?"

Myra nodded, and they returned their split attention to Eugene and the movie.

The scenes progressed on. Cassy and Jeannine, without inhibition, set up their canvas tent homestead and broke the ice for Billy. He did not have to make a choice; it was their intention as well as their desire to share him. Then as Billy swung each of them gracefully around the gymnasium floor, Eugene needlessly pointed out his purpose. "Do you see what I did here? By reversing the sexes I created a veiled biography of my own relationship with Stacie and Jack."

Myra and Hooper answered in unison, "Uh, huh."

Connie patted his hand.

Eugene was in complete enjoyment. Watching his story come to life on the screen was even enough to erase his anger over the title change. To the others he said, "I can't get over how well this is done. I'm truly pleased with it. Although I'm a little disappointed that I didn't get to produce and direct it myself, I can't begrudge Frank or Jack a bit."

Hooper, considering this, found himself wondering if there really was any significance to be gained from watching Eugene watch *Resurgent Man*.

Then the setting shifted to Alaska, and Eugene divulged, "Hey, this is where the good part starts."

Hooper was startled that anyone could consider the gory conclusion good. Unable to contain the shock, he uttered, "Good part?"

"Yes," Eugene confirmed. "This is where the Gods of the Pond get the Free Alaska Movement started."

Hooper started to speak, but Myra stopped him by squeezing his forearm.

RESURGENT MAN

ACT THREE

SCENE FIFTY-ONE. MASTER SHOT: EXTERIOR. DAY. A panoramic view of snow capped Alaskan mountains against a clear blue sky. DOLLY BACK and TILT DOWN. Center on river and PAN LEFT along its course to the dam. Below the dam is a salmon ladder, a series of long pools that appear as steps over which the water flows. Leaping from several of these steps are salmon. Beside the dam is a building with a sign that reads:

GODS OF THE POND SALMON HATCHERY

From the hatchery, along the sides of the salmon ladder, is a railing where three children, dressed for cold weather, stand. One, a little girl, is pointing out the jumping fish to her two male companions, one blonde the other a brunette. PAN RIGHT as all three turn and run across a grassy field, autumn yellow, to a long log building with smoke rising from a stone chimney.

The children stomp loudly up wooden plank steps, push open a heavy wooden door, and go inside.

CUT TO: SCENE FIFTY-TWO. MASTER SHOT: INTERIOR. DAY. Inside cabin.

In contrast to the clear blue-cast outdoors, the cabin walls glow with the soft yellow-red hues of glazed log walls and plank flooring, crackling embers against a creosote stained hearthstone, and light from oil burning wicks inside foggy globes. Cassy, pen in hand, is busily working on some papers behind a wooden table as the children enter.

DILLON and BILL JR.:
(screaming in unison): "Hey Dad, Daaaaad!"

Cassandra turns in the wooden swivel chair toward them. Her belly is swollen in pregnancy.
Cassandra: "Boys, not so loud."

BILL JR.(the blonde boy):
"But Mom, the salmon are running."

Jeannine, dressed in jeans and a flannel shirt, enters from a door in the back.
Jeannine: "What's going on out here?"
Both boys rush over to her, each grabs one hand.

DILLON (the brunette boy):
"Mom, the salmon are running! We've got to tell Dad."

Jeannine: "Your father already knows. He's gone into town to hire some help."
Bill Jr. (hopeful): "He can hire us, Mom."
Jeannine (winks to Cassy): "I don't know. What do you think Cassy; are they old enough to become gods?"
Dillon (turns to Cassy; pleads): "Please, Mom."
Cassandra: "They'll have to prove themselves worthy."
Bill Jr.: "Aw, Moms, come on; you can let us. You both started when you were our age."
Cassandra: "Not quite, we were about two years older, but I think you're old enough; go put your boots on so you'll be ready when your father gets back."
The two boys dash out of the room abandoning their little girlfriend.
Jeannine: "Well, Beverly, it looks like you have been left here with the girls."

BEVERLY:
"I want to catch fish, too. It was me who saw the salmon running first - before Dill and Bill did."

Cassandra: "It's okay with us if you get your parent's permission, but don't hold your breath. I'm afraid your father has different ideas about raising children than we do." (she turns back to the work on her desk) "Jeannine, look here a moment. I've been going over last year's figures, and if we do as well this season, we'll have enough to begin construction on our own cannery."

Jeannine (excited): "Are you serious? I thought we'd have to wait a few more years."

Cassandra: "Look, you can see for yourself." (she pauses as Jeannine moves beside her) "For the last eight years, we've pumped all profit back into the business. Therefore we haven't had to pay any taxes. This year, however, all our equipment debts will be paid up, which means we will have a taxable excess. We have to reinvest it if we don't want to pay taxes on it. The good news is the excess will be large enough to build the cannery."

Jeannine: "That's wonderful."

CUT TO: The front door where Beverly stands and listens.

Beverly (smiles): "Are you going to be canning salmon too?"

CUT TO: Cassy looking over her shoulder.

Cassandra: "Not until next season, dear."

Beverly: "Oh, boy that's great!"

As Beverly exits, DISSOLVE TO: SCENE FIFTY-THREE. EXTERIOR. DAY. Large canning plant with sign reading: BATE'S CANNERY.

CUT TO: INTERIOR. As Beverly walks into an office where a short, balding, portly man is talking on the telephone.

MR. BATES:
"... officially the season begins today and I'll need a full crew here by Monday. Oh, yeah, hire as many of those back-to-nature hippies as you can; they'll work for practically nothing."

#

Eugene mumbled, "Hippies?"

#

Mr. Bates hangs up.

Beverly: "Hi, Daddy; may I help Dill and Bill catch salmon?"

Mr. Bates: "What are those weirdos doing now, exploiting their own children in violation of the child-labor laws?"

#

Eugene cried out, "Wait a minute! This isn't correct."

#

Beverly (defensive): "They're not weirdos, Daddy; they're real nice people, and they're gonna build a cannery just like us, because they don't pay taxes."

Mr. Bates: "What!"

Bates snatches up the phone, quickly consults a flip file, and dials rapidly.

Mr. Bates: "Who is this?"

CUT TO: Cassandra holding her phone.

Cassandra: "This is Cassandra. Who is calling?"

CUT TO: Bates.

Mr. Bates: "Bob Bates; my daughter just came in and announced you were building a cannery."

CUT TO: SPLIT SCREEN Mr. Bates on RIGHT and Cassandra on LEFT.

Cassandra: "Yes, Bob that's true. We hope to begin construction next spring."

Mr. Bates: "What's wrong? Am I not giving you the service you need? You think I've got too many customers, and I need the competition? Well, you're not going to cut into my business. I'll give you the fight--"

Cassandra (interrupts): "Bob, hold on a minute. We're not going to compete for your customers. We'll only be canning our own salmon, which shouldn't be a problem for you since you're operating over capacity already. With us setting up down the street, we can ship together and save transportation costs. In fact, it may be enough of a savings that you'll be able to put in that badly needed addition you've been talking about for years."

Mr. Bates (yells): "I'm no fool!"

Cassy looks at the telephone receiver and shrugs. As she hangs up, WIPE: SCREEN RIGHT PUSHES LEFT leaving only Bates and his daughter in the picture.

Beverly: "May I, Daddy?"

Mr. Bates: "Certainly not!"

FADE.

#

Eugene stood up. "What the hell is going on? I didn't write this." He turned to Connie with an accusatory look on his face and demanded, "Who changed this?"

Connie's face paled in distress; all she could do was shake her head.

#

SCENE FIFTY-FOUR. MASTER SHOT: EXTERIOR. DAY. Alaskan town square. Beside a muddy police car, Bob Bates is button-holing a local law official whose beige colored apparel resembles a Canadian Mountie.

Mr. Bates: "Look here Winslow, I want to know why you're not doing your job?"

WINSLOW:
"What are you talking about, Mr. Bates?"

Mr. Bates: "Isn't bigamy illegal in this state?"

Winslow: "Of course it is."

Mr. Bates (jabs Winslow in the chest with his finger): "Then I demand that you arrest Bill Brooks and those two wives of his."

Winslow (brushes the annoying finger away): "D'you realize you're asking me to arrest three of this community's leading citizens? The law states that only Bill is guilty, not his wives. They married him voluntarily. My advice to you is to look at it the way the rest of the town does: it's voluntary, it's their business, and it's doing nobody any harm."

Mr. Bates: "Doing nobody any harm! Why their immoral behavior is influencing our youth, my daughter in particular."

Winslow: "Then I suggest, sir, that you forbid your daughter from spending so much time at the Brooks' house, and that you use that time to teach her what morals you believe she should accept."

Mr. Bates: "Are you going to uphold the law and arrest them or not?"

Winslow: "No, I'm not. The people of this town elected me to protect them and their property from crime, not to be out harassing peaceful individuals because they're different."

Mr. Bates: "Winslow, I'm going to report you to the town council!"

Winslow: "Mr. Bates, you can report me until you're blue in the face, but unless I'm breaking the law, myself, there's nothing the council can do. I doubt they'll even be interested in your case considering they just appointed Cassandra Brooks last week to take over the seat vacated by Quentin Lester's death. However, you do have one recourse; you are free to vote against me in the next election."

FADE as Bates stomps off in a huff.

#

Eugene grabbed the sides of the TV set as if he were going to pick it up and smash it, but he cried to the screen instead, "No! No Bates, you're supposed to be their friend."

Releasing his grip, he swung back around to Connie, and insisted, "Tell me who changed this."

Connie whimpered, "I don't know, Frank."

"Don't call me Frank. I'm sick of it." He stomped his foot. Then as if the violence of his action slammed the answer straight up his leg to his brain, he conjectured angrily, "That's it! Frank did it. He had to; it couldn't have been Jack. Jack knew I wrote it as a tribute to his ideas."

He turned to Myra like an interrogator, and grilled, "You were there - you produced it. Frank fucked it up, didn't he?"

Myra had been physically restraining Hooper from reacting, but when Eugene turned his attention to her, she let go and commanded, "Don't you dare speak to me like that Eugene Eastly."

It worked. Eugene shut up and tears spilled from his eyes. For several seconds his body shook, then as he regained control of himself he muttered, "I'm sorry."

Hooper picked up the remote and switched off the VCR. "I think we've seen enough. Eugene has gotten the idea behind Margo's flippant remark."

Myra thought, "No, we can't stop now," and started to object, but Eugene said first, "No. Please, I want to see the rest. Connie, I'm sorry. It's... it's just that it was so important to me."

Seeing his tears caused Connie's composure to return. She stood up and patting his arm said, "It's okay; anyone would be angry under the circumstances. I'm only sorry we don't have the answers for you."

Hooper backed the tape up and turned the VCR on once again, and everyone took their seats.

#

SCENE FIFTY-FIVE. MASTER SHOT. INTERIOR. DAY. Study in Bate's home. Expensive antiques surround a large ornate desk behind which Mr. Bates sits smoking a pipe and shuffling a stack of papers. Beverly enters and removes a coat from the polished hook of a mahogany hat rack.

Mr. Bates: "Where are you going?"

Beverly: "Out."

Mr. Bates: "You know you're forbidden to go over to the Brooks'."

Beverly: "Why do you hate them Daddy?"

Mr. Bates (defensive): "I don't hate them. It's just that they're trying to destroy my business. I know they say they're not, but don't you believe them. It's our livelihood, whether I can feed our family, that man and his two pretty wives are trying to take away from us."

Beverly: "But Daddy, I thought we were rich?"

Mr. Bates: "I suppose they told you that too?"
Beverly: "No, you did."
Mr. Bates: "Nothing is permanent, honey. Now you go out and find some nice playmates."

Beverly pulls on her jacket.

Mr. Bates: "Wait a minute."
Beverly: "Yes, Daddy?"
Mr. Bates: "What was it you told me the other day about how the Brooks' were going to pay for their cannery?"
Beverly (smiles brightly): "Mrs. Brooks said they saved enough money because they didn't pay taxes."
Mr. Bates (gleeful): "Ah ha, that's it! Darling, you're splendid."
Beverly (jumps joyfully): "See Daddy, I told you they were nice people.
Mr. Bates (bellows): "Nice!"

Beverly's smile disappears.

Mr. Bates: "Don't you understand? It's against the law not to pay taxes. Your friends are hurting everybody in the whole town because they are too greedy to pay their fair share, and now they're using other people's money to put me out of business. Well, I shall put an end to that."

CUT TO: SCENE FIFTY-SIX: MASTER SHOT: EXTERIOR. DAY. Front of hatchery. Billy is grinning as he was walks out of the hatchery door. In each hand he holds a huge salmon. Across the grass walking toward him is Jeannine and waddling right behind her is Cassy. He lifts the fish high, as if they are winning trophies, for the girls to see.

Billy (proud): "This is the year!"

CUT TO: SCENE FIFTY-SEVEN. MASTER SHOT: EXTERIOR. DAY. Large limestone columned government building. In front a Rolls Royce pulls to the curb, and Bob Bates climbs out of the back. A meter-maid walks up and points to a No Parking sign. Bates hands her a twenty-dollar bill and turns toward the entrance of the building. The meter-maid pockets the bill.

CUT TO: SCENE FIFTY-EIGHT. MASTER SHOT: INTERIOR. DAY. Office. Lettering on open door reads: Internal Revenue Service.

Mr. Bates enters room. In front of him is the back of a man who is bent over the desk of the receptionist. The man is fondling the girl's hand and whispering imperceptibly. She interrupts him by pointing toward Bates. Ranger Roy in a suit turns around and faces Bob Bates.

#

Eugene gasped, "Oh my God."

#

Roy: "May I help you."

CUT TO: Both men sitting on opposite sides of a desk as Roy digs through a file cabinet.

Roy (impatient): "What was the name of that company again?"

Mr. Bates: "Gods of the Pond Salmon."

Roy: "Damn that name sounds familiar... ah, here we go."

Roy, file in hand, spun around to face Bates, the chair's hinges squeal in protest at the intrusion of Roy's massive weight. He flips open the file then looks at Bates with annoyance.

Roy: "Where'd you say you got this tip?"

Mr. Bates: "From my daughter."

Roy shakes his head as he gives the stack of papers his attention. He runs his plump forefinger down the columns of every page.

Roy: "Everything's in order; your daughter must be mistaken."

Mr. Bates (protests): "You just haven't looked close enough. I'm sure if you dig a little deeper you can find something on that damn bigamist and those two fish-women he calls wives."

Roy (brightly): "Bigamist? Fish-women? Wait a minute!" (He snatches the top sheet) "Gods of the Pond Salmon, Private Corporation. Officers: William Brooks, President, Cassandra Brooks, Vice President, Jeannine Brooks, Vice President... I can't believe I didn't notice this before. Mister, I'll find something here if I have to look all night."

CUT TO: Wall clock reading: 10:25. DISSOLVE TO: Wall clock reading: 5:14.

CUT TO: The desk covered with a spread of paper, empty coffee cups, and candy bar wrappers. Both Roy and Bob have removed their jackets. Roy's armpits are stained.

Roy: "I'm sorry Bates, believe me, I'm sorry, but I can't find a thing wrong here."

Mr. Bates: "Oh, come on! I hear you guys can always find something."

Roy: "That's usually true, but this time I'm afraid it's not. These people are incredibly meticulous; everything here is absolutely correct and in order. But don't give up yet."

Mr. Bates: "I thought you just said--"

Roy (winks): "Tell me how bad you want to get these people?"

Mr. Bates: "Pretty bad; what's it gonna cost me?"

Roy: "You're gonna get off cheap, Bates, 'cause I've got a personal score I want to settle with these people. You understand I can't do anything officially, but the Brooks don't have to know that. I've got some dirt on a guy or two around here I can get to help us, and you're certainly welcome to come along."

FADE.

SCENE FIFTY-NINE. MASTER SHOT: EXTERIOR. DAY. Brook's cabin. The blue pick-up truck rolls on knobby tires up the dirt path to the front of the cabin. Dill and Bill hop to the ground from the back as Jeannine jumps out of the front. The boys vanish around the back of the house while Jeannine bounds up the steps to the front door. Billy is helping Cassy, still swollen with child, get out of the cab. Jeannine stands and reads a bright yellow sign nailed to the front door. Suddenly, she rips the sign down, and runs back to the truck.

Jeannine (gasps, holds up sign): "Billy... Cassy, look what was on the door."

CUT TO: CLOSE UP of sign: GOVERNMENT PROPERTY / NO TRESPASSING

CUT TO: Billy: "What the hell?"

CUT TO: Cassandra: "It must be some kind of mistake."

CUT TO: MASTER SHOT. A black sedan drives up and parks beside the pick-up. Four men emerge. Three wear dark gray-green suits, one carries a shotgun. Bob Bates wears tailored blue serge. Jeannine gasps and her face turns white as Roy turns and faces her. She drops the yellow sign and grabs Billy's arm for support.

#

Eugene moaned, "Oh no."

#

Roy waddles over to the three and flashes a badge.

Roy: "Internal Revenue Agents. You are hereby ordered to vacate the premises immediately. If you do not leave, you will be placed under arrest."

Billy (demands): "What for?"

Roy: "Suspicion of evading federal income taxes."

Jeannine: "Suspicion! If you've bothered to look at our tax returns, you know that's not true."

Roy: "It's being investigated now, and if in the next few months it turns out we're wrong, your property will be returned to you."

Cassandra: "Months! You've got to be kidding. You can't keep us out of our house."

Roy: "Lady, you so much as touch that house and you'll find yourself in jail."

Cassandra (turns to Bates): "Bob, what do you have to do with all this?"

Billy steps between Jeannine and Roy.

Billy: "Mister, personal vendettas can work both ways, and in the end they can go a little too far."

Roy ignores Billy and looks down at the torn yellow sign on the ground.

Roy: "It's a violation of federal law to remove that sign; I could run you in right now just for that."

Cassandra: "This is too much!" (Cassy waddles around the truck and climbs behind the wheel) "I'm going to get Constable Winslow."

Roy (orders): "Stop her!"

#

Again Eugene moaned, "Oh no."

#

Cassandra quickly locks the door.

Roy (screams): "I said, stop her!"

The agent holding the shotgun runs around the truck. He smashes the butt of the gun against the window. Bates stands and smiles. Billy runs over and grabs the man from the back and tries to pull him away from the cab.

Billy (yells): "Start the engine Cassy, start the engine!"

Before Billy can pull the man off the truck, the other agent runs up behind him and kicks him in the back of the knees. Billy falls down, and gets back up as the agent with the shotgun, holding it high above his head, swings around and slams the stock into Billy's skull. The sound of crushing bone permeates the air. Billy falls dead; his cracked head spatters blood and brain matter over the mirror polish of the agent's black shoes.

#

Eugene begged the screen, "No. Please no."

#

CUT TO: CLOSE-UP of Cassy's panic-stricken face as she presses it against the window. Her lips smear the glass as she screams.

CUT TO: Jeannine, her arms flailing like a maniac, running toward the house.

CUT TO: Bob Bates, his face horrified, grabbing Roy's arm.

Mr. Bates: "What the hell are you doing?"

Roy socks him in the stomach, and he slumps to a squat.

Roy: "I'm giving you exactly what you ordered." (Roy turns to agent standing over Billy's body) "Hurry up and get that bitch out!"

CUT TO: The agent beating the window. The window breaks. Cassy screams in terror as pieces of glass hit her. The revenue agent

ignores her and reaches and grasps her cowering body. The other man joins him.
Cassandra: "Leave me alone!... Help!"

Agent One (grabs Cassy's long blonde hair, orders):
"Shut up, bitch!"

Without bothering to unlock the door and open it. The two men drag her through the smashed glass of the broken window.
Cassandra (begs): "No, please, no! No. Please!"
The agents behave as if they hear nothing and continue to drag her, swollen belly and all, over the shards of glass. Cassy's voice hits its highest pitch as her waist crosses the jagged threshold. The men drop her silent quaking body on the ground. Cassy's pale complexion is striped in gory crimson from her neck to her knees. With the last of her strength she stretches her hand across the dirt and grasps Billy's hand.

#

Eugene's ribs rose in a retch, but he put his hand over his mouth.

#

CUT TO: CLOSE-UP. Cassandra on ground.
Cassandra (closes her eyes and whispers): "Oh Billy, I thought here our love was safe."
CUT TO: Roy shuffling over to the two bodies, the fabric of his pants makes a swishing sound as his fat thighs rub against each other. He stops when his toe bumps into the shotgun and with great effort, he squats down and picks it up. Groaning, he rises back up and looks at his two awe struck companions.
Roy: "What the hell are you two doing? We've got to catch the other girl."
Suddenly there is a banging noise of wood hitting wood. The three men turn toward the cabin.
CUT TO: The cabin door bouncing off the outer wall.
Jeannine: "Aaiiiiiiiii!"

Jeannine runs across the porch, her feet pound down the plank steps. She holds a baseball bat high in her hands, like a Banshee dashing into battle. Her eye sockets are ghostly white, and her mouth is open wide emitting a shriek of death.

#

Eugene leaped to his feet and screamed, "No Jack. No!"

Myra grabbed Hooper's wrist and uttered, "Oh Jesus, he's remembering."

#

Bates lurches backward along the ground from where he lay holding his stomach. The two nameless revenue agents turn and run, but Jeannine's path is clearly targeted toward the fat Ranger who had once tried to rape her and was responsible for the killing of her friends.

Roy pumps the shotgun.

Roy (orders): "Stop!"

Jeannine is beyond hearing.

CUT TO: SLOW MOTION. Smoke puffs from the muzzle of the gun.

CUT TO: A red splotch rips along Jeannine's ribcage.

CUT TO: The gun puffs again as Roy recoils in slow motion.

CUT TO: The top of the baseball bat shatters and flies from Jeannine's hand. Her hands flutter down, yet she continues to run. Her steps look like those of a drunkard.

CUT TO: The gun puffs once more.

CUT TO: A red flower bursts into bloom on Jeannine's neck. She wavers, but continues.

CUT TO: CLOSE-UP. Jeannine's eyes - still clear with consciousness, they look to the right.

CUT TO: Jeannine veering to the right, away from Roy, and toward the bodies of Cassy and Billy. She swings her shoulders hard in a struggle to maintain the momentum of her strident dash long enough to carry her the last few feet to her friends. Her body tumbles and stops, her arm flops forward.

CUT TO: CLOSE-UP. Three hands, palms up, fingers touching, each with a puffy white scar across the wrist.

#

Eugene fell to his knees and threw up. Connie jumped from her chair and held his quaking shoulders as he continued to heave between wails of, "No Jack... Why Jack?"

Connie yelled at Hooper, "Turn that goddamn thing off already!"

"Leave it on," Myra countered.

#

CUT TO: Bates rising to his feet.

Mr. Bates (screams at Roy): "You... you, I can't believe you... this was supposed to be--"

Roy pulls a revolver from inside his coat and fires. Bates drops to the ground. Roy wipes the revolver clean with a handkerchief then places it in Jeannine's hand. He then wipes the shotgun and places it in Bate's hands.

Roy and the two other revenue agents get back in their sedan and drive away.

CUT TO: The agonized faces of Dillon and Bill Jr. peering out from beneath the front porch steps.

FADE.

#

Ralph ran into the room crying, "What the hell is going on in here?" Then as the stench of fresh vomit hit his nostrils, he cringed, and muttered, "Ugh."

Sara came in behind him and simply stared.

#

SCENE SIXTY. MASTER SHOT: EXTERIOR. DAY. Front of salmon hatchery. Dillon is standing on a ladder as he loosens the bolts holding up the sign reading: GODS OF THE POND SALMON. Bill Jr. is holding the ladder steady. Beverly walks up.

Beverly: "I came to say good bye. My mother says the welfare people are coming to get you today."
Bill Jr.: "We're not going with the welfare people."
Beverly: "But what will you do?"
Dillon: "We're going to build a new pond, and then a town around it."
Beverly: "Where?"
Dillon: "North."
Bill Jr.: "As far away from people as we can get."
Beverly: "All people?"
Dillon: "Except for people like us."
Beverly: "I'm like you; can I go?"
Bill Jr.: "We're leaving as soon as we get our sign down."

CUT TO: Bill Jr. and Dillon with packs on their backs, and the sign between them underneath their left arms. Walking with them is Beverly. Beyond the yellowing grass in front of them are huge craggy snow-capped mountains like a massive cemetery of broken headstones.

ZOOM TO CLOSE-UP of red slash across the right wrist of each child, as the credits begin rising up the screen.

#

Myra squatted beside Eugene and brushed the hair out of his eyes while Connie wiped his mouth with a tissue she found in her pocket.

With the hair out of his face, Myra could see that his eyes were glazed and unfocused. She pushed Connie's hand out of her way and shook him. "Frank! Frank!" she implored, but he did not respond.

"Eugene! Eugene!" she urged, but with the same result. He continued to rock and commiserate the same lament, "No Jack... Why Jack?" Then entreating no one in particular, she dropped her hands and moaned, "Oh God, what have we done?"

Hooper said, "Off hand, I'd say we applied shock therapy."

Connie pulled Frank into her arms, and charged, "You're awfully flip! Are you saying you knew this would happen?"

Responding slightly defensively, Hooper answered, "Please don't be presumptuous; we knew only that *Resurgent Man* was connected to his past. We hoped it might serve as a catalyst to restoring his memory."

"Well, I hope you're satisfied," Connie huffed.

Myra wailed, "I feel so guilty."

Ralph, who had remained at the door offered, "Shouldn't we call a doctor."

"Yes, yes," Myra responded brightly. "I'm afraid I haven't been thinking. I'll call Sammy Garcia right away."

She turned to Sara and ordered, "Sara, go turn Frank's bed down." Then to Hooper, "Hooper, help Connie get him into bed."

As her steps carried her through the doorway Ralph asked, "Is there anything I can do?"

Myra turned around. Her eyes fell on the vomit-covered carpet, but she shook her head, and said, "No, you can go on to bed if you like."

After Connie and Hooper had gotten him settled into bed, Hooper said, "Connie, I would like you to understand what I was hoping for. I like Eugene; I think of him as a great kid. I also like Frank; well, that is, I admire him. Once Frank regains his memory of Eugene, or vice versa, I believe he'll surpass anything he's done. Can't you imagine that? The greatest becoming even greater."

Connie stroked Frank's huddled figure through the sheets. "I guess I owe you an apology."

"None needed. Myra and I weren't exactly broadcasting our intentions."

"Still, I should. I'm afraid, in my quest to win this poor man's heart, I lost sight of his health. I've been petty - especially with you, and until recently, I was even hostile to Myra."

Myra walked into the room, and said, "Sammy said it sounds like he's regained his memory, but we won't know until he calms down. He suggests someone stay with him and comfort him until then. He also suggested that we might give him a sedative." She pulled a plastic pharmacy bottle from her pocket and added, "We have some."

Hooper said, "That's good news."

Myra asked him, "Hooper would you mind letting me speak to Connie in private."

"Certainly," he answered and left the room.

"Connie, I'm still his wife and feel it's my responsibility to stay up with him, but I think it would be better for him if you did it."

"I'd like that."

"Why don't you get dressed for bed, and I'll stay with him until you're ready."

"Thank you, I'll be back in a jiffy."

Ten minutes later she returned in robe and slippers. Myra told her she had gotten Frank to swallow a sedative and that he appeared to be sleeping. When Connie removed her robe, Myra whistled. She was wearing a full length satin nightgown. Its pale green color shimmered in perfect contrast to her dark red hair. A lace inset spearing downward from her neck and shoulders to a point below her navel added an airy elegance while hinting at the curves of her shapely figure.

Myra told her, "I don't know if that will do anything for his memory, but if he doesn't show some kind of response when he wakes up, I'd say he was gay."

Connie giggled and said, "If he wakes up gay, I'm going to give him some real shock therapy." She then kissed Myra's cheek, and said, "Thank you for being so understanding."

Myra returned, "I hope everything works out."

As Myra turned to leave, Connie asked, "Are you going to let Hooper sleep over?"

"He can stay if he wants, but it won't be in my bedroom. I need some time alone. Besides, I need to feel free from this situation before I can give him what I want."

When Myra closed the door, Connie slid between the sheets and curled up against Frank's back. She tucked her chin over his shoulder and gradually matched her breathing to the steady rise and fall of his chest.

Myra shooed Sara away from cleaning the living room carpet, and finished it herself. When she was done, she found Hooper sitting at the bar that separated the kitchen from the dining room. He was contemplating a glass of whiskey. She wrapped her arms around him from behind and kissed him on the back of the neck.

"I'm going up to bed," she said, still holding him. "You can stay down here on the sofa if you like." Then adding softly, she asked, "You understand, don't you?"

"Yes," then after a moment, "Can you guess what was going on in his mind, when he lost it?"

"What do you mean?"

"I'm wondering what keyed it. It seemed as if it happened right as Jeannine went after the fat ranger with the baseball bat. Was it the culmination of the violence, or something more specific?"

"I don't know."

"It obviously triggered his memory of Jack's death. But what he was moaning seems to wreck both our theories."

"Go on."

"He kept saying, 'No Jack.' and 'Why Jack?' To me that sounds like Jack might have been doing something to cause the car to crash."

"I don't think so. Why would Jack having done something stupid enough to get himself killed cause Eugene to lose his memory? I think it has to be something worse. But I believe you're on the right track."

"How's that?"

"That Eugene did not purposely kill him."

"I've been saying that all along."

"Wait a minute; I've got it. What about the gunshot in the movie that seemed to precipitate his reaction? Maybe he had to shoot Jack in self defense."

"I can't imagine any circumstances for that to happen."

"Maybe over Stacie?"

"I doubt it, but enough speculation - I'm going to sleep."

Myra gave him a hug, and said, "I suppose you're right, although I'll probably have nightmares about it all night long."

"Me too."

He turned around and pressed his lips to her mouth. He felt her lips biting, pulling, grasping his mouth as she slid her arms around his waist. It was their first kiss. Gene and Carol had kissed, sure, but this was different. This was the answer to the question Hooper had asked ten years earlier. This was the fulfillment of a dream, and a commitment to the future. It was a kiss that would last forever in his memory.

He could feel that she was hesitant to break away, so he pushed her back gently, and whispered, "I'll see you in the morning."

As the light of dawn entered the living room window, Hooper felt the cold morning air on his bare feet. He tried to kick the covers back over them, but something was keeping him from doing so. He opened his eyes to see Frank holding the end of the blanket up.

"About time you woke up Hooper."

"Who am I talking to?" Hooper asked.

"Just me. All of me though, which is what you're hoping to hear."

"So, what do I call you?"

"Frank. What other name do you think I could get away with?"

"How about Frank Eugene Stacy?"

Frank pondered it a moment then said, "Yes, I like that."

"Have you seen Myra yet?"

"No, I'll see her later. I wanted to speak to you first; to let you know that you gave me an excellent performance, and deserved the role from the beginning. I wanted to make sure you understood you were given the role because your audition warranted it. There was no other reason."

"Thank you, Frank. I needed to hear that."

"That's all." He started to rise.

"Wait a minute. I want to ask you a question."

"I'm sure you've got plenty, but they can wait until breakfast."

"I'm not sure this one can wait. That is, I can't imagine you want just anyone hearing it."

Frank sat back down, and said, "What is it?"

"Did you kill Jack?"

"Jesus, no! What gave you that idea?"

"Some things you said. How did Jack die, then?"

"That's one of the things you'll have to wait for until breakfast."

"Then just tell me this; could you have prevented Jack's death?"

Frank looked at him sadly, and answered solemnly, "I wish I could have."

"I'm sorry; I had to know."

"It's okay. You'll understand everything later." Then bouncing to his feet he said, "I gotta go." With a sheepish, boyish look on his face he added, "I think I'm going to get laid."

Hooper bolted upright on the sofa. "Whose bedroom are you going to?" With his hand curling into a fist, he stood and added, "I'm ready to fight if you tell me the wrong one."

"Jesus Christ, Hooper. I thought we settled this in the walkway outside your dressing room." Frank grinned and walked away.

In the morning, Myra was walking sleepily down the hall to the bathroom. As she stopped to turn the knob, the door opened and Connie appeared.

"Oh!" Myra gasped.

"Did I scare you?" Connie asked.

"Just startled me. How is he?"

Connie cooed, "Oh, he's just wonderful."

"You didn't," Myra implied with a smile.

"No," replied Connie gleefully, "he did."

Both women giggled then hugged each other.

As their laughter subsided, Connie said, "I must have fallen asleep when he woke up. I was sleeping on my side, and he rolled me over. I opened my eyes, and he said, 'Connie' that's it, just 'Connie,' but it was Frank's voice. Then he proceeded to make love to me, and he was so... so, well anyway I couldn't think about anything else until he was finished."

"Well, it certainly put some color in your cheeks."

"Oh hush, Myra; you're embarrassing me."

Myra giggled again, and Connie said, "Listen to this. When he finished, he said, 'Connie, forget about getting in touch with that writer; we've made enough changes to that script already."

"He did?"

"Yes, and then he went on to say that he wanted me to call the cast and crew together for this afternoon, because they deserved an explanation concerning his behavior."

"Oh, I can't wait to see him."

"You'll have to wait. He's talking with Ralph right now, but he said he wanted to speak to all of us over breakfast. He also had me invite Zack over."

Frank pushed open the door to Ralph's bedroom and walked in. Ralph woke immediately from a sound asleep as Frank snatched the covers off him.

"What's going on here?" he cried.

"Wake up you old movie-maker, there's work to be done; that is, if you want to help me make the greatest war picture of all time."

"I must be dreaming," Smurling scowled.

"Breakfast in twenty minutes, Ralph." Frank said, walking out the door.

CHAPTER EIGHTEEN

Five expectant faces watched Frank at the end of the table while Sara served breakfast.

"I first met Jack when I was thirteen. It was a Saturday afternoon and the movie was over. I always attended the Saturday matinee, because it was the first showing each week, and at half price, the only show I could afford. I stood in the front of the screen trying to decide which exit to take. Out-guessing my father was a matter of luck; sometimes I made it - sometimes I didn't. To my old man it was a game. He knew I always went, but he didn't beat me unless he caught me. I believe he must have gotten some kind of sick pleasure from beating me in public."

#

If you were driving through Schley County on the morning of Saturday April 20, 1963, it would not have mattered whether you traveled north or south on Highway 19; or east or west on Highway 26; because before the two highways crossed, you would have to stop. On the way you would have passed miles and miles, and acres and acres of land once ruled by cotton, now serving orchards. You would have seen rows of pecan trees extending beyond the horizon, their gray-black limbs just beginning to sprout leaves, reaching into the sky like a colonnade of capillaries; next to diagonal queues of easy-to-reach, flat-topped peach trees, with short gnarled trunks like hat racks sporting shaggy green toupees; next to pine trees in military parade, bristle-tipped bayonets soaring toward the clouds until the day they would become 2x4's, newspapers, and paint thinner.

Unless you were from Schley County, which is pronounced "Sly" by the natives, you would not know you would have to stop until you saw the sign with the three big P's, and the road block just beyond it. If you were traveling north on 19 you would round the bend and see the city limits sign, but before you could read anything else you would be able to make out that three words beginning with the letter P encircled the name of the town. Then you would get closer and see that it read: Ellaville, Georgia. *People - Pride - Progress*, but if you were from Schley County you would know what every school child knows: that the 3-P's of Ellaville are really Peach - Pine - Pecan, because cotton came and went and while the mobile home factories currently provided the major source of income, it was the 3-P's you could always count on.

If you were from Schley County, you would already know the road was blocked because you knew, from as far back as you could remember, that the third Saturday of April marked the first rite of spring: *The Schley County Squirrel Fry*. It was the annual event ending a week of gunfire as every male in the county old enough to tote a gun worked to make the pecan and peach orchards safe for another season. The roads however, had not always been closed for this celebration. It took the invention of the automobile and the addition of the *Ellaville Road Rally* for the occasion to close the roads.

A huge banner which read: *Schley County Spring Festival* hung from the telephone wires over Broad Street. On the east side of Broad was the town square, its traditional grassy park dotted with picnic tables covered with bowls of potato salad, pecan stuffing, deviled eggs, pickled peaches and mounds of fresh fried squirrel. But the hundreds of people crowded there all faced west toward the clock tower atop the county courthouse across the street. The countdown to noon had begun, and twenty men, the best hunters of the season, ten on each side of the street stood with their rifles raised to the sky. It took the sound of twenty rifles to start the race because between them, the drivers of forty-two cars were revving their engines in deafening anticipation. The huge second hand ticked away as the crowd called out, "Ten... nine... eight..."

Eugene Eastly stood beside his mother and watched the 1957 Chevy at the front of the pack. Jim Eastly was always in the number one position because no one had beaten him in over five years. His third gear was legendary; shifting into it propelled the car with a g-force intensity that would pin the driver to the seat. Eugene suspected that shifting into third triggered a nitrous oxygen tank connected to the carburetor; it wasn't outside the rules - there weren't any. In fact, nearly every car in the race was hopped up on airplane fuel. What made the difference in Jim's car was not only having the nerve to use that third gear, which could blast the car from sixty miles per hour to over a hundred in less than ten seconds, but having the ability to hold the steering wheel steady at the same time.

The rifles cracked and the cars shot forward in a haze of blue smoke. Unless Jim lost his grip and crashed, it would be a race for second place. Eugene yawned and looked wistfully over his shoulder toward the movie house. *Lawrence Of Arabia* had finally come to town, but the theater delayed the matinee until the end of the race.

Five hours later, Eugene stood with his hand on the back of the left aisle seat of the first row looking left then right toward the two exit doors on either side of the screen. He was a slender boy, almost slight, with big feet and long fingered hands that had grown in advance of the rest of his body. Near white hair cut in a crew made his ears stand out like flaps. Flaps the bigger boys would grab in the school hallway, then while grinding their knuckles into his scalp, would call out to their friends, "Hey fellas, come check out this sand paper." He would liked to have grown his hair out, but Jim insisted on cutting it himself once a week.

Often, if enough people came for the matinee, he was able to slip out the front door in the middle of the crowd, but on this day, attendance was poor. Eugene's only hope was that his father was still occupied in backslapping congratulation with the other drivers and the fans. Within minutes the auditorium was nearly empty.

A kid a few inches taller than Eugene walked up behind him and in a poor imitation of Monty Hall, TV host of *Let's Make a Deal*, said, "Behind which door is the grand prize? Is it door number one, door number two, or door number three where Carol Merrill is riding the four hundred dollar exercycle?"

Eugene flinched when he saw the older boy and started to tell him to leave him alone, but a disarming smile on the boy's face stopped him. He'd seen him around for as long as he could remember, but the two had never spoken before. Eugene mostly avoided older boys, because they always picked on him. This one in particular because the townsfolk considered him bad, although Eugene didn't know why. Probably because he was one of the older kids from the orphan farm, and was often out on the streets regularly after dark. Eugene thought back to when he had last seen him at the grammar school. It had been about two years, and Eugene remembered he used to see him selling candy to kids who had lunch money. Eugene could not, however, recall ever seeing him hanging out with any particular person or group. The word loner came to mind as he looked up at the boy who was nearly six feet tall with dark, longish hair. There was something scary about his dark eyes and pale face. No one ever bothered him, thought Eugene.

The kid, however, smiled, so Eugene relaxed.

"So which door are you going to pick today?" he asked again.

"I haven't decided."

"You want me to go find out which door he's behind?"

"You mean you know?"

"About your father? Sure I know what an asshole he is. I'm here almost every Saturday and I've seen him plenty of times."

"Really?"

"Yeah, so do you want me to check the doors for you?" The boy paused and dropped his voice down to a conspiratorial whisper. "Or would you like to learn a new way out that he'll never discover?"

"Are you serious?"

The boy looked over his shoulder, up the aisle, then said, "Follow me."

He led Eugene to the exit on the right then stopped. "It's best to do this while the lights are still down so the ushers won't see you." He then looked one more time toward the back then said, "You gotta act like you're going to go out this door, then real quick, slip behind this curtain." The boy disappeared behind the curtain hanging to the right of the exit. Eugene followed him along the wall until they were behind the screen. The boy pointed to a ladder connected to the wall leading to the ceiling. He climbed on it and gestured for Eugene to follow.

The boy disappeared into the darkness above, and Eugene reluctantly pulled himself up the rungs in time to the beat of his heart pounding loudly in his ears. He heard a tiny creak before sunlight poured on his face.

The boy whispered, "It's the roof exit. Hurry, before someone sees the light."

Eugene scrambled up the remaining steps. When he reached the final one, the boy reached down and pulled him onto the roof.

While the boy was closing the opening, Eugene stood up, looked out over the town square, and exclaimed, "Wow, you can see everything from up here."

"Get down before you get us caught!" The boy grabbed him by a belt loop, yanked him down to the tar and gravel surface.

"Sorry," Eugene said, his voice a whisper.

They crawled across the rooftop until they reached the end of the block. The boy peered over the edge, then ordered, "Come on."

He leapt four feet across a two story drop into a broken window of an abandoned cotton warehouse that ran the length of the block on the backside of town square. Eugene followed and they climbed down another ladder to the first floor. The boy peeled back part of the corrugated metal wall, and Eugene slipped through it onto the sidewalk. The boy came through immediately after and hit the sidewalk in a run. Eugene had to run hard to keep up. The boy dashed across Wilson Street and into the woods behind City Hall and did not stop until he reached the railroad tracks.

The boy laughed breathlessly, "Now you never have to worry about your old man catching you again."

Eugene sat down on the railroad ties, "How did you find that way out?"

"A kid I live with at the farm gets into the movies that way."

"The orphan farm?"

"It's a soybean farm, and a foster home," he corrected, his voice defensive.

"Sorry, I didn't mean to--"

"It's all right. I used to think I envied anybody with parents until I saw you and your old man."

"So, is that the way you get in?"

The boy glared at Eugene, "No, I don't have a problem with paying."

"I was just curious."

"I thought you would be different. Most people just assume I steal because I'm an orphan. Well I don't - I've got a job."

Eugene dropped his head and scuffed his shoe against the gravel.

The boy asked, "So, what's your name?"

"Eugene."

"Eugene, I'm Jack; you wanna mess around?"

Eugene looked up and smiled, "Sure."

#

"So that's how I met Jack," Frank said to the group around the table. "And, soon thereafter, I noticed that the bigger kids in town quit picking on me. I never found out if it was anything Jack did, or if they feared him and left me alone because of our friendship."

"Before Jack, I mostly played alone, and on occasion with one of the neighboring kids. It wasn't like any of them were friends. It was more like I would be playing and one of them would happen along, or vice versa. It never amounted to more than that. My father didn't help matters; the kids were all afraid of him. No one was interested in coming over to my house because Dad might be drunk. One kid told me, 'I never know if I'm going to see the nice Mr. Eastly, or the scary Mr. Eastly.' That hurt."

"I remember a time when a kid did come over. We got the idea to fix a rusty old clothes dryer Dad had left laying out in the front yard. All we had to do was reconnect a bunch of broken wires. It did, however, take several tries before we found the correct combination. When we finally did, we pushed it over onto its back, plugged it in, and took turns riding in it. We would spin around and around until we were about to puke, then try to climb out while it was still going. What you had to do was grab hold of the side while lifting your feet, and then somersault onto the ground. It wasn't nearly as graceful as it sounds, because as soon as you grabbed hold of the side the whole world kept spinning and you couldn't tell which direction was the ground; you had to let gravity do the rest. The best part was trying to stand up once you hit the ground. Of course it was impossible, but it was so funny to watch as we staggered around like drunks."

"Anyway, Dad shows up right after I'd taken a turn. I was still lying on my back, clutching the grass as if it might stop the inside of my head from churning, and watching the clouds and treetops spin. All of a sudden, I saw Dad's face spinning among the clouds, and before I could say a word, he pulled me to my feet and started hitting me with his belt. To make it worse, I was still unable to stand; I was too dizzy. This made Dad angrier; he told me if I didn't stand up he'd hit whatever part of my body happened to be where my butt was supposed to be. That part turned out to be my shoulders and the back of my head. By the time he finished, my playmate had long run away."

"When Jack and I started hanging out, it was different than with the other kids. He actually liked me; it wasn't because I was conveniently nearby. After that day at the theater, I didn't see him again for a long time. It wasn't until sometime in late fall. I'd already started high school. I remember I was dodging bodies in the hall on my way to my first class when I saw him standing in front of an open locker that was packed with candy, gum, cigarettes, ball point pens, and maybe a school book or two. I stopped and watched as some kid gave him a quarter for a nickel candy bar. He saw me and winked, and then turned back to his transaction. I was going to say hello, but a wave of people washed me on down the hall and I found myself at the door of my classroom, so I went on in."

"That same day at lunch, as I was eating alone and reading a book on Stanislavski's Method Acting, someone sat across from me. I didn't bother to look over the top of the book. No one ever sat by me unless all the other tables were taken. Then I heard the person ask, 'So you want to be an actor?'. I recognized Jack's voice and immediately looked up from my reading."

"No, I want to be a director, but I need to know about acting to be any good."

"That makes sense. What kind of movies do you want to make?"

"Ones that are fun to watch, but can make a statement at the same time. Only I'm not sure what kind of stories those will be yet."

"Maybe like the pictures Ralph Smurling makes?"

"Who?"

"The guy who made *Court Appointed Lawyer*."

"Oh, I liked that one."

"But do you know why you liked it?"

"Because the trial scenes were so exciting."

"Come on Eugene, tell me why they were exciting."

"Because the lawyer helped poor people?"

"No, because he fought against a system that ignores justice when it comes to poor people. He said to hell with plea bargaining prosecutors and took his clients to trial."

"Oh."

"Think of the climax: the prosecuting attorney had finished a highly emotional, yet fact-less closing argument. The camera cuts to the jury and you can see by their faces that they're leaning his way. Then the court appointed, defense attorney stands up. He's a scrawny fellow who looks like he never got over being born premature. He opens his mouth and the words boom in resonant passion, yet he offers no appeal to the emotions of the jury. Instead he hammers them with the facts, circumstantial and sketchy. He pounds away until he's nailed each and every member of that jury to their seat. When he's finished, it's obvious the jury has been turned. The prosecutor leaps to his feet, imploring the judge to give him a chance at rebuttal, but the judge rules him out of order. The courtroom bursts into applause."

"Yeah that's the kind of movie I want to make."

"Then you should think about studying under Ralph Smurling."

#

"So, you see Ralph, it was Jack who encouraged me to come to you. His admiration for your work became mine, because I admired him and his ideas. Jack seemed like such a serious guy at first, but as time went on, I learned he had a silly side as well. It wasn't so much that he was silly, but that he knew how to enjoy life."

"The next time I saw Jack was after school one day. I was riding my bicycle home, and he caught up with me on his."

#

"Hey, Eugene. Wait up!"

Eugene looked over his shoulder. When he saw Jack pedaling hurriedly behind him, he lowered his foot and dragged the rubber toe of his canvas sneaker in the grit along the road side.

"You wanna make some money?"

Eugene sized up the boy he still perceived to be the town hood, "Is it legal?"

Jack looked at him in disgust, and said, "Legal is a political term. Better to ask if it's moral."

"Moral?"

"Yeah, like whether theft or fraud is involved."

"But aren't those illegal?"

"They're immoral first. There are plenty of ways to make money that are illegal but not immoral, and vice versa."

"So is it moral?"

"Yes, and by random chance it also happens to be legal."

"You talk funny."

"You only say that because you think funny," retorted Jack, "but you'll get over it."

Eugene rolled a piece of gravel back and forth with the sole of his sneaker, and asked, "So what do I have to do?"

"I need a partner. This morning I was offered a part time job, but I have two part time jobs already. I can't do all three, but with a partner I could, and still make more money."

"A real job," Eugene exclaimed. "Doing what?"

"First, as soon as school lets out, I go to the diner and wash all their breakfast and lunch dishes. My other job is sweeping out the barber shop after it closes, but this morning Mr. Scott at the grocery store offered me a job doing his stocking. He says he's getting too old for all the lifting. The stock work pays a little more than the dishwashing, but I get a meal at the diner, and I don't want to give that up. If you split the dishwashing and stocking with me I'll split the money with you, but I get the meal. With both of us working together I'll still have time to sweep out the barber shop. So, you wanna do it?"

"Sure, when do we start?"

"Right now."

Three hours and twenty minutes later, the two boys parked their bicycles underneath the spiraling red, white, and blue pole of Owen's barber shop.

Jack said, "You can hang out if you want, but this isn't part of our deal."

"I know, but I'm too excited to go home. Four dollars and fifty cents; I've never had so much money. My father only gives me fifty cents allowance, and it always gets used up at the movies."

"I once asked Mr. Guthrie for an allowance, but he said if he gave me one he'd have to give everybody one, and he couldn't afford it."

"How many kids does he keep?"

"There are twenty of us," Jack answered, pulling open the barber shop door. A little bell jangled inside as he entered."

"Hi Jack," Owen called out from the back room. "You're mighty early. Today isn't Thursday is it?"

"No sir, I'm just early." Then to Eugene he whispered, "He pays me fifty cents a day plus a haircut on Thursdays."

Eugene grabbed his arm and whispered back, "How'd he know it was you? He can't see out here."

"I asked him once and he told me he can tell who is coming in by the way the bell jangles against the door because everybody in town has a different way of pulling open the door."

"Do you really believe that? He probably knows it's you 'cause you're the only person who comes in this late in the afternoon."

"You should watch him on a Saturday when it's busy. He never looks up from his work, yet he greets each man who enters by name."

Owen emerged from the back room and declared, "Since you're already here, I can leave," Then seeing Eugene, he added, "Hi there Eugene, how's your mother?"

"She's fine."

"Good to hear. Well boys, I'll see you later. Don't forget to lock up, Jack."

"I won't."

Jack had a push broom in hand and was sweeping the traditional black and white tiled floor before Owen was out the door. Eugene had climbed into one of the barber chairs, and while playing with the handle to make it rise, said, "Wow, look at all the hair."

"This is nothing. Look what's behind you in the corner. When he's in between customers, Mr. Owen sweeps everything out of his way."

"Seems like such a waste."

"Yeah, I asked him how come he didn't try to sell it to a wig maker, but he said none of it was long enough."

"How long have you been working?" Eugene asked.

"Since about the time I asked Mr. Guthrie for the allowance. All I wanted was what you get: fifty cents a week, but when he said he couldn't afford it, I started asking around for work. The problem was, I didn't have time for most jobs, because I had so many chores back at the farm. This one turned out to be perfect because it only takes me about half an hour."

"What about all your chores now?"

"I quit doing them when I found out what Mr. Guthrie was getting for nothing."

"What do you mean?"

"The state of Georgia is paying him to keep me and nineteen other boys."

"You mean like a salary for running the farm?"

"Hell no! The farm is his; he grows soybeans for profit, and subsidies. The state pays him to take on foster children. It's perfect; he gets free labor, and all he did was add a bunkhouse to the side of his barn with a wood stove for heat. We plow his fields, plant his seeds, then weed, water, and reap. We shovel the shit out of his barn then fertilize his garden with it. We milk his cows, feed his chickens, and collect his eggs. The man doesn't shell out a penny for any kid there. Our clothes come from *Goodwill*, and our furniture came from the *Salvation Army*. We even cook our own meals from the food we raise."

"That's slavery," Eugene stated, his face flush with the indignation he felt for his new friend.

"Just about. However, I have to admit that the circumstances have taught me to become self sufficient."

"When did you find out he was getting paid?"

"I always suspected, but I never really cared about it, or how much it was until he started bitching about my working. At first it didn't bother him. In fact, he liked it, until I had to leave one day in the middle of harvest to come here. He acted like he was getting gypped out of something, and that was what got me thinking. A few days later when both he and Mrs. Guthrie were out, I sneaked into the house and went through his desk until I found the check stubs from the state welfare department. I couldn't believe it; he was getting over a thousand dollars a month."

"Wow," Eugene exclaimed.

"That's what I thought. The next day I went to him and asked him for a five dollar allowance while explaining how I thought I was earning it by the work I was doing."

"What did he say?"

"He said again that he couldn't afford it, and I insisted that he could too because of the money he got from the state. He got mad then, and started yelling about that being his compensation for taking care of ungrateful brats like me."

"What did you do then?"

"I took the job at the diner, and did as many chores as I could when I got home. He really raised hell; he threatened to have the welfare department put me in another home. He said, he had some pull and that he could get me placed somewhere that would really make me miserable. I got mad and started yelling about my rights and how I was earning my keep and how he had no complaint. He just laughed, and his next words may as well have been a punch in my stomach. He told me I didn't have a single right in the world because I'm a minor and a ward of the state; and until I'm eighteen years old I will never be allowed to make a decision affecting my own life."

"What did you do?"

"A few days later I ran into some luck. I had caught the flu, probably from not enough sleep. I was staying up late every night after finishing my chores so I could keep up with my school work. Anyway, I laid out of school, and while I was in bed I could hear Mr. Guthrie through the wall to the barn. All of a sudden he started moaning like he was in pain, and I jumped out of bed and ran into the barn. He was standing with his chest pressed against the pen where we kept the newborn calves. Both his arms were stretched out along the railing and his hands were gripping the rail so hard his knuckles had turned white. But it was his face that scared me. His eyes were closed tight, his mouth was hanging open, and his head was tilted all the way back. Jesus, I thought he was having a heart attack, and I cried out to him."

"Did you save his life?"

"Hell no. There was nothing wrong with him. When he heard my voice, he snapped his head in my direction, and I could see his eyes; they were wide open and wild looking. He screamed at me, 'get out of here - get back to bed.' I'd never seen him so angry before. I ran out of there as fast as I could."

"Then what did you do?"

Jack had stopped to push the mound of hair into a large dust pan. After dumping it into the trash can, he beat the loose hairs off the broom by banging the handle against the top of the can, then continued, "Now I was pretty sick - fever, aches and chills - and believe me, I thought I had done the right thing - rushing in there to help him and all. I swear he looked like he was really hurting. By the time I got back to bed, I was feeling kind of stupid and embarrassed, 'cause I figured he was concerned about my health instead of his own. It was maybe thirty minutes later when he came into the bunkhouse. I thought he was coming in to check on me or to apologize for yelling at me, but that wasn't it at all. He told me I had become too much of a discipline problem for him to handle; and as soon as I was well, he was going to contact the welfare department to ship me to a foster home equipped for bad boys. I was crying before he'd left the room. I couldn't hold it back. I wasn't a bad boy; I couldn't believe he would send me away. He was the only father I'd ever had. There had been good times. I mean, after all I've lived on that farm for the length of my memory. It's the only place I can call home."

"Anyway, the hurt started to go away when I remembered about the money. I began to realize Mr. Guthrie was in the Foster Parent Business strictly as business. I saw the farm as a jail and after a bit, my self esteem recovered. Then I got suspicious about what Mr. Guthrie had been up to. I probably would never have given it a second thought if he hadn't come in to the bunkhouse and told me he was getting rid of me. Anyway the next day, I was still sick, but I acted like I was better and left like I was going to school, then I hung back and let the others get ahead of me. Once they were out of sight, I turned back and hid in the loft of the barn. I fell asleep for a while, but I woke up to sounds of Mr. Guthrie moaning again. As quietly as I could, I slid up to the edge of the loft and looked down. He was just like I saw him the day before with his head back and his arms stretched out, but this time I wasn't off to the side, I was directly across from him. I couldn't believe what I was seeing. His fly was wide open and he had his hips pressed between the lower rails, and the newborn calf was taking his pecker like it was the mama cow's udder."

"You're kidding!" Eugene gasped.

"Hell no. Mr. Guthrie was grinding his hips against the rails, and that baby bull was sucking away."

"But why would the calf keep sucking if he wasn't getting any milk."

"Hell if I know. I guess it's because they're dumb animals; and they'll suck anything if you take their mothers away for a long enough time."

"Did you say anything to him?"

"I wanted to. I wanted to stand up and yell, 'caught ya!' but I was afraid he'd kill me. Instead, I thought I could threaten to tell the welfare department if he tried to ship me off, but after thinking about it, I figured they'd believe him over me."

"So what did you do?"

"Well, one of the kids owns a *Polaroid* camera, so the next day I borrowed it and laid out of school again. I wrapped toilet paper around the shutter release so he wouldn't hear it click, then waited in the loft. I tell you old Guthrie's cattle prod must've stiffened up by a timer because he came in at the same time as the two days before. Down went his zipper, and I aimed the camera. The instant he pulled that cow pacifier out of his pants I snapped the first picture. I went through the rest of the roll in five minutes. Eight shots of that son of a bitch feeding his boner to that bovine baby, and he never saw me."

"Hoo-Whee!" cried Eugene, slapping the arm of the barber chair. "I wish I could catch my old man doing something like that. So what happened next?"

"The following morning he came into the bunkhouse while we were cooking breakfast, and he tells me I'm not to go to school because he's driving me to the welfare office in Columbus. After the kids left, he returned and told me to pack my things. I handed him one of the pictures, and asked him what he thought the welfare people would think of it."

"First thing he did was turn red, and then he punched me in the mouth so hard it knocked me on the floor. I scooted behind one of the beds, before he could hit me again, but he didn't follow. He looked back at the picture, turned it over and said, 'This is a Polaroid, so it's the only copy.' He tore it in half and then into several more pieces and shoved them into his pocket. He said, 'Looks like your little game isn't going to work, but you're going to be sorry you ever thought of it. I'm going to report to Welfare that you're an incorrigible delinquent and recommend you be sent to reform school.' Well, I was scared. I had hidden the other pictures, but if I got locked up, I could never get to them again. I stood up and said, 'I've got seven more.' The next thing I said was pure fiction inspired by a movie I'd seen. 'Three of them are in an envelope addressed to the governor, and I gave it to a friend who will mail it if he doesn't see me at school today. He doesn't know what's in the envelope, and I would rather he did not have to mail it.' He glared at me like he wished he could kill me, but I could tell he believed me. He asked me what I wanted, and I said, 'All I ever wanted was a little spending money. Now I just want you to leave me alone. You can have all the photos, but not until I'm eighteen and free to leave. In the meantime, I intend to keep my job, but I won't be your slave anymore. To be fair, however, I will do a few chores in exchange for my bed and breakfast.' Then I started crying, and I said, 'The sad part is that I used to like you, Mr. Guthrie. It doesn't even bother me those things you do with the livestock. It doesn't hurt anybody, and if you like it, well that's your business, but for my sake, it's a good thing other people don't think like I do.' Then I picked up my books and went to school."

"Can I see those pictures some time?" Eugene asked.

"No, and you're on your honor never to mention it to anyone. The only reason I told you about it was to make you feel better about your own situation."

"You have my word."

"Well, I'm done. I'm going on back to the diner for supper, then I've got to get over to the library and study a bit. I'll see you at school tomorrow."

#

"Not only were we working together every day after school, but we ate lunch together. Suddenly I was no longer eating alone, but with a crowd. Mostly with girls who wanted to hang out with Jack. I thought it was because Jack would say so many funny things, but that was only because I never noticed Jack was a good looking guy. Some girl nicknamed him *Leader of the Pack* after the song by the Shangri Las, although I could never understand why because he didn't have a pack, and he only rode a bicycle, but it stuck. I guess it was because he looked like he ought to have a pack. For me it was great; I was part of something; and Jack was really funny. I wish I could remember everything he ever said, but there was this one time at lunch when they served us *Jello* with something that was supposed to be whipped cream on it."

#

"Hold it everybody!" Jack pointed at the fluffy white topping on his day-glow green gelatin. "Eugene, give me your tray."

Eugene slid his tray across the table and Jack scooped all the food from his tray onto Eugene's. Then leaning conspiratorially over the table, he said to the group, "I figured out what this stuff really is. It's a top secret glue invented by the military and they're using students as unwitting guinea pigs to test it for toxicity."

Then with his knife, Jack scraped the topping off the two servings of gelatin on Eugene's tray and smeared it onto the bottom of his tray. "Let's see if this stuff really works."

The girls giggled. Jack stood up and looked over his shoulder, and then, satisfied that no one else was watching, he put his chair on top of the table and climbed on to it. The chair teetered slightly as he stretched up on his tip toes and pressed the back of the tray against the ceiling. Before he let go, he brought one hand down to his mouth and placed his extended forefinger against his lips to signal silence. Then he brought his other hand down, and the tray stuck to the ceiling. He got down just as the assistant principal walked up.

"What are you doing with that chair on the table?" he demanded.

Jack gave him a look of pure innocence and said, "Sir, I was trying to get the wobble out of this chair," he rocked the chair to demonstrate, "and I didn't think it was proper to get under the table to work on it. Some of these girls might think I was trying to look up their dresses."

Every student within hearing range laughed. The assistant principal said, "Son, I don't suppose it occurred to you that putting a chair on the table is unsanitary."

"Uh, no sir. I didn't realize sanitation was a priority here."

"Don't get impertinent with me. Put that chair on the floor where it belongs and finish your lunch," he ordered before stomping away.

Jack sat down and peered up at the ceiling, "Looks like it's going to hold. Maybe we should save some of this stuff for the wood shop."

#

Frank laughed as he finished, "That tray stayed up there for weeks before any of the school staff saw it, and had it removed."

"It was always something he was doing for laughs or more likely, to amuse himself. There was the time he and I were on our way from the diner to the grocer's when we rode past Georgette Peach who was running against the incumbent Mayor for the upcoming term. Jack hit his brakes and spun around. She had on one of those straw hats with a campaign bumper sticker pasted around the band and she was passing out more bumper stickers just like the one around her head. Jack took one and rejoined me. I asked him if he liked her better than the Mayor, and he said it didn't matter because as far as he was concerned, all people who ran for office were the same. I started to ask why then did he want the bumper sticker, but he was already pedaling again. Over his shoulder, he yelled for me to hurry or I'd be late for work. I followed, of course, but instead of riding straight down Broad Street to the grocer's, he turned left on Church Street and pulled into the parking lot of City Hall. Can you guess what he did? He put the sticker on the bumper of the Mayor's car."

"Then there was Stacie. Beautiful and unapproachable, and a natural member of the school social click. You know the group, it's the same in every high school, the one composed of kids from all the better families. Stacie was destined to become a cheerleader, and a candidate for Homecoming Queen. Instead she became a cross-over the day she sat down at our table."

#

"You're funny," Stacie said to Jack.

Smiling at the unexpected arrival, Jack asked, "Does *funny* mean that you think I'm strange or that you find me amusing?"

She paused a moment before answering, "Now that you mention it, I actually think you're both, but when I said it, amusing was all I had in mind."

"Thank you; my ego is slaked. In return, may I compliment your courage."

"My courage?"

"Yes, your sojourn seems to be promulgating the indignation of your peers," he said, nodding toward the dozen or so eyes that were glaring from a table across the room.

She shrugged and said, "They don't make me laugh."

"And you want to laugh?"

"As much as possible," she answered as she poured milk from a cup sized bottle into her glass.

"Anything else?"

"I'd like to talk the way you do: like a dictionary." She grinned at Jack, while carefully re-crimping the soft foil cap back on the bottle.

Jack grinned in return and said, "I see; you want a vocabulary teacher who makes you laugh. Okay then, here is your first lesson: Always remember each word in the English language has its own function. This includes slang and vulgarity. If you wish to attain the greatest amusement, I suggest reserving those most base and common words for formal occasions like when the Pope comes to Ellaville."

Stacie did not respond and instead spooned the whipped cream off the top of her banana pudding, spread it onto the bottom of her milk bottle, and stuck it up under the table with a thump everyone could hear.

"Are you trying to flatter me?" Jack asked.

"Maybe," Stacie answered demurely.

"In that case I hope my ability to amuse you continues."

"It's really more than that."

"What do you mean?"

"I like the way you think. It's different. Take today in History class for example. Mr. Ackerman told us the U.S. Constitution was a hallmark of democracy, but then you stood up and said you thought it was supposed to be a hallmark of individual rights. He said you were right, that it was both. You didn't agree. You stood there and told Ackerman that to call it both was a contradiction because majority rule negates individual choice."

"I didn't think anyone paid attention to what I said in class."

"I do."

#

"I became a satellite that day, but I didn't mind. I still had Jack all to myself when we were at work. Even better, because I was Jack's friend, I could walk right up and talk to the most attractive girl in school. Jack was my idol; I wanted what Jack wanted, and I was in love with Stacie because Jack was."

"I recall a day shortly after that, that I saw Stacie by her locker, and was going over to speak to her when one of her old friends got there first."

#

"I can't believe you're going with the Leader of the Pack," the girl exclaimed.

"Oh, for Christ's sake, Suzy, must you resort to using sobriquets?"

"That's another thing; you don't speak English anymore."

"That's ridiculous, I'm merely adding spice to dull everyday speech."

"You're changing Stacie, and we're losing you."

"Don't be absurd; no one's losing me. All I'm doing is exploring new avenues of life instead of trying to be like everyone else in this tiny boring town."

"I think Ellaville is charming just the way it is."

"You mean secure."

"What's wrong with that?"

"Nothing, only I want more. Can you tell me what's wrong with that?"

Suzy shrugged.

Stacie put her hand on Suzy's shoulder, "Let's get to class."

Eugene's face glowed in approval as he watched Stacie. "She's beginning to sound like Jack," he thought.

"Eugene! Come out here a minute," Jack called from the alley behind the barber shop where he was putting out the trash.

Eugene poked his head out the barber's back door. The dark of night had already settled. In the dim light from the bulb over the door he saw Jack pulling a stiff body out of the dumpster. A shiver ran down his spine as he cried, "Wh-who... who is it?"

A look of surprise crossed Jack's face when he saw Eugene clinging to the doorframe. He smiled and said, "It's a mannequin. The clothing store on the corner must have thrown it out."

Relief replaced fear on Eugene's face and he laughed timidly. He crossed the alley as Jack stood the figure up against the dumpster.

"Looks like the arm's broken," Eugene commented.

"I can fix it."

"What's it good for?"

"It would make a good scarecrow, but I'll bet there's something better."

"Like what?"

"You looked pretty scared back there; maybe we can use it to scare your father sometime when he's drunk."

Eugene smiled, and said, "Yeah, like make him think he ran over somebody some night when he shouldn't be driving."

Jack said, "We ought to hide it until we're ready. You know any good places?"

Jack leaned back in his chair as he pushed his tray toward the center of the table. He was the last of the group to finish eating. A line of trays ran down the middle of the table. Everything had been eaten from each except the portion of stewed prunes.

"God, those things are ugly," remarked Eugene. "I'm surprised I still had an appetite after looking at them."

"Look at Anorexic Eddie," Wanda said, pointing to another table, "he ate everything including the prunes."

"Oh that's nothing; he always eats the prunes," added Libby, "and everyone else's who's sitting near him."

"If he eats so much, how can he be anorexic?" asked Stacie.

Jack grinned and suggested, "Perhaps it's the purported purpose of prunes that prevents his becoming profuse."

"Jesus, Jack! What kind of gibberish did you just jabber?" Wanda cried out in laughter.

"I think he said Eddie shits himself skinny," offered Eugene.

Everyone laughed, and then Jack announced, "Two more weeks and I need never look at another stewed prune for the rest of my life."

Eugene's smile faded, and Stacie's face whitened.

Wanda, however, missed the point and said, "Oh, that's silly; you'll see them again next September. There's enough canned prunes in the cafeteria storeroom to fill every latrine at Fort Benning."

"Maybe, but I won't be here. I turn sixteen next month which means I'll be old enough to drop out. It's the first step in becoming master of my own dominion. Unfortunately, I'll have to wait two more years for the next step, but then I'll be eighteen and no longer a ward of the state."

"Don't you want to keep on learning though?" pleaded Stacie.

"I don't need to stay in school for that. School taught me how to study; now I can study what I want to learn. If I stay here, I'll only be exposing myself to two more years of the state's shaping and molding process; and I'd rather start unlearning that process."

"You sound like a communist!" Libby accused. "This is America and the schools are here to teach us about freedom."

Jack stared into her eyes and asked solemnly, "Are you telling me that forcing children to attend school until they are sixteen years old will teach them about freedom?"

"Well, if we don't force people to learn about freedom, how will they ever know about it?" demanded Libby.

"Are you perhaps related to Rousseau?"

"Who?"

"He was a gigolo turned philosophe who expounded a theory he called *The Social Contract*. You could call him a forefather of Fascism because he proffered the gestalt view that the whole of society is greater than the sum of its individual members. Among his many contradictions of logic he said, 'we must force men to be free'."

Libby stood and picked up her tray. "You're not as funny as you used to be, Jack Franklin."

Jack shrugged as Libby stormed away.

Stacie ran her fingers along his wrist and said, "We're going to miss you."

"I'll be around."

Eugene winced in jealousy at Stacie's caress. To change the subject, he said, "I hear there's an assembly on Friday, and the whole student body is going to be required to attend."

"What's it about?" Jack asked.

"Oh, you'll love it," Wanda answered facetiously. "Some biblical scholar is going to refute evolution."

"Then I won't be going."

"You'll have to," she stated apprehensively. "The principal hired a truant officer to deter all the skipping everyone's been doing since the weather has gotten nice."

"Don't worry; he won't catch me."

Thinking about his leaving, Stacie begged, "Oh, come on and go; it could be fun. We can take the air horns and heckle him."

Jack's face brightened. "That gives me an idea. Okay I'll go; it's going to be a lot more fun than you think. Eugene, can you stay late after work tonight?"

"Sure."

"Good, cause I'm going to need your help."

Pride glowed in Eugene's face. Jack had said he needed him.

Jack arrived late. Eugene was already washing the diner's dishes. Later, on their way to the grocery store, Eugene saw a paintbrush and can in Jack's bicycle basket. He asked, "Are we going to paint something?"

"No, this is glue," answered Jack.

Jack added two brown paper bags from the grocery store to his basket. Eugene's curiosity rose to its boiling point, and he demanded, "Are you going to tell me what you're up to?'

Jack chuckled as he put his left foot on the pedal, "I found a use for our dummy and for some of that barbershop hair you were worried was going to waste."

Before Eugene could say, "What?" Jack pushed off the ground three times with his right foot to send the bike speeding down the sidewalk. Swinging his leg over the saddle, he called out, "Come on, Eugene."

#

In retrospect it's easy now to say I should have seen the change that was occurring in Jack. He was going beyond simply being funny. Everything was now an issue with him. He'd gone from being the class clown to becoming some kind of intellectual fanatic. I, of course, couldn't see it. Jack was my best friend, my only friend. If he included me in anything he was interested in, I was in heaven.

#

Friday afternoon the wall speaker in Eugene's fifth period classroom crackled as the principal commanded the student body to assemble in the gymnasium. Eugene scooped up his books, already closed, stacked, and ready to go, and bolted out the door ahead of his classmates. Avoiding collisions with kids exiting classrooms on both sides, he ran a zigzag pattern down the length of the hallway. At the last doorway he stopped. When Stacie emerged, he grabbed her elbow and admonished her to hurry. Guiding her by her arm, he led her out the back door and together they trotted across the grassy backyard of the school to the gym.

Inside the gym, hall monitors stood along the basketball court to direct students who were not wearing sneakers away from the polished floor and toward the bleachers. In the center of the court a gray-green tarp was spread to protect the floor from seven rows of seven chairs reserved for the teaching staff.

Stacie and Eugene entered the gym facing the stage. Sitting at the top of the left-side bleachers on the end nearest the stage was Jack. They joined him breathlessly.

"What's all the rush?" Stacie asked as she pulled the hem of her skirt over her knee.

"Is everything ready?" Eugene whispered.

"I've got the air-horns if that's what you mean." Stacie patted her pocketbook.

"Here, Eugene," Jack pointed between his feet to the end of a length of stout wrapping twine. "Keep those horns handy Stacie; we may still want to use them."

"What are you guys up to?" she whispered.

"We're going to upstage the professor."

"How?"

"Wait and see. I don't want to ruin the surprise for you."

"Jack Franklin, what deviltry are you up to?"

Jack grinned. "I'll give you a hint. If there is any fact to the biblical story of creation, then Satan was the good guy because he persuaded man to evolve beyond the status of animals."

"Are you going to embarrass this man?" Stacie queried reprovingly.

"Probably, but my aim is at the Bible-thumping principal, who made this little meeting mandatory instead of voluntary."

A high-pitched squeak turned their attention to the stage as the principal turned on the microphone. He blew into it, then said, "Testing... testing... one... two... three, can everyone hear me out there?"

A cheerful, "Yes!" rose like a chorus from the crowd of students happy to be reprieved from their sixth period classes.

"Quiet, quiet now. May I have your attention, please?" His voice boomed over the waning murmurs emanating from the crowd.

The crowd became silent, and he continued, "Students, and fellow staff members, our speaker is a professor of theology at *Mercer University*, and the country's leading proponent of Creation as the factual origin of man. Today he will dispel once and forever the myth of evolution. Please welcome, Dr. Boynton Thrush."

Obligatory applause rose from faculty section in the center of the gymnasium, and was joined by a smattering of hand clapping from isolated seats in both bleachers. Dr. Thrush stepped up to the lectern, his attention drawn to the bleachers on his right by the enthusiastic applause of two boys and a girl on the top row. He smiled at them, and began.

"Thank you, everyone. Today we'll take a look at established scientific fact, and the words from the book of *Genesis*, then combine the two for a theory on the origin of man that will demolish the house of straw known as Evolution. Let us start at the beginning with the words of the Bible ..."

For several minutes the professor read from Genesis. When he reached the part where God commanded Adam, "... but of the tree of the knowledge of good and evil you shall not eat ..." Jack winked at Eugene then yanked the cord between his feet.

People gasped; some screamed. Stacie jumped slightly and grabbed Jack's arm. A gorilla dropped from the rafters of the stage behind the professor, but it never reached the ground. Without touching the floor, it jumped and the crowd saw the long spring attached to its back. People began to laugh. Stacie giggled into Jack's ear. The bouncing inanimate hunchback was covered in a thick multicolored hair, and wore a sign around its neck that read: 'ADAM.' In one hand it held an apple and in the other a banana. Above the hirsute effigy, hanging from the theater-flies, a banner unfurled. Pictured on it was a snake saying:

PICK THE CORRECT FRUIT, APE, AND EVOLVE TO MAN.

The Professor could not see what was happening behind him, but the reaction of the audience caused him to turn around. The dancing dummy caused him to make a startled backwards leap, for which he was rewarded with peals of laughter.

The principal, meanwhile, charged to the stage from his front row seat; his black heeled shoes scuffing the polished floor. His mouth was working in wide open rage, but his words were lost in the roar of the crowd.

The professor, however, had regained his composure by the time the principal topped the steps, and like a traffic cop held up his hand to stop him. The principal halted, and Professor Thrush said into the mike, "Quiet Please! Quiet Everyone."

The noise subsided gradually, and with a broad smile on his face, the professor pointed to the furry mannequin and continued, "This is good. This visual aid, albeit uninvited, shows that someone in this school is thinking. A style of thinking different from my own, but that is not to say that it is bad. Let's look at what our anonymous thinker is saying. He is combining evolution with the story of Creation. God created the earth and populated it with animals. He is saying that before Adam acquired the knowledge of good and evil, he was nothing more than an animal. His theory says that eating the fruit was good because it forced man to rise above the level of animals. On the other hand, the theory of Creation says that eating the fruit gave man an equal footing with God. God, however, didn't care for competition and threw man out of his garden before he could eat from the tree of life and become immortal. Man was then forced to spend the length of his mortality eking out a living from the earth. Now let us move on to the rest of my lecture."

"Give me one of those air-horns," Jack whispered to Stacie.

She did, and Jack pressed the button which forced compressed gas to scream out through the bell of the horn. Hundreds of faces turned toward the noise, including the professor. Jack, satisfied that he had everyone's attention, released the button and raised his hand.

The patient professor made a dramatic show of dropping his chin and raising an eyebrow while drolly asking over the mic, "Did I say something to offend you sir?"

Jack smiled, and in the wake of the professor's facetious question, deliberately voiced his answer in a tone of severe innocence. "Not at all, sir. Please pardon the noise, but I have a question and I wanted to make sure you would see me."

The crowd giggled. Jack's rudeness with the horn had already dissipated from their minds. The professor responded with slight irritation, "By all means then; ask."

"How could Adam and Eve have known whether or not God was good or evil, that is whether or not they should heed anything he told them, before they ate from the tree of knowledge of good and evil?"

"That's simple, God created them and they loved him as a child loves a parent: unequivocally."

"I did not ask you whether they loved God or not."

"It doesn't matter because the Garden of Eden story is strictly symbolic. Man is mortal and God gave him knowledge so he might survive."

"He's refusing to answer," Jack whispered, and started to lift the air-horn.

Stacie grabbed his hand and said, "Don't! You've scored plenty of points. If you continue, you'll lose face."

Jack lowered his hand. "You're right. Thank you."

The professor walked back to the dummy and pried the banana from its hand. With a grin he held it high for the audience to see and began to peel it. "This, boys and girls, would have been my choice. I've always felt Adam gypped me out of the easy life."

As the professor took a bite, Eugene jumped from his seat and started scratching his ribs while screeching, "Eek eek, ooh ooh ooh."

Across the room another student jumped up and did the same. Within seconds, students throughout the auditorium were joining them until nearly the entire student body was jumping up and down, scratching their ribs, and chanting, "Eek eek, ooh ooh ooh ... Eek eek, ooh ooh ooh."

The principal grabbed the microphone and screamed over and over, "Stop! Stop this! Stop!" But his voice, even with the aid of the public address system, was drowned out by the crowd. The teachers offered no help to him either, instead they faced away from the stage and snickered to each other.

A week later school let out for the summer. Jack and Eugene began washing dishes earlier in the afternoon which gave them a few hours to play before they were due at the grocery. Stacie would join them during this time, and the three would take their bicycles and explore the countryside.

Each day, Eugene would not see Jack until they met at the diner. Jack explained that his mornings were reserved for study, and should Eugene ever need him, he would be in the library.

"But it's summer, Jack," Eugene decried.

"I know, but I've got this whole life in front of me and I want to find out what's in the world outside Ellaville. Just because I'm free from school doesn't mean I want to stop learning. Now is the time for me to decide how to spend my life, but I really need a better library. I wanted to take some of the money I've saved and buy a car so I could drive down to Albany and use the library at the state college, but I found out I can't legally own a car until I'm eighteen and Mr. Guthrie won't help. Barriers! It's always barriers. The next two years aren't going to pass fast enough."

A few days later Jack, Stacie, and Eugene rode their bicycles down Highway 19 to where it crossed Buck Creek. While Jack and Stacie ate lunch in the shade under the bridge, Eugene showed off by doing full gainers off a make-shift diving platform some kids had nailed to a tree on the edge of the bank. Every time he climbed the platform Stacie would beg him not to jump because the water was too shallow. Goaded by her pleas, Eugene would laugh before hurling his body into the air.

Later that day while they were stocking the grocery store shelves, Eugene asked Jack, "Are you in love with Stacie?"

Jack paused in mid-reach to the top shelf and brought the can of tomato paste back down. "Yes."

"Because she's beautiful?"

"More than that. It's because she's like me. She questions authority, and doesn't accept everything she's told."

"Am I like you?"

"As much as you want to be, Eugene. It's as simple as deciding to be the master of your own dominion."

"But, you said you weren't yet... that you couldn't be until you were eighteen."

"That's true, but you have to begin now to know how. Essentially, I already am my own master, but it requires manipulation like what I had to do with Mr. Guthrie. Ultimately, I want to be free of having to resort to manipulation."

"I love Stacie too."

Jack glanced curiously at Eugene then placed the tomato paste on the top shelf.

Two weeks later, Jack disappeared for a nearly a week. Before he left, he phoned Eugene to say he'd have to do both jobs by himself for a few days. He also asked him to sweep out the barber shop for the same length of time. He did not mention why or where he was going.

On Friday morning of the next week, Eugene received another call. Jack asked him to meet him at the soda fountain in the drug store at eleven o'clock. When he arrived, he saw Jack and Stacie sharing a chocolate milkshake. Heat flushed under the skin on his face as he looked at the two straws in the single glass.

Jack saw him and waved for him to join them. Eugene reluctantly walked over. When he sat down, Jack added another straw and poured more milkshake from the metal mixing can.

Eugene pointed to the straw. "You sure I won't be in the way?"

"Of course not," answered Stacie. "It's one for all and all for one, you know, like the musketeers."

Eugene smiled and took a long pull on his straw.

Jack spoke, "I guess you're wondering why I asked you here; and where I've been for the last few days."

Stacie and Eugene nodded.

He continued, "I found out who my mother was..."

"Oh that's wonderful!" interrupted Stacie. "How'd you do that?"

"Well, it is and it isn't wonderful. I found out because she died and left me something. It turns out that she was a local prostitute--"

Again Stacie interrupted, "Oh that's horrible!"

"Perhaps the life she had to lead was, but she, herself, was not. Eugene, do you remember our discussion about legality and morality?"

"Yes."

"This is one of those situations where the act is illegal, but not immoral."

"I don't understand how you can say prostitution is not immoral," Stacie said.

"Men create laws, Stacie, but nature creates morality. The nature of man demands that he not do anything that's unhealthy for the species. The species is simply a collection of individuals, so if one man harms another he is violating nature. If a woman wants to rent out her body, and a man is willing to pay the rent, then the transaction is voluntary, and no harm involved. There's no difference between the druggist selling me this milkshake and my mother selling the druggist sex, other than the political legality. If I had to venture a guess, I would say that somewhere back in history someone got envious of the amount of money made by prostitutes and for that reason lobbied to put them out of business."

"I understand what you're saying, but I was always raised to think of prostitution as being dirty." She paused and her eyes drifted away from his face toward the mirror behind the fountain then back again to his face. "It's kind of hard to break free of that kind of thinking, but now that you've gotten me started, I can imagine good things about prostitution, and I think you're wrong about the reason it was made illegal. I think it was because married women, who used sex to control their husbands, found that their ability to manipulate was rendered useless as long as their husbands could visit a prostitute."

"Good thinking," Jack complimented.

"I still like your idea, Jack," Eugene offered ingratiatingly.

Jack winced.

Stacie noticed and gracefully turned them back to the subject by asking, "So, what else did you find out?"

"That it gets worse before it gets better. I found out the state took me away from her when I was only a few months old. Her intentions were to someday get me back and raise me. In the meantime, she bought a small farm outside town where she planned to retire. Unfortunately, she never got the chance. It seems that because she was getting older, she was unable to attract the men as easily, and was asked to give up her room at the town brothel. Because her profession is illegal, which rules out advertising or hanging out a shingle, she had to move to Columbus and hit the streets. Consorting with seedier sorts of men, in order to make a living, cost her her life. Somebody murdered her."

"Oh my God!" Stacie cried.

"Yes, that's what's horrible, but it's difficult to have much feeling for someone I never met. I miss not getting to know her, but I take consolation in knowing she was willing to make her living by bucking the system."

"Did you find out who your father is?" Stacie asked.

"No, it could have been any man in town. My mother was apparently quite popular back then."

The words crashed into Eugene's consciousness, and he found himself staring at Jack's face as he never had before. He knew his own father frequented the local whorehouse on a regular basis. Jack was taller than Eugene, but not taller than his father. The dark eyes were similar to his father's as was the broad forehead, but Eugene's father was a blonde and Jack's hair was nearly black. The hair comes from Jack's mother, Eugene told himself. He desperately wanted to believe Jack was his brother.

"Anyway, the reason I was away for so long was because the executor of the will told me I could not inherit the farm until I was eighteen. I saw the farm as a way to get out from under old Guthrie's roof, so I took a bus to Columbus and hired a lawyer. He drew up some papers that entitled me to use the farm immediately, and I used some photographic blackmail to coerce Guthrie into signing them."

"When do we get to see it?" Eugene asked.

"Right now."

#

"Getting his own place was probably just as bad as it was good for Jack," Frank said. "Isolating himself out on the farm divorced him from the harsher realities of the world he wanted to change. Stacie was his last anchor to regular people, and even her influence was waning in the wake of Jack's charisma. I certainly couldn't fill the role she was abandoning; my father had made me into an emotional cripple. You can never see something for what it is when you're controlled by passions, and I was desperate for approval. As far as I was concerned, Jack always knew what was best. He was growing up to be an angry young man, and now looking back, I'd say it was too bad Jack hadn't been named after Patrick Henry because he was developing a real give me 'liberty or give me death attitude'."

#

Jack led them by bicycle three easy miles on open stretches of paved road then two difficult miles down back woods roads of gravel. The gray granite crunched underneath them, and where it would have given traction to fatter automobile and truck tires, it performed the opposite for the skinny bicycle tires. They slipped and slid along until the treachery of it forced them to slow down and ride single file inside a bare rut pounded into the earth over the years by hundreds of heavier vehicles.

After cresting a tree-lined hill, Jack braked down the gentle incline. The trees stopped on the right, and were replaced by a split rail fence enclosing a pasture of waist-high, wind-bent grass. He turned past a battered mailbox onto a smooth dirt road with blackberry briars and Queen Anne's Lace encroaching on either side. The road dipped and curved sharply to the right, bringing the house into view. It was a box shaped cottage on a foundation of three foot brick pillars with a rocking-chair porch wrapped all the way around it. The wood siding was painted colonial blue and trimmed in beige. Etched fringe ran along the base of a tin roof, while shutters with flower cut-outs framed the windows. Both gave it a feminine gingerbread appeal. Rising behind it in red was a miniature version of a two story Dutch barn.

Jack skidded to a stop. "There are thirty acres of enclosed pasture in front, thirty acres open pasture in the back, and forty acres of planted pine running from front to back on the left side. Behind the barn is a stream that fills a one acre pond already stocked with fish."

"Wow, that's a hundred and one acres," exclaimed Eugene.

"No, just a hundred, you're counting the pond twice," Jack corrected.

"Oh," Eugene said with a sheepish grin.

Jack bounded up the three wooden steps to the porch. "Let me show you the inside."

For Jack, who had never had a room of his own, it was a palace. He pushed open the door and swept his arm in a gesture for them to enter. They walked into a single long room paneled in knotty pine, and separated into kitchen and living area by a large wood stove. Along the left wall were four windows curtained with lace-edged blue calico. Underneath the first window was a tiny desk. On the right were two doors, both open and revealing bedrooms. Filling the center of the living area was a blue upholstered sofa and two matching chairs around a rectangular coffee table. In the kitchen, completing the furnishings, were four chairs around a pine table.

"You need a TV," stated Eugene.

"What for?" Jack asked.

"So you can watch all the old movies."

"Oh, I see," Jack laughed, then added, "I have one problem, though: no electricity."

"Then how do you run all these?" Eugene pointed around the room toward the light fixtures.

"Those are all oil lamps. I do, however, have some electricity. There's a propane generator behind the house, but it's for pumping the well. That big silver thing up by the road that looks like a miniature submarine is my gas tank."

"Why don't you have the Power Company run some lines out here?" Stacie asked.

"I thought about that when I realized there wasn't any electricity here, but then I wondered why my mother didn't have it done. I figured it was for the same reason she bought such isolated property in the first place: for privacy and solitude. Since I don't have much money, I decided I'd try it out as she intended."

"The oil lamps will add some romance, and I can already see you studying like Abe Lincoln," Stacie said.

For the next hour Jack led them around the property and showed them the barn, the pond and a blue pick-up truck. When they got back inside the house, Jack briefly showed them the bedrooms. He pushed open one door to reveal a feminine room in pink with lace dust ruffles and curtains. Across from it, the other room was decorated in blue. At the foot of the bed was a wooden trunk. He walked over to it, opened it and said, "This is the saddest part of it all." Inside was a progressive collection of never-used toys for the various levels of maturity a boy would grow through. Included was a baseball bat, ball and glove, a BB gun, a can of *Lincoln Logs*, toy soldiers, a wooden boat with a string and a sail, and a little yellow dump truck.

They were all silent for a moment, and then Eugene looked at his wrist watch. "Jack, we need to be leaving soon to get to the diner."

"Oh, Jack do you have to?" cajoled Stacie. "I feel like I haven't really seen the bedrooms."

Jack looked in her eyes a moment then over to Eugene. "Eugene, if you'll do the dishes, I'll stock the grocery, then on Monday we can get back on track together."

Eugene scuffed his sneaker toe across the wooden floor and answered reluctantly. "Sure, Jack."

"Thank you, Eugene," Stacie said, then hugged Jack.

Eugene coveted that hug as he trudged down the steps to his bicycle.

Over the course of the summer, Jack put in a small garden, and acquired four goats, a dozen ducks, and a multiplier of two rabbits. Eugene was allowed to come out in the mornings as long as he used the time to study. Jack brought him books on motion picture making from the libraries he visited out of town. Since his father did not approve of his reading them, Eugene had to read them at Jack's. He never missed a morning. Stacie usually arrived later than he, but on occasion he found her already there, and sometimes finishing breakfast with Jack.

The goats were Jack's last addition, and the sight of them shocked Eugene. He asked, "Why these kinds of animals, and not traditional ones like cows, horses, pigs and chickens?"

"I've a lot to learn about farming," explained Jack, "and cows in particular need a lot of special care and attention. I chose low maintenance animals. Goats and ducks are more resistant to disease than cows and chickens, and because they are foragers, they can take care of themselves if necessary. What this means is that I don't have to take as much time from my studies to tend them. The benefits are nearly the same if not better. From the ducks I get eggs, down, and meat. From the goats I'll get milk, and, if I can re-orient my thinking, meat and leather as well. Two of the goats are

Angoras, and I'm hoping to sell their hair, and from the rabbits their pelts, and again meat. The rabbits, however, do have to be penned and well tended."

"I don't see you as a farmer," Stacie commented. "And from the books you read, I don't believe you do either."

"You're right, however, learning to run a farm is teaching me quite a few things; some of which are giving me ideas as to what I ultimately want to do with my life."

"Like becoming a world class feta cheese maker?" Stacie smirked.

"More than that," Jack answered seriously, "like how to manage a number of projects at one time, and because the farm has an economy of its own, I'm learning survival techniques I'd never even thought of."

"I'll bite," Stacie asked respectfully. "How does this relate to your lifelong ambition?"

"It's given a goal to the direction I've been going. I guess it's from growing up in the orphanage, but I've always wanted to do something for the cause of freedom. Now I know what. I'm going to study political economics, so I can teach people struggling for freedom how to achieve it."

"What's political economics? asked Eugene. "I've heard of politics, and of economics, but never together."

"Strictly speaking, Politics is the proper use of force in society. Economics is the manner in which goods and services are distributed in society. Political economics refers to how much choice individuals in a particular society have in using their property, and to how much of the goods and services they produce they are allowed to keep. Simply speaking, one extreme says that an individual owns his own body and all that he produces in order to sustain his life; the other extreme claims the state owns the individual and thus all that he produces. Everything in between is the degree of force society uses against individuals when it decides how to use some portion of the individual's property. Do you understand?"

Eugene shook his head. "Not really."

"Say I set up an alcohol still on my property. What will the sheriff do if he finds out about it?"

"He'll come chop it up."

"Why can he do that if I grew the corn, and I bought the sugar, and I welded together the still, and I spent my time distilling the alcohol, and then when Joe down the road offers me two dollars for a jug of it, I sell it?"

"Because it might be unsanitary?"

"Can he still chop it up if I'm so clean and scrupulous that my moonshine is awarded the *Good Housekeeping* Seal of Approval?"

"I guess not, if you pay the tax."

"Bingo! If society can't get its tax, it will chop my still up, and any other commodity."

"Is that what political economics is about, taxes?"

"Taxes are only part of it. You were correct about the sanitation of my still. It has to do with any way in which the government makes decisions for individuals."

In September, back at school, Eugene started the ninth grade and Stacie the eleventh. At lunch time they found themselves sitting alone. There was no group without Jack's antics. Jack, meanwhile, back at the farm, was becoming increasingly more serious when it came to his studies and his plans, but on occasion, for the smaller audience of Stacie and Eugene, he retained his sense of humor.

Jack continued to work both jobs with Eugene through the school year, but by the end of the following summer, the farm was turning a profit and he quit. Another September had arrived, and Eugene at age fifteen was beginning to take on the physical signs of manhood. His maturity did not pass unseen by Jim Eastly, who ordered Eugene to quit his jobs and spend his afternoons as a plumbing apprentice. Without Jack's companionship, the work had become drudgery, and he offered little argument to his father before acquiescing to his demands. It was Jack's help, however, that enabled him to find the words to convince his father to give him some payment for his labor, primarily in consideration of what he lost in having to give up his jobs.

Eugene was beginning to understand the nature of boundaries that Jack hated so much. His personal freedom of choice seemed to be dwindling. Jim was forcing him to learn plumbing, yet still did not allow him to study film making. He might never have had time to see Jack or study the movies, had his father not preferred to take weekends off. Additionally, there was the occasional afternoon of freedom, when Jim had an out-of-town job that Eugene couldn't work because of school. While his father ceased his cruel waiting game outside the theater on Saturdays, he made up for it on the job with painful practical jokes.

Once when he and Eugene were repairing a leaky hot water main, he instructed Eugene to remove the pipe leading away from the hot water heater. As soon as Eugene saw that his father had turned off the water, he began loosening the pipe with his wrench. When the pipe was free, but before he could lower the long pipe to the floor his father reopened the valve. Scalding water showered over him, and Jim yelled at him not to drop the brittle cast iron pipe because it would crack. Eugene, his burning shoulders demanding that he jump out of the way, controlled himself long enough to gracefully lower the pipe to the ground. When he finally allowed himself to jump, his father started laughing and turned off the water.

"What's so funny?" Eugene demanded as he ripped his steaming shirt off.

"Nothing, just that I was mistaken; brittle cast iron is never used for hot water mains - you could have dropped it."

Before he could get comfortable enough to sleep that night, he used an entire can of aerosol benzocaine to cover the first degree burns on his back.

On other occasions Jim used Eugene as a human jack to hold up heavy pipes, while he welded them in place. For amusement, Jim would run the torch flame along the sides of his son's boots making him jump, then scold him for moving.

Eugene did his best to anticipate Jim's cruelty. He would show up for work wearing a hard-hat or a raincoat, but it was needless preparation because when he least expected it, his father would conceive a new form of torture.

He hated plumbing, but a bit of wisdom from Jack kept him going.

"If you're learning something, it's always good, because any knowledge has several applications."

"What do you mean?"

"Take farming for instance. I'm learning more about organizing my time and assets than I am about raising goats or rabbits. Try to look at plumbing from the perspective that it will make you a better movie director."

It was Stacie's senior year in high school; Eugene was a sophomore, and Jack was beginning to talk about Alaska as the place to teach the political economics of freedom. At school, Stacy seldom associated with her former friends. Instead, she went to Eugene for companionship. It was Jack's influence that had changed the manner in which she thought, and it was only Eugene who could understand the things she wished to talk of. Eugene was flattered, especially when other boys at school nudged him and made comments about the pretty girl who only hung out with him.

Once, on a school night, he phoned Stacie at home to ask her help with an assignment, but her parents told him she'd spent the night with a girlfriend. The next morning in front of the school, he saw her get out of Jack's pickup truck, and it finally dawned on him how she had been able to get to Jack's so early on those mornings the previous summer. A thick pain filled his chest. The force of gravity had somehow increased, and he found it difficult to make his diaphragm draw air into his lungs. His head felt dizzy when he noticed she was walking his way, and he slumped against the brick facade of the building.

"Good morning, Eugene," she said brightly and took his elbow. "Will you walk me to homeroom?"

"Sure," he answered numbly, and started walking despite the throbbing in his body.

While they were walking down the hallway, she spoke of Jack's plans to sell the farm and move to Alaska, of how she wanted to go, and that Eugene should too. Several boys stopped along the way to say hello to Stacie, and one winked slyly at Eugene. Suddenly, he found himself feeling better. “It was obvious,” he thought. “Stacie loved him too. That was why she wanted him to join them in Alaska.”

Summer arrived. Stacie graduated high school. Jack turned eighteen and gained legal title to the farm. Eugene began shaving. Jack returned the pictures as he promised to his former foster father. Mr. Guthrie, however, refused to believe Jack was giving him all the copies. Jack shook his head and as he turned to go said, "I have kept my word, but you're entitled to be a jackass and believe anything you want, just as long as you keep your hands to yourself, Mister."

"I'm finally free!" Jack exclaimed to Eugene and Stacie back at the farm. "I've surpassed the barriers and I'm the master of my own dominion. Now, I can make plans to sell this place and move to Alaska."

The goat herd had grown significantly in two years. There was one male angora he was particularly fond of. Jack named him Barney and allowed him to graze in the yard around the house instead of in the fenced pasture. Barney had long curling horns which Jack refused to trim. He would butt anyone who wasn’t paying attention. Because of this, but more likely for Stacie's and Eugene's amusement, Jack put up a sign which read:

WARNING: ANGORAN WATCH-GOAT ON PREMISES.

"I'm going to take my time selling," Jack continued, as he scratched the nuzzling Barney behind the horns, "because by the end of next summer I'll have a nicely profitable load of wool, down, and rabbit furs, and it goes without saying, that a profitable business with a low overhead will bring a higher price. It will be money I'll need to finance the town I want to build in Alaska."

Jack seldom left the farm except to go to market. Frequently, when Eugene and Stacie arrived for a visit they found him sitting against the trunk of the spreading oak tree on top of the knoll in the back pasture with a book lying open in his lap, and the vacant stare of contemplation in his eyes.

Whenever Stacie discovered him in such a state of reverie, she would join him quietly so as not to disturb his thoughts. Stretching out on the grass beside him, she would lie still until he noticed her. Whereas when Eugene was looking for him, Jack would be snapped out of his reverie by loud shouts of "Hey, Jack!"

Jack always had a smile for Eugene, and would answer fondly, "Hi, Eugene."

Their conversations always followed a similar route.

Eugene would ask, "Whatcha' thinking about?"

"Alaska, and what I'll do when I get there," Jack always answered.

Then Eugene would begin to run off at the mouth.

"Tell me about it Jack, so I can make a movie about it. I'll take your abstract ideas and give them story form. Then once I've made a name for myself in Hollywood, I'll turn the story into a screenplay and produce it. It will work like a recruiting film, and all the people who think like we do will flock to Alaska to live in your town. Of course, it will take a long time, but while I'm establishing myself in Hollywood, you'll be founding the town. Have you thought of a name for it yet? I wonder if I should use the real name, or one that sounds like it? Do you think we'll both be ready before the Vietnam War turns into World War Three, so we can successfully secede from the union? You know, I could run two stories parallel to each other in the same film: one set during the American Revolution and the other set to your Alaskan Revolution. That way no one will miss the point. Or would that be too obvious? Heck, I've got plenty of time to decide. Maybe I should take flying lessons as soon as possible, because sooner or later I'm going to be living in Alaska with y'all; and I'll have to commute to Hollywood if I want to keep making movies. I couldn't make any up there because film gets brittle and cracks in the cold air. Wait a minute, that can't be right, because I'm almost certain *Nanook Of The North* was filmed on location. That's perfect because we'd want our own film industry anyway. Alaska could be just like Hollywood was at the turn of the century when all the independents left New York to seek creative freedom. Now all the stifling red tape and bureaucracy that used to be in New York has been transferred to the backlots of Hollywood. The independents will need a new haven for experimentation."

Eugene paused to take a breath. Stacie rolled back into the shade to escape the shifting rays of the sun, and said, "Gee, Eugene, you never talked this much when we used to sit together at lunch. I practically had to drag conversation out of you."

Eugene blushed. Jack chuckled.

Most of Eugene's summer was spent working for his father, but each day at the stroke of quitting time, he left for Jack's. He felt like he could breathe at the farm. It wasn't the fresh air - it was the carefree atmosphere Jack inspired that lifted the weight of gravity that had begun to burden his breast on a regular basis. Anything could happen; they might be sitting and discussing the circumstances for various ethical theories when Jack would leap up unexpectedly and start a game of tag.

On one occasion, Jack took a red tablecloth out of a kitchen drawer, the black baseball cap out of the wooden trunk by the bed, and then walked outside. Stacie and Eugene followed. They watched him tuck the visor inside the cap as he mashed it onto his head like a montera, and then roll his pant legs up to his knees. He picked a rose from the bush by the porch and handed it to Stacie. Then with a gracious bow, he said, "Senorita, I dedicate this bull to you."

His deep sweeping bow caught the attention of Barney the Angoran watch-goat, who began to charge toward his rear.

Stacie cried, "Jack watch out!"

But Jack remained bent over. Then when the goat was within eight feet, he stood, whirled around, and snapped the red cloth out to his side drawing the goat's attention just in the nick of time. He whirled again to face the goat while snapping the tablecloth as if he were a toreador with a muleta cape.

"Toro! Toro!" he called while Eugene cheered and Stacie screamed in fear.

Before Eugene knew it, it was time for school again. Eleventh grade was lonely without either Stacie or Jack for company. Making it worse was having to work as soon as school let out, and then having to study as soon as he was free from work.

He began to live for Saturday mornings when he would rise early and rush over to the farm, often waking Jack, who answered the door in his boxers and T-shirt.

Jack would guide him to the kitchen table, then throw a log in the stove so it would get hot enough to make coffee. While the pot perked, they would discuss the events of the week. Eventually, Stacie would emerge from the bedroom fully dressed.

Eugene would see the made bed through the bedroom door, and then feel a brief wince of jealousy which he quickly suppressed; because in his heart he knew they would make room for him as soon as he reached the legal age of becoming "master of his own dominion."

It was on a cold Saturday morning in January that he pushed open the front door to find them already up. Stacie was sitting on the sofa crying.

Alarmed he asked, "What's wrong?"

"Jack's been drafted," she answered, holding up a typed letter.

Eugene noticed that all she was wearing was one of Jack's shirts, and how her nipples were pressing against the fabric.

Jack stepped from the kitchen holding two mugs of coffee and said, "I haven't been drafted. I've been ordered to report for draft registration."

"Isn't that the same thing?" Eugene asked.

"Philosophically - yes, technically - no."

"Well, it happens to everyone," Eugene said reassuringly as he took a seat across from Stacie.

"God dammit, Eugene. Can't you recognize that this is another barrier? They're telling me I'm still a ward of the state; that I don't even have the right to life."

"Come on Jack, it's like death and taxes," Eugene argued, but his mind was still on Stacie's breasts. "You should take my old man's advice. He's always telling me I should sign up for the *Marines* rather than wait and get drafted into the army. Of course, it's usually an afterthought whenever he's bitching that he can't make a man out of me."

Jack set a cup down on the coffee table in front of Stacie and handed the other to Eugene. As he headed back to the kitchen he said, "Eugene, sometimes I don't understand you at all, but if you've got it in your head to sign up - make it the *National Guard*. At least defending your homeland from attack is nobler than storming the beaches of someone else's homeland for the sake of a bunch of politicians, or worse, for some corporation's interests."

"Is that what you think you'll do?"

"No."

"Then what are you going to do?"

"I don't know yet."

The following Saturday, he arrived in the afternoon to find both Jack and Stacie outside. It was an unusually warm day, and their moods had improved. Jack was wrestling Barney on the grass, and Stacie was sitting on the edge of the porch laughing at them.

"Hi, y'all," he called out.

Turning Barney's horns loose, Jack rolled away and stood up. Laughing he said, "Do you realize I overslept because of you?"

He then bent over to brush the grass off his pants. Barney crouched, Eugene started to point, and Stacie squealed, "Jack!"

It was too late, Barney sprung, and Jack went flying forward with a perfect belly-flop onto the grass.

Stacie leapt from the porch and cried, "Jack, are you all right?"

He rolled over and moaned, "Yes." Then chuckling he added, "However, I'll bet there's a lesson to be learned here."

Barney walked over, looked at him curiously, and then leaned down and licked him in the face. Stacie and Eugene laughed before both gave him a hand and pulled him to his feet.

When they reached the porch and took a seat, Eugene asked, "So, have you made a decision about your draft notice?"

"Yes," Jack answered optimistically, but Eugene saw the mirth in Stacie's face disappear.

"Is there something wrong?" he asked, witnessing a tear roll from Stacie's eye.

Eugene looked from Stacie to Jack. "You aren't going to leave the country are you?"

"No, he's going to jail," Stacie wailed as more tears ran down her cheek.

"Oh, no." Eugene cried. "You're not going to burn your draft card, are you?"

"Of course not," Jack said with annoyance. "I'm going to test the system, that's all."

"Test the system?"

"Yes, by following the official rule book: the Constitution of the United States of America."

"What are you talking about?"

"I'm talking about why a war was fought within this country just over a hundred years ago."

"The Civil War?"

"Yes, and out of that war a new rule was amended to the official rule book. The thirteenth amendment says: 'Neither slavery nor involuntary servitude, except as a punishment for crime whereof the party shall have been duly convicted, shall exist within the United States, or any place subject to their jurisdiction.'"

"What does the draft and slavery have to do with each other?"

"Everything. If my choice is to be drafted or go to jail then the draft is clearly involuntary servitude. Since I have not broken any laws, I cannot be tried and convicted and then forced to serve in the army of the United States of America."

"Jesus Christ," Eugene exclaimed.

"They'll send you to jail, Jack Franklin," Stacie cried, "and then Alaska will never get saved."

Jack put his hand on her shoulder and said tenderly, "I'm not going to jail. They have to abide by the Constitution; every government official from the President down to the lowliest dog-catcher has taken an oath to uphold it."

"Then why are people still getting drafted?" she asked.

"It's simple; they never bothered to read the official rule book."

"What are you going to do?" Eugene asked.

"I going to write out an affidavit, which is a legal statement. I'll explain how the Selective Service has no jurisdiction over me because of the thirteenth amendment to the Constitution. Then to make it completely legal, I'll have it notarized, and sent to them by certified mail. After that, anybody who tries to draft me will be liable for prosecution."

"How'd you figure that out?"

"Eugene, life is full and varied and always offers options and choices. All one has to do is look for them. Some people would like you to believe the adage: Ignorance is bliss, but I prefer the words of Socrates: 'The unexamined life is not worth living.'"

"I get it, examining life and understanding it makes you master of your own dominion," Eugene said brightly.

Jack leaned over and gripped Eugene's shoulder, as he did so a gold medallion fell out of his shirt.

Eugene saw it and pointed, "What's that?"

"It's a Saint Christopher Medal," Stacie answered sadly. "Oh, I don't really believe in protective saints, but I wanted to give him something symbolic of the protection I wish I was able to give him.

Jack's affidavit seemed to work, for he received no reply from Selective Service. Life went on as usual. Jack continued making his plans and tending the farm. Eugene went to school, then to work, and on the weekends, to the farm. Stacie took a job in town at the apparel shop on the corner of Oglethorpe and Broad Street. It was the same store that threw out the mannequin Jack covered with hair and hung from the rafters of the high school gym. Stacie could see the gym from the store window; it was across the street from the Sheriff's office at the end of the block.

During these quiet months, Eugene finished the screenplay he'd promised Jack he would write. It was written in secret, late at night, so his father would not try to stop him. He called it: *Gods Of The Pond* after an idea he got fishing with Jack and Stacy in the pond behind Jack's barn. It was two themes in one: the concretizing of Jack's dream - freedom in Alaska, and the concretizing of Eugene's dream - a plural marriage bringing Jack, Stacie, and himself together. If asked, he would have vehemently denied that his story was a marketing strategy aimed at persuading Stacie. He had already convinced himself that Jack wanted them all to be married.

Excited by the completion of his screenplay, and wanting to share it with his friends, Eugene arrived early at the farm on a Sunday late in April. He was so eager that he didn't knock, and walked right in. Immediately he heard Stacie yelling, "Jack! Jack! Jack!" and Jack crying out, "Oh, God! Oh, God!" Thinking something was terribly wrong, he rushed into the bedroom.

Stacie was on her knees and naked; her hands grasping the brass rails of the footboard, while her breasts swayed forward and back. Jack was naked as well, and standing on his knees behind her. He was thrusting his pelvis against her buttocks, while his hands firmly gripped her hips.

"Jack, what are you doing?" Eugene exclaimed.

Stacie whipped her face toward him, and shouted, "Get out of here!"

Eugene did not move. He stood staring at the naked bodies in front of him; and felt himself becoming aroused.

Jack said calmly, "Eugene, you need to leave."

"But Jack, what about me; don't you want me to join you?"

Firmly this time, Jack reiterated, "You need to leave, now!"

Tears burst from Eugene's eyes as he said, "But, but what about--"

"Now, Eugene!" Stacie screamed.

He ran out the room, and out of the house. He jumped onto his bike, still crying, and rode furiously until he got home.

"What the hell is wrong with you?" demanded Jim Eastly as Eugene walked into the house with his tear-stained face.

"Nothin'."

"Don't you 'nothin' me," ordered Jim. "You tell me what's going on."

"I was just at Jack's."

"What's got you so upset?"

"He and Stacie were..." Eugene choked back a sob. "He and Stacie... he and Stacie..."

"Oh, he's porking that dress shop girl you got a crush on. Well, get over it. She's too old for you, anyway."

"But, but--"

"But nothing. I thought I told you not to hang out with that hoodlum."

"He's not a hoodlum, Dad."

"What's he still doing around town anyway. He should be serving his country like the rest of the men his age. Hasn't he gotten drafted yet?"

"Yes, but he's not going."

"He's got no choice."

"Jack's smart, Dad. He figured out a loophole."

"A loophole! There ain't no such thing. Only a goddamn commie would refuse to serve his country."

"But Dad, you don't understand. Jack says it's the Communists who want to make people slaves of the state. He says only a Communist government would draft people to work for it. It doesn't matter what kind of work it is - it's still slavery. People are not government property. Can't you see it Dad? By opposing the draft, he's opposing Communism."

"Boy, you're sounding more and more like those goddamn college students I keep seein' on television, who're rioting all over the country. I'll tell you this once and once only. If I ever catch you with that Jack fellow, I'll beat the livin' shit out o' you. Is that clear?"

"Yes, sir," Eugene answered reluctantly.

"And another thing, don't you go gettin' any ideas from that boy. When you graduate high school you're going to enlist in the *Marine Corps* where you'll learn how to become a man. Then when you come home, you'll work for the family business."

"Yes, sir."

Spring warmed to summer temperatures. Eugene suppressed his discomfiture with Jack and Stacie, by rationalizing that they only wanted to protect him from his father's wrath until they could all be in Alaska. And, so things went back to normal. On May 7th, Eugene celebrated his seventeenth birthday in secret with them.

About a week later, on a hot afternoon, Eugene was waiting at home for his father to pick him up and take him out to the job site. He sat on the fender of Jim's Chevy and stared vacantly across Airport Road to the treeless acres that ran its length. It had been named in the hopes that the town would one day grow into needing an airport. The post World War II baby boom had caused the population of Schley County to grow as rapidly as the rest of the country, but as the economics of the nation moved away from agriculture, the youth of Schley County moved away from Ellaville. Eugene gazed along the stretch of grass known as Gill Airstrip and thought it needed mowing.

Jim arrived later than usual, and said nothing when Eugene got into the truck. His father swung left off of Airport Road onto Oglethorpe Street, and headed toward town. Eugene thought it odd, because it was the opposite direction to the job they had not finished the day before. Jim stopped in front of the barber shop. He handed Eugene a dollar, and said, "Son, get out and get yourself a haircut. I'll come pick you up later."

"But, Dad..." Eugene started to protest, but words failed him. He was stunned that his father would send him to the barber after years of insisting on cutting Eugene's hair himself.

"I said, get out!"

Eugene obeyed; his father's mood implied a probable hormone imbalance; a special need that frequently drove him to the town's prostitutes. Eugene had learned the hard way that it was safest to comply with Jim's demands until the pressure of excess testosterone was purged from his system.

There were several men ahead of him in the barber shop, so Eugene sat down and flipped through a comic book. Mr. Owen looked up and uttered in surprise, "My, my,... look who's here." Eugene was embarrassed, so rather than wait inside, he decided to walk to the corner and say hello to Stacie at the apparel store. As he reached the corner, he saw his father's truck. It was pulling away from the curb, just down the street in front of the Sheriff's office. Several other vehicles pulled out at the same time. It made him curious, but only mildly, and he turned to enter the store.

Suddenly, Stacie came running out of the door. Following right behind was the woman who owned the store. The woman caught her by the elbow and yelled, "Stacie, stop! There's nothing you can do."

Eugene ran to them and demanded, "Stacie, what's going on?"

Stacie's face was a picture of terror, and tears streamed down her cheeks as she screamed, "Mrs. McKay just came into the store and told me Sheriff Dooley was going to arrest Jack. She said the man from Selective Service, who brought the order, is claiming Jack is dangerous, and he demanded that Sheriff Dooley take a bunch of armed men with him." Hysterically, she added, "Can you believe it - a fucking posse in this day and age."

"Stacie! Your language," the store owner cried.

"Let go of me!" Stacie commanded, then yanked her arm free.

Eugene felt numb as he asked, "W-what do we do?"

"Get out there before they do," Stacie answered and grabbed him by the arm as she started running.

They leapt over the doors of Stacie's Mustang convertible into the front seats. The engine roared to life; and she sped down the road. "I know a short-cut," she hollered over the wind, and turned down a gravel road. Dust clouds spewed out behind the car, and the rear tires slid with every curve. Eugene clung to the door to keep from flying over the side or into Stacie's lap. Finally, they pulled into Jack's driveway. No one was in sight, not even Jack.

Stacie ran into the house while Eugene regained control of his wobbly legs.

"Jack! Jack!" she called, but no one answered.

When she came back out, Eugene was sitting on the porch. She sat down beside him to wait. Barney wandered up, bleated at them, then scratched himself by rubbing against the picket fence Jack had put up to keep him out of the flowers. When he reached the end of the fence, he stretched his neck and sampled a rose that had grown too close.

"Barney!" Stacie scolded, and the goat ran around the side of the house.

Only a few minutes passed before the parade arrived: four cars, five pick-up trucks, a van, the Sheriff's car, and the Deputy's car. They all parked along the edge of the driveway that curved in front of the cottage. Eighteen men gathered together before approaching the house. There was the Sheriff and his deputy, four men wearing gray suits, whom Eugene did not know, and twelve local men, two of whom were his father and Mr. Guthrie. Eugene could see that every man held a shotgun or a rifle, but of the local men, only his father and Mr. Guthrie seemed to be enjoying themselves.

One of the men pointed to Eugene, and said, "Hey Jim, isn't that your boy?"

Jim looked at Eugene, and started to storm ahead of the group, but the Sheriff grabbed his arm and said, "Hold up there a minute." Then he yelled to Eugene, "Boy, you go tell Mr. Jackson Paine Franklin to come on out and give himself up."

"He ain't here," Eugene answered.

"Where is he?"

Before he could answer, Stacie squeezed his thigh to hush him, and said, "You got here too late. I warned him; and he's already on his way to Canada." Then to Eugene she whispered, "Maybe that'll make 'em go away, and he'll have a chance to get away."

"If that's true Miss, I'll have to arrest you for aiding and abetting a wanted criminal."

Stacie stood up, put her hands above her head, and said, "Then you better take me on in."

As she started down the stairs, she whispered to Eugene, "Good, now they'll leave. You stay here until Jack gets back so you can warn him."

"Oh, no, it's too late," Eugene moaned, and Stacie looked up to see Jack's blue pick-up truck pull around the curve of the driveway.

Jack drove past the group of men and parked in front of the porch. He stepped out of the truck and with a pleasant smile said, "Good afternoon gentlemen, I wasn't expecting a welcoming party. After all, I only went to Columbus."

"Mr. Franklin, you're under arrest," said Sheriff Dooley.

"What for?"

"Draft evasion," answered one of the men in gray. "Now come along peacefully."

"Let me ask Sheriff Dooley a question first." Then turning his attention to the Sheriff, he asked, "Sir, can you arrest someone for not doing something that is against the law?"

"Of course not."

"Then, sir, you cannot arrest me. Apparently, these Selective Service people neglected to tell you that I have put them on legal notice that I do not fall within their jurisdiction. The draft, Sheriff, violates the thirteenth amendment to the Constitution, and these gentlemen, as well as yourself, sir, have all sworn to uphold the Constitution. Therefore you cannot arrest me. The only thing I have done is refuse to violate the thirteenth amendment by refusing to allow myself to be drafted."

"That sounds like a lot of gibberish to me," said one of the gray suited men.

"That's only because you haven't read the official rule book. Sheriff, if you'll hold on a minute, I'll give you a copy of my legal notice to the Selective Service. Then you can satisfy yourself that these men have no jurisdiction over me."

Before the Sheriff could object, Jack disappeared into the house. In less than a minute he returned, walked over to the Sheriff, and handed him a notarized copy of the affidavit he sent by certified mail to the Selective Service. "Here, you can take this copy to study; if you have any questions, you can phone me. Please, for your own sake, keep in mind that refusing to uphold the Constitution after taking an oath to do so is nothing short of treason."

The Sheriff stood mute and befuddled as Jack turned to walk back to the house, but Jim Eastly started screaming, "Treason! What kind of crap is that? You're the only son of a bitch guilty of treason!"

"Yeah! Yeah!" rang out a couple of voices from the crowd.

Mr. Guthrie demanded, "Ain't you gonna arrest him, Sheriff?"

"I don't know if I can. The boy's got a point. I'll have to check it out." The Sheriff then turned to the deputy and said, "Eddie, get headquarters on the radio for me. Tell them to get the county prosecutor on the phone."

"Well, I know one thing," Jim bellowed, "I can take my boy out of here."

Jim stormed across the yard. He grabbed Eugene by the collar with his free hand, and pulled him off the porch.

"No, Dad, no!" Eugene protested, but Jim ignored him.

Jim Eastly released his grip, and punched Eugene in the mouth.

Eugene fell on his back. Jim bent over and grabbed his son's collar. Spittle flew from his lips onto to Eugene's face as he yelled, "Get up you goddamn sissy. You make me sick."

Meanwhile all the commotion aroused Barney's curiosity, and he stuck his head out from around the corner of the house to investigate. Directly across the yard from him was Jim Eastly's wide rump. He crouched to charge, but all the noisy screaming people made him hesitate. Suddenly charging ahead of him was Jack.

Jack was big, but not big enough to pull the iron muscled plumber off of Eugene. "Stop it!" he screamed, but Jim just swung out his shotgun like a hunk of pipe. Jack took the stunning blow on the shoulder and fell to the ground.

"Sheriff, can't you stop him!" Stacie cried.

"I don't interfere in family business, Miss."

Jack stood up holding his shoulder. "Get off my property!" he screamed. "This is private property and every one of you is trespassing."

"Son, we're not moving one inch until I hear from headquarters." The Sheriff turned his back, and leaned into the window of the squad car while the deputy continued talking on the two-way radio.

"If you won't stop it, then I will." Jack ran into the house, threw up the lid on the toy box and grabbed the baseball bat.

He was only inside for a few seconds, but when he returned Jim was again bent over Eugene. Stacie was screaming, "Stop! Stop it!"

Jim was swinging his hand back and forth, slapping Eugene's head over and over again. Eugene was pressing his hands over his face to protect himself.

Jack dashed down the steps yelling, "Get off of him right now, or I'll crack your skull open!"

But at the same time, Mr. Guthrie split off from the mob in a hard run. With less distance to cover, he was able to leap in front of Jack before he got to Jim. Jack found himself facing the gaping hole of a large bore revolver.

"Stay out of it, Jack Franklin," ordered Guthrie.

Jack stood motionless with the bat frozen in air above his head. Out of the corner of his eye he could see Barney contemplating Jim Eastly's fat ass. He grinned and yelled, "Toro! Toro!"

The command was all Barney needed. Jim Eastly screamed as the goat's horns slammed into his rear. Mr. Guthrie jerked his head to see Jim somersaulting over Eugene's covered face. In that instant of Guthrie's distraction, Jack swung the bat and yelled, "Pop fly to center field."

The bat cracked against the revolver. Guthrie shrieked in pain as the gun tumbled across the lawn.

Eugene uncovered his face, but the passing seconds seemed to bleed together as the ensuing scenes imprinted on his memory.

Stacie was running to him.

Guthrie was dancing in pain while holding his broken hand above his head.

Barney had turned and was crouching for a second charge.

Jim was scrambling on his hands and knees to get out of the way.

The Sheriff, still facing the car, was waving the radio hand-set over his head while saying, "Listen up, everybody. The county prosecutor says we bring in the Franklin boy without asking questions."

The four Selective Service Agents braced their shotguns against their shoulders.

Eugene looked at Jack, who was yelling, "That's absurd, call 'em back and I'll speak to them."

Beyond Jack, he could see the Sheriff turn around, and look at Guthrie who was still dancing in pain and his father who was still crawling. The Sheriff cried out, "What's going on here?"

In that same instant Barney charged, and a shotgun blasted.

Barney crumpled, Stacie screamed, and Eugene, seeing the horror in Jack's face, stood up and cried, "No, Jack!"

Jack wasn't listening. He charged the four men with the bat over his head. The local men who were standing behind them scattered out of the way.

The four men raised their shotguns and aimed.

All four blasted simultaneously; Jack crumpled.

"No!" screamed Eugene, as Stacie fainted in his arms.

Silence filled the air, and no one moved except for Eugene who let Stacie's limp body slide to the ground. He staggered to where Jack's body fell, then dropped to his knees. He pulled Jack's mutilated chest to his own, and sobbed uncontrollably.

"Why Jack, why?" he blubbered over and over again.

It was as if he too had taken a blast to the stomach. Pain filled his rib cage, and the gravity that always seemed to attack his diaphragm fell full force against it, until he could barely breathe. He whispered, "I guess none of us will ever be master of our own dominion; there will always be boundaries."

His breathing became more and more shallow as he became overwhelmed by his sense of loss. The lifeless form in his arms was all that remained of his best friend; the only person who ever cared anything about him. It was too much to process; it felt like something was squeezing his brain from inside his skull. He started to fell dizzy. He clung to Jack's body, as the light around him began to fade. His hand balled into a fist enclosing the gold Saint Christopher medal around Jack's neck. He whimpered one last time, "Why Jack?" Then passed out.

Jim Eastly grabbed his son by the shoulders, shook him, and said, "Wake up, boy. Wake up!"

Eugene didn't move, so Jim slapped him hard across the face three times, and yelled, "I said, wake up!"

Eugene's mouth opened. He loudly sucked in a deep breath, and then his eyelids fluttered.

"Get up, boy!" Jim ordered, and pulled him to his feet.

Eugene's fist remained tightly gripped on the thin gold chain around Jack's neck causing it to snap.

"Let's go, Eugene. It's time to get home."

Eugene opened his eyes, looked at his father in bewilderment and asked, "Who are you?"

Jim grabbed Eugene's arm and said, "I'm not playing games with you, boy. I said, let's go!"

Eugene said nothing as his father drove them home. When they were inside the house, his father told him, "Go to your room."

"Which room is that, sir?"

Jim stared at his son's blank face and without a word took Eugene's shoulder and guided him to his bedroom.

He watched as Eugene wandered about the room picking up objects and looking at them as if he'd never seen them before. He sat on the bed and bounced three times, then stood back up. He opened drawers in the dresser, and then the door to the closet. "All this is mine?" he asked his father, but Jim didn't answer.

He continued about the room until he got to the desk. He pulled open the top drawer, and removed a mechanical pencil. He twisted it to make the lead come out, and then laughed when it did. He tossed it back into the drawer, and then removed a notebook. Looking at some writing on the cover he asked, "My name is Eugene Eastly?"

Again Jim did not answer. Eugene opened it to the first page and froze. After several minutes, Jim noticed he was not moving and walked up behind him. Over his son's shoulder, he read:

an original screenplay by EUGENE EASTLY

Jim put his hand on Eugene's shoulder and said, "Son, are you all right?"

Eugene turned around, and said, "Oh, hi Dad. When did you come in?"

"I followed you in."

"Oh yeah that's right. We just got home from work."

"Son, are you feeling all right? I know I was a little rough on you today, but with everything else that happened... I know how much you liked... " Jim's words trailed off.

"Hey, it's okay Dad, I can handle hardest work you can dish out. We'll finish putting in the rest of those pipes tomorrow."

Jim stared at his son's glassy eyes, and said, "Eugene, perhaps we should both take the next few days off."

"Whatever you say, Dad, but let's not put it off too long. You know I've only got a year left to learn the family business before I have to ship off for *Marine Corps* boot camp."

Jim walked to the door, turned and said, "Son, if you continue to feel this way, you'll make me a proud father."

Eugene did not answer. He sat down at the desk, and picked up a ball point pen. Jim walked away.

Eugene ripped the first page out of the notebook, and then snapped open the binder rings. He pulled a fresh sheet from the back and wrote:

RESURGENT MAN

an original screenplay by JACKSON PAINE FRANKLIN

#

"Three days later, I finished the rewrite," Frank continued to the group around the table. "Rewriting it was a compulsion. With the conclusion of Jack's life came the conclusion of his dream. It was as if I had corrected the story of my own life, for as far as I was concerned, it too had ended. My mind was a mess. All my thoughts were muddled and I'm actually amazed that I was even able to rewrite the story because my entire body was numb. Even as horrible as my thoughts were, a glimmer of hope, as at the bottom of Pandora's box, did remain. It was the children of the Gods of the Pond, who represented that small feeling of hope in my mind. In the end, they took my hope and went off to create their own community despite the deaths of their parents. That hope held my mind together until I went to see Stacie.

As soon as I finished the rewrite, I drove over to Stacie's parent's house. I had been so intent on finishing that I had not bathed or even changed clothes since the day of the killing. It was raining out, so I took a windbreaker out of the closet, and then almost as an afterthought, I rolled up the manuscript and put it in the inside pocket of the jacket.

#

Stacie came out on the front porch, and sat with Eugene on the swing and watched the lightening.

"They buried him today," she said in a voice barely holding back the tears.

Eugene took her hand and said, "Marry me, Stacie. You and I can take Jack's ideas to Alaska ourselves."

She smiled and said, "You're sweet, Eugene."

"I'm serious," he said. "I love you. The three of us were going to be together, so why not the two of us? Just because Jack is gone doesn't change the way you and I feel about each other."

She patted his hand and said, "I know you're feeling hurt, Eugene, and I don't wish to add to that hurt, but you're mistaken about how I feel about you."

"You mean you don't love me?"

"Of course I do; I love you like a brother."

"But don't you see, I can take Jack's place."

"No," she said standing up. "No one can take Jack's place."

Eugene stood up then and threw his arms around her. "I can take Jack's place. Kiss me - you'll see."

She pushed him away as he tried to kiss her, and the more she pushed the more insistent he became. Finally she screamed, "Stop it, Eugene, stop it! What has gotten into you?"

Ignoring her protests, he continued to force himself on her. He was convinced that if she would only taste his kiss, she would remember how much she loved him. Finally she pushed hard enough to break his grasp, and before he could grab her again, she slapped him.

The burn in his cheek gave the final signal that all hope had completely disappeared. Tears filled his lower eyelid. He turned away, and with his shoulders bent in defeat, turned toward the porch steps.

“Where are you going?” asked Stacie.

"I'm running away, and never coming back," he said; crying. Then he ran down the stairs to his car; and yanked the door open.

The rain started pouring its hardest in that moment.

At the edge of the porch, Stacie stopped, and called out over the sound of the storm, "Wait.”

He turned and looked at her through the curtain of water.

“Don’t do anything foolish!" she said.

“Like what?”

“You know, like hurt yourself.”

“How could I possibly hurt any more than I already feel?”

“You’ll feel better in time. Time heals all wounds.”

“Don’t patronize me,” he screamed, and then turned toward the driver’s seat.

“Eugene... wait!”

He climbed behind the wheel, and muttered, "There is no Eugene." But she couldn't have heard.

#

A hurricane was blowing in the Gulf of Mexico that night and turning into tornadoes as soon as they hit land. Winds were raging north through Alabama all the way to Tennessee before dying down, and I was driving straight into them. I wasn't trying to kill myself. I was simply running away. Driving right into a tornado was stupid, but my brain had turned to mush, because I didn't even hear the weather warnings blaring out of my car radio. Every bit of my consciousness was telling me that nothing mattered anymore, but without knowing it, I drove only down highways heading west.

Subconsciously guiding my car was that part of me that still wanted to make motion pictures, but that was all it was doing. Thoughts of movies and directing were buried under tons of fallout from a battle being waged in my brain over whether I would retain any memories at all. Suddenly a tree in the road decided the argument, for I was too close to stop. I crashed, banged my head and woke up without any memory, except that I was heading west.

Gradually over the weeks it took me to get out here I remembered only that I was going to Hollywood to make movies, and that I would study under Ralph Smurling, but not my past or who I was. I named myself from the last name of the author on the screenplay, and from an inscription on the Saint Christopher medal I later found in my pocket. The rest you know.

"What you don't know is that if Jack had lived, I probably never would have made a movie. As you know, going to the movies is the world's favorite form of escapism, and I was no different. I was escaping my father and the misery he inflicted on me. Escapism, however, gradually led to dreaming of becoming a director, and that gave meaning to my life - gave me a goal. It helped me fight loneliness, and my father's aggression. Then I met Jack, and Jack became my substitute father. He was older and bigger than me, and cared about what I cared about. I was no longer lonely, and my dreams ceased to be important. Jack, however, had his own dreams and goals, and because he had direction, he expected everyone around him to have direction of their own. I continued to study motion pictures because it made Jack proud of me. I can see now that I would have never made it to Hollywood. My self-esteem was so low, that I would have followed Jack to Alaska instead. After Jack died, and Stacie refused me, I had no one to cling to. I was suddenly without direction. Fortunately, my subconscious remembered Hollywood and the only direction that was ever truly my own."

Frank paused and glanced at the faces around the table. When his eyes met Ralph's, he asked, "So now, do you understand, Ralph, why I couldn't make a war movie?"

"Yes," Ralph answered. "It brought to the surface the unnamed pain from Jack's death that was buried in your subconscious."

"Thanks to everyone here, I've faced that pain and survived it. Myra, I'll go see that head-shrinker friend of yours now; I'm sure I still have issues I need to work on. And, Ralph, if you're still willing, I'm ready to make that war movie. But, my idea is to make a war movie to end war."

A unified gasp rose from the table.

Frank picked up a pencil off the table as he began to speak, the parenthetical creases around his mouth deepened, and a look of animation formed on his face that was new to everyone present.

"Imagine this: we start the film with a group of soldiers who are sent to some god-forsaken foreign country to fight a war over senseless reasons caused by corrupt politicians who are in turn controlled by corporate lobbyists. We focus on only five or six men who become friends. We follow them through months of every imaginable horror of war. Battles constantly rage around them, leaving no time for rest. They're dirty, sweaty, bloody, and exhausted, yet they're never allowed to stop."

"The country they're in is incredibly hot and humid, and rains twice a day yet gives no relief to the heat. They're plagued by insect bites, skin fungus, and dysentery. We show one soldier getting skinnier and skinnier as he slowly shits himself to death. All of them sustain some wound or another, yet they are too far inside enemy territory to even hope for a medical evacuation. We'll have them get captured and tortured, and then we'll let them escape only to suffer even greater travesties."

"At one point a plane will drop napalm over them. They will see it coming in time to run through a thorny underbrush which rips their skin and clothes before they can dive into a green slimy pond. When they come out, each man is covered with leaches. One man won't have made it into the water in time and his back will be seriously burned. Days later, the men find maggots living in his rotting flesh. Their medic, long without his medicinal gear, will say, "Leave the maggots. They'll eat away the dead tissue and keep him from getting a greater infection."

"Finally, adding insult to injury, just when they are about to make it back to the base alive, they are all killed by friendly fire as their own army drops a bomb on them."

"They'll wake up in a fog, and through it they can see the Pearly Gates. Relieved that their misery is over, they walk toward Heaven only to find St. Peter pulling a gate shut; the lock clicks as they reach it. He points to an elevator which has only a down button. As they turn to the inevitable, they take one glance through the fence. Heaven is populated solely by corporate board members, military generals and politicians."

"They exit the elevator in Hell. Satan snickers as he casts them into a fiery room. The men walk through a smoky room of boulders glowing red hot. One stretches out on a rock and says, "Say, it's not too bad in here. The heat actually soothes my sore back muscles." Another drops his gun, and says, "I can finally relax. If I'm here, what's left to fear." Their sergeant adds, "Yeah, and it's dry. I'll bet it never rains here." They're all happily bantering when Satan returns. Angrily, he booms, "This is Hell." The men laugh, and one says, "Kiss off Buddy, this is nothing. You can't even conceive a suffering we haven't learned to endure." The men turn back to their pleasant chatter. Free at last. The title will be:

I'LL TAKE HELL, THANK YOU

and the credits will read:

Produced by Frank Eugene Stacy
Directed by Ralph Smurling and Frank Eugene Stacy

What do you think, Ralph? Want to do it?"

THE END

AFTERWORD

I got the idea for ***...and Never Coming Back*** when I was taking an Abnormal Psychology class, as a 19 year old college student, at *Georgia State University*. We were studying dissociative types of hysteria such as amnesia, fugue states and multiple personalities. I learned that amnesia can be a reaction to an intolerably traumatic experience, and that an extreme case could trigger a fugue state. A fugue is a type of amnesia where a person, who encounters an unpleasant situation from which he sees no escape, loses his memory and takes flight. One of the interesting facets of this condition is that the individual appears normal and is able to engage in complex activities including pursuing long repressed desires or goals.

We studied the case history of a woman who had been raised by religious fanatics, sent to college to prepare for missionary work, and then forced into an arranged marriage with a man she did not love. She lived in this repressive life for 37 years when her favorite child died. The next day she disappeared. She crossed the country, took a new name, and began a new career playing and teaching piano. She was very successful which attracted attention until one day someone recognized her and reported her whereabouts to her family. She denied knowing her family for some time before her memory was brought back through therapy.

I also learned that a person waking up from a fugue will often have no memory of the time during which he was in the fugue.

I was so fascinated by this condition that I found myself daydreaming: "What if I woke up and had no idea where I was, yet all my memories seemed perfectly intact." That question evolved into something a little more fun: "What if I woke up rich and famous, and had no clue how I became so fortunate." That question led to: "Should I tell anyone? If I do, will I wind up in a straight jacket? Or should I keep quiet and fake it until I figure out who I've become?"

My influences for this book are Robert Penn Warren, Pat Conroy, Victor Hugo, and Ayn Rand. I was inspired by Warren who, in *All The King's Men,* intermingled the tales of Willie Stark and Jackie Burden, with that of Cass Mastern - the allegorical story within a story. Conroy is my archetype of a southern writer; I've read his *Lords of Discipline* a dozen times. Hugo's gift is developing parallel stories that eventually crash together with amazing emotional impact. A good example of this is in the *Hunchback Of Notre Dame,* when Esmeralda, who separated from her mother as a baby, is tragically reunited with her when they compare the little embroidered shoes each carries as a memento. Finally, Rand showed me that the concepts of individual liberty can be portrayed entertainingly in a fictional format.

My endeavor with this story was to write not merely with depth, but with caverns branching, and twisting, and becoming runaway tunnels before bursting back into daylight. My intention was to create a literary novel of page turning passion, that will be read and reread for the sake of discovering all of its hidden elements.

ABOUT THE AUTHOR

Robert Evans Wilson, Jr. has been fascinated with human motivation since high school, where he devoured pop-psychology books and magazines. In college, he formally studied psychology and philosophy. He also worked in two psychiatric hospitals. Rob was interested in what makes people tick because he wanted to create interesting and believable fictional characters.

While waiting to get his fiction published, Rob turned to advertising and used his knowledge of motivation to create ads that moved people to the next level in the buying process. His ads were so successful, he started winning major advertising awards. Those awards got the attention of several colleges which invited Rob to teach.

In 1997, Rob accepted an offer to teach at his alma mater: *Georgia State University*. He taught advertising, marketing and public relations. His teaching led to invitations to speak around the United States. Rob began delivering motivational speeches on innovation, creative thinking, goal achievement, and leadership.

In February 2007, Rob began writing *The Un-Comfort Zone* a monthly column on motivation, innovation, and leadership. In 2009, Rob started writing his blog, *The Main Ingredient* for *Psychology Today*. In 2011, Rob published his humorous children's novel *The Annoying Ghost Kid* which will soon be made into a movie by *Lead Lion Media*.

Rob lives in Atlanta, Georgia with his two sons, dog, and cat.

Made in the USA
Columbia, SC
28 October 2022